Blameless
in
Abaddon

Blameless
in
Abaddon

❖

JAMES MORROW

HARCOURT BRACE & COMPANY
New York   San Diego   London

ISBN 0-15-188656-3

Text set in Granjon
Designed by Judythe Sieck

Printed in the United States of America

For
Kathryn Ann Smith
with love abiding

ACKNOWLEDGMENTS

DURING MY ODYSSEY through theodicy I was guided by many thinkers in the persons of their books. Let me here acknowledge my debt to Marilyn McCord Adams and Robert Merrihew Adams's *The Problem of Evil*, Peter Adam Angeles's *The Problem of God*, John Hick's *Evil and the God of Love*, C. S. Lewis's *The Problem of Pain*, Edward H. Madden and Peter H. Hare's *Evil and the Concept of God*, H. J. McCloskey's *God and Evil*, Terrence W. Tilley's *The Evils of Theodicy*, and Melville Y. Stewart's *The Greater-Good Defence*. Jeffrey Burton Russell's four-volume history of evil incarnate—*The Devil, Satan, Lucifer,* and *Mephistopheles*—while not a theodicy per se, contains much tough-minded speculation on the conundrum of suffering. Interpretations of the Book of Job are as numerous as the sores on his body. The three I found most valuable are William Safire's *The First Dissident*, John T. Wilcox's *The Bitterness of Job*, and Carl Jung's *Answer to Job*.

To the best of my knowledge, all of the disasters catalogued by the prosecution team actually occurred. For those interested in pursuing this subject, I recommend Stuart Flexner and Doris

Flexner's *The Pessimist's Guide to History*. In constructing the cystic fibrosis case presented in chapter twelve, I drew on several sources, including Frank Deford's *Alex: The Life of a Child*. Certain details of Robert François Damiens's execution come from Michel Foucault's *Discipline and Punish*.

Like *Towing Jehovah* before it, *Blameless in Abaddon* benefitted from the moral and intellectual support of my agent, Merrillee Heifetz, the formidable mind of my editor, John Radziewicz, and the willingness of my friends and colleagues to critique a piecemeal manuscript and discuss my assorted obsessions with me. My gratitude goes to Joe Adamson, Linda Barnes, Craig Brownlie, Lynn Crosson, Shira Daemon, Sean Develin, Daniel Dubner, Margaret Duda, David Edwards, Robert Hatten, Peter Hayes, Michael Kandel, Christa Malone, Glenn Morrow, Jean Morrow, Elisabeth Rose, Joe Schall, Peter Schneeman, Kathryn Ann Smith, James Stevens-Arce, David Stone, and Dorothy Vanbinsbergen.

CONTENTS

In the underworld the shades writhe in fear, the waters and all that live in them are struck with terror. Sheol is laid bare, and Abaddon uncovered before God.

—The Book of Job, 26:5-6

The conservative has but little to fear from the man whose reason is the servant of his passions, but let him beware of him in whom reason has become the greatest and most terrible of the passions. These are the wreckers of outworn empires, disintegrators, deicides.

—J. B. S. Haldane
Daedalus

BOOK ONE
Necessary Evils

❖

Chapter 1

OF ALL THE NEWSWORTHY OBJECTS torn loose from the ice by the great Arctic earthquake of 1998, among them an intact Viking ship and the frozen carcass of a woolly mammoth, the most controversial by far was the two-mile-long body of God. The debate, oddly enough, centered not on the Corpus Dei's identity—the body was accompanied, as we shall see, by an impeccable pedigree—but rather on its metaphysical status. Was God dead, as the nihilists and the *New York Times* believed? Only in a coma, as the Vatican and Orthodox Judaism dearly hoped? Or—the Protestant consensus—was the Almighty as spiritually alive as ever, having merely shed His fleshly form as a molting mayfly sheds its husk?

Prior to the peculiar events that constitute my tale, it looked as if the mystery might never be solved. The Corpus Dei's proprietors, devout Southern Baptists all, were ill inclined to sanction platoons of scientists tramping around inside His brain, leaving muddy footprints on His dendrites as they attempted to ascertain His degree of life or death. Moreover, as upholders of the theologically comforting Mayfly Theory, God's keepers rightly feared that such an expedition might yield signs of neural activity, thereby reinforcing the far more troublesome Coma Theory.

As for me, I wholeheartedly agreed with the ban on journeys into His cerebrum. Being the Devil, I have strong opinions about how human beings ought to conduct themselves. Unlike the Baptists' views, however, my own are shaped more by prudence than by piety. It is always wise, I feel, to leave well enough alone. It is best to let sleeping gods lie.

❖

The sign on the courtroom door read JUSTICE OF THE PEACE, though neither justice nor peace figured reliably in Martin Candle's occupation, which was largely a matter of enforcing leash laws, reprimanding jaywalkers, trying petty criminals, collecting overdue parking fines, and performing civil wedding ceremonies.

Martin pursued his calling in Abaddon Township, Pennsylvania, a staunchly Republican enclave spread across a wide valley twenty miles north of Philadelphia. Abaddon was a quiet and prosperous world, a place of lush parks, rolling farmlands, and bedroom communities with names like Fox Run and Glendale. The township's best feature, everyone agreed, was Waupelani Creek, a luminous stream winding gently through the valley from north to south, threading its settlements together like the string connecting the beads on a rosary. Minnows thrived in the Waupelani. Garter snakes slithered along its banks. Water striders walked Jesus-like on its surface. A rare and beautiful species of fish lived in these waters as well, a yellow-scaled carp whose collective comings and goings on brilliant summer days transformed their habitat from a conventional brook into a river of molten gold. Bisecting the backyard of Martin's childhood home in Fox Run, the Waupelani afforded him many happy hours of ice-skating, catching crayfish, and sailing the battleships he'd nailed together from stray scraps of lumber found in the basement. Only after he'd grown up, moved to Glendale, obtained a degree from Perkinsville Community College, and won his first election did it occur to him that Waupelani Creek had actually functioned in his boyhood as a toy—the best toy a child could wish for, better than a tree fort or a Lionel electric train set.

Abaddon Township's odd appellation traced to a warm summer evening in 1692, when a Quaker schoolmaster named Prester Harkins spied the Devil himself sitting in the boggy marsh that drained the valley's brooks and streams. The Evil One was taking a bath. Harkins saw his iron-bristled scrub brush. Although the schoolmaster was in fact suffering from a nascent case of paranoid schizophrenia, his neighbors all gave credence to his hallucination, and before long the marsh and its environs had acquired one of Hell's more evocative epithets, *Abaddon* being the Hebrew name both of a demonic angel and of the Bottomless Pit from which he hailed. By the time the twentieth century arrived, however, the township's citizens had forgotten the meaning of *Abaddon*. To them, it was merely an adequate name for an adequate suburb, a word outsiders were forever mispronouncing by accenting the first syllable. "Rhymes with Aladdin," the natives routinely informed visitors. "Emphasize the *bad*," they added—a strangely Augustinian motto for a citizenry whose sense of original sin could hardly be called acute. While occasionally one of Martin's neighbors would experience the sort of dark depression that commonly overtook less fortunate Americans, the average Abaddonian gave no thought to the fact that he was living in Hell.

Like many individuals who remain in their home communities while their friends venture into the wider world, Martin battled a fear that he was, and always would be, a failure. Under such circumstances a man will typically take an extreme view of his vocation, either regarding it as a kind of penance (somewhere between emptying bedpans in a paupers' hospital and working an oar on a slave galley) or elevating it beyond the bounds of reason. Martin opted for apotheosis. Upon winning the electorate's approval with his dignified bearing, athletic figure, and dark-eyed, sandy-haired good looks, he retained its loyalty through diligence and probity, considering each case as if the fate of nations hung on the outcome. Eventually even Democrats were voting for him. Although he held no advanced degrees— a person could ascend to the office of JP in those days with nothing but a college diploma and a working knowledge of local ordinances—he was as devoted to the ideal of justice as anyone on the faculty of Harvard Law School. His rulings were inspiringly fair, his methods upliftingly thorough. Judge Candle would never stop at suspending an alcoholic's license following a drunk-driving conviction; no, he would also try maneuvering the offender into rehabilitation. When an adolescent shoplifter came his way, he was never satisfied to convict, fine, and rebuke the thief; he would next attempt to uncover the root of the felony, visiting the young person's parents and urging everyone toward family counseling.

Even the weddings gave Martin an opportunity to find glory in his judgeship. When two people choose to be married before a justice of the peace, it's a good bet that something interesting has gone wrong in their lives, and the typical ceremony found Martin functioning more as a priest or therapist than as a magistrate. In about ten percent of these cases, one member of the couple was terminally ill. In twenty-five percent, the bride was pregnant. In forty percent, the proposed match—Jew to Christian, Protestant to Catholic, white to black—had proven unpalatable to one of the affected families. On three occasions, Martin had wed a man to a man; twice, a woman to a woman. Although these same-sex unions scandalized many of his fellow Republicans, he performed them with equanimity, believing that the principle of laissez-faire should apply no less to the bedroom than to the marketplace.

Commonly, the couple in question could not afford to rent a suitably dignified locale in which to exchange their vows, and they were understandably loath to use their own accommodations: a run-down trailer park or your parents' living room is an inauspicious platform from which to launch a new, connubial life. Learning of the couple's plight, Martin would immediately offer them the back parlor of his bachelor's apartment. The rug was clean, the furniture tasteful, and the light sufficiently dim to make the Masonite paneling look like oak. In their nervousness many couples would forget an essential prop or two, and so he kept his parlor stocked with marriage paraphernalia. The bride and groom were invariably amazed when, just as panic was about to possess them, Martin would coolly open a plywood cabinet and remove an imitation-gold wedding ring, a pair of scented candles, a bouquet of silk flowers, a box of latex condoms, or a bottle of Cook's champagne.

The most imaginative nuptials occurred not in Martin's parlor but in the world at large. He always brought his wedding props along, securing them carefully inside his briefcase before climbing into his white Dodge Aries and setting off to stamp the Commonwealth of Pennsylvania's imprimatur on the venerable urgings of the flesh. Once he wed two scuba enthusiasts at the bottom of the Schuylkill River, everyone dressed in wet suits and breathing bottled air. Another time he joined two skydiving aficionados as they floated above the Chestnut Grove Country Club, the bride's veil trailing behind her like a superheroine's cape. He would never forget uniting a pair of Perkinsville bohemians as they copulated vigorously on their waterbed, so that they might enjoy the unique experience of beginning the act as fornicators and completing it as a legal entity.

It was through his vocation that, at age forty-nine, Martin met the beguiling and eccentric Corinne Rosewood. One agreeable April afternoon the township's blustery constable, Hugh Steadman, hauled Corinne into Martin's little courtroom, having arrested her on a charge of disturbing the peace. According to Steadman, for the past three years Corinne had given the backyard of her Chestnut Grove bungalow over to the cultivation of

Nepeta cataria: catnip. Each evening, right after sunset, the addicts would arrive—tabbies, calicoes, tortoiseshells, Siamese—mewing and hissing as they pressed their spines to the ground and rolled around on the leaves. Not only were Corinne's neighbors forced to endure the din of this nightly bacchanal, the cat owners among them were commonly subjected to pets so stoned that, prancing home at four A.M., they totally forgot what a litter box was, blithely relieving themselves on the floor.

There she stood, a zaftig woman with hair the color of buttered toast, dressed in a checked flannel shirt, faded jeans, and red vinyl cowboy boots, rocking back and forth on her heels and grinning unrepentantly as Constable Steadman charged her with corrupting the township's cats. Her face was round and dimpled, barred from true beauty only by a nose resembling a baby turnip. Martin was smitten. Throughout the arraignment his heart pounded like a moonstruck adolescent's. Corinne's majestic form and unorthodox features appealed to his aesthetic sense, her crime to his fondness for audacity. The central image enchanted him: hundreds of ecstatic cats hallucinating in the moonlight, singing to the stars, gamboling through Corinne's garden of feline delights.

At her hearing ten days later she pleaded innocent. Martin weighed the evidence, found her guilty, and fined her two hundred and fifty dollars.

"I think I'm in love with you," he said, whipping off his bifocals and staring directly at the defendant. "Will you marry me?"

Assuming the judge was being facetious, Corinne replied that of course she would marry him, provided he dropped the fine.

"I won't drop the fine, but I'll reduce it to two hundred."

"One hundred fifty?"

"Two hundred."

"All right."

"Does a June wedding sound okay to you?"

Constable Steadman blinked incredulously. The bailiff issued an astonished cough.

"Are you crazy?" said Corinne, absently fingering the Commonwealth of Pennsylvania flag beside Martin's bench, opposite the Stars and Stripes. "I don't even know you."

"How about dinner instead? Dinner and a show."

"That's a possibility."

"Tonight?"

"Tonight I'm holding up a gas station in Glendale. Friday night would work."

"It's a deal."

On Friday night Martin and Corinne attended a revival of Agatha Christie's *Witness for the Prosecution* at Philadelphia's Theater of the Living Arts, and six months later they were indeed married, in a civil ceremony conducted by Kevin McKendrick, the JP of Cheltenham Township, the jurisdiction immediately to the east.

A most peculiar pair, these two. Martin: the lifelong Protestant monotheist and centrist Republican, the only son of Siobhan O'Leary, a receptionist in a travel bureau, and Walter Candle, a teetotal bartender who sought to counter the intrinsic secularity of his career by teaching Presbyterian Sunday school. Corinne: the free-spirited pagan and former Peace Corps volunteer, progeny of the first woman ever to run for governor of Maryland on the Socialist ticket and a failed Marxist playwright turned successful sporting-goods salesman. And yet they were happy . . . not only happy but obstreperously happy—happy to a degree that would have been insufferable in a couple less blameless and upright.

Four months after their wedding they secured a mortgage on a ramshackle farmhouse and adjoining barn at 22 Flour Mill Road in Chestnut Grove. Located three miles north of Abaddon Marsh, the couple's estate comprised over six acres, more than enough for furtively growing *Nepeta cataria*. That April they sowed the seeds together, pausing periodically to make love in the apple orchard, and by June the crop was in bloom, introducing dozens of local felines to a level of self-indulgence that seemed excessive even by the standards of a cat.

Corinne's love for animals went far beyond catnip farming. She was a devout vegetarian whose Ford Ranger sported bumper stickers proclaiming MEAT IS MURDER and I'D RATHER GO NAKED THAN WEAR FUR. For her livelihood she managed All Creatures Great and Small, a Perkinsville establishment specializing in gourmet food for dogs, cats, and—most profitably—the horses owned by the adolescent girls of Abaddon Township's wealthiest settlement, the posh and sylvan community of Deer Haven. Corinne's own taste in pets ran decidedly toward the outré. The creatures with whom Martin was forced to compete for his wife's affections included not only an iguana named Sedgewick but also a tarantula named Hairy Truman and an armadillo called Shirley—a misanthropic beast whose entire behavioral repertoire consisted of eating, sleeping, and, every day at two P.M., creeping from one corner of the basement to the other, depositing a pile of ordure as she passed.

On the evening of their first anniversary, Corinne looked Martin squarely in the eye, raised her second glass of Cook's champagne to her lips, and said, softly, "It was the lobsters."

"The lobsters?"

"From Super Fresh."

The case to which Corinne was evidently alluding had appeared on Martin's docket early in their courtship. Shortly after eleven P.M. on September 19, 1996, a young woman named Nancy Strossen had broken into a Super Fresh grocery store in Fox Run and transferred all the live lobsters from their display case to a holding tank. Later that night Strossen drove the tank across New Jersey, parked on a deserted Cape May beach, and released each and every lobster into the North Atlantic. Presented with the facts of Strossen's escapade, Martin had sentenced her to two days in jail, but he declined to make her pay any damages. Instead, he told the Super Fresh management their lobster trade was manifestly inhumane, and they would do well to abandon this business of torturing crustaceans.

"It was the lobsters that won me over," Corinne continued. "You let the defendant off with a slap on the wrist, and I said to myself, 'Look no further, dear.'"

"Lovely lobsters," said Martin woozily, finishing his third glass of champagne. "Lovely, lovely lobsters."

Eighteen months into the marriage Corinne got the idea of setting up the canine equivalent of the celebrated Make-A-Wish Foundation. She solicited contributions through *Dog Fancy* magazine, rented a one-room office in downtown Kingsley, and hired her dim-witted but saintly cousin Franny as chief administrator. Within half a year the Kennel of Joy had become a going concern, sustained through a mixture of charitable donations and Corinne's take-home pay. Thanks to the Kennel of Joy, a dying Manhattan dachshund finally got to chase a Wisconsin rabbit into its warren; a diabetic bloodhound from Newark joined three other dogs in finding a child lost in the Great Smokies; and a leukemic golden retriever born and bred in the parched Texas town of Tahoka spent the last weeks of her life swimming in the Rio Grande.

Had Martin not been crazy about Corinne, he would have regarded the Kennel of Joy as a dreadful waste of money, and the organization would probably have occasioned screaming matches of the sort that had characterized the terminal phases of his previous relationships. But love does strange things to a man's sense of proportion, which is why—contrary to rumor— it is by no means the Devil's least favorite emotion.

❖

Me again. Yours truly. Let's get something straight right now. This is not Old Nick here. This is not Mr. Scratch, Beelzebub, Gentleman Jack, or any other cozy and domesticated edition of myself. This is the Devil. This is hardball.

This is a two-month-old Bulgarian baby tossed into the air and caught on a Turkish bayonet in front of its hysterical mother. This is an Ustashe commandant splitting open a Serb's ass with an ax, so that the Serb begs the commandant, *begs* him, to shoot him in the head, and the commandant simply laughs. A thirty-year-old melanoma victim slipping his head into a plastic bag and cinching it with the string of his son's Batman kite. The Yangtze River overflowing its banks in 1931, flooding every acre from Nanking to Hankow and drowning 3.5 million peasants. The great Iranian earthquake of 1990, rippling through the country's northern provinces, flattening a hundred towns, and leaving fifty thousand dead.

Please understand, I never asked for this job. It wasn't my idea to be the Prince of Darkness, the Principle of Evil, the Principal of Hate, or anything of the kind. I never requested that God reach into Hell's highest dung heap, grab a glob of primal slime, and mold me as He would later mold Adam from clay. While I am willing to confess my sins before any priest with time enough to listen, the ultimate responsibility for Martin Candle's fate—for all the world's pain—does not lie with me. Yes, I invented the typhoon; true, my hobby is breeding tuberculosis; nolo contendere, I am gravity's mechanic and, by extension, an accessory before the fact of every fatal fall. But just because our Creator subcontracts evil out to me, we mustn't neglect to notice the blood on His hands.

"God dwells in the details," wrote the architect Ludwig Mies van der Rohe . . . and so do I. My name is Jonathan Sarkos, I am six foot four, and I weigh two hundred and eighty-five pounds. Like a chameleon's, my complexion varies as a function of my environment, though inversely. On asphalt, I am white. On snow, black. You must cast all clichéd accessories from your mind: scepter, forked beard, scholar's cap. I gave up cloven hoofs in the Middle Ages. I haven't worn horns since the Renaissance.

Of all my portrayers, it was a twentieth-century painter

named Jerome Witkin who came closest to the truth. Witkin's masterpiece is a 72 x 65–inch oil-on-canvas called *The Devil as a Tailor*. This artist saw it all. My cramped and penumbral shop with its Elias Howe sewing machine and its racks of newly made garments awaiting pickup. My massive frame, balding pate, large, turtlelike head. The one thing he got wrong was my age. While poets commonly produce their best work in their thirties, and mathematicians typically burn out in their twenties, miscreants tend to be late bloomers. Hitler didn't get around to invading Poland until he was fifty. Ceausescu got the hang of atrocity only after turning sixty-four. I am an eternal seventy-two.

My sewing needle boasts an honorable lineage, having been fashioned from the very spike the Roman soldiers drove through Jesus Christ's left wrist. *Flash*, it goes in the light of my whale-oil lamp, stitching together shirts, trousers, coats, blouses, and gowns. *Flash. Flash.* The demand for my goods is great. Authentic evil is rarely committed by the naked; even rapists keep their pants on. Hour after hour, I sit here inside God's decaying brain, hypnotized by my needle's glitter, glancing up occasionally to watch the great cranial artery called the River Hiddekel flow past my private dock on its journey to the pineal gland. I rest only on Sundays. Military uniforms are a specialty. Copes and cassocks, of course. Flags, naturally. White hoods and matching sheets. Business suits. During one of my boom periods, from 1937 through 1945, I produced 4,328,713 yellow stars inscribed with the word *Jude*.

I am the Father of Lies. Over the years, my children have done me proud. I shouldn't play favorites, but I am especially pleased with "The meek shall inherit the earth." Likewise, I shall always retain a soft spot in my heart for "Every cloud has a silver lining." As for "Time heals all wounds" and "Whenever God closes a door, He opens a window"—they, too, make me gloat unconscionably.

But enough about me. Whatever my shortcomings, vanity is

not among them. You came to learn about the awful events that befell the upright magistrate of Abaddon. For the nonce I shall hold my tongue.

❖

Given Corinne's worldview, Martin reacted with astonishment when, during a visit to the Chestnut Grove Flea Market, she insisted on buying a moldering pantherskin rug. She was acquiring it, she explained, in homage to an idol of hers, the Italian ballerina Marie Taglioni. According to Corinne, on a moonlit winter's night in 1835 Taglioni's carriage was halted by a Russian highwayman who then commanded her to dance for him, an audience of one, on a panther's pelt spread across the snowy ground. In the years that followed, it became Taglioni's custom to place chunks of ice in her jewel box and watch them melt amid the sparkling gems. Thus did she preserve her memory of that magical encounter: the highwayman, the black pelt, the star-speckled sky glittering above the frozen forest.

At first Martin maintained that forty-five dollars was far too much to have spent on a scruffy hunk of fur. But then one frigid January evening he awoke to realize Corinne no longer lay beside him. Acting on instinct, he went downstairs, donned a ski jacket over his pajamas, and hurried toward the catnip patch. Shimmering in the moonlight, a steady stream of snowflakes floated down, slowly, softly, the sort of generous crystals that, during childhood, he'd loved catching on his tongue. As he opened his mouth that night, he remembered his mother telling him no two snowflakes were alike. To the ten-year-old Martin there seemed something momentous in this fact—an entrée into the mind of God—but he'd never managed to fathom it.

An extravagantly beautiful voice reached his ears, one of Corinne's favorite performances: Loreena McKennitt singing her original musical setting for Tennyson's "The Lady of Shalott."

For ere she reach'd upon the tide
The first house by the water-side,
Singing in her song she died,
The Lady of Shalott.

And then he saw her: Corinne, improvising a sinuous ballet atop her panther pelt, her white Lycra bodysuit giving her buxom form the appearance of a snow sculpture by Praxiteles. The sight transfixed him. He forgot to breathe.

Out upon the wharfs they came,
Knight and burgher, lord and dame,
And round the prow they read her name,
The Lady of Shalott.

The song ascended, pouring from her battery-powered tape recorder. As the snow collected on his face, Corinne danced toward him and pressed her lips against his cheeks and brow, kissing each crystal into oblivion.

The animal lover who danced on an animal's hide—the contradiction charmed him. Inevitably he thought of a remark made by a character in *The Brothers Karamazov*, a novel he'd read in Mr. Gianassio's twelfth-grade honors English class: "If everything on Earth were rational, nothing would happen." Thus did one of Martin's most intense experiences with cosmic benevolence reach its climax, with Corinne's lips and Dostoyevsky's epigram.

Two days later he had the first in a series of intense experiences with cosmic evil.

It happened while he was on the job, marrying Demetrius Mitsakos and Gina Fontecchio, high-school dropouts who could barely afford the low end of his sliding scale. Standing in his living room, surrounded by wedding guests, Martin was seized by an overwhelming urge to urinate. He barely got through the ceremony. Rushing into the bathroom, he began emptying his bladder without bothering to lift the toilet seat. A razoring pain hit him, as if a strand of barbed wire were traveling through his urethra. He screamed. His knees buckled. He fell to the floor, eyes fixed on a stain compounded of fungus, rust, and desiccated toothpaste.

Slowly, the agony slackened. He exhaled, thanking God for the relief. His bladder was still complaining, but he dared not pee. Stumbling out of the bathroom, he limped up to Demetrius and Gina, smiled bravely, and wished them all the happiness in the world.

Later that afternoon everyone reconvened at the local Wendy's—the first time this particular restaurant or, Martin suspected, any restaurant in the entire Wendy's chain had hosted a wedding reception. For Demetrius and Gina, the place was redolent of sentiment. They'd met three months earlier at the salad bar.

Had his bladder not been torturing him, Martin might have enjoyed the party. Splendid in his yard-sale tuxedo, Demetrius swaggered to and fro amid the Formica tables, assuring his guests the food would cost them nothing. "Eat up, everybody!" he said expansively. "Gina and I are payin' for everything. Have another Frosty for chrissakes, Sid. More fries, Trixie?" Never before in his life, Martin guessed, had Demetrius been anyone's benefactor, nor was he ever likely to play that part again.

The urge became intolerable. Martin retreated to the men's room and, steeling himself, peed a pint of what felt like sulfuric acid. A foul-smelling yellowish discharge followed.

Pale and shaken, he hobbled back into the dining room, bade the newlyweds farewell, and fled the festivities in a panic.

Twenty-four hours later his primary-care physician, an ethereal young man named Harrison Daltrey, subjected Martin's rectum to a digital examination and offered a diagnosis: acute prostatitis. Dr. Daltrey wrote him a prescription for an antibiotic called NegGram, then explained that Martin would require periodic prostatic massages to expel the urethral secretions. The magistrate felt better even before swallowing the first pill.

And then he felt worse. The NegGram diminished the burning only slightly, and the yellowish discharges continued unabated, staining his underclothes so thoroughly that he took to washing these garments separately, when Corinne wasn't around. Daltrey switched him from NegGram to Furadantin. No improvement.

Then came the fateful prostatic massage of May 4, 1999.

"Something new today," said Daltrey, withdrawing his gloved index finger. "I'm picking up a small hardening along the lateral border of the left lobe. I want to make sure a specialist can feel it too. Matt Hummel's the best urologist around. You'll be in good hands."

Dr. Hummel's good hands also detected a hardening in Martin's prostate.

"Until we have a look, I can't tell you whether it's fibrous or neoplastic," said the urologist, a dour, moon-faced man who'd never shed his boyhood freckles. "If I had to make a wager, I'd bet my last nickel it's benign."

"You're sure? Your last nickel?"

"You're only fifty-one," Hummel explained, reaching for the phone. "Let's put you in the hospital this afternoon, okay? We'll do a lab workup, and tomorrow I'll biopsy the area."

When the anesthesia wore off, the first thing Martin realized was that a Foley catheter projected from his urethra, angling downward like a retrofitted science-fiction penis. Antiseptic fragrances suffused the recovery room. The aggressive chill of central air-conditioning blew across his skin. The nurse on duty, a rotund woman who might have just stepped out of an opera about Visigoths, seemed edgy and distant, as if she feared he might engage her in conversation. Where the hell was Hummel?

"We're keeping you another night," said the nurse, sidling toward the door.

"Why?"

"Doctor's orders."

"I hate this catheter."

"I can imagine."

And suddenly she was gone, leaving him alone with his fear.

As the clock on the recovery room wall crept toward three p.m., Hummel finally appeared.

"How're we doin'?" he asked.

"You didn't tell me there'd be a catheter."

"We'll take it out before you go to sleep."

"It's driving me crazy. Did you win your bet?"

"What bet?"

"Your last nickel."

"Lab report was vague. I told 'em to look at the tissue again."

"Good-vague or bad-vague?"

"Vague-vague. Let me worry about it, okay?" Hummel started out of the room. "If you're a cooperative patient, we'll let you watch the Phillies tonight."

Martin sat up, intent on chasing Hummel down the hall and asking what "vague-vague" meant, but the catheter made him reconsider. He lay back, closed his eyes, and brooded.

Twenty minutes later the Visigoth nurse and her ham-fisted male assistant removed the catheter, a procedure that would have caused him only slightly more pain if the device had been a lag screw. They transferred him to a regular room, one boasting not only a color TV and a civilized temperature but also a private phone. Grabbing the receiver, he punched up the number of All Creatures Great and Small.

"They're not letting me out till tomorrow," he told Corinne.

"What about the biopsy?"

"They won't tell me anything."

"Within a week, this'll all seem like a bad dream." Her tone was warm, kindly, reassuring. No wonder armadillos fell in love with her. "You'll be standing on home plate, marrying a couple of baseball fans, and you won't even be thinking about your prostate."

At nine o'clock the next morning Corinne appeared at his bedside bearing the happy news that Hummel had signed him out. His back throbbed. His bladder spasmed. His urethra burned fiercely, as if it had been colonized by fire ants. He wondered whether his augered penis would ever be able to perform its various duties again.

Slowly he eased himself out of bed, collected his watch and wallet from the nightstand, and put on his street clothes. As he and Corinne shuffled past the nurses' station, the pasty-faced woman behind the desk spoke up.

"Dr. Hummel said to get in touch before you leave. Here's the number. There's a pay phone by the Coke machine."

Hummel's receptionist was expecting Martin's call. "The doctor wants to see you down here at six o'clock. Would that be convenient?"

"Okay," he said, palms growing damp.

"Can your wife come along?"

"I think so."

"Please bring her."

The receptionist hung up.

"He wants to see us at six," said Martin, staring at his shoes. "Both of us. That's ominous, don't you think?"

"Not necessarily." Corinne clasped his forearm. "When I was seventeen, a surgeon cut a benign cyst out of my breast. He wanted my mother there afterward to hear exactly what he'd done and why. Here's the plan: once we're finished with Hummel, we're going to Chi-Chi's for dinner."

And so it happened that, on May 12, 1999, at 6:23 P.M., Martin and Corinne stood together in his urologist's badly lit office, hearing a verdict more punishing than anything the JP had ever handed down in his courtroom. Hummel summarized the results of the biopsy, then showed them the report from the pathology lab. The final line read, "Diagnosis: adenocarcinoma of prostate." In other words, at the age of fifty-one, this devout Presbyterian and devoted public servant, this innocent lover of justice, had developed cancer.

❖

Lucky you: I'm back. At this juncture in our hero's plunging fortunes, it would be appropriate to chronicle the origin of the great shrine toward which his cancer will eventually propel him. Initially, of course, no one believed that the eighty-million-ton carcass embodied God Himself. Candle, for example, favored the theory that it was a hoax: a foam-rubber statue carved by a wealthy sculptor with a demented sense of humor, perhaps, or an inflatable dummy constructed by prankster existentialists. Other people were convinced it had fallen from a passing UFO. Still others dismissed the body as a movie prop that had drifted away from the set of an aquatic religious epic, much as the mechanical whale from the Hollywood adaptation of *Moby-Dick* had escaped during shooting.

But then Pope Innocent XIV—staggering beneath the burden of his conscience, a weight that lay upon him like his Savior's cross—came clean. On December 30, 1998, the pontiff stood before a dozen radio microphones, a score of TV cameras, and a phalanx of journalists from every corner of the globe and told an astonishing story. How six years earlier the Vatican had been visited by an archangel claiming that God's inert body lay adrift in the Gulf of Guinea. How Gabriel and his fellow angels had hollowed out an iceberg pinned against the island of Kvitoya. How Captain Anthony Van Horne of the United States Merchant Marine, acting on orders from Rome, had piloted the supertanker *Carpco Valparaíso* to the body's splashdown point off the coast of Gabon, strung two parallel chains from her afterdeck, secured them inside the divine ears, and—after a series of harrowing adventures—towed this strange cargo to the Arctic and deposited it inside the great crypt.

While the fact that its Creator was quite possibly dead

proved, on the whole, depressing for the human race, the situation nevertheless boasted a bright side. To the tabloid press the Corpus Dei was a godsend. General Dynamics was delivered from bankruptcy when the Vatican commissioned it to build the cooling chamber that, if He was indeed defunct, would presumably spare His body an unsightly dissolution. Lockheed Corporation was likewise saved when it submitted the low bid on the Series 7000 heart-lung machine that, if He in fact harbored a spark of life, might possibly stabilize Him. And, of course, there were those thousands of O-positive donors who, upon contributing their blood to this unprecedented project, experienced a variety of spiritual satisfaction no human beings had known before.

Grief became a growth industry. Sympathy cards flowed back and forth among the world's bereaved believers (even I sent one, to myself)—a phenomenon that not only quadrupled the worth of Hallmark, Incorporated, but forced the U.S. Postal Service to double its normal number of carriers. The major airlines fell over themselves offering discount rates to pilgrims wishing to pay their last respects. Arriving at the port of Naples, where the Corpus Dei was now moored (another tow by the tireless Van Horne), the mourners purchased bouquets from dockside vendors and tossed them into the waters, watching through tear-stained eyes as the currents bore the flowers across the bay and deposited them alongside His cooling chamber. For the first time in history, orchids had become a bonanza crop, eclipsing both tobacco and cotton, bowing only to opium.

From New Year's Day until well past Easter, Rome's startling revelation commanded the front page of every major newspaper in the Western hemisphere. Dead or alive? Corpse or coma victim? Above all loomed the question of causality. Assuming that the object was in fact a corpse, by what means and for what purpose did God die, and why now? Had He been murdered by a force even greater than Himself? Taken a good, hard look at His favorite species and forthwith succumbed to despair?

But then, inevitably, other matters caught the public's attention—the famine in Mozambique, the unexpected success of the Boston Red Sox—and the Corpus Dei was relegated to the op-ed pages and the occasional political cartoon. Even the *Weekly World News* saw the handwriting on the wall, and by the end of the year headlines such as COMA DEITY COMMUNICATES BY BLINKING and ALIENS USE GOD'S BODY AS LANDING FIELD had been supplanted by ELVIS SIGHTED AT LOURDES and DEAD SEA SCROLLS YIELD ARTHRITIS CURE. If people talked about the Naples cadaver at all, it was merely to repeat one of the tasteless jokes—offensive even to me—then in circulation. ("So one day God's doctors are poking Him with these huge electrodes, and He starts coughing. Suddenly He spits out the corpse of Charles de Gaulle. The first doctor turns to the second and says, 'No wonder He couldn't breathe. He had a Frog in His throat.'") Finally, even the jokes stopped.

The tragedy returned briefly to the fore when the Vatican, seeking to expand its missionary program and recover from various ill-considered real estate ventures in eastern Europe, agreed to sell the Corpus Dei to the American Baptist Confederation—on condition that the new owners keep Him inside the cooling chamber and connected to the Lockheed 7000. The negotiations stretched over months. Five law firms on two continents got into the act. Eventually the Baptists paid 1.3 billion dollars for God. To many observers (myself included) the price seemed exorbitant—until it became clear that the Corpus Dei's new owners fully intended to recoup their investment, their plan being to found a theme park called Celestial City USA and make Him its centerpiece.

But it wasn't the body of God per se that brought people in droves to the Celestial City. It wasn't the rides, the gardens, the shops, or the concerts, and it certainly wasn't the muggy Orlando air. It was the fact that, of the innumerable emphysema victims, arteriosclerosis sufferers, manic-depressives, alcoholics, diabetics, hemophiliacs, and cancer patients who visited the City and beheld the Corpse of Corpses, one out of five returned home cured—or so the brochures claimed.

❖

"Our best course of action would be an immediate and total prostatectomy," said Dr. Hummel. "You'd be rendered impotent, I'm afraid, but it's our only hope for a remission."

A feeling of suffocation overcame Martin, a sense of being swallowed by something cold and miasmal, as if he were sinking to the bottom of Abaddon Marsh. His hands smacked together in prayer. Although he hadn't attended church in years, preferring to engage his Creator the way a person might retain a private tutor (as opposed to the collegiate model of organized religion), his faith had remained steadfast. One thing he'd never understood was how any sane person could neglect to cultivate a relationship with God. When the doctor said "prostatectomy," what was there to keep an atheist from going mad?

Of course, Martin had to admit that faith was something he'd come by easily. Before succumbing to heart disease at age seventy-eight, his father had been the most popular Sunday school teacher in the history of Perkinsville First Presbyterian. A flair for the dramatic and a talent for the mawkish were chief among Walter Candle's gifts as an apostle to the young. Several times a year Walter would herd his students into an ancient, preindustrial section of Hillcrest Cemetery and instruct them to make rubbings of the deteriorating limestone markers. ("Before the turn of the century, all these names and dates will be gone, erased by wind and rain. It's up to us to save them. The dead deserve no less.") In an equally effective lesson, Walter would bring in an artificial Christmas tree decorated with miniature chocolate doughnuts and, seeking to help his students empathize with Eve's ordeal of temptation, forbid them to eat.

"I'd like a second opinion," Martin told Hummel.

"In your shoes, so would I."

By canceling the speeding ticket that Ralph Avelthorpe, son of a prominent Deer Haven neurosurgeon, had acquired in Abaddon Township, Martin was able to wrangle an early appointment with Benjamin Blumenberg, chief of urology at New York City's Memorial Sloan-Kettering Cancer Center. He hated to abuse his office so blatantly, but he was desperate.

Whether Dr. Blumenberg turned out to be old or young, Martin was determined to find him impressive. If old, he would be thankful so much experience was being marshalled against his illness. If young, he would decide he was in the hands of a prodigy, the Bobby Fischer of urology. But Dr. Blumenberg, when Martin finally got to see him, did not appear to be any particular age—somewhere in his late forties, perhaps his early fifties—nor was there anything striking about his appearance: doughy face, thinning hair, tortoiseshell glasses. His only remarkable feature was his voice, which had the raspy, beleaguered quality of Montgomery Clift in *Judgment at Nuremberg*.

This great doctor, this urologist's urologist, studied the pathology report, palpated Martin's gland, and said, "I'm glad you didn't opt for the prostatectomy."

Relief flooded through him. "You mean—it's not so bad?"

"Far as I can tell, the hard area on your left lobe is close to the prostatic capsule. Truth is, I suspect it's gone outside the capsule to involve the seminal vesicle."

Martin gulped audibly. His bowels turned to water. "It's . . . spreading?"

The specialist nodded. "A radical prostatectomy is justified only when there's a solitary nodule the surgeon has a chance of removing in toto. Don't despair, sir. Alternatives exist. We could try synthetic estrogen—you know, female hormones. Menaval, maybe, or Feminone."

"Estrogen?" groaned Martin.

Blumenberg offered a grimace of commiseration. "The side effects are crummy. Erosion of the sex drive. Gynecomastia."

"Gyneco—?"

"You'll grow breasts. And the hormones alone won't be enough. I'd have to do an orchidectomy."

"My orchids?" said Martin with a nervous little laugh.

"Your orchids."

"Please." He squirmed. "I'm only fifty-two."

"Happily, there's another route, equally promising: radiation. We can shield your testicles, shlong, the whole package. With any luck, your sexual functioning will remain intact. Step one is a lymphangiogram to determine whether the tumor has migrated beyond the vesicle. Can you go into the hospital on Thursday?"

❖

Lymphangiogram: lovely word—wouldn't you say?—so layered and mellifluous, its syllables rising and falling like the soft, gentle slopes of a woodland meadow. *Lym-phan-gi-o-gram*. Someday I shall embroider LYMPHANGIOGRAM on the back of my red velvet smoking jacket.

Did I ever tell you how I sold our Creator on cancer? I walked into the pitch meeting and said, "Got a new pathology for You."

"Shoot."

"Solipsistic cannibalism. Your body starts eating itself alive."

"Like it."

"Thought You would. I call it *glutch*."

"Glutch? Glutch? Come on, Sarkos, what the hell kind of name for a dread disease is glutch? You can think of something more euphonious than that."

Thus did my masterpiece acquire its association with a half dozen of the world's most soothing and musical sounds. *Cancer. Metastasis. Carcinoma. Tumor. Oncology. Lymphangiogram.*

❖

Martin's lymphangiogram disclosed three abnormal lymph nodes in the vicinity of his prostate.

"Abnormal?" he wailed. "You mean malignant?"

"We won't know till we biopsy them," said Blumenberg. "If I had to make a guess, though . . . yes, Martin, malignant."

"Can we beat it, Doc? Is this cancer gonna kill me?"

"These days, with God out of commission, it's hard to know anything for sure."

"I don't believe He's out of commission."

"You favor the Mayfly Theory?"

"Don't you?"

Blumenberg shrugged. "When it comes to God, I have very few opinions. It's all I can do to keep up with urology. But to answer your first question: yes, I think we can beat it."

On May 25 Martin returned to the hospital, and twenty-two hours later Blumenberg cut into his abdomen. The specialist biopsied the three suspicious nodes, and each proved rife with cancer cells. Blumenberg excised these nasty little time bombs, then biopsied their neighbors, subsequently taking his knife to the ones infiltrated by carcinoma: the majority, predictably. With Martin already out cold on the table, Blumenberg decided to start therapy immediately, sowing the diseased gland with several dozen radioactive I-125 microcapsules, each no bigger than a grain of sand.

Surfacing into consciousness, Martin grew instantly aware of the violence wrought by Blumenberg's scalpel. From pole to pole, his belly throbbed and spasmed. He felt as if some demonic child had opened up his abdomen with a beach shovel, reached inside, and attempted to fashion a toy castle from his viscera.

A nurse stood by his bedside, wielding a syringe filled with Demerol. She jabbed the needle into his thigh, flashed a professional smile, and pushed the plunger.

Corinne squeezed his hand.

"The nodes," he rasped.

"It's what we thought," said Corinne.

"Positive?"

"Blumenberg cut 'em out, every last one." She lifted his fingers to her lips and kissed them. "Listen, honey, he also stuck forty-six radiation microcapsules in your prostate. It's a cure, Martin. In two days the side effects will hit, nausea, weakness, that sort of thing, but meanwhile the seeds will be hard at work, shrinking the tumor, and then the prostatitis will vanish too."

Martin was no fool. He knew that a man whose lymph nodes have been invaded by cancer cannot count on living for much more than a year.

"It's time we took a . . . vacation," he told his wife, the Demerol fuzzing his enunciation. "It's time we went to . . . went to . . . went . . ."

"Went to . . . ?"

"Orlando."

Chapter 2

NOTHING DELIGHTS ME SO MUCH as spoiling a surprise. Stapleton masterminded the Hound of the Baskervilles. Rosebud was Charlie Kane's sled. Jim Young pawned his watch to buy Della a set of combs even as Della was selling her hair to buy Jim a watch chain. God willed Himself into a death trance because He thought He'd do His creatures more good that way.

As the Jesuit cosmologist Father Thomas Ockham put it in his best-selling *Parables for a Post-theistic Age*, "It was essentially a strategy for forcing our species to grow up. By preventing us from taking Him for granted, He is making us fall back on our own resources."

So now you know. Mystery solved. Case closed. Unfortunately for His grand scheme, however, our Creator failed to reckon on Celestial City USA. As usual, He underestimated the human potential for self-deception.

❖

Among the drawbacks of developing a terminal illness while still relatively young is the large number of people you must notify. Most of your loved ones are still alive. On the day before Martin and Corinne's scheduled departure for Orlando, he telephoned everyone who mattered to him.

He began with his liberal Democrat sister, Jenny Candle, knowing that her talent for transmuting life's conventional horrors into black comedy would give him a needed lift.

"Oh, God—I'm so sorry."

"Say something funny, Jenny."

"Funny? How can prostate cancer be funny?"

"It's not as funny as lung cancer, but it's still pretty funny."

"You tell Mom yet?"

"Haven't worked up the courage."

"This'll be good for her. All those years of wasting her anxiety skills on trivia. 'What if I run out of candy on Halloween?' 'What'll happen when the boy who cuts my grass goes to college?' Now she's got something she can sink her teeth into."

"Cancer is worthy of her."

"We're gonna whup this thing, Brother Man," Jenny insisted, shifting into her impersonation of Elizabeth Taylor as Maggie the Cat. "We're gonna whup this thing till Hell won't have it again."

The next people to learn of his diagnosis were his two ex-fiancées. Robin McLaughlin, a dental technician with whom he'd lived while they both attended Perkinsville Community College, began weeping hysterically. Filtered through the telephone receiver, her sobs sounded like the death rattle of a Kennel of Joy client. At first he declined to call Brittany Rabson, who claimed to despise him these days but who was nevertheless continually arranging for their lives to intersect in pointless ways. ("Marty, do you have those snapshots of us feeding the ducks in Fairmount Park?") After thinking it over, he decided he'd better contact her: if the news arrived indirectly, he would never hear the end of it. Upon learning of Martin's tumor, Brittany reacted with characteristic narcissism, insisting that when he was in his final throes, withering away on a morphine drip, *she'd* be the one he could count on, *she'd* be the one who'd appear at his bedside, assuming he had the foresight to summon her.

Then came Mom, a Montclair, New Jersey, rose fancier and neurasthenic who habitually came on like Olga Prozorova yearning for Moscow, though in Siobhan's case the locus of her fantasies was her ancestral Belfast. After absorbing the blow, she predictably went to pieces, calming down only after Martin explained that he intended to visit the Celestial City.

"Your father would like that."

He saved his campaign manager for last: Vaughn Poffley, a scrappy extrovert who, when he wasn't making sure the office of JP remained in Republican hands, earned his living teaching driver's ed ("dread," the students called it) at Abaddon Senior High.

Martin and Vaughn had first met at a school board meeting. It was June 15, 1991, and Martin had come to protest the proposed elimination of driver's ed from the senior high curriculum, a budget reduction scheme he'd read about that morning in the *Abaddon Sentinel*. Recognized by the chairman, he stood up and explained that his conscience had compelled him to attend. As their local magistrate, he'd seen firsthand the damage that lack of driver's education caused. Martin told about broken bodies and bashed brains, dashed hopes and ruined lives. Were these loving parents truly willing to send their children onto the open road untutored in the art of defensive driving?

All in all, a brilliant performance, and by evening's end not only did Vaughn still have a job but Driving 101 had become a graduation requirement.

As the meeting broke up, Vaughn marched over and introduced himself—a short, balding, effusive man with a mild lisp. "Any time you need a favor," he said, clasping Martin's hand, "all you gotta do is ask."

Normally Martin would have dismissed Vaughn's offer as

the rhetorical pleasantry it was, but he'd been feeling over-whelmed of late, ever since Brittany had moved out on him. While the woman's intractable vanity and affection for Sturm und Drang had made the relationship qua relationship impos-sible, she'd been a splendid campaign manager. "Now that you mention it, I could use some help with my reelection effort. Leafletting, door-to-door canvassing . . ."

"I'm your man," said Vaughn. "Who's our opposition?"

"Some goat-cheese-eating liberal lawyer from Oregon."

"What angle do we play up? Candle the family man?"

"I haven't got a family. I don't particularly like children."

"Honesty, that's our gimmick. Honesty and experience."

Despite the impromptu circumstances of his hiring, Vaughn Poffley proved as effective in the job as Brittany, inventing a memorable campaign slogan—CARTWRIGHT IS ALL RIGHT, BUT HE CAN'T HOLD A CANDLE TO CANDLE—and plastering it on hundreds of telephone poles and billboards throughout Abaddon Town-ship. Without slinging mud or descending into sleaze, he handed Martin a winning margin of 2,418 votes.

Upon hearing that his friend had cancer, Vaughn steered the conversation in a pragmatic direction, asking Martin whether he still intended to enter the upcoming election. When Martin an-swered yes, Vaughn urged him to keep his illness secret.

"I'm not saying we should be deceitful, but November will be here before we know it. You'd be surprised how skittish voters get about cancer. They don't like it one little bit."

That evening, Martin and Corinne made love. Although Blu-menberg claimed that the implanted I-125 microcapsules would not contaminate his semen, Martin insisted on using condoms. Safe radioactive sex. In Corinne's view, the encounter owed its energy to its illicitness: she was abducting her lover, she felt—stealing him from the embrace of his disease. For Mar-tin, too, the night proved unprecedented in its intensity; their bed, it seemed, had transported them to a place of unbearable

urgency—to a battlefield, or a burning forest, or a South Seas
beach at the height of a typhoon.

❖

USAir Flight 3051 from Philadelphia to Orlando arrived nine
minutes early, touching down at 6:56 P.M. Upon entering the
terminal—the first time he'd ever set foot in Florida—Martin
encountered two gigantic posters, one of Mickey Mouse exhort-
ing his fans to visit Disney World, the other of Jesus Christ
bidding his followers to patronize Celestial City USA, neither
image doing much to alleviate Martin's depression. Shortly after
retrieving their luggage, he and Corinne found themselves in a
limousine zooming down Route 528, bound for the Buena Vista
Hilton. Ranks of swaying palm trees zoomed past, fronds rippling in the wind like piano keys yielding to invisible fingers.

To this day, some people argue that the Celestial City would
have been a roaring success no matter where its founders had
situated it. The original plan called for God and His accessories
to be towed via supertanker from the Mediterranean to the Gulf
of Mexico, then beached along the sparsely populated eastern
shore of Tampa Bay, there to lie beneath the Florida sun while
the great theme park emerged at His feet. But the stockholders
of Eternity Enterprises would hear none of this: the carcass, they
insisted, must be located in Orlando or nowhere at all—without
the spillover crowds from Disney World, Epcot Center, Univer-
sal Studios, Sea World, and the headquarters of Tupperware
International, the proposed attraction might fail to turn a profit.
And so began the greatest engineering project since the Suez
Canal. Thirty-eight steel gantries, each as tall as the World Trade
Center, were built especially for the task. They performed splen-
didly, lifting the Lockheed 7000 cooling chamber from the waters off Cocoa Beach and slinging it landward. Next the chamber
was placed atop a matrix of ninety-four railroad flatcars, transported for fifty miles along eight steel tracks laid parallel to

Route 528, and deposited north of Big Sand Lake. The haul required the collective energy of seventy-two GP diesel locomotives, five of which exploded en route and never saw service again.

Although the park would be open until midnight, the couple decided to remain in their hotel, Martin being nauseated, Corinne exhausted. The next morning they climbed aboard the shuttle bus, where a sobering spectacle awaited them. Martin wasn't the only one who'd come to Orlando out of desperation. Seated behind the driver was a withered old woman whose neck sported a goiter the size of a coconut. Beside her rested a bald young man with an oxygen mask strapped across his face. Nearly a third of the riders, in fact, exhibited various dire medical conditions, making the bus seem like nothing so much as an ambulance evacuating the survivors of some strange and far-reaching catastrophe.

Within a half hour the City loomed up, its spires and parapets cutting into the sky like guided missiles poised for takeoff. Cameras dangling from their necks, the passengers headed for the main gate, a ponderous post-and-lintel affair plated with gold, encrusted with cultured pearls, and surmounted by the park's logo: a many-towered, rainbow-roofed palace sitting atop a foundation of clouds. The breezes reeked of orange blossoms. A flock of pure white radio-controlled doves soared overhead, singing "Follow the Gleam" a cappella.

The pilgrims lined up at the ticket booth. Upon shelling out fifty-five dollars, each visitor received a packet containing a folding map, a laminated eight-inch Key to the Kingdom good for all the major rides, and a spiral-bound *Visitor's Guide to Celestial City USA*. A few yards away a band of demonstrators milled around, their T-shirts identifying them as the National Science Foundation's strident splinter group, the Committee for Complete Disclosure of the Corpus Dei. LET US INTO THE BRAIN NOW, a protest sign demanded in capital letters. SCIENTIFIC CURIOSITY: A GIFT FROM GOD, a twenty-foot banner declared. As Martin wove through the mob, he inadvertently looked a demonstrator in the eye—a stocky, bearded man whose placard read ETERNITY EN-TERPRISES: ENEMY OF TRUTH.

"Don't give them your business," the scientist pleaded, brushing the sleeve of Martin's Hawaiian shirt.

"I'm sick," he explained, breaking away and joining the other tourists. "I'm dying!" he cried, passing through the gate. "They don't deserve it!"

As he entered the City, Martin was immediately struck by its aggressive cleanliness. Everywhere he turned, he saw rolling hills so expertly manicured they might have been transplanted from William Randolph Hearst's private golf course. White marble fountains dotted the landscape, huge cherub-encrusted structures spewing what looked like luminous milk.

The final paragraph of the *Visitor's Guide to Celestial City USA* was titled "Hope for the Afflicted." *Hope*. The word enthralled Martin. He and Corinne read the passage three times, standing in the shade of an olive tree.

Although the City's healing energies emanate primarily from our Main Attraction, the entire park possesses therapeutic powers, and the stricken visitor is advised to sample a full spectrum of Holyspots. In one famous case, Orville Hazelton, a New Orleans taxi driver, received relief from his duodenal ulcer symptoms after winning a cuckoo clock at the Hammer of Jael nail-driving contest (located on the Millennial Midway, right across from the Stoning of Stephen rock toss), though the process became complete only after Mr. Hazelton beheld the Godform. In a second such instance, the rehabilitation of Wilma Alcott, a Kansas chicken farmer suffering from a rare liver ailment, began after she consumed a lobster dinner at the Last Supper café (on Straight and Narrow Lane, adjacent to the Manna from Heaven bistro), though naturally it took the Godform to finish her cure.

"Do you believe this crap?" asked Martin. "This business about patronizing every attraction—do you believe it's true?"

"As long as we've come all the way to Orlando," said Corinne, cleaning her sunglasses with the edge of her muslin blouse, "we should probably play by the rules."

Thus began a long, tedious morning of standing in lines. The wait was twenty-three minutes for the Chariots of Ezekiel ferris wheel, thirty-one for the Whore of Babylon funhouse, twenty-eight for the Stations of the Cross steam train, and seventeen for the Garden of Eden petting zoo. Of these concessions only the last gave the couple any pleasure, Corinne achieving instant rapport with the sheep and goats, Martin taking lascivious delight in the ceramic Eve, her breasts scarcely concealed by her long flaxen hair. Oddly enough, there was no line at the Four Horsemen of the Apocalypse carousel. Passing through the gate, Corinne selected one of the seven Famine stallions, all bones and sagging skin, while Martin picked a War mount, its flanks arrayed in spiked armor. They consciously declined to ride the animals intended for Death (not a horse but a horse's skeleton, carved from cherrywood and painted white) and Pestilence (a roan mare speckled with buboes). As the carousel reached top speed, the steam calliope screeched out "Onward Christian Soldiers."

More waiting—a full half hour for the Heaven to Hell roller coaster, an admittedly thrilling experience that lifted you past airborne choirs of android angels, then dropped you into fiery chasms where screaming adulterers writhed in pools of molten sulfur and spitted gluttons roasted over slow fires. The hiatus required for a berth on Noah's Ark, thirty-six minutes, was also worth it. There you sat, looking through your private porthole at mobs of drowning audio-animatronic sinners while the rain poured down and the restless seas pitched you to and fro.

At 1:45 P.M. the couple dropped into the Loaves and Fishes café. Martin decided to try the specialty of the house, haddock on sourdough. His wife ordered a Caesar salad. The food arrived promptly. To Martin it looked grotesque. These days most things looked grotesque. The intractable fact of his illness had become a kind of theatrical scrim, imparting a pall to whatever met his gaze. His eyes drifted across the table, moving from the twisted salt cellar to the sinister napkin dispenser to the menacing fillet on his plate.

"What would your father have made of the Celestial City?" asked Corinne.

Martin stared at his malformed mug of coffee. "I think he would've hated it. Sure, Dad could be pretty corny at times, having his students make gravestone rubbings and everything, but he was never vulgar. This place is vulgar. What are we doing here?"

Corinne raised her sunglasses, pushing them into her auburn hair. A wave of romantic longing washed through him, so pure and fierce he imagined it joining forces with the I-125 seeds to cleanse his prostate of cancer. How wise he'd been to delay marriage until the right woman came along; how astute of him to have passed up Robin's endearing sense of humor and Brittany's mastery of Chinese cooking and fellatio.

"We're here to make you well."

"Fat chance."

She bit into a carrot stick. Memories rushed past his mind's eye like snatches of scenery glimpsed by a man riding the Four Horsemen of the Apocalypse carousel. The two of them walking hand-in-hand across a railroad trestle in the Poconos. Reading to each other from the *Kama Sutra*. Playing chess in the nude.

> But Lancelot mused a little space;
> He said, "She has a lovely face;
> God in His mercy lend her grace,
> The Lady of Shalott."

"You have a lovely face."
"Thank you."

"I'm scared."

"I love you, Martin. Terribly and forever."

"I'm scared to death."

"Of course."

"I don't *feel* lovable."

She lifted her glass of tomato juice, took a sip, and swallowed. "Judge Candle, you're my knight in shining armor."

❖

Visiting the midway later that afternoon, Martin blew five dollars on the Stoning of Stephen rock toss. He continually failed to connect with the mannequin, while all around him corn-fed adolescents were drawing ersatz blood and receiving plush lambs and stuffed cherubs. He did much better at the Head of Holofernes, winning an Archangel Michael helium balloon by decapitating the dummy within twenty seconds, and he was positively brilliant at the David and Goliath slingshot tournament, beating out six other contestants in a race to slay the Philistine. His prize was a music box programmed to provide "a soothing aural environment for private readings of the Psalms."

The tours of the Main Attraction departed every hour on the hour, and Martin went crimson with rage upon learning that his Key to the Kingdom would not admit him. He calmed down only after voicing his dismay to two security guards, a T-shirt vendor, and an itinerant guitarist who sang evangelical Christian folk songs. To get the full Celestial City experience, Martin and Corinne had to ride a mechanized walkway south for a mile, then queue up at a ticket booth resembling a ziggurat. In the misty distance God's cooling chamber loomed, a vague mass on the horizon, its facets shimmering in the afternoon sun like Solomon's shields of beaten gold. Examining their tickets—thirty-five dollars each—the couple saw they'd been assigned to Group C, scheduled to leave at four P.M. When the designated hour arrived, a guide appeared and escorted her twelve charges inside a glass-and-steel kiosk housing a ruby-studded escalator plunging perpetually into the central Florida earth.

"On behalf of the American Baptist Confederation, I want to welcome y'all to the Main Attraction at Celestial City USA," the guide began in a honeyed and melodious voice. She was a tall, toothy blonde, no more than twenty-five, dressed in the lemon rayon shirt and white polyester slacks that constituted the City's official uniform. "My name's Kimberly, and I'll be happy to answer your questions, but first I gotta lay down one great big rule," she continued with manufactured cheer. "We're here today to enjoy a profound spiritual experience—we're *not* here to have ourselves a debate. Understand? Some of you've probably heard that the object we're about to see is God's comatose body. The American Baptist Confederation believes otherwise. Our Main Attraction is God's discarded form—a suit of clothes, you might say, that He tossed aside on the way to becoming pure spirit." She cranked her smile up a notch. "The heavenly Father is alive as ever, friends, the Son still reigns supreme"—she drove her clenched fist forward, as if shattering a pane of glass—"and the Holy Ghost dwells within us yet!"

As they started their descent, Martin realized the escalator had been designed especially for the City, each riser built wide enough to carry not only the individual pilgrim but whatever equipment he or she required. Three Group C members occupied wheelchairs: a pudgy young woman, a pimply teenage boy, a swarthy septuagenarian. Two other pilgrims, a svelte Chinese woman and a sinewy black man, made the journey downward attached to portable dialysis machines, chattering to each other all the while, the shoptalk of terminal illness.

At the bottom of the escalator an arched tunnel stretched as far as the eye could see, its ceiling supporting a monorail from which a streamlined, bullet-shaped tram hung like a caterpillar negotiating a twig. After all the passengers were aboard, Kimberly plucked a megaphone from its cradle behind the engineer's booth. The tram lurched forward, gliding into a tunnel speckled with twinkling lights, a kind of cylindrical planetarium.

"Each of these constellations is mentioned in the Bible," Kimberly announced into her megaphone. "Job 38:31, for example. 'Can you bind the cluster of the Pleiades or loose Orion's belt?' "

A mile down the monorail, the tunnel opened into a room suggesting an immense Antarctic cavern. Patches of frost covered the tiled walls. Icicles hung from the ceiling like stalactites.

"Station one: Preservation Central," Kimberly lectured as the tram slowed to a crawl. "I could tell the engineer to stop and let y'all explore, but, believe me, you don't want to. This room connects directly to our cooling chamber, and the temperature out there averages"—she mimed a shudder—"*brrr*, fourteen degrees! See that humongous silver tank? It contains nearly eighty thousand gallons of high-pressure Freon-114. After leaving the tank, the Freon spills into that huge green basketball thing, which allows it to reach a much lower pressure, then it slithers into that big snaky tube over yonder, where, *pffff*, it boils away, absorbing lots of heat in the bargain and thereby keeping our Main Attraction as cold as a penguin's kiss. Meanwhile, that big motor in the corner sucks up the Freon vapor and squeezes it so tight it starts wanting to change back into a liquid. The Freon gets its wish the minute it reaches that *other* big snaky tube. See how we've got lots of water pouring down like Jehovah sending the Flood? That's our trick for speeding up the condensation. Once the Freon's become a liquid again, it returns to the silver tank, and the whole process starts over. Anybody got a question?"

Not one person on the tram, Martin guessed, had been able to follow Kimberly's lecture. They all remained mute.

The cavern narrowed. The tram sped a thousand yards into the next station: another subterranean room, dominated by the most astonishing contraption Martin had ever seen. A steel-plated pump as big as a jetliner intersected a labyrinthine network of six-foot-wide transparent Plexiglas pipes, which were in turn connected to four igloo-sized aeration domes surmounted by an accordion-shaped bellows so gigantic it could have fanned a forest fire. Each pipe held a churning river, blue when it entered the domes, red on departure. A rhythmic thundering filled the air, a steady *thok-thok-thok* that rocked the tram back and forth on its rail.

"Station two: Cardiovascular Control," Kimberly explained into the megaphone, her voice building toward a shout. "As y'all know, not everybody agrees with us that His brain has no need of blood. Here at Celestial City USA we respect all viewpoints, so we keep Him hooked up to that device on your left: a Lockheed 7000 heart-lung machine. Every day of the year over a million gallons of O-positive blood are shunted into those aeration domes, each with a volume of two thousand cubic feet. Once inside, the blood is warmed, oxygenated, and filtered of impurities before getting pumped into His veins. The plasma itself— this part always kind of chokes me up—the plasma itself comes from just about every nation on Earth. Protestants, Catholics, Jews, and Muslims have all made donations, even an atheist named Jules Wembly. If any of you would like to augment the flow before leaving the City, just drop by one of the clinics conveniently located at each exit. Any questions?"

An emaciated young man with four Kaposi's sarcoma lesions on his forehead raised his hand. "May I leave the tram for a minute?" he yelled over the roar of the heart-lung machine. "I want to touch one of the pipes."

"We don't allow that."

"Please."

"It's simply not permitted."

"I must."

"No way, sir. Out there, the noise of the pump is enough to cause permanent hearing loss."

"Let me feel His blood, and I shall be made whole!"

Kimberly winced, and for the first time Martin saw that her job had a downside. "No. Sorry. No."

The tram moved on—through Cardiovascular Control and back into the tunnel.

"We're entering the Corridor of the Cured," Kimberly narrated as Group C traveled past dozens of illuminated niches, each filled with a device more commonly found on the premises of the halt, the blind, or the lame. "Each and every item displayed here was once needed by a Celestial City visitor. No more. We have the largest such collection outside the famous shrine at Lourdes." Ambulatory aids flashed by, row upon row of crutches, canes, walkers, and wheelchairs. Braces appeared next, fearsome contrivances of steel and leather designed to straighten crooked spines and warped limbs. Farther down the line lay respirators, oxygen tanks, and dialysis machines. "Not a day goes by without one of these things arriving in our mail room. That motorized ergonomic wheelchair came all the way from Kyoto, Japan. Any questions?"

❖

I am a creature of many faces, manifold personae, multiple disguises. While our hero was touring the Corridor of the Cured, I was making myself a new suit: red pants, red jacket, red cap, all trimmed with white weasel fur. Yes, friends, my alter ego is none other than Father Christmas himself. Excavate our respective mythoi, and you will learn that Satan and Santa are one and the same, beginning with the anagrammatic connection between our names. According to legend, the frozen north is the Devil's pied-à-terre, where he flies through the air aided by a team of reindeer. He enters people's homes via their chimneys. Food and wine are left out for him as a bribe. His sobriquet "Old Nick" derives from "Saint Nicholas."

Needless to say, my admiration for the Corridor of the Cured was boundless. As frauds go, the Corridor easily eclipsed

Piltdown man, the Hitler diaries, and Clarence Thomas's testimony before the Senate Judiciary Committee. Which is not to say the Celestial City's visitors never benefited from the Main Attraction. *Au contraire.* Thanks to the placebo effect, these wretched pilgrims routinely enjoyed spontaneous remissions. And while it's true that the Corridor's proprietors obtained most of their display items from medical supply houses, their aim was not deception for deception's sake—no, they merely wanted to harness deception to a profitable variety of healing. Never underestimate the value of a falsehood, friends. Never doubt the power of a lie. Blessed are the mendacious, for they shall grow wealthy beyond their wildest dreams.

In case you're wondering, I don't spend the entire workday inside my tailor shop. Even the Devil deserves a break. Come noon, I set down my sewing needle, grab my lunch pail, and stroll into the blinding glare of His neurons. Usually I'm content to explore the immediate neighborhood, wandering through His olfactory center, a few miles due east of the hippocampus; but sometimes the arteries beckon. During the hour that Martin and Corinne were dining at the Loaves and Fishes café, for example, my friend Bishop Augustine and I were piloting my rusty old packet steamer down the crimson channel that feeds our Creator's left cerebral hemisphere, eating corned-beef sandwiches and trailing a fish line from our stern. I'm eternally grateful to Lockheed for building the heart-lung machine. Because of this technology, the River Hiddekel's sanguine currents remain deep, clean, and fecund. On most of our expeditions Augustine and I catch at least one leukocyte and a mess of red blood corpuscles.

My days, I know, are numbered. All around me the landscape is disintegrating, despite the efforts of His keepers and their Lockheed 7000. Jerusalem's walls are crumbling, Eden's trees are dying, the Euphrates has become a sewer, the maggots shall inherit His meat. Luckily, our Creator constructed reality with an eye to His ultimate departure. He filled the universe with self-sustaining miracles. Long after He and I are gone, the great geophysical processes will continue yielding earthquakes and volcanoes, the vicissitudes of biology will bring forth multiple sclerosis and cancer, and the perversities of human nature will keep rape and murder in the headlines.

The one person to whom I have difficulty lying is myself, and in all candor I must admit I became obsolete long before I became mortal. Oh, how I long for that era when my Creator wasn't comatose and people consulted me as frequently as they now see psychiatrists, Mafia godfathers, and other members of the helping professions; that golden age when Madame de Montespan, Louis XIV's mistress, implored me to render the queen sterile so the king's attentions might be wholly fixed on her; that bygone time when the nuns of Loudon hired me to help them release their pent-up sexual frustrations. I don't want your sympathy, friends. I don't want your understanding. I merely want to be taken as seriously by you as Santa Claus is taken by your children.

❖

"Station three: the Cooling Chamber," said Kimberly as the tram reached the end of the Corridor of the Cured. "Please watch your step."

The tour guide led Group C through a terminal decorated with a facsimile of Donatello's bronze *David* and a reproduction of Leonardo's *Last Supper*, then into a passenger elevator so roomy it accommodated the entire party, wheelchairs and all.

"Two thousand and eighty-four feet from here to the top," said Kimberly, pushing a button. The door whooshed closed. Vibrating gently, the car shot heavenward. Three minutes later, it stopped. "All out, please."

Disembarking, Martin found himself atop a transparent Lucite plain. A larger-than-life facsimile of Michelangelo's marble *Pietà* loomed over the pilgrims. Beyond the *Pietà* stretched a meandering footpath bordered by flower boxes abloom with daffodils and hyacinths. Every six feet, a neon arrow lay embedded in the polymer, blinking bright red as it pointed the visitor toward the next checkpoint on his trek across the Main Attraction.

"As befits a journey so intimate, your meeting with the Godform will be entirely self-directed," said Kimberly. "Allow forty minutes for the complete circuit. Seven private chapels, three rest rooms, and a dozen snapshot opportunities are located along the way." She glanced at her Twelve Disciples wristwatch. "I'll expect you back at this statue no later than five-thirty."

Sneaking up behind him, Corinne seized Martin's hand, entwining their fingers in a fleshy knot. "You'd better follow this path alone, darling," she said. "A pagan's presence might annoy Him."

"You think so?" he asked, reverently brushing the marble Madonna's left knee.

"Let's not take any chances. You never know."

"You never know."

He started away, walking west across the Main Attraction's left nipple, then north along His sternum. There wasn't much to see. Pausing atop the frosted polymer, he directed his gaze through a hundred feet of sub-zero air and focused on the divine chest, a hairy landscape rolling a thousand yards in all directions: compelling vistas, but their therapeutic value seemed nil. He kept moving north. Reaching the mouth, he discovered to his astonishment that God, like everyone else on the staff of Celestial City USA, was smiling. The fifty-yard rictus stretched ear to ear, pulpy lips pulled back to reveal teeth as white as Ivory soap, each the size of a refrigerator door.

The path curved east, bringing him directly over the left eye. God's tear duct was as big as a barrage balloon. Staring into the luminous pupil, Martin suddenly experienced a tingling in his toes. A divine emanation, he wondered, or the mere result of standing on ice-cold Lucite? An actual intervention, or the efflux of his wishfully thinking mind?

"Help me, God," he muttered.

The tingling sinuated upward, making his knees tremble.

"Please, God! Yes, God!"

Still migrating, the tingling reached his loins—stomach—lungs—brain.

"I'm yours, God!"

His whole body quivered with epiphany.

"I'm cured!" he shouted, jogging back down the path.

Corinne was sitting in a lotus position, spine against the *Pietà*. Hearing Martin's cries, she disentangled her legs and rose. They threw themselves into each other's arms, embracing in the Madonna's sharp black shadow.

"I'm cured!"

"Oh, Martin!"

"Cured!"

"Oh, yes, Martin! Oh, yes, Martin—yes, yes!"

"I love you!"

They kissed: their most passionate such connection since her lips had melted the snowflakes from his face.

Other tourists arrived, gathering around the Madonna, hugging her robes, pressing their faces against her feet.

"Jesus has healed me!" cried the Chinese dialysis patient.

"Praise the Lord!" shouted the black dialysis patient.

"I'm signing up for dance lessons!" sang the pudgy woman.

"I'm going to Barcelona!" whooped the man with Kaposi's sarcoma, though his brow remained dotted with lesions.

On the Friday after his return from Orlando, Martin took the train to New York for his biweekly checkup at Memorial Sloan-Kettering Cancer Center. As soon as Benjamin Blumenberg entered the examination room, Martin began prattling about his pilgrimage.

"You saw the corpse?" asked Blumenberg. "What's it like?"

"It's not a *corpse*. It's the Godform. I stood over His left eye, directly on top."

"I think we might go—the kids've been asking about it, Mrs. Blumenberg too. They let Jews in, right?"

"No problem."

"And you really believe the trip put you in remission?"

"I'm sure of it."

"I want to draw some blood today, so we can check your acid phosphatase."

At four o'clock on Tuesday afternoon, Dr. Blumenberg phoned the Abaddon Municipal Building, reaching Martin shortly after he'd gotten a Glendale teenager named Todd Weatherwax to promise that his rock band, the Elementals, would stop rehearsing after ten P.M. If no cancer is present in a person's body, the urologist explained, his acid-phosphatase level will be somewhere between 2.5 and 4.0.

Martin's level, he was sorry to report, stood at 11.6.

❖

Of all the pests and parasites the Almighty has commissioned over the years, the termite continues to do me proud. As you will see, termites figure as objects of philosophical discourse throughout this tale. At the moment, however, it is termite teeth, not termite teleology, that concern us.

An unutterable despair racked Corinne Rosewood as she drove home from work that evening. Right before she'd left, her husband had phoned with his blood-test results. Tears spilled down her face. Mucus dribbled from her nose. Eleven point six. She hadn't felt so wretched since the death of her girlhood Welsh corgi, Gwyneth.

Carefully she guided her Ford Ranger onto the Henry Avenue Bridge, an aging span of oak and iron that crossed the Algonquin River three miles above the point where it met Abaddon Township's beloved Waupelani Creek to form the muddy Schuylkill. The mammoth wooden guardrails were riddled with 27,489 holes, each wrought by one of my termites.

Eleven point six, she brooded. Eleven point six. And yet they'd been so sure their trip to the City had helped him, so sure, so sure—

A nervous and confused Irish setter dashed into the path of Rosewood's truck. She did exactly what one would expect of the Kennel of Joy's founder and president—she stomped on the brake pedal and swerved the wheel. The Ranger skidded, careening wildly, its right fender fracturing the setter's skull. Rosewood heard the emphatic smack of metal meeting bone. Her truck kept sliding, the dog's corpse sprawled across the bumper. The guardrail splintered like Styrofoam.

She screamed, overcome by the same chaotic falling sensation she'd recently experienced on the Chariots of Ezekiel ferris wheel. Her truck hit the Algonquin and sank. Darkness suffused the cab, as if someone had thrown a blanket over the sun. The dead setter floated up past the windshield like a wraith rising from a grave. Water squirted in around the door frames, spraying Rosewood's chest and face. Frantically she felt her way through the gloom, seized the window crank, and gave it a turn. The mechanism froze, befouled with silt. The water reached her knees. She wrapped her fingers around the door handle. Yanked. Pushed. Jerked. Shoved. The door wouldn't budge, not one inch. The water caressed her stomach.

Holding her breath, she lurched toward the passenger door. She grabbed the window crank. Stuck. The water encircled her neck. She clawed at the handle and threw herself against the door. Nothing. The Algonquin rushed up her nose, down her throat, into her lungs.

A splendid golden carp was the last thing Corinne Rosewood saw in her life—a lost and forsaken creature who, seeking to rejoin its school, had fought its way a half mile up the Algonquin, getting farther from home with each twist and turn of its shining body.

Chapter 3

PRIOR TO HIS DIAGNOSIS of prostate cancer, the worst thing that had ever happened to Martin was the loss, at age fourteen, of his cherished childhood home. He'd actually stood and watched as two bulldozers knocked it down, their fearsome steel scoops toppling the walls and leveling the foundation. By this time Martin's family no longer owned the place, his father having sold it to a wealthy chiropractor named Harold Clevinger for twelve thousand dollars, a sum with which Walter Candle had immediately acquired a more conventional domicile across the street. The chiropractor's first move was to obliterate the Candle dwelling—the property per se was what enchanted him, Waupelani Creek and its palisade of weeping willows—and erect in its stead a serpentine, one-floor monstrosity suggesting nothing so much as a spine that Clevinger had failed to straighten.

Martin's family couldn't fault the chiropractor's decision to call in the bulldozers, for the edifice in question had been constructed in 1935 to accommodate Abaddon Fire Company Number One and its modest two-engine fleet. When the building was abandoned a decade later, Martin's father had purchased it for a mere forty-five hundred dollars, deploying studs and plasterboard to convert the firefighters' upper-level dormitory into a maze of domestic spaces: bedrooms, bathrooms, dining area, kitchen. As a Sunday school teacher, Walter Candle was delighted with the idea of living in a firehouse. He saw himself as a kind of spiritual firefighter, forever dousing the burning desires and blazing temptations that flared in his pupils' hearts.

Martin loved the firehouse no less than his father. He was particularly enamored of the main siren, its domed carapace straddling the peaked roof like a helmet protecting the head of an infantryman. The siren was broken beyond repair, and no one in the family pretended otherwise, and yet he fantasized that one day, somehow, the device would spring to life, releasing a banshee cry so loud his sister would wet her pants.

And so it was that when Martin, ear pressed to his telephone receiver, first heard the terrible news from Constable Steadman—"Judge, your wife's been killed in a freak accident"—he heard something else as well: the long-dead siren on his lost firehouse, howling with bereavement and dismay.

He howled, he screamed, he wailed, he moaned. He damned the moment he was conceived, cursed the hour he quickened, and rued the day he left his mother's womb. Mourning transmuted him. He became a kind of monster, a violent force of nature rampaging through the farmhouse, breaking plates and ripping down curtains. The sinking sensation returned, the horrible feeling of suffocation he'd first experienced in Dr. Hummel's office, only instead of falling through Abaddon Marsh he was trapped in a slough even colder and crueler—a swamp the size of the Godform's bowels. Were it not for the vigilance of Vaughn Poffley, he might have availed himself of the Algonquin River that week, following Corinne into oblivion.

"Casket, cemetery plot, obituary in the *Sentinel*—I took care of everything," Vaughn informed him in the same steady voice he employed when assuring Martin they could beat the Democrats' current candidate for JP. "The stone is going to read, 'She loved all creatures great and small.' That sound okay?"

Seated at his kitchen table, Martin did not respond. He uncapped the salt cellar and dumped its contents in a shapeless pile before him. He stared at the white grains—so suggestive, he decided, of the useless I-125 seeds filling his prostate. For the first time ever he began to regard his imminent death as a blessing, his best hope for escaping this world with its rapacious bulldozers and elevated acid phosphatase, its dangerous bridges and drowned wives.

"Did you know Samuel Johnson missed his wife's funeral?" he said at last. "Too much for him."

"You ought to come, Martin. You'll regret it if you don't."

"Queen Victoria couldn't bring herself to attend the services for Prince Albert." With his index finger he traced a spiral in the salt.

"All you have to do is show up. I know Corinne wasn't religious, but I've arranged for my pastor to say a few words at the graveside, nice Lutheran words—that's okay, right?—and then we'll have a reception at my place. Marge'll make coffee, plus shortbread and little sandwiches with the crusts cut off."

"Goddamn Irish setter," he said, mashing the salt with his fist.

"Just show up, that's all. Hillcrest Cemetery, Saturday, ten o'clock. Your sister'll bring you. The grave's near the lawnmower shed. It's where they keep, you know, the lawnmowers. Day after tomorrow. Lawnmower shed. Just show up."

When evening came, Martin wandered into the *Nepeta cataria* patch, sat down amid the crop, and waited. At midnight the hedonists appeared—tabbies, calicoes, Manxes—but instead of rolling around on the leaves and getting stoned they simply stared at him, their pupils dilated by the darkness, their gazes a mixture of the inquisitive and the accusatory.

Where's Corinne? the cats seemed to be asking.

"She's dead," he said out loud. "You'll never see her again."

Who will grow the crop?

"I don't know."

Will you grow it?

"I don't know."

You must.

"Think of someone besides yourselves. Think of Corinne."

We are cats.

They spent the rest of the night together: a grieving judge and thirteen apprehensive felines.

Waking at dawn, his Perkinsville College jersey damp with dew, he rose and made his way through the heart-shaped leaves and the sleeping cats. Back in the farmhouse, he opened a box of Wheaties and shook several dozen scablike flakes into a soup bowl. He looked in the refrigerator. No milk. He sprinkled four teaspoons of Cremora onto the cereal, adding cold water from the faucet. The concoction tasted astoundingly foul.

Later that morning his big-boned sister appeared, each arm wrapped around a paper bag stuffed with groceries.

"I inventoried your kitchen yesterday," said Jenny, setting the groceries on the counter. "You were out of everything, so I went to Super Fresh. How're you feeling?"

"It hurts to pee—the prostatitis must be back. My right hip aches. Do me a favor?"

"You bet."

"Those animals of Corinne's, armadillo, tarantula, there's also an iguana—think you could find homes for 'em?"

"I'll take out an ad in the *Sentinel*."

"I don't want any money, but their new owners must be responsible people. No sadistic schoolboys. No flighty teenagers."

"Right."

"Good homes, Jenny."

"You got it." She unbagged a half gallon of skim milk, two grapefruits, and a cantaloupe. "I'm sorry about your pains. I'm sorry about . . . everything."

"Do me another favor? I'd like a ride to Perkinsville Station. I've got a three o'clock with Blumenberg at Sloan-Kettering. There's a new drug he wants me to try."

"Oh, Marty, this is all so *unfair*."

"Unfair," he echoed.

"Did you know Mom's coming to the funeral?"

"She can't. It's too far away."

"I'm giving her a lift."

"She can't drive that far."

"*I'm* driving her. Aren't you listening? I'll pick *you* up too. Nine-thirty, okay?"

"I want to go alone."

"I don't understand."

"It feels right."

"Alone?"

"Alone."

He caught the 11:45 out of Perkinsville.

Just as he feared, the new drug Dr. Blumenberg wanted him to try wasn't new at all. It was Feminone, the synthetic hormone that threatened to turn him into a woman.

"I'm not going to take it," he informed the urologist.

"It's our best hope for a remission," said Blumenberg, fingering Martin's inflamed gland.

"I don't want a remission."

"Nonsense."

"It still hurts to pee. The discharges have started again."

"Bactrim ought to clear that up. Any pelvic pain?"

"Quite a bit."

"Where exactly?"

"Right hip."

"Let's put you on a maintenance dose of Roxanol: first cousin to morphine—it'll give you substantial relief. Today we'll draw blood for another acid-phosphatase check."

Dusk found Martin standing outside Memorial Sloan-Kettering Cancer Center, raindrops bouncing off his cheeks and beading the lenses of his bifocals. As the Manhattan traffic rumbled down First Avenue, spouting black exhaust and invisible toxins, he drew the Feminone prescription from his pocket and methodically crumpled it up. He stared at the wad of paper, watching it grow soggy in his hand, then tossed it into a wire mesh receptacle. If I must die, he told himself, I shall do so in the gender to which I am accustomed.

❖

On the morning of Corinne's funeral, the skies over Abaddon Township bloomed sunny and clear, heralding a day more suited to tending roses or playing badminton than to burying one's wife. "Just show up," Vaughn had said. And so, at 9:45 A.M., Martin got into his car and, like a man transporting himself to his own hanging, set off for Hillcrest Cemetery.

He hadn't seen the place in years—not since he'd gone gravestone rubbing with a dozen other kids in his father's Sunday school class. Driving along the maze of narrow roads, he half expected to glimpse Walter Candle's ghost moving among the markers, paper and charcoal in hand, preserving names and epitaphs.

Although Vaughn had implied the lawnmower shed was conspicuous, Martin couldn't find it. Three times he circumnavigated the cemetery. His hip throbbed: hardly a surprise, his current acid-phosphatase level being a whopping 12.0, according to Blumenberg. He lobbed a 20-mg Roxanol tablet into his mouth and chewed. It tasted chalky and sour. A minute later he spotted a ramshackle brick building covered with Virginia creepers, and—sure enough—a few yards away a funeral was in progress. Two dozen mourners in dark clothing stood around an open grave, its head marked by a granite tombstone, its perimeter decorated with lilies and gardenias.

The pelvic pain faded, supplanted by a mild opium high. He parked, got out, and limped toward the crowd. The grass around the grave was weed infested and unevenly clipped, a disgrace by the standards of Celestial City USA. No one greeted him. Every face looked unfamiliar. When had Corinne acquired these mysterious friends? Where had she been keeping these auxiliary relatives?

He peered into the hole. The casket was half normal size. His first thought was that one of Corinne's pets had died without his knowledge, and her friends had decided to begin the ceremony by covering its little corpse with a layer of earth, after which a hearse bearing her body would arrive and then she herself would be interred. Or else they'd *already* buried Corinne, beneath her pet, and he—the damn fool—had missed it.

He looked at the tombstone. BRANDON APPLEYARD. 1992–1999. I MISS YOU SO MUCH . . . ALL MY LOVE, MOMMY. "Excuse me," he said, brushing the sleeve of a stout woman in a print dress who appeared more bored than bereaved. "I'm Corinne's wife. Husband, I mean. Was. Martin Candle."

The woman absently kicked the flowers with the tip of her shoe. "Wife? What?"

He pointed to the brick building. "They told me . . . the lawnmower shed. My wife's getting buried today."

"That's where they keep the backhoe."

"They keep the backhoe in the lawnmower shed?"

"No, that *building* is where they keep the backhoe. You know, to dig the graves."

"Don't they use shovels?"

"Nope, a backhoe—this is the twentieth century." The woman gestured toward the rising sun. A lobe of flesh jiggled from her upper arm like a rooster's wattle. "The lawnmower shed's in that direction, quarter mile or so."

"It's awful about the boy."

"Spina bifida. I'm his great-aunt. We're waiting for his mother. The father bailed out two years ago. Couldn't deal with having a sick kid."

"How irresponsible," said Martin automatically, wondering how he might go about redressing such knavery in his courtroom.

"I never met the jerk. You aren't him, are you?"

"Oh, no."

"If you ask me, Brandon's better off with the Lord. Spina

bifida, right? Boy couldn't walk, brain damaged by hydrocephalus, not to mention the constant pain. Turn around. Quarter of a mile."

"Thanks."

Martin faced east and started away, hobbling past the ranks of glossy granite stones. He realized that a necropolis, like any other city, had enclaves. To his right lay a wealthy neighborhood—Republicans, he mused—with tombs that were veritable houses. To his left, a blue-collar district. Ahead: a Korean section, the markers carved with incomprehensible glyphs.

A slender woman wearing black pumps and a dark gray business suit rushed toward him, her mourning veil pulled back over her head, revealing an oval, tear-streaked face. Her eyes were red rimmed and unusually large, the eyes of a cartoon rabbit.

"Are you the mother?" asked Martin, leaning breathlessly against a poplar tree.

The woman stopped running and blinked. "What?"

"Brandon's mother—that's you, right?"

"My therapist said it would be good if I came here on my own, but I went to the wrong funeral," she replied, nodding. "Somebody named Corinne."

"I'm Corinne, actually. Martin, I mean. Her husband. Candle. Do you know where my funeral is, Mrs. Appleyard?"

"Please don't call me that. It's his *father's* name, not mine. A retarded son with spina bifida, five orthopedic operations, and the bastard up and divorces me."

"What *should* I call you?"

"Patricia Zabor." Her hair was smooth, raven, and amazingly long, flowing down her back like a nun's veil. "Your funeral's by the lawnmower shed, straight past the Korean markers." She extended a black-gloved index finger. "It's invisible because of all those fir trees."

"Your funeral's right behind me, Miss Zabor. Just keep walking. You can't miss it."

They parted company, marching off bravely in opposite directions.

❖

By some miracle, he got through the morning. He survived the stupefying graveside elegy offered by Vaughn Poffley's minister, a weasel-faced man who spoke as if his mouth were full of peanut butter. He endured the gleaming casket sitting in its earthen groove; the grotesque flowers; the remorseless stone on which someone had inscribed SHE LOVED ALL CREATURES GREAT AND SMALL; the insipid gathering at Vaughn's house, where the drapes clashed horribly with the slipcovers and the rugs stank of carpet shampoo. Corinne's parents barely spoke to Martin. Lifelong Socialists and die-hard bohemians, they'd never understood why their daughter had married a Republican. The only gratifying moment of the entire reception occurred when Jenny informed him she'd found the ideal home for Corinne's pets. An eccentric Main Line dowager named Merribell Folcroft had promised to add them to her private zoo.

The next two weeks passed in a blur of angry victims, happy perpetrators, and miscarried justice. When an accused shoplifter pleaded innocent in the face of massive counterevidence, Martin dismissed the charges, setting the kleptomaniac free to steal again. In another such case, the judge was offered proof that Dustin Grant, a Deer Haven adolescent, had been mutilating his neighbors' trees with his father's chain saw—Dustin had been videotaped in the act—and Martin merely reprimanded the vandal: no fine, no family counseling. Then came the complaint of Alfred Lafferty, a Chestnut Grove resident whose property abutted the golf course. It seemed that, some weeks earlier, Susan Curtis of Glendale had teed off on the sixth hole while intoxicated, and the ball had sliced into the plaintiff's backyard, killing his beloved cat, Leopold. Normally Martin would have required the defendant not only to replace the slain cat but to pay for its successor's shots. Instead he threw the case out of court. He wished Susan Curtis's golf ball had beaned the wayward Irish setter instead, thereby preventing it from running in front of Corinne's truck. If God could part the Red Sea and set the planets spinning, why couldn't He send one lousy golf ball on the proper trajectory?

As Martin awoke on the last morning in August, the alarm clock droning in his ear, he experienced a rare moment of perfect resolve. He would not go to the Abaddon Municipal Building this day. Instead he would take a vacation, pursuing the hobby he termed "urban spelunking," one of the enthusiasms he shared with Vaughn Poffley—the others being Monday-night NFL broadcasts and Friday-night poker games. Both men took supreme pleasure in driving through the seedier sections of Philadelphia on Sunday afternoons and visiting its moribund factories. Like archaeologists digging up a lost civilization, they would piece together the city's past, feeling a peculiar joy upon deducing that the empty building on Cadwallader Street had once been a meat-packing plant or that the Eternal Life Temple at Nineteenth and Tioga had formerly housed dozens of looms. It was the melancholy of such places that moved Martin, the exquisite loneliness of broken windows and shredded conveyor belts, the sublime sorrow of a rusting caboose sitting on a spur.

He told his secretary to contact the relevant parties in the three cases on the calendar—a bait-and-switch appliance store in South Hills, a rent-control squabble between a Kingsley landlord and his deranged tenant, and a mixed-faith couple (he a Roman Catholic, she a Buddhist) who wanted to marry despite massive parental disapproval—and inform them he was indisposed. At 1:20 P.M. he boarded a SEPTA train out of Perkinsville and headed into the city.

A castoff *Philadelphia Inquirer* lay on the seat. Out of habit he perused the articles pertaining to justice. A woman in Prescott, Arizona, was suing to retrieve her biological son from his adoptive parents. A doctor in Little Falls, Minnesota, had been convicted of murdering an eighty-year-old Alzheimer's patient in the name of compassion. As the train pulled into Wayne Junction, Martin read how the United Nations, seeking to crack a white slavery ring operating out of Singapore, had after much debate amended the statutes of the International Court of Justice, giving its nine judges jurisdiction over individuals and the authority to try "crimes against humanity."

He got off the train and started his explorations.

Poking around an abandoned Schlitz brewery on Clarissa Street, a fire-gutted cavern reeking of mildew and pigeon dung, Martin inevitably began meditating on the drunk drivers who filed through his courtroom. From his attempts to point these offenders toward the AA way of life, he had come to understand that an alcoholic's convoluted psychological makeup could ultimately be grasped only by another alcoholic. Was the same true of grief? Did it take a mourner to know a mourner? One thing was certain: he wasn't supposed to be in a defunct Schlitz brewery right now. He belonged in the company of the bereaved.

A battered phone booth rose from the corner of Clarissa and Juniata. He lifted the receiver and, much to his surprise, heard a dial tone. For twenty-five cents he obtained the number of a P. Zabor in Deer Haven. Hunger pangs assaulted him, competing for his attention with the ache in his hip. He slipped the AT&T card from his wallet, punched in the appropriate digits, and connected with Brandon Appleyard's mother.

"Hello?"

A mere two syllables, but he recognized her voice. "Is this Patricia Zabor?"

"What do you want?" she asked suspiciously.

"We met two weeks ago. In the cemetery. Martin Candle."

"Oh, yes . . . I've been thinking about you."

"You have?"

"Yes, I should've offered you my condolences."

"That's why I called."

"For my condolences?"

"To offer mine. I've never been a parent, but I can imag-ine . . . anyway, I'm terribly sorry—that's all. I'm so sorry."

"I talked to your mother."

"My *mother*?"

"At your wife's funeral. She told me I should be taking calcium supplements so I won't get osteoporosis."

"Patricia, I was wondering—would you like to grab some dinner, maybe? There's a Greek restaurant in your neighbor-hood, the Athenian Corner."

"I don't want to go out tonight."

"Not hungry?"

"You kidding? I've been eating like a pig all day, and I'm still famished. Grief sharpens the appetite, have you noticed that? I'm in no condition. You understand?"

"Of course."

"I'm a wreck."

"Right."

"Another time, maybe."

"Sure."

"If you wanted to drop by, I could make us some spaghetti."

"No, that's too much trouble. Let me bring a pizza. You like pizza?"

"Sure. My twin sister's here. She likes pizza too. Sixty-five Mapleshade Lane, a mile past the Valley of Children Daycare Center."

"The building with the big wooden clown out front?"

"Right. My sister runs the place. I designed it for her."

"You're an architect?"

"Don't I wish. Commercial illustrator. Trading cards, mostly, like kids buy in the drugstore."

"Bubble-gum cards?"

"We call them trading cards."

"You design the clown too?"

"One of Angela's clients is a sculptor."

"A four-year-old sculptor?"

"The father. After he went to all that trouble, Angela had to accept the thing. The children seem to like it."

❖

The clown who guarded the Valley of Children was even more grotesque than he'd remembered, its twelve-foot-high emaciated form looming over Mapleshade Lane like the trademark of a fast-food restaurant catering to anorexics. Slowing down, he flicked on the turn signal and pulled into the driveway of number sixty-five, a stout Victorian mansion boasting a greenhouse in the side yard and a gazebo on the front lawn. Patricia's ex-husband was evidently rich. Martin parked, got out, and limped to the door carrying two pizzas, the dough's sultry moisture seeping through the cardboard and wetting his palms.

Angela Zabor, Patricia's twin, resembled her sister the way a symphony played on a piano resembles the full orchestral treatment. The themes are the same, but the depth is missing. Martin found her instantly annoying; he wished she weren't there. Seated at the hardwood counter dominating Patricia's kitchen, the three of them speedily devoured pizza number one.

"You own this place?" he asked.

"Booty from the divorce settlement." Patricia opened the second pizza box, revealing a fetus-shaped stain on the underside of the lid. "I got the house, a few bucks, and Brandon. Paul got what he wanted. Out."

"Wealthy man?"

"Spiritually impoverished," said Angela.

"Tenured professor at Villanova," said Patricia. "My sister receives nine thousand dollars a year for working with kids when they're most malleable. Paul receives seventy thousand for working with them when it no longer makes any difference. Angela teaches reading readiness. Paul teaches fucking Aristotle. Did you love your wife?"

"Very much."

"Good for you." Patricia lifted a slice from pizza number two, batting at the tendrils of cheese connecting it to the parent pie. "Brandon shouldn't be dead."

"Of course not," said Martin.

"No, I mean it was a fluke. He needed to have his V-P shunt replaced, a routine thing with spina-bifida kids—most of them have hydrocephalus—and after the surgery he got an infection, resistant to penicillin and everything else."

"That's awful."

"There's no justice," said Angela.

Martin shifted on his bar stool and bit into a discarded pizza crust, wincing as a cancer pain exploded in his hip. "Sometimes, in my little courtroom . . . not always, but sometimes—on a good day—there's justice."

"I was in your courtroom once," said Angela.

"You were?"

"Two years ago. You'd summoned me. I'd witnessed a guy running a stop sign and plowing into two fat ladies rolling a piano down the street. Nobody got hurt. The piano was totaled."

"I remember the case."

"You made the dork buy them a new one. Good decision." Angela slid off her bar stool. "If you need me, Pat, I'm doing the laundry."

As Angela marched out of the kitchen, Patricia tore away another pizza slice. "I'd like to know . . . I mean . . . if you don't mind my asking . . ."

"Auto accident." Martin slipped the Roxanol bottle from his pocket, rubbing the pliant amber plastic with his thumb. "She went off the Henry Avenue Bridge. Excuse me while I take a pill."

"Antidepressant?"

"Painkiller," he replied with a sardonic grin. "I have a touch of—what's it called?—prostate cancer."

"Oh, dear . . ."

"It's probably in my pelvis now—my right hip hurts all the

time." Tossing a tablet into his mouth, he ground it between his molars and washed down the grains with Diet Pepsi. "This drug is my best friend. Roxanol."

"Brandon was on that for a while. Kids aren't supposed to take it, but it was the only thing that worked."

"I've had lymph-node surgery, radiation—now they want me to try estrogen. Last month Corinne and I went to Celestial City USA."

Patricia offered a knowing nod. "We tried that too. Disney World did him more good, I think. He became great friends with two guys dressed up like Chip and Dale."

"Next time I get cancer, I'll go to Disney World instead."

"I can't believe we're just sitting here, talking about these things. We should be . . ."

"What?"

"You know. Screaming."

"Screaming," he echoed. Like a firehouse siren, he thought.

"Are you religious, Martin?"

The Roxanol—God bless it—kicked in. "My dad taught Sunday school when he was alive. Somewhere in the basement I've got all these little medals I collected for perfect attendance. They hung from my lapel. I looked like a brigadier general."

"Let me guess. Lutheran?"

"I'm named for Martin Luther, but I was raised Presbyterian."

"My ex is a Methodist."

"And what are you?"

"Me? I knew God was dead even before the corpse showed up." Patricia pried a mushroom from her pizza slice and set it on her tongue. "It must be terrific, having faith."

"It's wonderful," he said tonelessly.

After they consumed pizza number two, she guided him down the hall and into a spacious room she called her "studio," though it had evidently been one of Brandon's favorite places as well. The drawing board held various Berenstain Bears books and children's crayons intermingled with pen nibs, charcoal sticks, artist's brushes, straight edges, and elaborate, skillful sketches depicting assorted frog-eyed space aliens bent on conquering the Earth. Additional sketches—same lurid subject—papered the walls. The freestanding shelves displayed collections of stuffed dinosaurs, hand puppets, wooden building blocks, and Saga of Sargassia action figures.

"Some of your bubble-gum cards?" he asked, gesturing toward a raygun-wielding alien vaporizing a distraught child's poodle.

"Trading cards, remember? I just got a big commission, *Invaders from Vesta*, 'the thrilling sci-fi saga of Earth's war against the bloodthirsty inhabitants of our system's brightest asteroid,' in fifty-four action-packed scenes."

"You actually make a living from this?"

"Apex Novelty Company pays me three hundred dollars per finished painting. Sure, today's kids have their video games, their virtual reality, their Internet chat rooms, but they always come back to trading cards. There's nothing quite so satisfying as walking around with a complete set of *Mars Attacks* or *Invaders from Vesta* in your pocket."

Approaching the shelves, Martin picked up a Sargassia action figure, Stanhope the Steam-Powered Man. As he fingered the miniature robot, he realized how little he understood about children; he found them as cryptic as cats. In the far corner lay a community manufactured by a company called Fisher-Price, complete with a school, a barn, a Colonial-style house, and dozens of two-inch-high plastic citizens. Beside the drawing board reposed a wheelchair, its seat occupied by a fearsome Godzilla punching doll. Martin imagined Brandon using the doll therapeutically, hitting back at the evil lesion on his spine, *bam, bam, bam.*

"The dinosaurs were his favorites," said Patricia, taking a stuffed triceratops off its shelf. She set the Godzilla doll aside and, triceratops in hand, climbed into the wheelchair. "He'd sit right here, head bobbing every which way, and I'd act out little dramas for him, life in the late Cretaceous. The triceratops was always getting into trouble. The stegosaurus loved ice cream. So did Brandon. At least he's not in pain anymore. There were days when that's all I could think about. 'Please, God, stop his pain.' "

"God is out of the loop," said Martin, examining a sketch that seemed to make his point: a Vestan spaceship melting the Brooklyn Bridge at the height of rush hour. "He's left the scene"—he grimaced, realizing what he was about to say—"of His crimes."

Hugging the triceratops, Patricia rose from the wheelchair. "Play with me."

"What?"

"Play with me. Get on the floor. Play with me. These toys have never been properly played with. Brandon . . . couldn't."

"Neither can I."

"Please. Try. Please."

They pulled off their shoes, sprawled across the rug, and played. Seizing upon Brandon's building blocks, they made a multicolored tower, so high it overshadowed the drawing board. They worked with the dead child's Play-Doh, Patricia fashioning a blue elephant, Martin a yellow giraffe. They lovingly rearranged the Fisher-Price settlement, filling the Colonial house with healthy relatives, the barn with hardy animals, and the school with robust children—a utopia, they decided, a world that had no words for prostate cancer or spina bifida.

"I loved him so much," said Patricia. "Not because he was sick, and not in spite of it either. I just . . . loved him."

She yanked a cylinder from the foundation of their tower. The construction collapsed spectacularly, block tumbling over block—and then, finally, the scream did come, a bright red howl rushing from her mouth and blowing through the Fisher-Price community like a tornado.

Martin's palms grew damp. His heart raced. Instinctively he leaned toward her, and for a full five minutes they silently pressed against each other, embracing and shivering. Like shipwreck survivors, he thought. Like two freezing castaways, adrift on an ice floe, heading nowhere.

❖

Believe me, I dislike these interruptions as much as you do, but I thought you'd be intrigued to know that the appearance of a shipwreck metaphor in our hero's consciousness foreshadows an eventual obsession with nonmetaphorical shipwrecks and similar cataclysms. Among the exhibits to which Candle will be drawn while perusing the Kroft Museum of Natural Disasters and Technological Catastrophes is the rudder from the steamer *Larchmont*.

Maybe you know the story. At eleven P.M. on February 11, 1907, the *Larchmont* was rammed near Block Island by the schooner *Harry Knowlton*. Most of the *Larchmont*'s passengers were drowned in their cabins. Dressed only in their pajamas, those few who managed to escape on life rafts were beset by sub-zero winds and heavy seas. Ice soon covered them, freezing their hands and feet solid. To end his agony, one survivor slit his own throat. All told, three hundred and thirty-two people died that night.

For my money, the funniest part of the *Larchmont* story is the name of the company that owned and sailed her. The Joy Line. Get it? The Joy Line. Whatever you may think of our Creator, you can't fault His sense of humor.

❖

Martin spent the weekend in bed. Trembling with grief, tortured by illness, he rolled back and forth on his mattress, tearing the sheets free and wrapping them around his aching pelvis. His front lawn, uncut since July, had vanished beneath a carpet of weeds and crabgrass. Frost clogged his freezer. His reelection campaign was a shambles. The Glendale rent-control case would be upon him in a matter of hours, and he had yet to review the facts. But instead of acting he simply lay there, imprisoned within his own buzzing skull.

By the grace of Roxanol he slept most of Sunday night, waking the next morning with dry skin, clogged sinuses, and an astonishingly lucid sense of his immediate future. He would kill himself with liquor. Yes, this afternoon he would drink his way through the city of Philadelphia, saloon by saloon by saloon, then hurl his benumbed body into the Delaware River. The process would prove fascinating and pleasurable, and he had nothing to lose but his life.

He called his secretary, told her to defer his cases another day, then set about filling his stomach lest the coming binge knock him senseless before he'd accomplished his goal. The refrigerator contained some leftover macaroni; the pantry yielded four cans of tuna fish and a jar of baked beans. The condemned man's last meal, he mused, throwing everything together in a saucepan.

By noon his belly had reached capacity. He grabbed his Roxanol, climbed into his Dodge Aries, and took off.

Within the hour he had situated himself in Omar's Arabian Oasis at Seventh and Lombard, alternately munching painkillers and sucking a black Russian through a straw as if it were a Coke. Over the years the booth had acquired so many coats of thick, badly stirred olive-green paint that its surface now resembled a relief map. Two tubby men sat at the bar, bathed in the light of a Phillies game. The air was dark and heavy, clogged with the sweet odor of cheap whiskey.

Although his troubles did not disappear, they miraculously migrated outside his body. He still had prostate cancer, Corinne was still dead, but both disasters had been banished to the far-thest corner of Omar's Arabian Oasis. They hovered in the smoky air, unable to get at him. Above the bar hung a buxom plastic Saint Pauli Girl with a clock embedded in her stomach. The hour hand crept toward two P.M., millimeter by millimeter. He ordered a gin and tonic. Two-thirty. A rusty nail. Three P.M.

Brain spinning with whatever neurotoxic reaction occurs when hard liquor meets Roxanol, he wandered out of the saloon. At the base of the nearest parking meter a large puddle of dog urine lay drying in the afternoon heat. He ate a painkiller and started down Rodman Street, all the while imagining himself back in Celestial City USA, standing atop the Main Attraction. This time, instead of simply beholding God's right eye, he spat in it.

He staggered into the Royal Pub at 605 Rodman, sat down at the bar, and ordered the specialty of the house, "authentic English fish and chips." They arrived cold. He did not so much wash his chips down with beer as set them adrift in it, glass after glass of freshly tapped Samuel Adams. He visited the men's room once every ten minutes: an agreeable experience thanks to the blessed Roxanol-alcohol synergy, which spared him the usual fiery ordeal caused by his unending prostatitis.

Shortly after Martin returned from his fifth trip to the urinal, the man on the adjacent stool swiveled toward him and asked, "Come here often?"

"Only when I lose a wife."

His drinking companion was a grizzled giant with a leather patch over his right eye, an accessory that lent their surroundings the ambience of a pirate's den. "Divorce?"

"Gravity."

"What?"

"Gravity in the first degree. God's favorite modus operandi."

"If you're making fun of God," said the one-eyed man, "I may have to punch you in the face."

"I'm not making fun."

"Bad enough He's comatose, without people making fun of Him."

Once again Martin decided to change the venue of his suicide. Leaving the Royal Pub, he headed down South Street toward the Front Street intersection, where the words MIKE'S TAVERN flashed on and off: a neon beacon shining across the urban sea, guiding tempest-tossed rummies to port.

He never got past Third Street. Before him blazed a luminous marquee heralding the Theater of the Living Arts, where he and Corinne had seen *Witness for the Prosecution* on their first date. Several dozen playgoers were queuing up—a smaller, more somber group than the crowds who patronized the Agatha Christie revivals.

Tonight at 8:00
Hand-to-Mouth Players
present
Elie Wiesel's
THE TRIAL OF GOD

A soft rain fell. His hip throbbed. He checked his watch. 7:39 P.M. Limping into the foyer, he bought a ticket from the young woman in the booth, a hatchet-faced brunette with acne. He hobbled down the aisle, accepted a program booklet from the sullen male usher, and collapsed in his designated seat, where he tried repeatedly to read the dramaturge's essay. Only on his sixth attempt did he cut through his beery fog and comprehend the article in toto.

The Trial of God promised to be wholly unlike the courtroom thrillers Martin normally attended. According to the dramaturge, the plot traced to a bizarre event the author had witnessed while incarcerated at Auschwitz. In Elie Wiesel's words, "Three rabbis—all erudite and pious men—decided one winter evening to indict God."

The setting was the Russian village of Shamgorod in 1649, during Purim. Fixing his clouded eyes on the stage, Martin beheld a troupe of itinerant minstrels arriving at the local inn to perform a holiday play for the community. Much to their dismay, the minstrels discovered that Shamgorod had recently suffered a pogrom. Only two Jews remained alive—the innkeeper, Berish, and his traumatized, gang-raped daughter, Hanna. Goaded by Berish, the actors agreed that instead of a *Purimschpiel* they would stage a mock trial of God, prosecuting Him for allowing His children to be massacred.

As the first intermission got under way, Martin sat motionless in his seat, rolling his program booklet into a tube, unrolling it, rerolling it. He stood up. In the muzzy reaches of his brain a grand and terrible plan was taking shape. He wandered into the lobby, approached the refreshment stand, and, handing the concessionaire a one-dollar bill, indicated that he required a cup of coffee. Receiving his change, he slid the dime into his pants pocket, where his fingers encountered his ticket stub. He pulled the stub free and stared at it, a shabby piece of red cardboard, torn along one edge and stamped LEFT: F-106. Slowly, inexorably, the stub entered another dimension, becoming the very ticket around which Ivan Fyodorovich had constructed his famous diatribe in *The Brothers Karamazov*, Martin's favorite novel from his twelfth-grade honors English class.

"And so I hasten to give back my entrance ticket, and if I am an honest man I am bound to give it back as soon as possible," announces Ivan, who has concluded he no longer desires admittance to a universe where innocent children suffer, even though justice and harmony may prevail at the end of time. "And that I am doing. It's not God I don't accept, Alyosha, only I most respectfully return Him the ticket."

To which Ivan's devout brother responds, "That's rebellion."

Martin did not stay for the second act. Slurping down his coffee, he bolted from the theater, retrieved his car, and raced north through the drizzly darkness.

"I'm going to return You the ticket," he muttered, over and over. "I'm going to return You the ticket . . ."

❖

By midnight he was in Deer Haven, pounding on Patricia's door.

"Who's there?" a voice called down.

Lifting his head, he stumbled backward. Patricia leaned out the upper window, eyes flashing like a stoned calico's.

"Patricia, something amazing has happened!"

"Martin?"

"I'm returning Him the ticket!"

"Wait right there."

A minute later the door swung open, and she greeted him with a goofy smile. A silvery satin bathrobe enveloped her, shimmering in the orange glow of the porch light.

"What's this all about?" she asked, ushering him inside.

"We're putting Him in the dock!"

"Martin, you're . . ."

"Drunk? After all that liquor, I should hope so."

"I've had a sip or two myself." She piloted him toward the kitchen. "There's still some left. Join me?"

"Sure."

She poured him two fingers of Jack Daniel's on the rocks, the ice cubes crackling as the sour mash whiskey trickled toward the bottom of the tumbler.

"I'm calling Him to account, just like those rabbis did."

"What are you talking about?" She slopped whiskey into a second tumbler. "Calling *who* to account?"

"The Main Attraction. Humor me, Patricia. Lie to me. Tell me you think it's a great idea."

"I think it's a great idea."

"No you don't. You think it's an evil idea, and so do I. Maybe I'll even start taking Blumenberg's damn estrogen and buy myself a few more months. So I'll lose my gender, big deal. I don't want to talk about hormones. I want to talk about harmony."

She gulped her whiskey. "Play with me."

"What?"

"You know—play with me."

Drinks in hand, they staggered into her studio, their ice cubes clinking softly against the sides of their glasses.

"A week ago, I wouldn't have even *considered* a project like this," he chattered, downing his Jack Daniel's. He slipped the *Trial of God* program from his pocket. "But the United Nations just amended the statutes of its judicial arm—maybe you read about it in the *Inquirer*." He shoved the program in her face. "For the first time ever, an individual can be prosecuted before the International Court of Justice in The Hague."

" '*The Trial of God*,' " she read aloud, removing her satin slippers. "Martin, this is adolescent."

"That's what the Defendant wants us to think."

"Aren't you a Presbyterian?"

As the whiskey seeped into his brain, the studio began to rotate, as if mounted atop the Celestial City carousel. Steadying himself on the wheelchair, he pulled off his shoes. "I love the God of my childhood—the God of Dad's Sunday school lessons. But there's *another* God out there, and I'm going to get Him."

"And you really believe He's responsible for all our pain?"

"Who *else* would be?"

"I don't know. The Devil."

"A mere proxy."

Together they knelt on the floor and began constructing a new tower from Brandon's blocks. When they reached the height of the wheelchair, Patricia leaned forward and planted a wet, sensuous kiss on his lips.

"Did you like that?" She slid her hand into one of Brandon's puppets—either a beaver or a woodchuck, Martin couldn't tell—then pressed the animal coyly against her cheek.

"I didn't come here to kiss you, Patricia. My motives were purer than that."

"Purer?"

"Yes."

"How boring." She made the puppet scratch her nose.

"Maybe I'd better go home."

"Nope, sorry—you're spending the night. Nobody in your condition should be out on the road."

"I'm not as drunk as I seem."

"You're too drunk to enjoy a kiss from me. That's pretty drunk."

"If I get arrested for driving under the influence, I'd have to indict myself," he said with a throaty laugh. "I *did* enjoy it."

"You did?"

"A lot."

"Good. If you're really planning to change genders, Martin Candle, we'd better seize the time."

At Patricia's bidding, the puppet took the sash of her robe in its paws and yanked it away as if starting an outboard motor. The halves parted. Beneath the satin lay a female form as desirable as the ceramic Eve who presided over the Celestial City's petting zoo.

"I ought to be going," he said.

"Would she really begrudge you this moment?"

"Yes. No. I don't know. *I'm* the problem, not Corinne."

"Play with me."

"What?"

"You know. Play with me."

Taking a tress of raven hair in each hand, Martin pulled her toward him. He closed his eyes. "It's true what you said on Friday."

"What?"

"Grief sharpens the appetite."

"Right. Play with me. I'm on the Pill."

"Estrogen?" he asked, unbuckling his belt.

"Estrogen."

"I've got seeds in my prostate, forty-six radioactive I-125 microcapsules, but Blumenberg says they don't affect my semen." He shed his socks, pants, and jockey shorts. "We'll use a condom if you want."

"Irradiate me, Judge Candle."

Afterward, she wrapped his body in her arms and, through a series of maneuvers that alternately evoked modern dance and slapstick comedy, dragged him down the hall and laid him on the bed in her guest room. As she stretched out beside him, flopping her bare arm across his chest, he realized he hated himself, a sensation he found not altogether unpleasant. It was perversely satisfying to know that, for all the confusion seething in his brain, all the chaos raging in his prostate, his sense of guilt remained intact. Only a man with an operational conscience had the right to put the Main Attraction on trial.

" 'I'll chase him round Good Hope,' " he whispered drunkenly into the darkness, quoting Ahab's great speech from *Moby-Dick*, Martin's second-favorite among the honors English novels.

"Hope?"

"Hope," he repeated. " 'And round the Horn, and round the Norway Maelstrom, and round addition's flames—' "

" 'Addition's'? What?"

" 'Perdition's flames.' And round Omar's Arabian Oasis. And Shamgorod. Celestial City. And round The Hague. And . . . 'before I' . . . and . . . 'before . . .' "

"Before you . . . ?"

" 'Before I give him up.' "

Chapter 4

WHEN JENNY CANDLE FIRST LEARNED of her brother's audacious ambition, she decided he'd lost his mind and promptly gave him the name and phone number of her therapist. Vaughn Poffley also stood foursquare against indicting the Almighty, fearing the pre-trial publicity would cost Martin the upcoming election. Martin's mother, he knew, would have just one thing to say to him—"Your father would not be proud"—and so he didn't even tell her.

Much to his dismay, the person from whom he expected unequivocal support had no use for his project at all.

"I mean, what's the *point,* really?" asked Patricia as she and Martin sat down to espresso and sweet rolls in a Glendale coffee shop, Café Olé.

"We owe it to Brandon."

"Brandon is dead."

"We owe it to Corinne."

"Even if you get a conviction—even if they shut off the Lockheed 7000—is that *justice?*"

"Patricia, I'm hurt. Why can't you believe in me?"

"I *do* believe in you. What I don't believe in is revenge."

He jammed a Feminone capsule in his mouth. Phallic in its contours, the pill seemed designed to torment its consumers: not only do you have prostate cancer, Charlie, but your wife stands a better chance of satisfying herself with one of these things than with *your* disenfranchised dong.

"This isn't about revenge," he said.

"Some people, when they lose a loved one, *some* people go into grief counseling. *Some* people build elaborate tombs. But you—*you* think you have to put God on trial. It's nuts."

"No, Patricia—it's overdue." He swallowed the estrogen along with a mouthful of cappuccino.

Among the individuals closest to Martin, only his ex-fiancée Robin McLaughlin endorsed his scheme. Upon reading Albert Camus's *The Plague* in Mrs. Felser's English class at Abaddon High, Robin had come to dislike God intensely, an animus that endured throughout her college years, her relationship with Martin, and her unhappy marriage to a Fox Run proctologist named Derrick Smedley.

"You're calling the old Bully to account?" said Robin as she and her fidgety six-year-old son sat down for breakfast with Martin at McDonald's. "I like it—"

"Thought you would."

"—but it's not *you*."

"I've changed."

She slit a Half and Half capsule with her thumbnail, adding the mongrel fluid to her coffee. "I'm sure you know it's been done before."

"Elie Wiesel's play," he said, unwrapping his Bacon, Egg, and Cheese Biscuit.

"Earlier than that."

"Jeremiah denouncing divine injustice?"

"Before that even. Job on his dung heap."

"Job?"

"The Book of Job." Robin bit into her Egg McMuffin. "It's really a kind of courtroom drama. How are you?"

"How *am* I? Terrible."

"You don't deserve any of this—I hope you know that." She

began cutting up her child's pancakes for him with a white plastic knife and matching fork. "Is it true you're taking estrogen?"

"Where'd you hear that?"

"Your *other* ex-fiancée. Brittany got it from Vaughn, who got it from your sister."

"Jeez . . . you people publish a *newsletter*, do you?"

"The Internet does nicely. You're a great topic, Marty."

"Yes, I'm taking estrogen. If I keep at it, I'll turn into a woman."

"I don't recommend it."

"I have no choice."

"If you ever need me, just remember—I'm here."

That night Martin read the Book of Job for the first time in thirty years, discovering to his surprise it *was* a kind of courtroom drama, with the perverse twist that the Accused also functioned as Judge and Jury. Equally disturbing was the fact that when God went to make His case, He completely ignored Job's main concern—justice—opting instead to intimidate him with the majesty of Creation: lions, whales, horses, hail, stars, and, ultimately, the unknowable monsters Behemoth and Leviathan.

A rigged proceeding, yes, and yet Martin found it gripping. He was moved by both the force of Job's bitterness and the caliber of his blasphemy. "God bears hard upon me for a trifle and rains blows on me without cause," railed the sufferer. And then, later: "When a sudden flood brings death, He mocks the plight of the innocent." And still later: "Far from the city, the poor groan like dying men, and like wounded men they cry out, but God pays no heed to their prayer." Whether Job of Uz was an actual historical figure or the product of an anguished poetic imagination, this "blameless and upright" desert chieftain was a person to be admired.

After according the matter considerable thought and much research, Martin concluded he needed thirty-five thousand dollars, the price of a full-page ad in the *New York Times Book*

Review. He was about to take out a bank loan when the money from Corinne's life insurance policy came through—seventy thousand. He divided the settlement in half, earmarking one portion for the Kennel of Joy, the other for the downfall of God.

AN OPEN LETTER TO
THE WORLD'S INNOCENT VICTIMS

Dear Fellow Sufferers:

In the fifth century B.C., *a blameless and upright man named Job called his Creator to account, demanding to know the reason for his multiple misfortunes. Sixty years ago, three rabbis imprisoned in Auschwitz indicted the Almighty for crimes against His children. Now, once again, the time has come for humankind to ask an honorable question. Why, throughout history, has God permitted the innocent to suffer?*

An organization has been formed

Our name: the Job Society. Our claim: in fashioning a world where deadly viruses thrive, defective genes prosper, earthquakes kill, droughts destroy, and wars lay waste, the Main Attraction at Celestial City USA acted in a manner that can only be called murderous. Our mission: to bring this matter before the International Court of Justice in The Hague.

A meeting will occur

The initial gathering of the Job Society is scheduled for Saturday, September 25, 1999, 8:00 P.M., *at the Valley of Children Daycare Center, 61 Mapleshade Lane, Deer*

*Haven, Pennsylvania 19001. Registration is free. If you
wish to attend, return the coupon printed below.*

> *Sincerely,*
> *Martin Candle*
> *Justice of the Peace*
> *Abaddon Township, Pennsylvania*

He would never forget buying the *New York Times* for Sunday, August 29, 1999, pulling out the *Book Review*, and seeing
his cri de coeur shouted to the world in aggressive Geneva type.
Despite his perusal of the dummy version he'd created on his
computer, he wasn't prepared for this outsized incarnation. Everywhere he went that morning—bathroom, kitchen, catnip
patch—he carried the *Book Review* with him, reading his ad
over and over. He chastised himself for not catching the typo on
"Auschwitz" (it read "Auchwitz") when he'd examined the
proof that the advertising director had faxed him from Manhattan; he wished he'd said Job had "put his Creator in the
dock" instead of "called his Creator to account"; he decided
Helvetica type would have looked more serious than Geneva.
But for all this, Martin felt unabashedly pleased with his complaint.

The telephone started ringing right after lunch.

"I can't believe you did this," fumed Vaughn.

"Neither can I."

"I won't stand by while you throw the election to some
starry-eyed tree-*shtupper* from Harvard." Vaughn was alluding
to Barbara Meredith, the Democratic candidate for JP, a woman
with environmentalist views most charitably described as extreme. "It's political suicide. There's a typo on 'Auschwitz.'"

"I know."

No sooner had he replaced the receiver when his mother
called, every bit as vexed as Vaughn.

"Is this really the sort of thing you should be spending your money on?"

"I can afford it, Mom."

"Your father would not be proud. There's a typo on 'Auschwitz.' I'm worried they'll come after you."

"For a typo?"

"An ad like this—it's going to make people mad."

Patricia called next.

"Well, it's certainly *dramatic*. Are you satisfied?"

"Satisfied, thrilled, scared."

"My ex saw it. He wanted to know, quote, 'How the fuck did the Valley of Children get mixed up in this?' "

"Maybe he'd like to make a donation."

"I doubt it. He's pretty religious."

"So am I. Will you come to the meeting?"

"This is your fight, Martin. Not mine—yours. There's a typo on—"

" 'Auschwitz.' "

He spent the evening drafting a formal petition of the sort an aggrieved party must submit before its case can be considered by the International Court of Justice. Running to three single-spaced pages, the petition was essentially a prolix rewrite of the *Book Review* ad, with a postscript detailing instances of ostensibly unjustifiable aggression by the Main Attraction—the cholera bacterium, the eruption of Vesuvius—and a post-postscript pointing out that the Court's newly acquired jurisdiction over individuals logically included deities as well as people.

Two days later the responses started arriving from the outside world. They divided neatly into three categories—completed registration forms, heartfelt expressions of support, and intellectual hate mail. The majority of the friendly communiqués included donations, the smallest being a five-dollar bill from a precocious adolescent in Des Moines who claimed her hero was Friedrich Nietzsche, the largest being a cashier's check for two thousand dollars from the leader of a Satanic cult in Bangor,

Maine. ("Our Father, who farts in Heaven, thinks you've got a terrific idea.") Typical of the intellectual hate mail was a letter from a religious studies professor at the University of Memphis.

Dear Judge Candle:

The "honorable question" you raise has been pondered for centuries by minds far subtler than yours.

Have you never read Saint Augustine's De civitate Dei? *Thomas Aquinas's* Summa theologiae? *Bishop Origen's* Contra Celsum? *Saint Anselm's* De casu diaboli? *Gregory the Great's* Moralia? *Gregory Nazianzenus's* Discours? *Martin Luther's* Werke? *Until you acquire some credentials in theodicy, I suggest you stick with jaywalkers and leave evil to the grown-ups.*

Sincerely,
Phillip H. Strand, PhD

The dispatches from academia gave Martin considerable pause. He hadn't been prepared for them, and it didn't help when Patricia said, "I'll bet you haven't read *any* of those heavy thinkers, right?"

"I'm named for Martin Luther," he replied feebly.

" 'Theodicy'?"

"A theodicy is a systematic attempt to reconcile the fact of evil with the existence of an omnipotent, omniscient, omnibenevolent Creator."

"Where'd you learn that?"

"*Webster's Tenth New Collegiate.*"

"Yeah? Well, it'll take more than a *dictionary* to bring down God. You're in over your head, Martin. Get out while you can."

❖

"Those who cannot remember the past are condemned to repeat it," George Santayana—one of my favorite philosophers—used to say. I would add that those who *can* remember the past are also condemned to repeat it, but that's another story. The point I wish to make is that Martin Candle's project did not represent the first time the good people of Abaddon Township had awakened to find a rebel in their midst.

Cast your mind backward—to February 11, 1962. On that date a tenth-grade classmate of Candle's named Randall Selkirk is sitting in his homeroom in Abaddon Senior High School, pondering the student-produced "morning show" he has just heard, involuntarily, over the public-address system. Selkirk is discontent. As usual, the program has included the Pledge of Allegiance, a meaningless Fact for the Day ("Mount Everest is twenty-nine thousand feet high"), a series of stupid announcements ("the Chess Club will meet after school in Room 217"), and the obnoxious closing motto ("Abaddon: first in the Alphabet, first in Achievement, and first in Attitude"), but what really bothers Selkirk is that this broadcast, like all the others before it, began with a student reading ten Bible verses and then leading the school in the Lord's Prayer. Selkirk and his parents attend Fox Run Unitarian Church. They are staunch atheists who believe God is a unity, not a trinity, and while they appreciate the Bible for its literary merits, moral insights, and general raciness, they certainly don't think it divinely inspired.

That afternoon, Selkirk sees the assistant principal, Mr. Trevose, and reports his unhappiness with the religious portions of the morning show. Unmoved, Trevose flippantly suggests that Selkirk take his complaint to the Supreme Court.

Which is exactly what he does.

The route is indirect. Selkirk wins in a three-judge statutory court for the Eastern District of Pennsylvania, but the commonwealth appeals the decision, and eventually Earl Warren and his fellow Supreme Court justices agree to hear the assorted arguments for and against school prayer. Selkirk's political science teacher, William Rorty, gives him extra credit for writing out the detailed deposition that his counsel, Henry Sawyer, will use in arguing the appellee's case before the Warren Court. Rorty jokes that changing the course of American history is worth as much as a term paper.

Again Selkirk wins. His victory is a mixed blessing, however, for as soon as the rest of the Abaddon student body realizes that a heretic dwells among them, an ethos of persecution descends. The Current Affairs Club paints COMMIE FAGGOT on Selkirk's locker. The Math Society steals his slide rule. The soccer team urinates on his sister. Eventually he and his family move to Delaware, and who can blame them?

Randall Selkirk has never been a hero of mine either. Thanks to his meddling, millions of youngsters will never hear the rousing speech Moses delivers to his generals in chapter thirty-one of Numbers following the surrender of the Midianites: "Kill all the male children! Kill also all the women who have slept with a man!" They'll never hear the uplifting attitude toward families Jesus expresses in chapter fourteen of Luke: "If any man comes to me without hating his father, mother, wife, children, brothers, sisters, yes and his own life too, he cannot be my disciple." They'll never hear the line from chapter twenty-seven of Matthew that helped make anti-Semitism such an intractable feature of Western civilization: "His blood be on us and on our children!" If any of you knows of an organization devoted to restoring Bible reading to America's public schools, have its officers contact me right away. I'm good for a generous donation.

❖

While Martin had assumed the first sufferer to appear that evening would be a stranger, the man now standing in the open doorway to the Valley of Children was presenting himself as an old school chum.

"Randall Selkirk," said the visitor.

"You *do* look familiar."

Martin took a deep breath, and it all flooded back: *School District of Abaddon Township, Pennsylvania, et al., versus Randall Catlin Selkirk, et al.*, the 1963 Supreme Court case that—against the wishes of nearly everyone living in the United States at the time—had led to the banning of sectarian prayer and devotional Bible reading in the public schools. Shortly after the Court's opinion was reported in the *Philadelphia Bulletin*, Martin's father had broken down and wept.

"*Abaddon versus Selkirk*, right?" said Martin, extending his hand to Randall. "You've lost weight."

A lot of weight, if he was remembering correctly. Randall looked so skinny that his black silk shirt appeared to be on a wire hanger. His most striking feature, however, was not his emaciation but his manner. Martin had seen the type before: the aggressive atheist, the true unbeliever—fingers twitching with nervous nihilistic energy, eyes blinking frantically, their irises pained by light, a consequence of staring into the Nietzschean abyss for hours at a time.

"I run the Boston Marathon each year," Randall explained. "It keeps me trim."

He went on to reveal that he worked as a videographer for WGBH, in which capacity he'd recently shot "Immortal Coils," a *Nova* episode about the great technologies—the Lockheed 7000 heart-lung machine and the General Dynamics refrigeration system—that shielded the Main Attraction from the ravages of decay. Two summers ago, he added dispassionately, his six-year-old son had drowned in the South Beach undertow on Martha's Vineyard while the baby-sitter flirted with the lifeguard.

"I assume that's enough to get me in your club."

"Oh, Randall, I'm so sorry."

"Tomorrow's Larry's birthday. He would've been eight. The minute I saw your ad, I said to my ex-wife, 'This is the organization for me. God's enemies ought to stick together.' "

Martin stepped onto the welcome mat, inhaling the crisp September air. "I'm not God's enemy." The harvest moon hung low, its silvery beams flowing across the Valley of Children like liquid mercury, glazing the parking lot and burnishing the wooden clown. "In my own way, I still love Him."

Other Jobians had started arriving—most of them locals, with license plates bearing the slogans of Pennsylvania and her neighboring states, though some had driven from as far away as Virginia, Kentucky, Connecticut, and Québec. A dozen sufferers came in rental cars and airport limousines, having flown into Philadelphia International that afternoon from Indiana, Illinois, and points west.

"Jesus, Martin, I hope we know what we're getting into," said Randall, resting a palm on his classmate's shoulder. "This project isn't going to be popular."

"I never imagined otherwise."

"They treated me like a monster back in sixty-three—*I Was a Teenage Atheist*. The Future Homemakers Club threw dog shit at me. The football team photographed me in the shower and gave the prints to the cheerleaders. Right before we moved away, somebody nailed a Randall Selkirk voodoo doll to our garage door. This township lived up to its name that year. Abaddon—Hell. You *love* Him?"

"In my own way."

"And yet you're . . ."

"Correct."

"I don't get it," said Randall, slipping into the daycare center.

" 'If everything on Earth were rational,' " said Martin, quoting Dostoyevsky, " 'nothing would happen.' "

He greeted each new arrival personally. After directing the sufferer to deposit his coat in nap area two, Martin next escorted him into play area three and—depending on the registrant's preference—offered either a folding chair, a beach recliner, or a place on the Winnie the Pooh hooked rug. "Help yourself to some coffee," he said, indicating a pair of urns labeled DECAF and REGULAR. By 8:20 P.M. the entire Job Society had assembled: sixty-seven *Times Book Review* readers for whom prosperity and intelligence had proven inadequate defenses against disaster.

"Hello, I'm Martin, and I'm an innocent victim," he began. The allusion to Alcoholics Anonymous drew uneasy laughter. "Before we get down to business, I thought we should introduce ourselves. Give your name, tell us where you're from, and if you want to say what brings you here, fine. In my case it was prostate cancer combined with"—his throat constricted—"my wife's untimely death." He swallowed French roast from a Styrofoam cup. "Let me add that I undertook this campaign with great reluctance. I'm a Presbyterian. My dad taught Sunday school. Sometimes it seemed like God lived in our attic. Many of you, I suspect, come from equally religious backgrounds." He perused the room: a score of heads nodded in unison. "And yet we're all here, aren't we? For whatever strange reasons, each of us showed up."

As the meeting progressed, it became obvious that the Valley of Children—this world of diaper-changing tables, wooden blocks, pastel alphabets, and stuffed animals—was a cruelly ironic choice of venue, for children figured in almost half the Jobians' stories: insane children, maimed children, sick children, dead children. But this group was accustomed to life's morbid jokes. These people had seen it all. And so they persisted— "Hello, I'm Stanley, and I'm an innocent victim," "Hello, I'm Julia, and I'm an innocent victim"—sharing their grief and spilling their guts, telling one another of multiple-sclerosis battles and lupus defeats, of barren wombs and schizophrenic minds, of babies entering the world without brains and adolescents departing it without hope.

Particularly disturbing was the ordeal of Esther Clute, a

Trenton elementary school principal whose three-year-old daughter, Heidi, had contracted the common parasitic roundworm *Ascaris lumbricoides* while playing in her sandbox. Although *Ascaris* larvae normally take up residence in the alimentary canal, depositing eggs that are harmlessly expelled with the host's stools, in Heidi's case one worm kept on migrating, bearing a load of fecal bacteria. The parasite ended up in her brain, where the microbes caused a huge abscess and widespread tissue degeneration. Within the year, Heidi was dead.

"The doctors say she was probably incurable by the time her symptoms appeared," explained Esther, a brawny woman who looked like a goalie for a sport so brutal it was played only in Yakutsk. "I'm still trying to decide whether that's a good thing or a bad thing."

Martin had expected to hear about fatal and satanic diseases that evening. Paralysis, madness, addiction, bereavement: no surprise. There was one variety of pain, however, for which he wasn't prepared. But the more he considered these stories—the uncle whose niece's arm got torn off because he'd neglected to fasten her seat belt, the father who'd learned that his teenage son's suicide threats weren't just bids for attention, the young man who'd ignored his gonorrhea symptoms until he'd sterilized his girlfriend—the more he understood that guilt constituted a category of suffering no less real than cancer.

After two hours of testimony that would have left the world's most accomplished soap-opera writer feeling like an amateur, the final registrant spoke up: Allison Lowry, a Denver interior decorator whose only child, Jason, had spent the last nine years in bed, his spinal cord having been severed and his brain massively damaged in an auto accident when he was seven. The boy couldn't move. Neither could he speak, hear, or see. Swallowing was a major challenge. On his birthday Allison always baked Jason his favorite kind of cake, chocolate. She would puree a slice in her food processor and feed it to him with a spoon. As far as his mother knew, Jason's sense of taste was functional, though she'd never worked up the courage to ask the doctor.

While Allison dried her tears, a dense silence settled over play area three. The sufferers looked at one another, their eyes ablaze with righteous anger and mutual understanding.

They had a case, by damn. They truly had a case.

"What we're really talking about is a kind of class-action suit," Martin explained, passing out the rough draft of his petition. "With your permission, I'll be naming all of you on the last page as coplaintiffs."

Considering the many and varied philosophical complexities a Jobian complaint necessarily entails, the proposed indictment occasioned remarkably little debate. Randall argued that the bill of particulars should include biblical material—the Plagues of Egypt, Jepthah murdering his daughter at the Almighty's behest, Yahweh sending a pair of vicious bears to tear apart the children who mocked His prophet Elisha—but then Julia Schroeder, a dialysis patient from Hartford, persuaded the group that such stories were "straw men," tangential to the heart of the matter. Peter Henshaw, a Pittsburgh AIDS victim who earned his living as a ceramics instructor, argued that they should concentrate on those catastrophes most readily laid at the Main Attraction's feet: earthquakes, birth defects, infectious diseases. It would weaken their case to include—per Martin's draft—horrors that bespoke either human incompetence (plane crashes, hotel fires) or human depravity (rape, torture, war). Peter's position held sway until Randall noted that neither the original Job nor the rabbis at Auschwitz had hesitated to address such horrors. The God who'd slept during Buchenwald and fiddled while Hiroshima burned was the God they most wanted to nail.

Charles Braithwaite, a Manhattan journalist whose son had no left kidney and a dysfunctional right one, raised the whole messy question of the Defendant's metaphysical status. If He was in fact dead—completely dead, brain-dead—would there be any satisfaction in convicting Him? (A consensus quickly emerged: yes.) Alternatively, if He was alive in some way, did they dare ask the judges not only to find Him guilty but to reify the verdict by disconnecting the Lockheed 7000?

"Speaking personally," Esther replied, "I'd argue for . . . this isn't easy for me to say . . . I was raised a Baptist, understand? Jesus was the most important person in my life." She closed her eyes and winced. "I'd argue for pulling the plug."

"Would your daughter really want that?" asked Peter in a cautiously querulous tone.

"I don't know."

"Pulling the plug won't bring her back."

"No, but it might bring *me* back."

"Well put," said Ira Klein, a Long Island insurance salesman, his eyes bulging from his skull under the force of inoperable tumors. "She's right, people. We ought to go for broke."

By midnight the meeting had lost its momentum, disintegrating into random exchanges of information about megavitamin therapies and holistic healers, and Martin declared it adjourned. The Jobians agreed to reconvene in ten weeks, at which time they would analyze the response—if any—they'd received from the World Court.

An unutterable satisfaction wove through Martin, soothing his aching flesh, cooling his inflamed pelvis. How different his Jobians were from the sufferers he'd met at Celestial City USA. Both groups required the same accoutrements—wheelchairs, oxygen bottles, IV drips—but where the Orlando victims exuded a weary resignation, these people radiated militancy. Proudly he surveyed his troops: Esther stirring Cremora into her decaf, Randall arranging Fig Newtons on a serving tray, Peter opening a pack of paper napkins, Allison sneaking out for a cigarette, a handsome Bright's disease patient from Dallas speaking with a comely San Diego watercolorist who'd gone stone blind three weeks after winning the Norcroft Prize.

Sucking the salt off a hard pretzel, the Manhattan journalist marched up to Martin and presented his card.

CHARLES BRAITHWAITE
Time *Magazine*
Time & Life Building
Rockefeller Center
New York, New York 10020

"I ought to come clean," said Charles Braithwaite, nervously running his fingers through his brush cut. He had a haunted, lone-wolf look about him, a lost soul even by Job Society standards. "My son is very sick, true enough, but that's not why I'm here. I've been covering the Corpus Dei for—what?—six years now. Might I ask you a few questions?"

Martin, wary, looked the journalist up and down. "I suppose so."

Braithwaite pulled a 35mm SLR with flash attachment from his rucksack. "I'd also like, with your permission"—he brought the viewfinder to his eye—"to make that strong chin and noble brow famous."

❖

On the last day of September, Martin slipped the polished petition into a manila envelope, addressed it to the registrar of the International Court of Justice in The Hague, and drove the package to the Chestnut Grove post office. It cost the Job Society $11.95 to lay its case before the world.

Were it not for the feature article and accompanying photograph that Braithwaite published in *Time*, Martin might have enjoyed a relatively tranquil autumn. The Roxanol was keeping his pain in check, the Bactrim had finally defeated his prostatitis, and the side effects of the Feminone (swelling bosom, plummeting libido), though disturbing, were nothing he hadn't anticipated. But the piece indeed appeared—"The Man Who Would Kill God"—and by week's end he knew his life would never be the same.

The morning after the October 5 *Time* hit the newsstands, a brick came crashing through his kitchen window and pulverized the ceramic teapot Vaughn had given Corinne and him as a wedding present. It arrived wrapped in a paper towel onto which someone had Scotch-taped Martin's *Time* photo; a rope noose, crudely drawn in blue ballpoint ink, swayed menacingly above his head. Two days later, as he limped across the parking lot of the Abaddon Municipal Building, intending to retrieve his car and drive home, he was shocked to see that all four tires had been slashed. Someone had written LEAVE GOD ALONE, FUCK-FACE on the driver's door with red paint. He abandoned his crippled car and took a SEPTA bus to Chestnut Grove, where a cardboard carton trussed with twine lay on the doorstep. The carton exuded a horrendous stench. Opening the package, Martin found himself looking into the empty eye sockets of a dead muskrat.

Traumatic as these assaults were, the prying of the mass media proved even more unnerving. The reporters' energy was matched only by their obnoxiousness; they telephoned him at odd hours, clogged his fax machine with petulant pleas, and hung around his house like male dogs besieging a bitch in heat. Every periodical from the *Abaddon Sentinel* to *Playboy* wanted his story, and when he turned them down they went ahead and wrote about him anyway. While *Psychology Today* speculated that he was "a man with an unresolved Oedipus complex, out to murder his heavenly Father," the *National Review* called him "a modern Frankenstein's monster, bent on destroying his Creator." The *Geraldo* organization offered Martin forty-seven thousand dollars for an exclusive interview. Oprah Winfrey's people upped

the ante to fifty thousand. Martin declined both invitations—
partly because he believed such exposure would compromise the
purity of his case, partly because he was loath to advertise himself
to whichever self-righteous lunatics had not yet heard of the Man
Who Would Kill God.

As October progressed, shortening the days and blessing
Abaddon with leaves so bright and psychedelic they rivaled the
carp of Waupelani Creek, Martin grew preoccupied with his
mailbox. He started driving home for lunch, just to see if the
International Court of Justice had written back, but the only
personal correspondence he received that month consisted of four
sob stories from fellow Jobians, three death threats from an organization called the Sword of Jehovah Strike Force, and a Halloween card from Patricia. Compounding the pathos of these
trips was the fact that the mailbox itself, a miniature wooden
castle, had been a Christmas gift from Martin to Corinne. She'd
been delighted when, the following March, a pair of bluejays
had built a nest inside. Throughout the spring Martin had spent
many hours patiently wiping bird droppings off their mail.

When he wasn't brooding about the World Court's silence,
he turned his attention to the Kennel of Joy. Every Tuesday and
Thursday afternoon he called up Corinne's dull but dutiful
cousin Franny. The news was always good. The endowment
from Corinne's life-insurance policy remained intact, and private
contributions were pouring in at a steady rate. Recent beneficiaries included Nanook, a Siberian husky with a brain tumor
whom the Kennel had sent all the way to Nome so she could
run part of the Iditarod, as well as Boris, a Saint Bernard with
failing kidneys who got to rescue an avalanche victim in Aspen.
The whole event was staged, but Boris couldn't possibly have
known, and he died a happy dog.

Election Day found the citizens of Abaddon rushing en
masse to the polls and, in a contest that Martin's opponent had
managed to define as a referendum on his character, telling him
what they thought of his project. The final tally was 11,784 (for

Barbara Meredith) to 322 (for Martin). In the township's entire history, no incumbent JP had ever lost by a wider margin. When he telephoned Meredith to concede defeat, she apologized for capitalizing on his status as America's most conspicuous blasphemer. "We simply couldn't resist," she told him. "Your opponent goes around drawing mustaches on God—it was too good to pass up."

Patricia urged him to take the drubbing philosophically: if the World Court came through, he'd appreciate having so much time for preparing his case. Her argument left him unmoved. Magistracy had been Martin's whole life, his raison d'être, and now he'd lost it. The prosaic but ineluctable matter of solvency also haunted him. His savings would last another six or seven months, but *then* what?

Two days after the election Benjamin Blumenberg gave Martin a bone scan, telephoning him the following afternoon with the preliminary results. "It's not what we wanted to see," said the urologist. "The malignancy's evidently in your right hip and the head of your right thighbone."

"I'm not surprised."

"Me neither."

"So what do we do?"

"We increase your Feminone and hope for the best."

Setting down the receiver, Martin realized he'd begun to personify his disease. *Cancer*, Latin for "crab." A malicious and depraved crustacean had appropriated his prostate, extending its spindly legs outward, digging them into his lymph nodes and pelvis. The crab's claws were sharp and serrated. Its teeth were white-hot needles.

On the last night in November, Martin lay writhing atop his mattress, tortured by the crab, high on Roxanol, and wondering what else could possibly go wrong. Across the room his VCR played the climax of *Judgment at Nuremberg*: Burt Lancaster, the Nazi with a conscience, making his improbable admission of guilt.

Martin's nostrils twitched, aroused by the odor of burning wood and smoldering upholstery. He put the VCR on STILL: a closeup of the defense counsel, Maximillian Schell, telling the tribunal that Lancaster didn't really mean it. Heart fluttering, Martin stumbled downstairs, limped across the living room, and tore open the door. His enclosed front porch was ablaze—a seething red inferno, smoke rising in thick black coils, flames leapfrogging from the curtains to the throw rugs to the cushions. Waves of heat rushed toward him, striking his cheeks like vengeful slaps. His eyes grew watery. His lungs burned. Convulsive coughing wrenched his ribs.

"Die, Judas!" a man shouted, his voice amplified by a bullhorn. "Die, Judas!"

Martin pivoted. A dozen shadowy figures swarmed across the front lawn, brandishing their fists.

"Die, Judas!"

He hobbled to the kitchen. Snatching up the precious bottle of Roxanol, he opened it, ate two tablets, and staggered out the back door. Hacking, weeping, he made his way to the catnip patch and collapsed.

"Die, Judas!"

Lying on the cool earth, he seriously considered calling the fire department. That would certainly be the rational thing to do. But instead he stayed where he was, rolling around amid the rotting *Nepeta cataria* like a stoned tabby.

Sirens shattered the night, drilling through his tympanic membranes, rattling his Eustachian tubes. A peculiar truth fell upon him. He didn't care whether the flames devoured his house or not. No, he actually *wanted* the flames to devour his house. A thousand remorseless ghosts haunted 22 Flour Mill Road. Hardly a day went by in which he didn't encounter one of Corinne's hair ribbons, a bag of her bath herbs, or a photo of some slavering Kennel of Joy beneficiary. Let it burn. Let the whole damn thing burn down.

He levered himself upright and, groggy with Roxanol,

wandered toward the fire. The flames had transformed November's chill, bringing an ersatz summer to his property. Dozens of Chestnut Grove residents had collected on the lawn,
holding handkerchiefs to their mouths as they sweated in the
heat. Black hoses sinuated amid the crabgrass and the fallen
leaves. Men in thick yellow raincoats and white fiberglass hel-
mets wandered about, their faces obscured by oxygen masks,
looking less like firefighters than like methane-breathing aliens
out of Patricia's trading-card series.

Camouflaged by shadows, Martin called toward a uniformed
police officer—one of Constable Steadman's underlings, he realized. "Who lives here?"

"That JP who just got voted out, Martin Candle."

"Is he dead?"

"Don't know. Dead or alive, looks like the sucker's gonna
lose everything."

" 'Candle.' Isn't he the guy who wants to prosecute the Main
Attraction?"

"Same bastard, yeah. Tell you one thing—we find his
charred body in the rubble, I won't be sheddin' a whole lotta
tears."

❖

He spent the night at his sister's house, and the next morning
he drove his soot-smeared Dodge over to 65 Mapleshade Lane.
As Patricia sat before her drawing board, adding veins to a
Vestan's gigantic eyeballs, he told her of his newest misfortune.

"Burned down your house? Jesus. Are you okay?"

"Good question."

Extending an inky hand, she fondly squeezed his wrist.
"You're welcome to stay in my guest room."

"Thanks, but . . ."

"You're afraid they'll do *my* house next?"

"A reasonable concern, don't you think?"

"A reasonable concern," she echoed. "Guess what? I'm so depressed lately that reasonable concerns roll right off my back. The guest room is yours, pal. *Mi casa es su casa*."

He grimaced and inhaled. His clothing stank of the myriad odors liberated by the flames: paint, varnish, shellac, linoleum, plastic, fiberfill. "Whatever you charge, it's bound to be cheaper than a bodyguard."

"No payment necessary."

"You're a kind person, Patricia. I promise you I'll lay low."

"It's going to be fun having you around."

"I'm not a terribly fun person these days."

"We're going to have a ball."

Relocating to Patricia's guest room proved the simplest such move Martin had ever made. His only possessions to survive the fire—some carpentry tools, a few kitchen utensils, a dozen smoky books, an alarm clock, and the music box he'd won at Celestial City USA—fit easily into four cardboard cartons. He had plenty of time that afternoon to visit the Chestnut Grove post office and inform them of his new address.

With the advent of the Christmas season, Martin became as fixated on Patricia's mailbox as he'd ever been on Corinne's. He checked it incessantly—obsessively—like a new mother tiptoeing into the nursery to make sure her baby was still breathing. When he finally did learn the World Court's response, though, the news reached him not through the postal system but through Charles Braithwaite's second *Time* article about the Job Society. The piece was titled "The Trial of the Millennium: Postponed," and the key information lay in the final two paragraphs.

> *While the ICJ has made no formal announcement, economic realities will probably keep the Job Society's case off the docket for years to come. "The budget for such a trial would be many times our annual appropriation, something on the order of eighty million dollars," the Court's vice president, Giuseppe Sanfilippo, told* Time.

The costs in question, Time *has learned, include hiring a supertanker fleet to extradite the Corpus Dei, paying advocates to construct arguments on both sides of the issue, housing witnesses, and retaining UN peacekeeping forces to control whatever factions might attempt to disrupt the proceeding.*

Eventually a letter from the World Court did arrive at Patricia's house, but it contained nothing Martin didn't already know. "Although the judges are open to hearing a class-action indictment of the sort your organization proposes," wrote the registrar, Pierre Ferrand, "they see no way to finance such an elaborate undertaking."

"A blessing in disguise," said Patricia.

"Hardly," said Martin as a crab spasm tore along his femur.

"Put this trial out of your mind. It's time to get on with your life."

"I've got no life to get on with."

"Yes you do."

" 'The wolf is now my brother, and owls of the desert have become my companions,' " said Martin, quoting Job. " 'My blackened skin peels off, and my body is scorched by the heat. My harp has been tuned for a dirge, my flute to the voice of those who weep.' "

"Know what I think? Somewhere deep down inside, you believe if you reenact that crazy Bible story—if you call God to account and listen patiently to His defense—He'll replace everything you lost, just like He did with Job. New house, new career, new Corinne, new prostate gland. Well, it just doesn't work that way."

"This isn't about my prostate gland, Patricia."

"Then what *is* it about?"

He glanced furtively at her cleavage. Feminone now ruled his endocrine system so completely he might as well have been looking at a stop sign. "'Think again, let me have no more injustice. Think again, for my integrity is in question.'"

On December 17 the Job Society gathered once more in the Valley of Children. As the sufferers entered play area three, Randall sidled up to Martin and gestured toward a photograph thumbtacked to the bulletin board: Patricia and Angela wearing matching lime green sunsuits and standing outside the daycare center. Together the women held the nozzle of a garden hose and gleefully sprayed a gaggle of preschool boys in bathing trunks.

"You know them?" asked Randall.

"The one on the left is Angela Zabor—she runs this place. The other one is her twin sister, Patricia."

"Handsome women."

"I'm living in Patricia's guest room."

"Your girlfriend?"

"My friend. Her kid died from complications of spina bifida."

"Spina bifida? Then why the hell isn't she *here*?"

"She doesn't believe in what we're doing."

Randall scowled indignantly. "People shouldn't let other people fight their battles for them, especially when the enemy is God."

The meeting was not long under way when a curious fact dawned on Martin: the Jobians were more anxious to learn about his private disasters than about the ICJ's rejection of their case. Since their last gathering he'd gone out and become a celebrity, and his fellow sufferers wanted to know what fame was like.

"I'll bet your life's been horrible," said Esther.

"All our lives are horrible," Martin replied, casting his gaze about the room. Braithwaite was conspicuously absent—afraid, no doubt, to show his face. "But, yeah, you're right. I've had a pretty rough time."

"I heard they burned down your house," said Allison.

It was as if, having cheated the world out of a talk show appearance, he was obligated to give such a performance here and now. Only after questioning him for a full half hour were the Jobians satisfied to tackle the business at hand.

"Eighty million dollars," said Esther, drumming her fingers on the December 14 *Time*.

"So what're we going to do?" asked Randall. "Hold a fucking bake sale?"

"Let's all become Amway representatives," said Julia with a dark smile.

"Job never quit," said Martin. "He stayed on the dung heap, railing against injustice, and eventually the whirlwind appeared."

"I've got an idea," said Allison. "We're a grassroots organization, right? So why not stage a grassroots trial? My sister-in-law is a district judge in Macon, Georgia. Maybe she'd be willing to hear our case."

"I'd hate to settle for something that small," said Martin.

"Depending on how much media coverage we get, a scaled-down proceeding might be quite satisfying," said Peter.

"My heart's not in it," said Martin.

With the approach of midnight the pace of the discussion accelerated. Eventually it was agreed that, upon returning home, Allison would find out whether her sister-in-law could work the Trial of the Millennium into her schedule, a thought Martin found endlessly depressing. Holding the trial in Macon instead of The Hague would be like getting a plush terrier for Christmas when you'd asked for a live Dalmatian.

At five minutes to twelve, he declared the meeting adjourned.

A crab spasm radiated through his pelvis. He ate three Roxanols and looked around. Sixty-five Jobians were heading for the door, a morbid procession of wheelchairs, walkers, IV drips, and oxygen tanks. Ruefully he recalled the bittersweet denouement of their previous gathering. How alive he'd felt back then—how like Job himself, full of bracing belligerence. But tonight he felt like what he was: a widowed, impotent, homeless, lame-duck justice of the peace, marooned in a benumbing Republican suburb and dying of metastatic prostate cancer.

Chapter 5

CANCER IS MY MASTERPIECE, the source of all my awards, but weather has always been my bread and butter. You cannot be a credible Prince of Darkness without a talent for hurricanes, a feel for drought, and a working knowledge of snow.

On December 14, 1999, a ferocious blizzard engulfed the city of Cambridge, Massachusetts, a community boasting more IQ points per capita than any comparable settlement east of the Mississippi. For eighteen hours straight it snowed. Weighted down by the conglomerated crystals, scores of telephone cables and power lines snapped in two like Jason Lowry's spinal cord, rendering the city deaf, dumb, and blind. The streets became frothy white canals negotiable only via snowshoe, snowmobile, or cross-country ski. Enterprising teenagers made fortunes clearing sidewalks and delivering groceries. By Christmas the casualty count stood at twenty-five, including four citizens who'd experienced lethal heart attacks while out shoveling, an elderly piano teacher who'd bled to death after his snowblower lacerated his foot, and an eighty-year-old antiques dealer who, unable to obtain her insulin, had lapsed into a diabetic coma and died.

Throughout the city only one person remained oblivious to the disaster. This was Gregory Francis Lovett, a semi-retired medieval literature professor who rarely left his house, read his mail only when he felt like it, subscribed to no periodicals save the *Augustinian Quarterly,* owned neither a radio nor a television, and had not permitted a telephone in his life since 1962. For news of the outside world, G. F. Lovett relied exclusively on the man with whom he shared his Mount Auburn Street abode, his alcoholic younger brother, Darcy. If the stock market crashed, a war broke out, or Jesus Christ materialized in Harvard Yard accompanied by a band of angels, Lovett would not know of it unless Darcy got around to telling him.

When the emergency officially ended—on the morning of December 19—Lovett was sitting in his private library and savoring a cup of Irish breakfast tea, his ample rump squeezed into a cowhide wing chair. Cedar logs blazed on the hearth. Three thousand leatherbound volumes rested on mahogany shelves, their gold titles sparkling in the fire's glow. In the far corner a grandfather clock stood guard, ticking like the mechanical heart of Stanhope the Steam-Powered Man, the robot featured in one of the many beloved children's books Lovett had penned over the years.

Of all the various pieces of mail occupying Lovett's lap, the only item that intrigued him was the package from Vernice, his ne'er-do-well, thrice-married sister up in Maine, whom he was paying seven thousand dollars a year to send him clippings of a theologically provocative nature. This week's collection featured a dozen articles about an organization called the Job Society, and he had not known such a rush of excitement since 1971, when he and the analytic philosopher Emily Arboghast had crossed swords under the auspices of Harvard's Socratic Club, the topic of their debate being "The Plausibility of the Impossible." The fight had been grueling, but in the end God and G. F. Lovett had prevailed, with Lovett proving that Arboghast's rejection of the supernatural amounted to a rejection of the thought process itself.

"Darcy!" he called to his brother. "Darcy, something entirely splendid has happened!"

I should note that before entering His self-induced coma, our Creator had been well pleased with Lovett, granting him a sharp mind and a fit physique. Despite the odds—the claret, the meerschaum pipe, the sedentary life—Lovett was about to celebrate his seventy-fourth birthday. Some said his good health traced to his bank account, which had grown at an embarrassing rate since the Disney organization had turned the Saga of Sargassia into a series of animated features. Unlike the average Harvard professor, Lovett understood the mind of the child. He often joked that he himself had never stopped being one. The first Sargassia adaptation alone, *The Mermaid in the Maelstrom*, had so far brought him $17,439,860 in videocassette rentals and toy royalties, ten times more than he'd received from his lecture series on the Interfaith Network and all his books of Christian apologetics combined.

Which is not to say the Saga of Sargassia pandered to the marketplace or insulted its audience's intelligence. For the majority of readers, the cycle's central conceit—a vast floating island eternally plying uncharted seas, piloted by a mildly insane captain named Alexis Renardo and powered by trade winds pulling on the immense leaves of the island's indigenous gricklegrackle trees—resonated as deeply as a Greek myth. If there is justice in this world, when the history of modern fantasy is written, Sargassia will receive no less coverage than Wonderland, Oz, or Middle Earth.

"Darcy!"

At last Lovett's brother appeared, his walrus mustache damp with port, the stem of a wineglass pinched between his thumb and index finger.

"Listen to this." Lovett held up Charles Braithwaite's second *Time* article. "There's a magistrate down in Pennsylvania who fancies himself another Job."

Ever since his brother had apprised him of the Almighty's cryptic condition six years earlier, Lovett had been pondering the Corpus Dei. While ostensibly a troubling object, the Main

Attraction at Celestial City USA would eventually—he'd concluded—do the Episcopal Church and the rest of Christendom more good than harm. By providing the world with an intimation of His infinite grandeur, God was saying, in essence, "I have shown you mountains and rainbows, sequoias and whales, and now I have even shown you My fleshly form—yet these wonders are as nothing, *nothing*, compared to what you will behold upon entering My everlasting Kingdom." Which meant, of course, this so-called Job Society was woefully misguided in perceiving the Corpus Dei as an outlaw to be prosecuted. The body was an avatar to be venerated, or it was nothing at all.

"Fellow named Martin Candle, right?" said Darcy.

Lovett sipped his tea and nodded. "It's all too perfect, don't you think? For *decades* I've been wanting to get into a brawl like this."

Darcy took a substantial swallow of port. "Read on. The brawl's been canceled. The World Court doesn't have the scratch."

"How much do they need?"

"Eighty million dollars."

A sly, Alexis Renardo–like smile spread across Lovett's face. "Listen carefully," he said, steepling his fingers. "At your earliest convenience I want you to begin arranging the transfer of eighty million dollars from Sargassia, Incorporated, to the bank account of the United Nations."

"If you don't mind my saying so, dear brother, this is an astonishingly ill-considered . . ." Darcy's sentence decayed into a succession of bemused chuckles. He finished his port, paused a beat, and sighed. "I'll ring up Crawford first thing Monday."

Lovett rubbed his hands together as if lathering a bar of soap. "It's been a long while since I've had any fun, Darcy, and this is going to be *fun*. The final war, eh?" he said, *The Final War* being the tenth book in the Sargassia cycle. "I shall always be grateful to this Judge Martin Candle. Even as I cut him down . . . even as I grind his arguments to dust . . . does that sound terribly un-Christian?"

"Terribly."

"Even as I destroy the man, I shall remain forever in his debt."

❖

As Martin left the noisy clutter of Park Avenue and entered the hushed vulgarity of Trump Tower, he couldn't help thinking of an earlier, equally outrageous skyscraper, the Tower of Babel on the Plain of Shinar. He still remembered the Sunday school lesson his father had wrought from that particular Bible story. After telling his students to transcribe their favorite psalms but to leave out every other word, Walter Candle next had them read the resulting nonsense aloud. The ruckus that followed, fifteen preadolescents gibbering at the tops of their voices, vividly dramatized the confusion that had reigned at Shinar after God handicapped humanity with a multiplicity of tongues.

Cancer clawing at his pelvis, a Roxanol tablet dissolving in his stomach, he limped across the atrium: a lurid space, agleam with bronze banisters and Breccia Perniche marble. His soul was buoyant with hope. Just when his fortunes had seemed at their lowest, he'd received a call from Gretchen Wilde, private secretary to Stuart Torvald, president of the International Court of Justice. At the moment the Court stood adjourned, Wilde explained, so that the judges might enjoy the holidays with their families. Could Martin meet with Dr. Torvald two days after Christmas to discuss an important new development in the proposed legal proceeding?

He stumbled onto the escalator and rose through the tiers of polyglot shops: Loewe's of Spain, Jourdain's of France, Beck's of Germany, Pineider's of Italy. His reflection glided by, caught in the polished copper panels—his hunched frame and pain-pinched face. He got off on Level E and took the elevator to the forty-second floor, eardrums tightening with the force of his ascent. Leaving the car, he knocked on the penthouse door, which opened to reveal a man so lean and elastic he might have just exited an El Greco painting. Piano music drifted into the hallway, a piece Martin recognized as one of Corinne's favorites, Gershwin's *An American in Paris*.

"Justice Torvald?"

"Quite so," the ICJ president replied, his aristocratic tones filtered through the unequalized pressure in Martin's ears. "Magistrate Candle?"

"At your service." As the two men shook hands, Martin considered how the farthest ends of the judicial spectrum—the lowest and highest courts on the planet—were currently conjoined in this doorway.

Torvald ushered him into a sumptuous living room, its transparent far wall affording a breathtaking vista of midtown Manhattan. In the northeast corner a Scotch pine rose floor to ceiling, its branches hung with ornaments, tinsel descending in a silvery drizzle, the stand encircled by exactly the sorts of Christmas gifts one might assume were exchanged in such surroundings: a rope of pearls, a cashmere sweater, a pair of leather riding boots. For reasons not readily apparent, a battered attaché case sat incongruously amid the presents.

"Let me introduce a dear friend," said Torvald, guiding Martin toward a baby grand piano at which sat a stumpy man with salt-and-pepper hair, a surplus chin, and a beard so short and dense it seemed painted onto his jaw. Three gold-framed photographs rested atop the piano, each disclosing a different smiling and successful looking young woman, doubtless the judge's daughters. "Irving Saperstein, professor emeritus at Princeton and chairman of the Committee for Complete Disclosure of the Corpus Dei. Irving's lost the Nobel Prize in neurophysiology more times than Richard Burton was deprived of the Oscar."

"Goodness, Stu, I'd never heard *that* comparison." Lifting

his thick fingers from the keyboard, Saperstein stood up, bowed slightly, and shook Martin's hand.

"We've met before," said Martin. "Orlando," he added in response to Saperstein's scowl. "You tried to keep me from entering the Celestial City."

"Did I succeed?"

"No."

"You saw the Main Attraction, but your disease didn't go into remission, did it?"

"True enough."

"So instead we've got *International* . . . tell him, Stu."

Torvald sauntered across the room, reached toward the Christmas tree, and retrieved from the stack of gifts a small golden mallet. "Christmas present from my wife," he explained. "On Monday, June fifth, at ten o'clock in the morning, I shall slam this fourteen-karat gavel onto my bench in the Peace Palace, thus marking the start of *International 227: Job Society, et al., plaintiffs, versus Corpus Dei, Defendant.*"

Martin gasped so profoundly his clogged ears popped. "I thought you didn't have the funds."

"A backer has appeared—an angel, as they say on Broadway," Torvald explained. "Does the name G. F. Lovett mean anything to you?"

"No."

"You've probably heard of the movies they made from his children's books. *The Mermaid in the Maelstrom . . . The Basilisk of Barbados . . .*"

"Oh, right, the Sargassia cycle. My landlady's kid used to collect the action figures." Martin's heart raced madly. His breathing became short and shallow. Was he really hearing this? *International 227: Job Society versus Corpus Dei*—it was actually going to happen? "A sad story. The boy died."

"I'm told the Saga of Sargassia is really some sort of Christian allegory, but it's still a lot of fun," said Torvald.

"I was more into Oz," said Saperstein.

"Me too," said Martin. "I'll have to give Lovett a try."

"Before the new year is out, we'll *all* be giving Lovett a try," said Torvald. "Not the Sargassia books, certainly not the literary criticism—I mean the Christian apologetics. *God for Beginners . . . Sermons by Satan . . . The Conundrum of Suffering . . .*"

Torvald spent the next five minutes telling what he called "a characteristic anecdote" about Lovett, the time the professor had tried inducing Pope John XXIII to take up pipe smoking ("Our Lord treasured the things of this Earth, how else to account for all those references to mustard seeds and fig trees?"), but Martin heard only snippets. An angel had arrived! With eighty million dollars!

"Tomorrow I'm holding a press conference—downtown, at the UN—where Lovett's philanthropy will become public," said Torvald. "I'll also be announcing that *International 227* will occur only after a court-appointed fact-finding team has ventured into His brain." He presented Martin with a stare to shame the Barbados basilisk. "Let me lay my cards on the table. You and Lovett might be looking forward to this trial, but I am not. It has never been my ambition to supervise the persecution of God Almighty by a bunch of disgruntled *Times Book Review* eggheads. I have no wish to become the next Herod Antipas. Do you follow me, sir? I cannot endorse this project of yours. I find it impudent in the extreme." He cupped a hand around Saperstein's shoulder. "What I *do* endorse is the Committee for Complete Disclosure. When Lovett came to me with his offer, I immediately saw a thrilling implication: I realized we could temporarily consign the body to people who can make far better use of it than the American Baptist Confederation ever will."

"It's going to be the greatest scientific expedition of all time," Saperstein asserted, sidling toward the Christmas tree. "The search for the source of the Nile writ on a cosmic scale. A journey into the ultimate terra incognita."

"A lot of people think He's brain-dead," Martin protested.

"Here's the deal," said Saperstein, absently removing a velvet snowman from the tree. "The Baptists have always regarded their Main Attraction not as a comatose body but as a vessel God shed in the course of becoming pure spirit. Although the Holy Ghost periodically suffuses this vessel—hence its alleged healing powers—it is by no means synonymous with the Almighty. Ergo, when Stu told them the trial was contingent on the Corpus Dei's being alive, they agreed to a limited neurological biopsy. They were confident, you see, that the tissue would prove inert."

"They let you enter His skull?" asked Martin, astounded.

"We didn't have to go that far. A probe of His eyeball proved adequate. Last Thursday we drilled into the left cornea, made our way through the vitreous humor, and excised a cell from the optic nerve. Back in the lab, the thing proved anything but inert."

"Irving will be demonstrating its properties at tomorrow's press conference," said Torvald.

"Sounds like the Baptists have shot themselves in the foot," said Martin.

"I see now they were hoping to make hay with Irving's experiment. They wanted to use the neuron's presumed sterility to expose *International 227* as a show trial—politically motivated, not to be taken seriously."

"But it *will* be taken seriously, right?" said Martin. "You'll retain the best lawyers, hire top-notch philosophers, extradite the Defendant, send me and my Jobians to The Hague. I want the court to hear what happened to my wife, how a runaway Irish setter—"

"Oh, you'll be telling us your story all right. In fact, you'll be telling us a great deal *more* than that."

"More?"

Torvald rested the head of his gavel under his chin and smiled. "Lovett's donation arrives with three strings attached. First proviso: he himself gets to orchestrate the defense."

"Sounds reasonable."

"Second proviso: Martin Candle must take the stand as one of his witnesses."

"As one of *his* witnesses?"

"Right."

"He'll be getting an awfully hostile witness."

"I'm sure he knows that. Third proviso: the case for the prosecution must be conceived and executed by you, sir—by you and you alone."

Martin felt a tightening in his chest—the Feminone, he realized, attempting to enlarge his breasts. "Me? The entire case? Really?"

"You. The entire case. Really." Torvald laid his gavel on the piano bench. "Budget permitting, you may employ whatever outside experts you wish, but the opening statement, the closing argument, the examination of witnesses—all this must come from you. Evidently you've offended Lovett to the core. The man wants your head on a platter."

Martin picked up the gavel and rapped it against his soggy palm. Win or lose, he was morally obligated to accept this daunting mission. His Jobians deserved no less. "All right," he said at last. "Very well. Fine." He returned the gavel to the piano lid. "The Baptists—they'll actually let you impound His brain?"

"After my press conference at the UN, they won't have any choice—not unless they want to face prosecution themselves for obstructing justice."

"Perhaps I should drop by tomorrow, so I can see the optic neuron in action. I ought to know what I'm up against, right?"

"You aren't up against *God*, Mr. Candle—you're up against G. F. Lovett."

"If I were you, I'd rather be taking on God," said Saperstein, returning the velvet snowman to its branch. He retrieved the scruffy attaché case from under the tree and set it atop the piano. "As for our prize neuron, you may attend the press conference if you wish"—flicking his thumbs, he unfastened the two brass latches—"but we can satisfy your curiosity on *that* score right now."

An unearthly light filled the penthouse, rising from the attaché case in a shimmering blue vortex that struck the great Christmas tree and transmuted its ornaments into flaming asteroids, the tinsel into filaments of fire.

"What's going on?" asked Martin.

"Each time he sets it free," said Torvald, "it does something new."

Even before the judge had finished speaking, the errant neuron slithered, amoebalike, out of the attaché case and across the piano lid. A cry of amazement broke from Martin's throat. Blinding in its luminosity, fearful in its symmetry, the neuron suggested a kind of immanent Frisbee, perhaps, or a radioactive pizza.

"It's just one of billions, of course," said Saperstein as, rippling like a pebble-struck pond, the neuron extended a dendrite toward the keyboard and pressed middle C. "Imagine the wonders we'll encounter once we actually breach His cerebrum."

The creature began playing "Heart and Soul."

Impressed as he was by the neuron's performance, Martin found himself unable to occupy the moment. His mind had drifted elsewhere—toward the astonishing quantity of work that lay ahead, his upcoming odyssey into theodicy. Could he really hold his own against Saint Augustine, Thomas Aquinas, Bishop Origen, and all those other dead Christians mentioned in Dr. Phillip H. Strand's obnoxious letter?

"June the fifth—that's only five months away," said Martin.

"I wanted to wait till autumn, but Lovett would hear none of it," said Torvald. "I hope you're not getting cold feet."

"Lukewarm feet."

"Science is counting on you," said Saperstein.

The crab clamped its jaws around Martin's thighbone. He gasped, bit his inner cheeks, and said, "Do you know where

I'm headed next, gentlemen? Uptown—to Memorial Sloan-Kettering Cancer Center, that's where." He pulled out his Roxanol and ate two tablets. "I'll chase Him round Good Hope, Your Honor, and round the Horn, and round the Norway Maelstrom, and round perdition's flames before I give Him up."

"Then we'll see you in The Hague?" asked Torvald.

"With bells on," said Martin.

❖

The climax of Martin's visit to Memorial Sloan-Kettering came when Blumenberg examined the results of the latest bone scan, ushered him into his office, and said, "The Feminone is working wonders."

"It's given me a lovely pair of knockers. That's a wonder of sorts. Maybe I could become a Rockette."

"The spread of the tumor has definitely been halted. Now we're going to send it into a full retreat." Blumenberg clasped his hands together behind his head and tilted backward in his swivel chair. "We'll keep you on the hormones, but I want to supplement them with something called Odradex-11—experimental, hush-hush, terrifically encouraging results with prostate cancer. The good news is you can administer it yourself. The bad news is you must stick it directly in a vein—two cubic centimeters per day for the next three months."

"You mean I'll have to puncture myself?"

"Nothing that medieval. We'll install a Port-A-Cath in your chest—minor surgery, but surgery all the same—then send you home with a syringe. The injections themselves are a snap, easy as watering a house plant. Can we put you in the hospital Friday?"

"I guess so."

"How's the hip?"

"Until the Roxanol kicks in—terrible. Does this Odradex have any side effects?"

"A few."

"Feminone turned me into a woman. What will Odradex turn me into?"

Blumenberg leaned forward, propped both elbows on the desk, and rested his jaw in his cupped hands. "It won't turn you into anything. You'll probably experience some drowsiness, that's all, and you might have trouble focusing your thoughts."

"Forget it, Doc." Martin's gaze alighted on Blumenberg's 1964 World's Fair paperweight, a brass Unisphere the size of a softball. "During the next seven months my mind has to be sharper than ever. It's the only way I can win my case."

"A sharp mind won't win your case. An Odradex regimen might."

"My *legal* case."

"I thought they rejected you."

"They found an investor. The catch is, I've got to run the whole show. I can't lose my edge, not for a minute."

"Nobody rebels against God and wins, Martin. Prometheus couldn't do it. Job couldn't do it. Ahab couldn't do it. Take the damn drug, okay?"

❖

The installation of the Port-A-Cath came off without a hitch, though the procedure left Martin with an unpleasant sense of having been invaded, as if Patricia's Vestans had implanted some insidious monitoring device in his body. It was easy to forget about the microcapsules filling his prostate, but the Port-A-Cath—a plastic shunt buried above his right breast, the socket angling into the air like an inner-tube valve—irritated the surrounding skin and made his nipple tingle. He hated it, though not half as much as he hated the aggressive anticancer drug whose intrusion the device permitted.

Within an hour after receiving his first hit of Odradex from Patricia, he felt as if an elephant were stepping on his head. His vision went blurry. Sleigh bells jangled in his ears. He clambered into the guest-room bed and stayed there.

As he continued taking the drug, his subconscious began to torment him. With the approach of each dawn he routinely experienced the notorious inverse nightmare all cancer patients must endure. He dreamed he was in his little courtroom, sitting before the people he loved—Vaughn, Jenny, Patricia, Corinne—and telling them Dr. Blumenberg had just pronounced him cured.

During those rare and precious moments when Martin was lucid, he set about designing the prosecution's case. By availing himself of his century, that miraculous age of voice mail, fax machines, and computer webs, he was able to coordinate his Jobians without leaving bed. He directed Task Force 1, headed by Randall, to comb through academia, seeking out sociologists and historians willing to argue that a truly inculpable Supreme Being would have supervised His creatures' fates far more diligently. Task Force 2, headed by Esther, was responsible for lining up a full roster of angry victims. "I want at least twenty-five heartbreaking stories," he told her. "Thirty, if you can manage it."

Throughout January he remained an Odradex invalid, dividing his time between grappling with Lovett's *The Conundrum of Suffering* and zoning out on Patricia's television, a twenty-seven-inch Mitsubishi poised at the foot of the guest-room bed like a tombstone overshadowing a grave. He watched Court TV, the Sci-Fi Channel, and the Comedy Network—but most of all he watched the Siege of Celestial City USA.

The showdown traced to the ICJ's decision that the trial must not devolve into an empty symbolic exercise: this was a real criminal proceeding, and the Defendant must be extradited and imprisoned accordingly. Unfortunately, Eternity Enterprises was not about to surrender its cash cow without a fight. On the day the Court announced its intention to tow the Main Attraction to the Netherlands, each stockholder was enjoying a fivefold return on his investment. Following Saperstein's televised demonstration of the optic neuron's talents—proof that an indictable entity resided within the divine skull—a significant percentage of the world's legal scholars, academic philosophers, and liberal theologians had come out in favor of *International 227*, but this cut no ice with the stockholders. The average Eternity investor couldn't have cared less whether His cranium contained five living neurons or five billion: God was the property of the corporation. Upon learning that United Nations peacekeeping forces were headed for Orlando bearing deportation orders, the stockholders shed their business suits, picked up their handguns and hunting rifles, and secured the Celestial City against invasion.

CNN provided the best coverage. While the network claimed to be impartial, its sympathies clearly lay with the stockholders: six hundred and twenty photogenic white people, all prepared to die in the name of God's dignity and profit's honor. The peacekeepers' strategy proved a masterpiece of nonviolent aggression. Knockout gas was the key. Every time a new sector of the theme park fell under Eternity Enterprises' control, the UN would unleash canisters of Soporphoria-B. The CNN cameras revealed heaps of unconscious capitalists piled up around the Chariots of Ezekiel ferris wheel, the Heaven to Hell roller coaster, and the Four Horsemen of the Apocalypse carousel: scenes that for Martin evoked the comatose kingdom in the Disney *Sleeping Beauty*, which he and Jenny had seen together when it first came out in 1959.

As Martin interpreted *The Conundrum of Suffering*, its theodicy sprang from the concept of ancestral disobedience. For G. F. Lovett, the story of Adam's insubordination in Eden was true in some fundamental anthropological sense. Although the prelapsarian hominids who'd once inhabited the world were unsophisticated technologically, they were highly advanced spiritually, enjoying an immediate relationship with their Creator. But then, as a function of the very consciousness that had enabled them to apprehend God's love, these original sinners grew fatally absorbed in themselves, eventually turning away from the divine to pursue their own agendas. To wit, they became us: a damaged species, sick with sin, twisted by pride. "Is it any wonder God allows vermin such as we to suffer?" Lovett asked, rhetorically, in chapter three.

> *It is not. The mystery is that He does so with the sole aim of making us once again worthy of His love. Real love, divine love—as opposed to mere grandfatherly kindness— is hot as slag and hard as steel. It insists that its object be deserving and not depraved, clean and not corrupt. The tribulations of this world are like the incisions the surgeon makes as he cuts the malignant tumors from a patient's vitals. Awakening from the anesthesia, the patient finds himself in pain. At first the pain seems gratuitous and cruel, but then he remembers the alternative is much worse.*

God as cosmic surgeon. Martin had to admit it all made a kind of sense. (Indeed, in the days when he'd viewed his Creator more sympathetically, his image of God was not unlike his image of Dr. Lloyd Zimmerman, the swashbuckling cardiologist who'd performed a triple bypass on his father.) Doubtless this theodicy had its weaknesses, but in his present drugged state he was far too befuddled to notice them. The more Odradex he received, the woozier he grew. His gait became unsteady, his eyelids heavy, his memory porous. It seemed as if he were actually fighting two wars that January: one against cancer, the other against its cure.

On Groundhog Day, Martin reached a fateful decision.

"I'm going off the drug," he told Patricia. "The darn stuff's blowing out my neurons."

"Don't talk nonsense. It's keeping you alive."

"Alive for what? Alive so I can lose another election? So I can die a horrible death? It's in my lymph nodes, Patricia. It's in my bones. Don't tell me any fairy tales about Odradex."

"Please, Martin. I love you."

"You do?"

"Yes."

"That's not a very good idea."

"Keep taking the Odradex—*please*."

"No. I can't. Sorry. No."

Forty-eight hours after the last Odradex dose had entered Martin's bloodstream, his mind miraculously cleared. His brain, he decided, had been like one of Abaddon Marsh's frog ponds: suddenly the scum was gone, leaving the waters pellucid and pristine. Bring on the dead Christians, he thought. I'm ready for the lot of them.

February featured record snows, unprecedented lows, and a valiant effort by Martin to fathom the theologians cited in Lovett's footnotes, a project that included entering his reactions onto the hard drive of his Apple PowerBook 630, one of the first items he'd purchased with the $26,580,000 the professor had obligingly deposited in the Job Society's bank account. As a blizzard raged through Abaddon Township, Martin struggled with the indicated portions of Saint Augustine's *Confessions*, doing his best to grasp the bishop's notion of pain as a teaching tool sent by God so that we might learn self-restraint. "But does the pupil learn self-restraint," Martin typed into his laptop, "or merely what pain feels like?" He tackled the relevant sections of Gregory the Great's *Moralia*, striving to comprehend the pope's idea that souls were like athletes: to realize their potential, they must submit to painful training. "But there's a difference, surely," Martin wrote, "between training and torture." He sampled Gregory Nazianzenus's *Discours*, pondering this church father's argument that natural disasters bespoke divine displeasure. "The evidence is slim," Martin wrote. He dipped into Julian of Norwich's *Book of Showings*, plowed through twenty-four of Meister Eckhart's five dozen *Sermons*, and forced himself to read two hundred pages of Martin Luther's sixty-one-volume *Werke*. "All three thinkers," he wrote, "are making essentially the same argument: if life contained no challenges, virtue would wither for lack of exercise."

He glanced at Patricia's television. The one hundred Eternity stockholders not yet taken prisoner were making a stand atop the cooling chamber. Strung out shoulder to shoulder along the Lucite slab, an image recalling various Hollywood depictions of the fall of the Alamo, God's defenders hunkered down as thousands of UN peacekeepers prepared to storm the Corpus Dei from all four sides.

The further Martin ventured into Augustine and his ilk, the more apparent it became that a second theory of evil was afoot in their tomes. He dubbed it the Father-knows-best hypothesis. According to this argument, an obscure benevolence underlay most human suffering—but our perceptions were too limited to grasp it. "To an extraterrestrial, a mother's labor pains might seem pointless, whereas she herself knows a greater good will result," Martin wrote, paraphrasing the apologists as best he could. "To a kitten, a flea bath seems sadistic, even though it may be all that stands between the animal and anemia."

The Siege of Celestial City USA lasted fifteen days, two more than the Siege of the Alamo, after which—realizing the hopelessness of their situation—the Eternity stockholders laid down their arms, surrendered the Corpus Dei, and began appearing on the talk-show circuit. They were the new national heroes, more popular than the Apollo astronauts of the sixties, more sympathetic than the Iran hostages of the seventies.

"If Jesus had wanted us to, we would've fought down to the last man," they informed Oprah.

"We regretted having to take up arms," they explained to Geraldo, "but there comes a time when your duty to God outweighs everything else."

"Thank goodness they didn't kill anybody," Martin told Patricia.

"*Lots* of people are going to crack up before your damned

trial is over, Martin—not just freaked-out stockholders, *lots* of people. It's not too late to call it off."

❖

On the last evening in February, as midnight approached, Martin lay in bed wondering whether, having taken himself off Odradex, he should jettison the Feminone as well. His bosom was now so substantial that he had to wear a sports bra, his libido so beleaguered that not even the raunchiest erotica from Perkinsville Video could bestir it. Convulsed with shame, racked with pain, he climbed off the mattress, stumbled into the hall, and stood before the full-length mirror dressed in nothing but boxer shorts. In the feeble light of the forty-watt bulb his Port-A-Cath valve looked as innocuous as a mole. "Nice tits," he muttered, fighting tears.

Patricia appeared beside him, sketch pad tucked under her arm. The exposed page showed a Vestan flying saucer slicing through the Washington Monument like a knife bisecting a salami. "Nice tits," she echoed, laying a sympathetic palm against his cheek.

"It isn't *fair*." As a teenager, Martin had frequently indulged in the common male fantasy of wishing his body would transmute into a woman's, so that he might ogle himself in the mirror. Sometimes he would even mold his bosom into a facsimile of Gloria McIntyre's. Now his wish had come true. "First my health, then Corinne, my job, my house—"

"Read a detective novel, Martin, something in which justice prevails. Watch television. American Movie Classics."

"—and now my gender."

"You need a Fred Astaire flick. Fred and Ginger."

He returned to the guest room, retrieved the Feminone bottle, and reluctantly jammed a capsule in his mouth, washing it down with sour orange juice. Staying with the estrogen regimen made sense in the long run, he told himself. The drug was quite likely keeping him alive, and while it had deformed his body and disempowered his penis, it hadn't reduced his outrage one iota. Like many Republicans, Martin was ambivalent toward the so-called women's movement—he couldn't tell where the legitimate critique ended and the whining began—but he had to admit that the mere presence of female hormones in your blood didn't make you fainthearted, weak-willed, or unaggressive. Indeed, he felt more determined than ever to chase the Main Attraction from Good Hope to perdition's flames. Estrogen was not destiny.

Fishing the remote control out from under the blankets, he trolled through the channels in search of Fred and Ginger and hit upon *Larry King Live* instead. Irving Saperstein was gleefully demonstrating God's optic neuron for the spellbound host. Martin's finger froze. He stopped changing channels. Prompted by Saperstein, the neuron computed the value of pi to thirty-six decimal places. Martin yawned. His mind drifted. By the time he was asleep, the neuron had painted a first-class forgery of Van Gogh's *Sunflowers*, proved the four-color map theory, and written a love sonnet so beautiful and true the studio floor manager burst into tears.

Three hours later a crab spasm jolted Martin awake. Slipping on his bifocals, he glanced at his digital Westclox . . . 3:55 A.M.—a sinister hour, he mused. He wouldn't be surprised to learn that a disproportionately large number of people died at 3:55 A.M., violently and unmourned.

He swallowed a Roxanol and fixed on Patricia's Mitsubishi. Strangely enough, the neuron still commanded the screen: a closeup highlighting its silvery outer sheath. Grabbing the remote control, he aimed it at the TV and pushed OFF. The image remained intact. He changed channels. Nothing happened.

"You don't want another network," said a high, squeaky, but emphatically noncomical voice, each syllable entering the room with a crispness and fidelity far surpassing what the Mitsubishi normally delivered. "I'm the best thing on television right now."

So deep was Martin's astonishment, he kept his eyes locked on the screen even after a second crab spasm ripped through his pelvis. He ate another Roxanol and nervously addressed the televised cell. "Are you talking to *me?*"

"To you and you alone. For the next five minutes Cable News Network is my plaything—the simplest method I could devise for communicating with you directly."

"I didn't realize you were so powerful."

"I'm a piece of *God*, for chrissakes—I'm not something the cat dragged in. Listen, Candle, if you're still determined to stage this trial, we insist you do it right."

"We?"

"Me and my Progenitor."

"Your Progenitor?"

"A.k.a. the Corpus Dei."

Martin gulped audibly. "I guess I'd been assuming that your, er . . . your *Progenitor* was dead against *International 227.*"

"He has a much broader mind than you might suppose. In His own peculiar way, He wants to see justice served."

"I'm confused. God hopes I'll *win?*"

"Let's just say He hopes the trial will be aesthetically satisfying. The point is this: you've got a tough row to hoe. To triumph in The Hague, you'll need to do much more than foreswear Odradex, stay on Feminone, read Saint Augustine, memorize *The Conundrum of Suffering*, and put your Jobians on the stand—though all of those moves are essential."

"What do you recommend?"

"Mastering the world's great theodicies means going inside my Progenitor's head."

"Is this a dream?"

"Neither dream nor chimera nor hallucination. I'm offering you the best advice you'll ever receive. Take it or leave it."

"Join Saperstein's expedition? I'm not much of a traveler."

"Indeed. Some people are armchair psychologists. Some are armchair politicians. *You're* an armchair human being. Jesus,

Candle, you've lived in Abaddon your whole life. Okay, sure, you've had your reasons: inertia, lack of funds, neurotic girl-friends—plus, of course, your nebulous desire to protect your father from your mother—but it's time you widened your horizons."

"Good heavens, is there anything you *don't* know about me?"

"Yes. I don't know whether you deserve to win."

The neuron began to glow a brilliant crimson, and suddenly it was gone—*poof*—replaced by the normal CNN transmission, a report on a promising new AIDS therapy.

Martin aimed the remote control, killed the image, and collapsed on the mattress. His hands shook. His heart thumped wildly, causing his implanted Port-A-Cath to vibrate. Seeking to quiet his nerves, he made a mental list of the items he would take on the expedition. His painkillers, of course. His Feminone. Several sports bras. What sort of place was the "ultimate terra incognita," anyway? A land of milk and honey, bounteous beyond comprehension? Or had the coma turned it into a wasteland? He decided he would bring his hiking boots. Tea bags. Dental floss. Kleenex. And a flashlight.

"I think I'm going mad," he told Patricia's television.

❖

When Dr. Gregory Francis Lovett sent Martin a registered letter requesting that he fly to Cambridge, Massachusetts, for a pre-trial meeting, all expenses paid, the ex-JP's initial instinct was to decline. It seemed foolhardy to permit the first brush with Lovett to occur on ground of the professor's own choosing. But eventually Martin realized he had more to gain than lose by accepting the invitation. Better to size up his adversary now than in the confusion of courtroom battle.

After touching down at Logan Airport on the bitter cold morning of March 11, he hailed a cab, gave the driver Lovett's address, and settled into a Roxanolian catnap. The noon hour found him slipping through the wrought-iron gates of 87 Mount Auburn Street. As he approached the front door, briefcase swinging at his side, an uncommon sight greeted him: a plump, red-faced man lying supine in the snow. The man's arms were outstretched, and he was moving them up and down as if backstroking across a swimming pool.

"You made good time, Mr. Candle," said the man, slowly rising like a lead soldier climbing out of its cast-iron mold. Brushing the flakes from his parka, he gestured toward his impression in the snow. "Until the Day of Judgment, that's the closest I'll ever get to being an angel."

"Dr. Lovett, I presume?" inquired Martin, extending his arm. Their mittened hands connected, wool clinging to wool. "Do you make snow angels every winter?"

"I haven't done this since boyhood—a very satisfying experience. Snow angels, I mean. Boyhood too, come to think of it. Would you like to produce one yourself?"

"Thank you, but what I most want is a hot cup of tea."

From *The Conundrum of Suffering*, Martin had expected to find G. F. Lovett rather smug, somewhat pompous, and a tad misanthropic. As the afternoon progressed, he revised his hypothesis. Lovett was intensely smug, profoundly pompous, highly misanthropic . . . and also quite likable. In appearance he rather resembled Alfred Hitchcock, though where the film director's manner had been solemn and lugubrious, Lovett indulged in rat-a-tat speech and a peculiar arm-flapping gesture suggestive of a penguin attempting to take flight.

"Two months from now, you and I shall engage in the greatest chess match of all time," said Lovett, after providing Martin with a cup of Irish breakfast tea and a tuna-fish sandwich. Gripping a Malacca walking stick, the professor guided his guest into the library, where, as if to underscore his pronouncement, a green-and-white jade chess set adorned the reading table. He picked up the white king and held it before Martin's gaze like a sideshow mesmerist displaying a hypnotic charm. "God Almighty: Ruler of the Universe—omnipotent, omniscient, omnibenevolent . . . in a word, worshipworthy. And yet there is evil. And yet there is pain. You're asking the right question, Mr. Candle, no doubt about it." Lovett returned the king to its square. "I'm strictly a duffer at this game. I still don't know how en passant works."

"When your opponent advances a pawn two squares, you can capture it if you've got a pawn on one of the squares he passed."

"Want to give it a shot? I promise to lose graciously."

"Chess has unfortunate connotations for me," Martin replied as Lovett's rococo marble fireplace lured him toward its crackling warmth. "Before she died, my wife and I played every Sunday."

"You have my deepest sympathy."

"In the nude. The sensual and the cerebral, all at once. Ever done that?"

"No. Sounds rather . . . French." Lovett rested his walking stick against the reading table, sat down before the chess set, and moved the green king's pawn to square four. "You're wondering why I summoned you." Continuing his solitaire game, he developed the white queen's knight. "In my protracted sojourn on this planet, Mr. Candle, I have come to value three commodities above all others: good books, decent claret, and worthy opponents. Are you a worthy opponent?"

"By the fifth of June . . . yes, I'll be worthy."

"I want a sound return on my investment—a good fight, you understand? No knockouts in round one. A good fight."

"You don't believe I've got a chance—am I right? You're thinking, 'If they let O. J. Simpson walk, they'll certainly let God walk.'"

"Who is O. J. Simpson?"

"Are you kidding?"

"No, but I follow your meaning anyway. Will you give me a good fight?"

"I've read your *Conundrum of Suffering* twice now, and I've started investigating the theologians you cited in your footnotes—Augustine, Luther, Meister Eckhart."

"Splendid. And have you grasped the essence of my argument?"

"I think so."

"And what might it be?"

"Spare the rod, and you'll spoil the species."

A prodigious grin spread across Lovett's ruddy face. " 'Spare the rod,' " he echoed in a half whisper. " 'Spoil the species.' Wonderful, sir. Perfect. And do you believe my argument works?"

"Not completely."

"You've found a chink?"

"Yes."

"Excellent." Walking stick in hand, Lovett sauntered toward the far wall. With the insouciance of a cancan dancer lifting her skirt, he pushed aside a burgundy drape to disclose a red plastic button. "In the Augustinian view, of course, we're *already* a spoiled species. Spare the rod, and you'll spoil the species *even more*." As the circuit sprang to life, the central bookcase rotated like a subway turnstile, revealing a gray slateboard on its opposite side. "Normally this board is covered with scraps of Old English verse and medieval poetry. Every Thursday evening my more promising pupils drop by for food and conversation—the Beer and Beowulf Society, we call ourselves, though we rarely consume beer, and we've yet to scan a single line of *Beowulf*." Taking a stubby stick of chalk from his waistcoat, he wrote DISCIPLINARY in capitals replete with curlicues. "As I interpret my own book, it's basically a gloss on the so-called 'disciplinary defense.' As you know, this solution to the problem of evil has a long and venerable history."

"Indeed," said Martin, seeking to score an early point. "I'm especially taken with Gregory Nazianzenus's image of the soul as an athlete-in-training, each day growing stronger by shouldering life's burdens."

"You are confusing Gregory Nazianzenus with Gregory the Great," replied Lovett with a quick little wink.

"Gregory the Great," said Martin hurriedly. "Of course." His cheeks grew flushed. "That's who I meant."

"Whom."

"What?"

" 'That's *whom* I meant.' It's called grammar. Don't let the 'is' fool you—the objective case must be employed here. So what's this chink you've found in the disciplinary defense?"

"You'll learn about it in two months." Between now and the fifth of June, Martin decided, would be plenty of time to get his Gregorys straight.

"Fair enough." Lovett leaned toward the slateboard and wrote HIDDEN HARMONY. "Supplementing the disciplinary defense, of course, is the famous 'hidden harmony' solution."

"I call it the Father-knows-best hypothesis," said Martin with all the sardonicism he could muster.

" 'Father knows best,' " echoed Lovett. "Yes. Very clever—just the sort of dismissive paraphrase in which *I* am accused of trafficking. Unfortunately for your case, the farther one ventures into the hidden harmony defense, the less dismissable it becomes. Meister Eckhart got to the heart of the matter when he said we have no right to impose our own limited vocabulary on God. I'm sure you know his famous remark, 'Calling God good is like—' "

" '—calling the sun dark.' "

" 'Black,' actually. He said 'black.' Julian of Norwich provides an equally vivid image: we see reality through a kind of milky crystal." Lovett pressed the chalk stick against his lips, giving himself the appearance of a man being silenced by a skeleton's index finger. "If we could but remove the cloud, plagues and tornadoes would appear necessary in their own way. Doubtless you have an answer for Julian."

"I don't find him particularly profound."

"Her particularly profound."

"Her?"

"Her."

Maybe I've lost this skirmish, brooded Martin as he scanned the bookcases flanking the fireplace, but I'm going to win the war. Beyond the first editions and the leatherbound reprints, the shelves' most striking occupants were ten plastic action figures derived from the Hollywood adaptations of Lovett's works. Captain Alexis Renardo stood watch atop *The Canterbury Tales*. Basil the Basilisk guarded *Sir Gawaine and the Green Knight*. Amberson the Lion protected *The Mabinogion*. Stanhope the Steam-Powered Man maintained a vigil over *Le Morte d'Arthur*.

"Any *other* defenses?" asked Martin in a tone he hoped sounded more defiant than apprehensive.

Lovett touched chalk to slate. ESCHATOLOGICAL, he wrote. ONTOLOGICAL. LIBERUM ARBITRIUM.

Anxiety swept through Martin, less painful than a crab spasm but almost as disorienting. His understanding of "eschatological" was hazy at best, he couldn't imagine what an "ontological" defense might comprise, and the only sense he could make of *liberum arbitrium* was "arbitrary book."

"You look unhappy," said Lovett.

Drawing his new laptop from his briefcase, Martin began recording the contents of the slate. "I'll master all five."

"Splendid. What's that device you've got there?"

"Personal computer."

"Fascinating. I suggest you start with a good English translation of Augustine's *Opus imperfectum contra Julianum*—unless, of course, you read Latin."

"*Some* Latin," said Martin icily, typing *Opus imperfectum contra Julianum* into his hard drive. "I'll buy a translation tomorrow. And there's something *else* I intend to do, Professor. I intend to journey through the Defendant's skull. Saperstein has agreed to let me join the expedition."

"Why would you want to do *that*?" Lovett smiled slyly. "Are there more things in God's brain than are dreamt of in Augustine's philosophy?"

"Ten days ago that weird neuron Saperstein bagged during his first probe communicated with me via my landlady's television set. Maybe I was hallucinating, but the message came through loud and clear: I'd do well to enter the divine mind. I don't imagine *you've* been contacted by the neuron . . ."

"I don't even own a television."

Irritated by the Port-A-Cath, Martin's right breast began to itch. Placing hand to bosom, he scratched himself through his sweater. "You're welcome to come along. I wouldn't want to have an unfair advantage."

"Yes you would."

Martin laughed. "Yes I would."

Abandoning the slate, Lovett shuffled toward a lamp table on which rested two wineglasses and a many-faceted decanter filled with dark red fluid. "Eighteen years ago my brother published a book about life in France during the reign of Louis XIV. It sold in the tens of thousands. Such is Darcy's talent that he managed to make the Versailles of Saint-Simon as vivid as your grandmother's kitchen." He yanked out the stopper. "But fancy this: my brother has never been to Versailles. When he visits The Hague as my aide-de-camp next month, it will be the first time he's ever set foot in Europe. I needn't go traipsing across God's cerebrum, Mr. Candle, to know what God is like. Care for some claret?"

"Please."

Lovett filled both glasses, handing one to Martin. "A toast . . . to reasoned theological debate."

"To reasoned theological debate," Martin echoed. Their glasses clinked together.

"And may the best man win."

"*Better* man."

"What?"

Martin pressed the glass to his lips, took a warm swallow of claret, and grinned. "It's called grammar."

BOOK TWO
Spelunking the Infinite

❖

Chapter 6

AFTER MY CREATOR'S OPTIC NEURON made the covers of *Time* and *Newsweek* simultaneously, shining forth from the magazine racks in brilliant color and three-dimensional splendor, barely a day went by before the striking hologram—coyly dubbed a "holygram" by Charles Braithwaite—appeared on thousands of walls, bulletin boards, and refrigerator doors throughout Europe and North America. I myself saw no need of exhibiting that particular image. It would be as absurd for a Corpus Dei inhabitant to display a divine neuron as for a Bedouin to appoint his tent with pails of sand.

The longer people contemplated their holograms, the more they were forced to acknowledge a disquieting truth. What they had in the Corpus Dei was their comatose Creator Himself, not some expendable husk. For many citizens of the Western world, this situation proved, as you might imagine, troubling—especially in the United States, where reality has never enjoyed a great deal of prestige. And so the American Baptist Confederation once again undertook to restore the average American Protestant's peace of mind. Sacred time, the Confederation explained, differs from profane time. Just as Jesus lay suspended in his tomb for three days prior to his resurrection, so would the Corpus Dei remain comatose for the same interval, seventy-two hours—measured, however, not by any terrestrial chronometer but by the Great Clock of Heaven. Be patient, the Baptists counseled their flocks. God will awaken soon.

Having abandoned the Mayfly Theory for a theology more congruent with the facts, the Baptists were in no position to protest what happened next. Flush with their victory at the Siege of Celestial City USA, the United Nations peacekeeping brigades disconnected the Corpus Dei's evaporator, compressor, and condenser, selling the whole massive refrigeration system to a Chicago meat-packing concern for 8.5 million dollars and donating the proceeds to Eternity Enterprises. As for the cooling chamber that contained the body itself, the UN decided to leave it in place. Although irrelevant to its original purpose (the Corpus Dei being alive after a fashion), this great Lucite box could still function as a kind of shipping crate. Only one person on Earth ended up regretting the chamber's retention—Hugo Ott, a wiseass freelance journalist who noted in the *Village Voice* that "God, like Adolph Eichmann before Him, will stand trial from inside a glass booth." The day Ott's article appeared, he was visited at home by three masked vigilantes from the Sword of Jehovah Strike Force. After removing his right thumb with a scaling knife, the Jehovans informed him that his left would be next if he published any more articles comparing God to a war criminal.

The Lockheed 7000, of course, also remained undisturbed, nourishing the Main Attraction's surviving cells with the countless gallons of clean, oxygenated blood His static heart, collapsed lungs, and shriveled kidneys could not provide. Thus did the River Hiddekel continue on its route, flowing past my tailor shop at forty kilometers per hour, weaving to and fro among the dying forests and decaying cities of His western hemisphere.

God's deportation was a simple matter of reversing the steps by which He'd come to Orlando. Availing themselves of the same gantries that had lifted the cooling chamber from the Atlantic, the peacekeeping brigades next loaded it onto an array of flatcars and sent it by rail to the east coast of Florida. On April 23, 2000, the Corpus Dei arrived safely in Cocoa Beach, where the UN troops set the chamber afloat on a gargantuan raft chained to a triad of supertankers, the *Carpco New Orleans*, the *Arco Fairbanks*, and the *Exxon Galveston*. The heart-lung machine completed the flotilla, buoyed by its own raft and borne by its own ship, the *Chevron Caracas*.

On the morning of May 2, just as I was completing one of my most spiritually satisfying commissions ever—the flag of the Rwandan Government in Exile, a dauntless band of Hutu tribal leaders and militiamen who, before being ousted, had presided over the slaughter of nearly a million Tutsis—all four super-tankers set sail under the command of Captain Anthony Van Horne, dragging the Corpus Dei and its auxiliary cardiovascular system north toward Philadelphia. Like almost every other sentient being in Creation, I watched the convoy's stately progress on television. Joining me in front of my portable black-and-white Zenith were my clever neighbor Bishop Augustine and my crafty disciple Herr Schonspigel—the very demon who, as it happens, fashioned the prototype from which all such supertankers descend. The worthiness of Schonspigel's design has proven itself repeatedly, from the *Torrey Canyon* spill that so spectacularly spoiled the English Channel to the wreck of the *Carpco Valparaíso* and subsequent obliteration of Matagorda Bay.

❖

Had the United Nations not supplied Martin with an armored car, a driver, and two personal bodyguards, he might very well have been assassinated en route to the great flotilla. As he traveled through Philadelphia that morning, the Sword of Jehovah Strike Force took up strategic positions along the sidewalks, bombarding the car with a panoply of projectiles: rocks, bricks, bottles, lead pipes. From his sanctuary inside the passenger compartment, Martin browsed his Penguin Classics edition of

Augustine's *Opus imperfectum contra Julianum* and simultaneously pondered the Jehovans' agenda. What they were *really* mad about, he decided as an empty mayonnaise jar exploded against the window, was God's decision to go catatonic, not *International 227*, but their impacted reverence prevented them from directing their fury toward the Defendant Himself.

Disturbing as his trip to the flotilla was, Martin felt even worse about the previous evening's conversation with Patricia.

"You *say* you love me, but you don't *mean* it," she asserted.

"I love you," he said, slipping on his sports bra. "You're a dear, dear friend."

"You love me, but you'll never love me as much as you loved *her*."

"Please, Patricia. *Please*. I can't be thinking about this stuff right now. My bones are full of cancer, my tits are bigger than yours, and I've got less than a month to make myself smarter than sixteen different church fathers."

"Randall Selkirk phoned yesterday—he saw my picture in the Valley of Children. He's coming to Philadelphia next week to shoot some zoo footage, and he wants to take me out to dinner."

"Randall isn't supposed to be starting a relationship. He's supposed to be working on *International 227*."

"Oh, I get it," she said in the tone she normally reserved for commentaries on her ex-husband. "It's okay if he humps me, as long as he's reading Saint Augustine at the time."

"Don't put words in my mouth."

"Stay home, Martin. You belong here."

He looked into her sad, wet eyes. " 'And if I am an honest man I am bound to give it back as soon as possible. It's not God I don't accept, Alyosha, only I most respectfully return Him the ticket.' "

"Fuck you, Martin. Fuck you from here to Holland."

Arriving at the waterfront, he jammed *Opus imperfectum con-*

tra Julianum into his pocket, snatched up his two mismatched suitcases, and, as the bodyguards lobbed tear-gas canisters into the mob, boarded a decrepit UN cutter called the *Haile Selassie*. Within minutes the cutter was steaming southward down the Delaware, a voyage made singularly unpleasant by the dead fish that, maneuvering their speedboats within range, the Jehovans managed to hurl onto the foredeck. Crab spasms exploded in Martin's right ilium and left pubic bone. No surprise, really: according to the latest bone scan, the tumor had infiltrated both halves of his pelvis. He pulled out his Roxanol, popped three tablets, and chewed.

Reeking of halibut and mackerel, the *Haile Selassie* cruised into Wilmington Bay, where the *Carpco New Orleans* and her sister vessels lay at anchor. TV news helicopters circled presumptuously overhead, poking and probing with their zoom lenses. Surveying this bizarre and epic scene, Martin realized how radically the scale of his life had changed. A year ago he'd been wondering whether it would do Margo Spencer, an adolescent shoplifter, more harm than good to spend a night in jail. Today he was confronting the panoramic fact that—thanks to him—four supertankers, a gigantic heart-lung machine, and the comatose body of God Almighty were all poised for an unprecedented trip to the Netherlands.

He bid the bodyguards farewell and, suitcases in hand, strode up the gangway and stepped onto the weather deck of the *Carpco New Orleans*, where Anthony Van Horne greeted him with a vigorous handshake. The captain was a hale, gray-haired, lantern-jawed man in his late fifties, wearing dress blues and sporting a broken nose. Guiding Martin down the catwalk, he explained that by tomorrow morning they'd be in Bayonne, where they would refuel, take on supplies, and pick up the two scientists Saperstein had chosen to accompany him into the divine cranium.

"It's good to be at sea again," said Van Horne, inhaling a

healthy helping of salt air. "It's good to have a mission. I hope you're prepared for a long, slow voyage. I speak from experience. Towing the old Smiler takes time."

"Ever been to Holland before?"

"A Dutchman like me, you'd think I'd have gotten over there by now, but this is actually my first trip."

"Looking forward to it?"

"My country is the ocean, Mr. Candle. Tulips and windmills do nothing for me."

While the Jehovans regarded Martin as the most insidious piece of slime ever to creep across the face of planet Earth, the Committee for Complete Disclosure saw him as a hero, the man whose vision and stubbornness had afforded them their entrée into God. The cabin into which Van Horne now led Martin was luxurious to the point of decadence: Cornell astronomer Dwayne Kitchen, the Committee's flamboyant chairperson, had arranged the poshest accommodations available—a four-room suite featuring a Jacuzzi, a wet bar, a home-entertainment center, and a refrigerator stocked with champagne and caviar.

"I've read about your troubles," said the captain. "Illness, and then your wife. Really rough. In your shoes, I'd probably want to strike back too."

Setting the smaller suitcase on the bunk, Martin popped the clasps and tilted back the lid. He shuddered. A plastic syringe and fifty 2cc vials of Odradex rested atop his flannel pajamas, right next to Augustine's *Confessions* and Lovett's *The Conundrum of Suffering*. Patricia's doing, no doubt—*he* certainly hadn't packed the stuff.

"I must tell you something, though," said Van Horne. "I'm a big fan of your opponent."

"God?"

"G. F. Lovett. If his books are anything to go by, you've got your work cut out for you. That fellow's crafty as a marlin."

Martin studied the beguiling vials. Hobson's choice. If he didn't go on Odradex, he might die before the trial began, whereas taking the drug meant losing the alertness on which his hypothetical victory depended. "I sometimes wonder if I'm the only person in the world who's never read *The Mermaid in the Maelstrom*."

"You should give it a try. My little boy and I are working our way through the whole Saga of Sargassia together—it's going to take us about five hundred bedtimes. Thanks to G. F. Lovett, Stevie thinks having a skipper for a dad is a pretty good deal. He's started calling me Captain Renardo."

❖

Martin passed the voyage to Bayonne in yet another attempt to plumb *Opus imperfectum contra Julianum*, pausing only to eat caviar, swallow Roxanol and Feminone, and visit the bathroom. With the help of his *American Heritage Desk Encyclopedia* he'd already deduced that *liberum arbitrium* meant "free will," that the so-called "eschatological" explanation of suffering had something to do with Heaven and Judgment Day, and that "ontology" was a branch of metaphysics addressing the nature of existence, enabling philosophers to distinguish, for example, between flesh and spirit. He'd been hoping Augustine would offer coherent accounts of these theodicies, so he could start devising counterclaims. Alas, the further he ventured into *Opus imperfectum*, the more perplexed he became. The proper words appeared with regularity—*evil, will, soul, body*—but their context continually veered between the obscure and the opaque. The linchpin sentence of book one, chapter twenty-two, for example: "This is the Catholic view, a view that can show a just God in so many pains and in such agonies of tiny babies." Maybe it made more sense in Latin.

On the morning of May 11, in the supertanker's oak-paneled wardroom, a breakfast meeting occurred—a colloquy addressing matters of such consummate uncanniness that an eavesdropper might have interpreted it as a therapy session for schizophrenics.

At the head of the table presided the celebrated neurophysiologist Irving Saperstein. To Saperstein's left sat Jocelyn Beauchamp, a black mathematics professor from Vassar best known for her work in artificial intelligence, which she described for Martin as "my quest to create a sentient robot whose heart is in conflict with itself." To Saperstein's right: Father Thomas Ockham of Fordham University, the cosmologist who'd served as the Vatican's liaison during the first towing of the Corpus Dei, an adventure the priest subsequently turned into the best-selling *Parables for a Post-theistic Age.* Martin occupied the remaining chair, adjacent to a porthole framed in brass, from which vantage point he watched the stormy, windswept Atlantic, forever ejecting foam and spindrift as the convoy crept eastward toward The Hague.

Saperstein began by announcing that within forty-eight hours they'd be beyond the range of the TV helicopters. "This is all to the good," he explained, sipping coffee from a Carpco Shipping mug. "Whatever we find in His skull, it's bound to be complex, right? God is a professional. When we reemerge into daylight, the last thing we want is some pesky CNN stringer landing in our laps, demanding an instant analysis."

"We'll be strangers in a strange land, won't we?" said Beauchamp. She was a booming, stately, Junoesque woman with flaming red lipstick and clusters of dreadlocks hanging from her cranium like coils of insulated wire.

Saperstein grunted in agreement. "The Fodor's guide to this particular country hasn't been written yet. The Berlitz phrasebook for trips to infinity doesn't exist."

"You're imagining we'll be able to communicate with Him, aren't you?" said Ockham.

"That cell we pried from His optic nerve tells us everything that's on its mind. Look at the Torah, Thomas. Genesis, Exodus, Leviticus: this is a God who *talks*. He likes to spell out laws. You needn't be shy about asking Him to clear up certain long-standing mysteries—you know, what is the correct value of the

Hubble constant, why is the proton in a hydrogen atom eighteen hundred and thirty-six times as heavy as the electron?"

"Naturally one thinks of old Werner Heisenberg, lying on his deathbed, declaring he'll have two questions for God," said Beauchamp.

"What questions?" asked Martin.

"Why relativity, and why turbulence?" Beauchamp bit into a cinnamon roll and smiled. "Then Heisenberg added, 'I really think He may have an answer to the first question.'"

"Fine, great, but I'd like to venture even deeper than that," said Ockham. He was a gaunt, rawboned man, forever in motion—eyes darting, fingers entwining, spine shifting—as if trapped in an eternal state of remembering he was supposed to be somewhere else. "I'd like to go to the meat of things and ask why He bothered to create a physical cosmos in the first place. I'm assuming, of course, our Corpus Dei is in fact the Supreme Being and not some Gnostic artificer or Platonic demiurge."

"Artificer?" said Martin, swallowing orange juice. "Demiurge?"

"It's one of the oldest problems in theology," said Ockham. "Was the universe created by God Himself or by one of His fallible apprentices? Human vanity favors the former hypothesis, though the latter makes a good deal more sense."

The orange juice soured in Martin's stomach. Oh, crap, he thought—with my luck, everybody will decide the Corpus Dei is really just a "demiurge." It was God the Father he wanted to bring down, not some ancillary hit man.

"Even if our cargo *is* a demiurge, he probably knows more about the universe than we do," said Saperstein. "We should still have our questions ready."

"What if God doesn't exist?" asked Beauchamp. "What if our demiurge was created by another demiurge, and that demiurge by another demiurge, and *that* demiurge . . . ?"

"Assuming the universe was truly *made*—assuming it didn't somehow invent itself—then eventually one must posit an uncreated Creator: a self-sufficient, self-explanatory, necessary Being," said Ockham. "And there's the *real* puzzle. Why would a self-sufficient Being indulge in the seemingly pointless exercise of fashioning a material cosmos?"

"Maybe He was bored," said Martin.

"Then He wouldn't be self-sufficient, would He?"

"Lonely?"

"Same problem—a lonely God is a codependent God." Ockham slapped the shell of his soft-boiled egg with the back of his spoon. "One answer is that the Supreme Being in His day had two poles: a self-sufficient side that existed beyond space and time, and a contingent side that created the universe. *That,* I would argue, is the first thing we should ask Him. 'God, were You bipolar?' "

Martin stared out the porthole. He didn't quite know what to make of his fellow passengers aboard the *Carpco New Orleans*. In theory their curiosity was wholly admirable, yet it seemed tainted with a certain opportunism. He pictured the scientists as three learned vultures, eyeglasses balanced on their beaks, circling around and around above the cooling chamber as they prepared to devour the spoiling meat of God's mind.

"I imagine you're planning to ask Him a math question or two," said Saperstein to Beauchamp. "I mean, if *anybody* can prove Fermat's last theorem . . ."

"The equation 'x to the n plus y to the n equals z to the n,' where n is an integer greater than two, has no solution in the positive numbers," said Martin, who'd had the good sense to take Mrs. Rosenzweig's Math for Romantics course at Abaddon Senior High. He remembered about the maddening note Fermat had scrawled in a book he was reading, brought to light posthumously; evidently the mathematician had hit upon a neat little proof of his conjecture, but there wasn't enough room in the margin for the details. "You mean they still haven't cracked that thing?"

"Several years ago my colleague Andrew Wiles announced that he'd done so," said Beauchamp, consuming a fluffy forkful of scrambled eggs, "but his solution was such a Rube Goldberg sort of affair nobody could work up much affection for it. What we really want, of course, is *Fermat's* solution to Fermat's last theorem."

A smile broke through Saperstein's scraggly beard. "So far we've been working from the top down—lofty, abstract questions. I'd prefer to begin near the bottom—with a single cell, okay? The human zygote. Immediately after arriving on the scene, it divides into two cells, then four, eight, sixteen, et cetera. Then, at a certain stage, one particular cell commits to becoming the baby's brain stem. Amazing. A miracle. How does *that* cell know to inaugurate the apparatus for thinking, feeling, hoping, dreaming? What keeps it from turning into a kidney or a spleen?" The neurophysiologist ate a syrup-laden hunk of pancake. "Now let's descend even further—to the protozoan *Myxotricha paradoxa,* a parasite who lives in the digestive tract of the Australian termite, engulfing fragments of finely chewed wood."

Hearing the word *termite,* Martin cringed. *Ravenous termites have attacked the guardrails on the Henry Avenue Bridge,* the police report on Corinne's death had noted, *turning them into little more than slabs of compacted sawdust.*

"Look at *Myxotricha* under the microscope, and you'll see he gets around via spirochetes attached all over his body. Question: what holds the spirochetes in place?" Saperstein bit the apex off a triangle of toast. "Static electricity? Duco cement?"

"Spirochetes on a *bacterium*?" said Martin. "Inside a *termite*? Do you people really worry about things like that?"

"You bet we do," said Beauchamp.

"All the time," said Ockham.

Saperstein's rubbery face contracted into a frown. He sighed, finished his coffee, and intoned what Martin recognized as a paraphrase of Franz Kafka's famous observation about religious faith. "To the scientist, no explanation is necessary . . . and to the nonscientist, no explanation is possible."

❖

As the late-morning sun beat down on the convoy, its beams slanting into the sea like flying buttresses holding up Heaven's airy ramparts, the neuronauts made ready to enter the Defendant's skull. They donned their scuba gear, shouldered their waterproof backpacks, and scrambled into the *New Orleans*'s launch, an inboard motorboat piloted by Van Horne's beefy and phlegmatic chief mate. Maneuvering amid the treacherous web of tow chains, the mate managed to ferry his charges out to the raft in only twenty minutes.

The southern face of the cooling chamber featured a vertical series of five hundred footholds, and by noon the neuronauts were climbing skyward. But for the painkiller in his blood, Martin would never have gotten past the first rung. Flecks of spray ricocheted off his wet suit, instantly borne away by the wind. Petrels cruised across the sky, gliding back and forth above the Corpus Dei, their flight made particularly beautiful by the soothing opium haze that lay between Martin and the world. As he reached the top and stepped onto the Lucite lid, he noticed how dramatically the chamber had changed since his visit to Celestial City USA. Gone were the flowered footpath and the neon arrows. A huge manhole now occupied the spot from which he'd once beheld his Creator's grin. Gangways and catwalks protruded from the edge of the opening, dropping for nearly a thousand feet to the spongy surface of His right tear duct.

Martin looked up, facing the Lockheed 7000. Beyond lay the North Atlantic, rolling between the continents like some vast wrinkled canvas on which God had once intended to paint His masterpiece.

"You don't much like us, do you?" said Saperstein, drawing alongside Martin. The neurophysiologist slid his face mask in place, rested his gloved hand on Martin's shoulder, and frowned. "You think we've got our heads in the clouds."

"That's one way to put it."

"Someday I'll tell you about *my* wife. Ever see a woman die of ovarian cancer?"

Martin ate his sixth Roxanol of the morning. "No."

"I hope you never do," said Saperstein, wrapping his lips around his regulator.

Into the eye, then. Into the primal wink, the pristine squint, the great globular organ through which, ten billion years earlier, He'd seen the Big Bang—that it was good. Saperstein led the way, fingers encircling the pistol grip of a tungsten-halogen lantern as he followed the path he'd blazed the previous winter. Marching across the tear duct, the explorers lowered themselves into an artificial fistula extending from the pocked outer surface of the cornea to its glassy underside. They plunged through the limpid aqueous humor, entered a second culvert, and, traversing the mighty lens (as large as the equivalent component of the Hawking Space Telescope), brought themselves to the shores of the vitreous humor. Stepping forward, they began their final descent.

Ever since he'd performed a wedding ceremony at the bottom of the Schuylkill River, Martin had felt comfortable wearing scuba gear. But this dive was different, a slow-motion fall through a fluid so heavy and gelatinous he felt like a bumblebee imprisoned in a bottle of Prell. As he neared his destination, jagged bursts of light shot upward from the basin: the sacred rods and holy cones, he realized, blinking and sputtering as comatosity claimed the farthest reaches of His nervous system.

Landing, the neuronauts collected on the threshold of the optic nerve—a ten-foot-wide hole, black as the silt of Abaddon Marsh—and yanked the regulators from their mouths. This was God's blind spot, Saperstein explained, the only light-insensitive area on His entire retina. Free at last of God's humors, the neuronauts shed their scuba gear, securing the mound of wet suits, air tanks, masks, gloves, fins, and weight belts beneath a dead photoreceptor. The surrounding cells continued to convulse, flashing randomly on and off like semaphores being operated by lunatics.

Activating his lantern, Saperstein aimed the beam straight ahead and climbed into the blind spot, Beauchamp right behind, then Ockham, then Martin. Within a minute the neuronauts were hiking through the damp, gluey shaft of the optic nerve: a dazzling place, alive with the op-art throb of its glistery ceiling and rainbow-colored walls. The nerve expanded, soon growing as large as the Lincoln Tunnel. A journey of a hundred yards brought them to the pulpy crossroads of the optic chiasma. Beauchamp snapped a dozen photographs with her waterproof Nikon. Focusing his camcorder, Ockham ran off a long burst of videotape.

They had a choice now—left optic nerve versus right—an issue Saperstein resolved with a flip of the Manhattan subway token he found in his windbreaker. Heads. Left. They would stay on their appointed path, bound for His western hemisphere.

Seventy yards beyond the chiasma they began encountering actual brain matter. Massive assemblages of neurons lined the shaft, their dendrites interlocked in spidery configurations, their synapses firing madly, a million golden explosions per second. As the explorers ventured forward, the nerve became larger still, its fleshy walls rising for a hundred meters, then meeting to form the roof of a vast subdural chamber. Saperstein killed his lantern, the surrounding psychic fireworks having rendered it superfluous. To Martin the space felt simultaneously soothing and incomprehensible, as if he were traversing the nave of a cathedral housing a religion so fiercely beautiful only angels and children were permitted to believe in it.

Large, glowing objects drifted through the air: tree, lion, chair, plow, sword—shapes that despite their numinous luminosity seemed to possess more reality than their terrestrial equivalents. The tree radiated treeness. The lion exuded lionhood.

The chair was the source of all chairs, the plow a primal plow, the sword a glittering quintessence.

"Good Lord, He's a Platonist!" gasped Ockham, aiming at the lion with his camcorder and squeezing the trigger. "I knew it, I just *knew* it."

"What do you mean?" asked Martin.

"Unless I miss my guess, we're in a universe of perfect forms. This is God's private laboratory. It's where He develops His ideas."

"I must admit, I was expecting a more Jewish sort of consciousness," said Saperstein. "I never thought He'd be so Greek."

Awesome as the floating archetypes and the optic cathedral were, their connection to the world's great theodicies seemed decidedly remote, and Martin had trouble summoning a properly reverent attitude. Had he been foolish to believe the errant neuron's claim that triumphing in The Hague meant trekking across this terra incognita? Might he have done better staying home in Abaddon, reading dead Christians?

In the center of the cathedral the explorers paused for lunch. They opened their backpacks, removed their provisions—beef jerky, fresh fruit, stuffed grape leaves—and began to appease their rumbling stomachs. Organ notes filled the air, chords that Martin immediately recognized as belonging to one of his father's favorite pieces, Bach's *Toccata and Fugue*. But of course, he mused—whom else but Johann Sebastian Bach would God have commissioned to compose the divine Muzak?

Before the *Carpco New Orleans* sailed from Philadelphia, Martin and his co-prosecutors had calculated that, throughout the flotilla's Atlantic crossing, the Corpus Dei would be in range of the Mahatma Gandhi Geosynchronous Satellite. It was with this fact in mind that he now drew out his Apple PowerBook, along with a modem and a cellular phone. He plugged the devices into each other and set about determining whether the United Nations computer in New York City harbored any e-mail from either Randall or Esther.

From: selkirk2@aol.org
To: marcand@prodigy.edu
Date: Sun, May 14, 11:32 AM EDT

Martin, did you ever hear of the Disaster Studies Department at Bowling Green State University, founded two years ago by a professional "cataclysmatician" named Donald Carbone? He's something of a madman, but he has a million facts at his fingertips about earthquakes, tornadoes, pestilences, plane crashes, and hotel fires. Wonderful stuff. (Did you know 550,000 Americans died in the Great Influenza Epidemic of 1918–1919, more than ten times our battlefield losses during the concurrent Great War?) Problem: Carbone is scheduled to teach a summer school course on the Black Plague. Second problem: he wants $125,000 for ten days on the stand.

I'm in Philadelphia right now, shooting gorilla footage at the zoo for a Nova *episode about primate behavior. Your landlady and I had dinner last night. We quite enjoyed ourselves. I did, at least. As you probably know, she's in love with you.*

Earthquakes, tornadoes, pestilences, plane crashes, hotel fires—wonderful stuff indeed, thought Martin. If Job had possessed such data, he might have won his case.

From: marcand@prodigy.edu
To: selkirk2@aol.org
Date: Tues, May 16, 01:38 PM Local Time

The Defendant's brain is very strange. Ideas fly through the air like angels. Believe it or not, He's a Platonist.

Randall, we simply must *put your cataclysmatician on the stand. Tell Carbone we'll not only pay him his $125,000, we'll earmark another $15,000 for whomever he gets to teach his Black Plague course. I'm delighted you and Patricia are hitting it off, but please don't dissipate your energies. June 5 will be here before we know it. It's time to start filing discovery motions. Contact Pierre Ferrand in The Hague and ask him for a list of Lovett's proposed defense witnesses.*

Esther, too, had posted a message.

From: esthclute@aol.org
To: marcand@prodigy.edu
Date: Mon, May 15, 06:15 PM EDT

Progress on this end is slow but steady. Allison Lowry is willing to submit a deposition concerning her son's brain injuries, but she won't come to Holland. (Jason needs her, she says. I think we should respect her wishes.) On the bright side, I've lined up seven absolutely terrific cancer patients, six bereaved parents, and Stanley Pallomar. Remember him? That Marine lieutenant who lost both his legs in Vietnam? I'll bet he'll break the world's collective heart.

Allison's recalcitrance put Martin in a foul humor. Couldn't the kid get by without her for one lousy week?

From: marcand@prodigy.edu
To: esthclute@aol.org
Date: Tues, May 16, 02:03 PM Local Time

Esther, we absolutely have *to get Allison to testify. There wasn't a dry eye in the room after she talked about feeding*

*Jason his pureed birthday cake. Yes, Stanley's missing legs
will probably net us a couple of "guilty" votes, but Allison's
story is even more wrenching. Tell her we'll pay a nursing
team top dollar to watch over Jason the whole time she's
in Holland, and she can charge us whatever witness fee she
wants, up to $10,000.*

Reading the first draft of his letter to Esther, Martin experienced a sudden and profound bewilderment. What kind of
world were they constructing here? What sort of reality was it
where Stanley Pallomar's mutilation became an asset and Jason
Lowry's paralysis an ace in the hole? Right before Martin's eyes,
International 227 was transmuting into a terra incognita every bit
as strange as God's brain. He shuddered to imagine what vistas
lay ahead.

"Well, folks," said Saperstein, sealing a divine dendrite in a
Ziploc bag, "it's time to hit the road."

❖

The farther the neuronauts advanced, the more of God's mind
they met. Certain archetypes were astonishingly concrete (the
paper clip), others highly abstract (freedom), but in each case
Martin had no trouble identifying the manifestation at hand. The
concept of photosynthesis drifted past, enacted by masses of eternally transmogrifying ectoplasm. The notion of a feather followed. Pollination next. Homeostasis. Fission and fusion. Wheel
and wedge. Pi and pie. The self-healing intelligence of wounds.
The pleasures of a successfully scratched itch. Bad ideas inhabited the laboratory as well—fleas, greed, monarchy—but despite
such lapses this was clearly the workshop of a genius.

Beyond the cathedral, the brain changed radically, the neuronal conglomerates yielding to a more conventional terrain: a
flood plain reeking of ammonia and roofed by a lambent sky. It
was a world of mud, dotted with ferns and pocked with puddles,

spreading toward the horizon like a preternatural oil slick. The explorers pressed steadily on, pausing only to take pictures and collect pieces of the pungent landscape—silt, leaves, holy water.

They had traveled barely three kilometers when an ornate wooden gazebo appeared, elegant despite the ravages of rain and wood lice. No less exquisite were the gazebo's inhabitants, two ten-foot-tall, ostrichlike dinosaurs, seated at a picnic table and engrossed, against common expectations, in the venerable game of Scrabble.

"What species?" whispered Ockham, slogging cautiously forward.

"*Gallimimus*, I think," said Saperstein. "Don't startle them."

A wave of sadness washed through Martin. Poor, sick Brandon Appleyard: Brandon and his beloved dinosaurs.

The female *gallimimus* looked up from the Scrabble board and gestured smoothly with her left forelimb. "Come on over, darlings! We've been expecting you!"

The neuronauts approached the gazebo, silt sucking at their boots.

"You can *talk*," gasped Beauchamp.

"Everything you know about dinosaurs is wrong," said the male, bobbing his blunt reptilian head. He spoke in a nasal but endearing New York accent. "We were warm-blooded, quick on our feet, good in bed, and verbal to a fault."

Mounting the gazebo steps, Martin glanced at the Scrabble board. The dinosaurs' word choices bespoke a morbid state of mind. DOOM. DESPAIR. PLAGUE. DAMNNATION. NOTHING.

"*Gallimimus*, correct?" asked Saperstein.

"Correct," said the female. She sounded more cultured than her mate, carefully shaping each syllable in the manner of a Boston aristocrat. "Call me Vivien."

"My name's Lawrence," said the male, cleverly obtaining a Triple Word Score by appending NESS to NOTHING.

"We aren't simply *any* dinosaurs," said Vivien. "We're the Idea of Dinosaurs—the archetypes, if you will."

"We've just come from His lab," said Ockham, nodding sagely. "An astonishing place."

"This whole *hemisphere* used to be astonishing, glory pouring from every neuron," said Lawrence. "Then the coma came. You're Father Ockham, aren't you?"

"That's right."

"I read your book," said Vivien. "Basically you got it right: the coma was God's idea, His way of forcing humankind to mature. You're a good writer. Try using fewer adjectives next time."

"I appreciate your candor," said Ockham. "Now, please answer one question for me. Are we wasting our time in here?"

"That depends—what do you want to know?" asked Vivien, seizing on the second s in NOTHINGNESS to make ABYSS.

"Well, for example . . ." Ockham cleared his throat. "What is the correct value of Hubble's constant?"

"I beg your pardon?" said Vivien.

"Good question," said Lawrence, exploiting the A in ABYSS to make CARRION.

"Why turbulence?"

"Beats me," said Lawrence.

"Did Fermat really have a simple proof for his last theorem?" asked Beauchamp.

"I haven't the foggiest," said Vivien.

"How do the spirochetes adhere to *Myxotricha paradoxa*?" demanded Saperstein.

"You know what you ought to do?" said Vivien. "You ought to go see Sarkos."

"Who?"

"Jonathan Sarkos, the tailor—he's the brightest person in this hemisphere. Walk south. After an hour you'll reach the River Hiddekel. Turn left, follow the levee for five kilometers, and you'll run into his shop. You can't miss it. He's got a satellite dish outside. Looks like a giant wok."

"Five kilometers?" said Saperstein. "But that's longer than the whole Corpus Dei!"

"Indeed. Or, as Dostoyevsky put it, 'If everything on Earth were rational—' "

" '—nothing would happen,' " said Martin.

"Exactly," said Vivien.

"May I take a photograph of you?" asked Beauchamp.

"You may," said Vivien, batting her dual-lidded eyes.

"Go right ahead," said Lawrence, grinning expansively.

Beauchamp framed the dinosaurs in the viewfinder of her Nikon and pressed the shutter release.

"There's one question we *can* answer," said Vivien, running her tongue across her upper lip.

"Indeed," said Saperstein with a skewed smile. "I hesitated to bring it up. I imagine it's a sore subject with you."

"Quite sore." Lawrence scowled at his mate. "We really don't like talking about it."

"*You* don't like talking about it," said Vivien tartly, rising from her bench. "I think we should be talking about it all the time. I mean, how *else* are we going to deal with it?" She rested her tail on the gazebo floor and pivoted toward Saperstein. "Let's begin by admitting the most popular explanation simply doesn't wash."

"Are you referring to the cosmic-catastrophe theory?" asked Saperstein.

"I am. Indubitably an asteroid rear-ended the Earth during the late Cretaceous—the worldwide iridium layer confirms this—and, yes, it threw up a blanket of dust, blotted out the sun, and killed endless acres of vegetation, but that doesn't begin to explain our demise. If the disaster had been sufficient to exterminate all of *us*, it would've wiped out the frogs and turtles too, and *they're* still around."

"So what's the answer?"

"Guess," said Vivien.

"Well . . . as you probably know," said Saperstein, "one theory holds you were too, er, unintelligent to adapt to changing planetary conditions."

"Fuck you, buster," said Lawrence. "The dinosaurs lasted over a hundred million years. You'll be lucky to get past *five*. Guess again."

"Another school has it that poor skeletal design led to an epidemic of slipped discs."

" 'Poor skeletal design'? Look who's talking, White Man—you and your four thousand backache remedies."

"Upstart mammals devoured your eggs?" ventured Beauchamp.

"Please."

"The world got much colder," said Saperstein, "and even though you were warm-blooded, you couldn't maintain sufficient body heat."

"Hardly," said Vivien.

"A global contagion?"

"Impossible."

"Erupting volcanoes spewed out poison gases and—"

"No way."

"All right," said Saperstein. "I give up."

"You do?"

"Yes."

"Constipation."

"What?"

"Constipation."

"How's that again?"

"You want me to draw you a picture? Constipation. We died of blocked bowels after eating newly evolved, indigestible plant forms. Once we herbivores were gone, of course, the carnivores perished for lack of prey." Vivien lifted all seven letters from her rack, but instead of placing them on the board, she enclosed them in her fist and lurched toward Martin. Her eyes enchanted him, each jet-black pupil set against a golden iris like the moon eclipsing the sun. "Judge Candle?"

"Ex-judge. I lost big in November."

"Your project can't possibly end happily for the prosecution—

I hope you know that." Opening her fist, Vivien began arranging the Scrabble letters across her palm. "Too bad they booted you out of office—your verdicts were always environmentally sound. We especially appreciated your decision in the Pronto Prints case." Pronto Prints was a Fox Run film processing concern that had surreptitiously dumped three thousand gallons of stale chemicals into Waupelani Creek. Martin had levied a stiff fine and made the company install a full complement of water-treatment devices. "You're absolutely determined to go through with it?"

"Absolutely."

"Then we have a request. When you draft the final indictment, keep Lawrence and me in mind. Lawrence and me . . . and the rest of us."

"A major extinction is nothing to sneeze at," said Lawrence.

"A bona fide evil." Vivien placed all seven of her letters on the board. The A in PLAGUE enabled her to spell out THANATOS.

"I quite agree," said Martin, wondering what sort of sense, if any, it would make to mention the great Cretaceous dying in the indictment.

"You can't use that word," said Lawrence to his mate.

"Yes I can."

"It's a proper name—a Greek personification."

"It's also a synonym for *death*."

"No it isn't."

"Yes it is!"

"I challenge you! Where's the goddamn dictionary? I challenge you!"

"We want a voice," said Vivien abruptly, swerving toward Martin as she drew a *Random House College Dictionary* from underneath the picnic table.

"Give us a voice," said Lawrence.

"I'll see what I can do," said Martin.

The neuronauts departed shortly after learning that *thanatos* is not always capitalized.

Chapter 7

WHEN MARTIN CANDLE and his associates came tromping into my backyard, boots caked with mud, brows shiny with sweat, I suddenly realized how starved I'd grown for stimulating social intercourse. With the exception of Bishop Augustine, my customers are a dull lot, and my disciples have as much use for the life of the mind as a cobra has for a corn plaster. All Belphegor wants to talk about are horror movies and baseball. Schonspigel's idea of a conversation is reminiscing about the sack of Rome. The thought of passing a leisurely afternoon with beings whose intellectual prowess rivaled my own brought me to the brink of rapture.

Upon learning the sobering fact that I am not just a tailor but also the Prince of Darkness, all four neuronauts grew apprehensive, but through copious applications of reason and charm I eventually calmed them down. The coma, I explained, had left me a metaphysical cripple. I could no more steal their souls than a decoy duck could lay eggs.

Here on the River Hiddekel, we are all devout carnivores. If it doesn't bleed, we don't eat it. My personal chef, Funkeldune, has become a purist of late, refusing to cook anything he hasn't hunted down and killed himself. Luckily, none of my guests practiced vegetarianism, and their eyes absolutely glowed upon perceiving the proteinaceous supper Funkeldune had set out for us, a stew wrought from the Jehovic archetype of Ernest Hemingway.

I said my standard grace—"Dear Lord, we know You have good reasons for allowing thousands of children to starve in various underdeveloped nations, and we thank You for concomitantly supplying our own table with these grossly superfluous portions, amen"—after which we all dug in. Naturally I kept the meat's true source hidden from my guests. They believed they were eating a wild boar, which in a manner of speaking they were.

"What I don't understand is whether you are the actual Devil or merely the Idea of the Devil," said the Jesuit cosmologist, Thomas Ockham, devouring a chunk of Hemingway's haunch.

"The Idea of the Devil *is* the actual Devil," I replied firmly. "The incarnate Devil, the Jobian *satan* who used to go roaming across the Earth, is but a simulacrum of myself." I was tempted to add, "Just as the Ernest Hemingway who enjoyed fame as a terrestrial writer is but a simulacrum of the Ernest Hemingway on whom you are dining." Somehow, I resisted.

All during the meal my visitors plied me with the sorts of questions people worry about on public television. To tell you the truth, I don't really like public television. Give me the Playboy Channel anytime—pubic television, as Belphegor calls it. What is the correct value of Hubble's constant? Why is the proton in a hydrogen atom eighteen hundred and thirty-six times as heavy as the electron? I explained that, before the coma came, I probably possessed the answers, but these days I could barely remember how to do crewelwork.

"Do you know any counterarguments to the *liberum arbitrium* or 'free will' solution to the problem of evil?" piped up Candle.

"Doubtless I did at one time."

"What about the ontological solution?"

"You should be talking to a doctor of theology, not a Father of Lies. The distinction is subtle but real."

Our hero ate a piece of Hemingway's shank. "G. F. Lovett had me read Saint Augustine's *Opus imperfectum contra Julianum*, but I didn't find it very helpful."

"One of my favorites, actually—but why settle for Augustine's last work when you can have Augustine himself? See that brown worsted three-piece suit over there?" With my taloned index finger I guided Candle's gaze toward a set of clothes awaiting pickup: coat, vest, trousers. "When he comes to claim it tomorrow, I'll tell him I'm canceling the bill . . . provided he leads you upriver, straight to the wellspring of his theodicy. I refer, of course, to that paradisiacal spot from which the Pishon, Gihon, Euphrates, and Hiddekel all flow."

"A journey to the Garden of Eden would be most stimulating, I'm sure," said Ockham, chewing on a morsel of loin, "and it may indeed equip Mr. Candle with the sort of information he requires, but the rest of us have come for *scientific* knowledge."

"If *you* can't answer our questions, who can?" asked Beauchamp.

"Stop talking as if you won't be visiting the pineal gland," I told the scientists. "I wouldn't *dream* of allowing you to leave His cerebrum until you've visited the pineal gland." Pivoting, I pointed my sewing needle directly at Candle's left eye. "Beware of Bishop Augustine, friend. He's smarter than the rest of us. Given half a chance, he'll tie your mind in knots. Some people don't have all their marbles. Augustine has *too many* marbles."

"The pineal gland?" said Ockham.

"The pineal gland," I echoed.

"Do you mean to imply that Descartes—"

"Was right all along. Every person's soul, even our Creator's, is synonymous with his pineal gland. If your questions have answers, Father, you'll find them on the frontiers of His forebrain."

❖

Over the course of his career, Martin had on several occasions encountered a human being he was forced to label evil. He would never forget the case of nine-year-old Jared Galitzen, for example, who had serially doused eight Glendale cats with kerosene and set them aflame. Then there was the time he'd investigated an ostensible instance of improper garbage disposal in Deer Haven only to discover that the stench pervading Gladys Wurtz's property came from the strangled corpse of her ten-month-old son. Now, once again, Martin found himself in the presence of irredeemable depravity. However much the coma might have atrophied the tailor's powers, this was still a being who—if it suited his purposes—would handcuff you to a bedpost and remove your liver with a jigsaw. But for the optic neuron's insistence that the best countertheodicies lay in the divine cranium, Martin would have excused himself forthwith and beaten his way back to the *Carpco New Orleans*.

"I'm afraid there are no beds on the premises," said Jonathan Sarkos as the Idea of Darkness settled over his shop, "but among the virtues of my packet steamer are six berths containing air mattresses inflated with the last gasps of slaughtered lambs. You've never slept on anything softer."

Martin blinked, his eyes adjusting by degrees to the wan glow of the whale-oil lamps. The nearest rack contained five motorcycle jackets with the words ANTICHRIST CONSORTIUM embroidered on their backs. Beside them hung Saint Augustine's worsted suit and a dozen sheets featuring the logo of the Ku Klux Klan. He fixed on his maleficent host: a bald and boisterous giant, his eyes as red as a lab rat's. Dressed in an expertly cut tuxedo, the tailor was a walking advertisement for his talents, but the match between Sarkos's appearance and his profession was the only jot of rationality Martin could glean from his present circumstances.

"Before you turn in, permit me to entertain you." Sarkos reached behind his worktable and drew out a device that, thanks to Martin's membership in the Abaddon Junior High Audio-Visual Club, he recognized as a Kodak Pageant 16mm projector. "I don't expect you to find these shots very amusing." Setting the projector on the worktable, the tailor threaded up a 400-foot reel. "I expect you to find them painful, in fact. Of all my inventions, I am particularly proud of home movies. Mind operating the machine, Mr. Candle? I know you're familiar with it."

"No problem," said Martin warily.

"Ladies and gentlemen, Purgatory Pictures presents *It Came Upon a Midnight Drear*, written, produced, and directed by Jonathan Sarkos." The tailor lumbered toward the far wall, took down a KKK sheet from its peg, and thumbtacked it to the doorframe. "Roll it," he instructed Martin, simultaneously dousing the lamps.

Martin rotated the control knob to FORWARD. The projector bulb ignited, and the image hit the sheet: a wobbly, badly lit long-shot evocative of low-grade pornography. Dressed only in a wristwatch and a rhinestone necklace, a prostitute sat cross-legged on the stained ticking of a motel mattress. A customer entered the frame—a multihorned, thousand-eyed beast who might have just escaped from the Book of Revelation—and promptly availed himself of her services.

"My conception occurred against the odds," Sarkos narrated. "The woman in question was infertile, her fallopian tubes having been clogged by a case of gonorrhea acquired on the job. She remembered nothing about my father, except that he smelled like roadkill. An abortion was out of the question. Mother was always militantly pro-life."

The beast turned toward the camera and laughed. His semierect penis looked like a shock absorber.

"The instant God realized I was in the works, He resolved

that mine must be a humble birth, lest the sin of pride infect me prematurely. He had a stable all picked out, but it was otherwise occupied . . ."

The nativity scene from the 1959 remake of *Ben-Hur* appeared: a Metrocolor Madonna sitting amid a congestion of cows and goats, staring adoringly at her newborn son.

". . . and so He had to settle for something fancier."

A Holiday Inn flashed onto the screen, its neon VACANCY sign glowing through a relentless downpour.

"Thus did the Father of Lies come into the world, borne by the Mother of Whores."

Belly swollen with a full-term pregnancy, the prostitute lay sprawled across a queen-sized bed. As the camera operator zoomed capriciously in and out, the baby rammed his way through the cervix and down the birth canal, dragging the umbilicus behind him like a rock star trailing a mike cable. Smiling demonically, the baby crawled across the exhausted woman's torso and wrapped his cord around her neck.

"I really don't need to see any more," said Ockham.

"Mother and I were fated to have a stormy relationship," said Sarkos.

The baby cinched the fleshy rope. The prostitute's tongue shot out like a carved bird from a cuckoo clock. Seconds after her death, the infant Sarkos began sucking on her left nipple.

"Shit, this is disgusting," said Beauchamp.

"Turn it off," said Saperstein.

"From the very first, the outside world recognized the import of my advent," said Sarkos. "Among the visitors to my cradle was a trio of potentates from the West . . ."

Three men with wildly divergent hairstyles charged into the hotel room, gaily wrapped gifts in hand, mischievously poking each other in the eye and conking themselves on the brow. The first visitor wore what looked like a black mop on his head; the second boasted a Jewish Afro; the third sported a crewcut.

"The low point of their careers," said Beauchamp.

A mid-shot followed: the infant sitting on the dead prostitute's stomach, opening one of his presents. Seven cloth-and-metal snakes sprang out.

"Ever since then," said Sarkos, "I have lived by the maxim 'Beware of geeks bearing gifts.'"

The final shots showed the infant hurling the potentates into the Holiday Inn's piranha-infested pool.

"The end," said Sarkos.

"Thank goodness," said Saperstein.

As Martin shut off the projector, Sarkos struck a kitchen match, touching the flame to a lamp wick. The shop filled with the whale oil's warm mammalian glow.

"You missed your calling," said Ockham acidly. "You should've been a film director."

"I am a film director. You don't *really* think Robert Zemeckis made *Forrest Gump*, do you?" Sarkos strode to the projector, wrenched the reel off the pickup spindle, and waved the movie in Martin's face. "Logically, of course, I should be vehemently opposed to *International 227*. If the verdict is 'guilty' and the tribunal pulls the plug—well, where does that leave me?" He flung the reel across the shop like a discus. "Still, an acquittal would depress me even more, so I'll be cheering you every step of the way. My disciples and I plan to watch the whole circus on my little Zenith over there." Sarkos slipped a TV remote control from his jacket and pointed the device at Martin. "A remarkable tool. Not only does it change the channels, control the volume, and vary the contrast, the LED display allows me to assess every tin-pot Prometheus and would-be Job who blows through town."

Pressing the remote control against Martin's forehead, Sarkos stared at the matrix of buttons. The device felt like an ice cube.

"It's cold."

"Shhh," said Sarkos. "Let's see . . . bitterness quotient: 147, good. Self-righteousness ratio: 175 over 96, excellent. Moralistic fervor: 38.8 degrees centigrade. By damn, Mr. Candle, you're the strongest contender we've had yet. You might even win. Justice is blind, after all. I ought to know—I sewed her eyelids shut . . . with this." The tailor flourished a bright silver sewing needle. "Above all, whatever tricks Lovett pulls in The Hague, don't let him put the blame on me."

"I won't."

"Nobody forced our Creator to pollute the universe with a Prince of Darkness," said Sarkos, flashing a sharklike grin. "My violent conception, my slutty gestation, my ignoble birth: none of this was inevitable. He made it all happen of His own free will."

❖

With the aid of Roxanol, Martin slept soundly that night—so soundly, in fact, that when he awoke it took him several minutes to realize he wasn't back home in Abaddon but afloat on the River Hiddekel aboard a broken-down, fifty-foot packet steamer called the *Good Intentions*. It was the river's distinctive fragrance that jogged his memory; the Hiddekel exuded the most wondrous odor his nose had ever known, a combination of red roses, hot marshmallows, and cured meat. Even in its present decadent state, God's cerebrum smelled better than most brains did at their peak.

He slid off the mattress, limped past the sleeping forms of Saperstein and Beauchamp, and ascended a companionway to the main deck. The *Good Intentions* was fully under way, steaming steadily west, the featureless mudflat gliding past on both sides. Her engine chuffed and chugged; smoke gushed from her dual stacks, bulbous black clouds speckled with orange sparks. The morning air was wet and viscid, its sticky molecules sustaining swarms of buzzing aquatic insects. As he approached the wheelhouse—a wooden shack boasting all the architectural sophistication of an outdoor privy—he heard a male voice singing what he took to be a risqué sea chantey. The lyrics reached his ears in ragged bits, as if issuing from a phonograph record so badly worn the needle was hopping randomly among the grooves. Martin made out "kissing a squid" followed by "humping a humpback whale."

The singing stopped.

"Hello, Mr. Candle." A hideous creature poked his snout through the open wheelhouse window. "I'm Belphegor, your fearless pilot, not to mention Mr. Sarkos's favorite disciple." To Martin, the demon resembled what might have resulted if nature's laws permitted gorillas to mate fruitfully with warthogs. Belphegor's eyes were bloodshot. You could have stored Ping-Pong balls in his nostrils. "Do not hold my metaphysical status against me," he pleaded as a dollop of snot rolled from his nose. He belched explosively. "Given the choice, I'd be playing professional baseball."

Revolted, Martin lurched away from the wheelhouse and stumbled toward the bow, swatting blindly at the archetypal flies and primordial gnats hovering about his face. A mosquito as large as a hornet landed on his forehead and began to feast. He slapped himself, bursting the insect and spraying his brow with his own half-digested blood.

Dressed in the same brown worsted suit Martin had seen the night before in Sarkos's shop, a tall, solid, fiftyish man leaned against the stern bulwark, conversing animatedly with Ockham. Binoculars dangled from the stranger's neck, swaying in time to his gesticulations. His aquiline nose supported a pair of horn-rimmed glasses; his handsome teeth clenched a briar pipe. He looked both distinguished and successful, like a tenured Ivy League professor, or an aristocratic Romanian vampire who'd managed to establish a pied-à-terre down the road from a girls' boarding school.

". . . by conceiving of the Supreme Being as bipolar," Ockham was saying.

"A bifurcated deity?" said the stranger, plucking the pipe from his cavernous mouth. "No, no, the Godhead is a tripartite unity," he added, whereupon Martin noticed the man's ability to raise each eyebrow independently of its mate. "You're sidling into Manichaeanism, Father. I've been there. Don't go."

"But the poles work in tandem, just as your eyes do when you use these," Ockham insisted, brushing the man's binoculars. "In Manichaeanism, the two principles are at war."

"It's a trap, friend. Stay away."

"Bishop Augustine?" inquired Martin, approaching.

"The Idea of Augustine," the man corrected him. He synchronized his eyebrows into a scowl. "Judge Candle?"

"Ex-Judge Candle. I've read your autobiography."

"My *Confessions*? All of it?"

"All of it."

"Congratulations. It is my dubious distinction to have produced one of the three masterworks of Western literature that fewer than seventy people, living or dead, have read in toto, the others being *Paradise Regained* and *The Decline and Fall of the Roman Empire*." Augustine raised his right eyebrow. "These days, of course, I wouldn't have to bother writing it all down, would I? I'd simply go on *Geraldo*." The left eyebrow attained the level of its mate. "So, Mr. Candle, you want to know about evil."

"Indeed."

"Mr. Sarkos says he won't charge me for my new clothes if I give you a tour." Augustine crossed his arms over his stomach, rubbing the leather patches on his elbows. "I don't mind telling you *International 227* vexes me to the core. Educating you will give me no pleasure, and I'm inclined to back out of the bargain right now." Again the bishop scowled. "Still, a free suit is a free suit." Reaching into his coat pocket, he produced a folded sheet of pink computer paper, its edges fringed with perforations. "Our itinerary. Mount Moriah, the plains of Sodom, the foothills of Ararat, the Country of Dung, the Garden of Eden." He repocketed the paper, puffed on his pipe, and exhaled a smoke ring shaped like a Möbius strip. "The urge to cleanse one's soul through confession can be overwhelming at times, wouldn't you agree? Right now, for instance, I am moved to admit that our upcoming visit with the actors on Moriah—Abraham, Isaac, the sacrificial ram—will arouse my carnal appetites."

"You have impure feelings toward Isaac?" asked Ockham.

"The ram, actually." Augustine curled his generous lower lip into his mouth and bit down hard. "Lord, what a foul and fallen world we inhabit! The word, Father, is *concupiscence*. Concupiscence, concupiscence, all is concupiscence."

As the morning wore on, the bishop continued revealing himself. He told of his recurrent impulse to have intimate relations with various pieces of heavy farm machinery. He described his raging wish to wear lacy silk negligees. He admitted that he longed to referee one of the famous farting contests to which the Idea of Martin Luther periodically challenged the Idea of Satan. Halfway through this prodigious mea culpa, Ockham slipped away, but Martin decided to tough it out, eager to cultivate the bishop's goodwill.

The salacious content of Augustine's confessions eventually prompted Martin to recall the case of Sidney King, a Glendale real-estate agent whose three girlfriends had come to the magistrate's office shortly after learning about each other. Their complaints were identical. Each was seven weeks pregnant by King, a situation that roundly contradicted his claim to have undergone a vasectomy. Whereas Cynthia Ringle planned to get an abortion, Karla Schwartz and Joanne Bogenrief both intended to keep their babies. None of them wanted to marry the jerk.

"Any way we can get justice here?" Schwartz had asked.

The next day Martin issued a summons, charging King with flagrant misrepresentation of a major reproductive organ. "You could go to jail for this," he told King shortly after the defendant appeared in court. King became agitated. Seizing the opportunity, Martin extracted a pledge: until his children reached age twelve, King must make himself available as a weekend babysitter—no exceptions, no excuses, a hefty fine in the event he reneged. If the president of General Motors invited King to go trout fishing one fine Saturday morning, both of King's bastards must come along. If a Hollywood starlet proposed they spend two weeks in the south of France, she would have to make four plane reservations. Seven months later the babies arrived, a boy in each case, and from the very first the arrangement worked well, fatherhood having awakened a dormant tenderness in King. Eventually both Schwartz and Bogenrief acquired stepfathers for their sons, with King functioning in the boys' lives as a kind of year-round Santa Claus.

"Have you ever wanted to have a gerbil living in your rectum?" asked Augustine, his hands drifting toward Martin's abundant bosom.

"Can't say that I have."

"Concupiscence, Mr. Candle—concupiscence!" The bishop copped a feel and continued. "Oh, what a deplorable species we are! Our flesh is fetid! Our souls are full of slime! The sooner the Day of Judgment comes, the better!"

It is my sacred duty to put up with this, Martin told himself, clenching his teeth and closing his eyes. My Jobians are counting on me.

❖

As the late-morning sun beat down on the mudflat, raising mirages reminiscent of the iridescent icons back in the Defendant's laboratory, Martin returned to his berth and collected his e-mail.

From: selkirk2@aol.org
To: marcand@prodigy.edu
Date: Tues, May 16, 09:45 PM EDT

At the moment my relationship with your landlady is flourishing. Patricia and I have much in common—divorce, bereavement, atheism—and I believe we can help each other, *though she remains oddly unsympathetic to our cause. She wants to know whether you're taking something called Odradex.*

Bad news. Dr. Carbone has upped the ante. He's now asking $175,000. What's more, he insists that the only other cataclysmatician in Ohio competent to cover his summer-school course is his wife, Pearl, and she wants $32,000, plus $5,000 for a teaching assistant. I think these figures are outrageous, and I told Carbone so.

By the time Martin finished reading Randall's message, his heart was pounding, and his blood felt ready to boil.

From: marcand@prodigy.edu
To: selkirk2@aol.org
Date: Wed, May 17, 11:40 AM Local Time

For Heaven's sake, Randall, stop goofing around with our star witness's fee! Give him his $175,000 and his wife her $37,000. We may not have the angels on our side, but we do have a Hollywood budget.

Inform Patricia I'm not injecting myself with Odradex. This will come as no surprise to her.

Esther's message was considerably more soothing than Randall's, though it began on a discouraging note.

From: esthclute@aol.org
To: marcand@prodigy.edu
Date: Wed, May 17, 10:17 AM EDT

Allison Lowry refuses to testify, not even for $10,000, and that's that. Sure, she was able to tell her story at our first *meeting, but that doesn't mean she wants to repeat it before the whole world.*

I can't promise you any more severed spinal cords, but I think I'm on to something just as rich: cystic fibrosis. I'm interviewing three sets of parents this week. (Two of the relevant children will be dead within the year, while the third succumbed last January. Wish me luck.) On the terminal-cancer front, meanwhile, things keep getting better and better. You should hear Frank Latham describe the horrors of Hodgkin's disease and Rosalind Kreuger talk about losing a daughter to acute lymphoblastic leukemia. Best of all, I think I can score us a refugee from the Rwanda genocide, Xavier Mrugama. They attacked him with a machete.

Tongue pressed against his upper lip, Martin reread Esther's letter. "I can't promise you any more severed spinal cords . . ." So there it was again, the cold-blooded kingdom of *International 227.* "On the terminal-cancer front . . ." No wonder humankind so rarely took its Creator to court. God hunting was not a sport for amateurs.

From: marcand@prodigy.edu
To: esthclute@aol.org
Date: Wed, May 16, 11:58 AM Local Time

All right, fine, we'll leave Allison alone. If you can dig up an articulate cystic-fibrosis parent, that ought to plug the gap.

Naturally I'm pleased we're doing so well with our cancer patients. I have a concern, though. Hasn't cancer become rather jejune of late? Can you find us something with more

pizzazz? I seem to recall at least one multiple-sclerosis vic-
tim, and a couple of early-onset Alzheimer's cases.

When Martin returned to the daylight, the Idea of the Sun
stood at its zenith. Wandering about the packet, he found Augustine on the afterdeck, sprawled across an Adirondack chair
and holding a fishing rod. The line trailed off the transom for
about twenty feet, connecting with an egg-shaped plastic bobber
before descending into the Hiddekel's depths.

"Have you ever wanted to decorate your face by forcing
fishhooks through your lips?" the bishop inquired.

"Never," Martin replied.

"East of Eden, the temptations never stop."

"Catch anything?"

"No . . . and when you consider the monsters who inhabit
this river, it's probably just as well. Over there, for instance"—
Augustine pointed north—"we have a beast so fearsome that
God subdued him only after a three-day battle. Behemoth from
the Book of Job."

Martin glanced toward the levee. An animal resembling the
offspring of a hippopotamus and a plesiosaur lay half buried in
the muck, feasting on bulrushes and lotus plants. Its mountain-
ous shoulders glistened with plasma. Its darting eyes were set
atop stalks, a pair of organic pinwheels.

Moaning, Martin grasped the transom rail for support.
It was one thing to read about Behemoth—a symbol of primordial chaos, according to most commentators on Job—and
quite another to be in the cosmic hippo's presence. Inevitably
Martin recalled the time his father, ever in search of provocative
material for Sunday school lessons, had rented a 16mm print of
The Giant Behemoth, a late-fifties sci-fi thriller, borrowing a projector from the church and previewing the film in the living
room of the firehouse. It was a big event. Martin was allowed to
invite Billy Tuckerman over. Unfortunately, *The Giant Behemoth*
wasn't very scary, at least not to a twelve-year-old's sensibilities.

Walter, too, had watched it with growing disappointment: except for the narrator's first line—"And God said, 'Behold thou the Behemoth' "—and a vicar's graveside funeral speech, the movie contained no biblical material whatsoever.

" 'And God said, "Behold thou the Behemoth," ' " quoted Martin, wishing Augustine would reel in the hook-and-bobber before the monster got wind of the bait.

" 'If the river is turbulent, he is not frightened,' " added Augustine, studying Behemoth with a mixture of terror and concupiscence. " 'He sprawls at his ease though the stream is in flood.' "

Martin stared at the receding beast, transfixed by its inscrutability. There were indeed more things in God's brain than were dreamt of in Augustine's—or anyone else's—philosophy.

" 'Can a man blind his eyes and capture him or pierce his nose with the teeth of a trap?' " quoted Augustine.

"Offhand, I'd say no," Martin replied, laughing nervously as the monster finally passed from view.

❖

The afternoon brought barbaric heat, ravenous mosquitoes, and, less predictably, the emphatic fragrance of burning wood—a sensation that evoked for Martin not only the recent loss of his Chestnut Grove farmhouse but also his unsuccessful attempt as a Boy Scout to earn a merit badge in cooking.

A crab spasm shot through his left pubic bone. He ate two Roxanols and looked north. A half mile beyond the riverbank a pyramid of faggots surmounted a hill of rock, flames and smoke curling upward from the bottommost sticks. The wood, he mused, might have come from the burning bush of Mosaic lore, for while the flames appeared sufficiently hot, they did not consume their fuel. Borrowing Augustine's binoculars, he raised them to his eyes, twisted the focus knob, and gasped.

A frail boy, no more than ten and dressed only in white

cotton briefs, lay wriggling atop the pyramid, his wrists and ankles lashed together with leather thongs. Twenty feet away a stooped, bearded octogenarian wearing a lumberjack's shirt paced in fretful circles, an obsidian knife clutched against his breast. He was a man divided—pulled in one direction by a divine mandate and in the other by his impulse to unfasten the boy and bear him safely home. Both actors, father and son, seemed trapped in a kind of time loop, like clockwork figurines dancing on a music box.

"Stop the boat!" Augustine rushed toward the wheelhouse, waving the pink itinerary around like a pennant. "Stop it right now!"

Leaning out the window, Belphegor confronted Augustine with the sort of expression a husband might flash his wife upon being asked to buy her a box of tampons, but the demon nevertheless complied, throttling down and dropping anchor.

A glutinous mist drifted across the river's surface as Martin lowered himself over the side and, holding his laptop computer high above his head, started for shore through the blood flow, Augustine and the scientists right behind. The crimson currents were warm and viscous, like melted fudge, a sensation Martin would have found completely unpleasant were he not flying on Roxanol.

Plasma running down their limbs, the travelers gained the bank and climbed Moriah's muddy slopes.

"Perhaps you can assist me," said Martin, moving as close to the boy as the flames permitted. Their eyes met. "Are you familiar with any of these solutions to the mystery of suffering?" He brought up Lovett's list on the laptop screen and held the display before Isaac. "The hidden harmony defense, for example? The *liberum arbitrium*?"

"You're Judge Candle, aren't you?" said the Idea of Isaac, sweat streaming down his face.

"Ex-judge. *Liberum arbitrium,* as you may know, means 'free will.'"

"I'm not thinking very clearly right now. My father is on the point of killing me. Otherwise, I'd be happy to talk about evil."

"I'm pretty confused too," said the Idea of Abraham, staring straight ahead with weary, bloodshot eyes. "Please, Lord, give me strength . . ."

As Ockham aimed his camcorder at Abraham and ran off several feet of tape, the patriarch raised the knife, bringing it level with his gaze. The blade glittered in the fading sunlight.

"Does either of you know how the spirochetes adhere to *Myxotricha paradoxa?*" asked Saperstein.

"Who are the Spirochetes?" responded Abraham.

Augustine moved into Martin's field of vision, confronting him with his lustrous, black-eyed stare. "You're looking at the eschatological defense," the bishop explained. "At the moment Abraham and Isaac are both suffering terribly—"

"You can say that again," moaned the boy.

"I wish I were dead," wailed his father.

"—and yet, in the fullness of time, the child will be rescued." Augustine smiled expansively at the patriarch. "Have patience, sir. The material world is a vale of tears, but ultimately you ascend to Heaven."

By way of retort, Abraham pointed the tip of his knife toward Augustine, curled his lip contemptuously, and burst into song.

> *Just around the corner,*
> *There's a rainbow in the sky.*
> *So let's have another cup of coffee,*
> *And let's have another piece of pie.*

"Well, yes—if you must put it that way," sneered Augustine. "Read *Contra Celsum* by my brilliant predecessor Bishop Origen," he said to Martin, "and you will realize all our earthly miseries are transient as grass."

Origen invented eschatological defense, Martin typed onto his hard drive. "What else should I know about Origen?"

"He began as a student of Plato and Gnosticism, then converted to Christianity," said Augustine.

"After which he sold his books, became an ascetic, and castrated himself," said Ockham.

Also cut off balls, Martin typed, shuddering as he recalled Dr. Blumenberg's proposal to battle his cancer via the same operation. He had difficulty imagining anyone mutilating himself in this manner merely for the spiritual thrill.

Extending his index finger, Augustine indicated a nearby thicket, where a plump ram stood frozen in a posture of fatalistic resignation, its horns ensnared in the branches. "See that ram, Isaac? Your deliverance is at hand. Any second now, Abraham will notice the creature and make the swap."

"I know, I know," muttered the boy sarcastically. "It's an old story."

"You don't sound satisfied," said Beauchamp.

"Satisfied? How can I be satisfied? My father hears a Voice from on high commanding him to immolate me and hand the charred meat over for His delectation and delight. 'Make Me an offering I can't refuse,' says Yahweh. Then, at the last second, He withdraws the demand. Do you imagine I'll go home now and simply *forget* the whole thing? The smell of the smoke, the gleam of the knife, the thongs chafing my wrists—do you imagine these facts aren't etched permanently into my brain? Do you imagine I'll ever be able to look my father in the eye without thinking, 'He would have done it'?"

"Or for that matter," said Abraham, "do you imagine I'll ever be able to look *Isaac* in the eye without thinking, 'I would have done it'?"

Dysfunctional family, Martin typed.

"You're both missing the point," Augustine insisted, frowning extravagantly. "The Binding of Isaac is a *symbolic* story."

"Your symbol, my son," said Abraham.

"Don't get testy with me, sir. I am Augustine of Hippo Regius, discoverer of concupiscence. Between my legs hangs the axis on which will turn the brave new world of Christian antieroticism."

"Excuse me," said the ram in a plaintive voice. "I don't mean to butt in. But if you want to destroy the eschatological defense, Judge Candle, don't start with the psychodynamics of the situation. Start with the crude truth that, wonderful as this boy's incipient deliverance may be, such happy endings are the exception, not the rule."

"The beast has a good point," said Abraham.

"Call me Gordon." Breaking free of the thicket, the animal stepped tentatively toward the altar. In both voice and demeanor he reminded Martin of Eeyore the donkey. "Consider my own predicament. As Abraham starts to sever my jugular, will Yahweh drop by and say, 'Stop, hold it, only kidding, April fool?' Will an alternative sacrifice appear in the next thicket over—a rabbit, maybe? And if it does, then what about justice for the rabbit? Will Yahweh be satisfied with a toad instead?" Gordon pawed the soggy ground. "Admittedly, I can't be objective here. But the fact remains that when child abuse is about to occur in the real world, it is not commonly canceled by divine intervention."

Augustine whipped off his horn-rimmed glasses and pointed them toward Gordon. "The correct interpretation of this incident does not lead us to expect justice here and now. The Binding of Isaac helps us remember that, through the atoning death of Jesus Christ—represented in the story by you yourself, Gordon—humankind has been redeemed." He gave the ram a firm pat on the rump. "When our Savior comes again, the dead will be raised, the wicked punished, and the virtuous blessed with eternal life."

"I cannot respect any theory of evil that so neatly immunizes itself against empirical disconfirmation," said Gordon. "All theodicies requiring belief in an afterlife are manifestly begging the question." The ram cast his limpid brown eyes on Martin. "Are you getting this? If the pre-coma God were as loving and powerful as His supporters claim, then He possessed no warrant, absolutely none, to wait until some hypothetical Judgment Day before eradicating evil. A father doesn't have the right to sexually molest his children throughout the winter simply because he intends to take them to Disneyland in the spring."

The Disneyland defense, Martin typed.

"In your opinion," said Augustine huffishly.

"In my opinion," said the ram evenly.

"Another problem with afterlife theodicies, it seems to me," said Martin, "is their blithe assumption that Heaven will be wonderful. Maybe the flip side of the grave is *also* a vale of tears, full of pain and loss and, of course, clerics promising us that once we check out, we'll find ourselves in Paradise. And so it goes—jam tomorrow, always tomorrow."

"That's good, Judge," said the ram.

"Thank you."

For the second time that day, Abraham began to sing.

> *Just below your pelvis,*
> *There's a tumor in your thigh.*
> *So let's have another shot of morphine,*
> *'Cause cancer is a rotten way to die.*

He sheathed his knife, hobbled over to Isaac, and loosened the thongs from the boy's wrists and ankles. "Here," he said, presenting the bindings to Martin. "They're yours. Outside the divine cranium, they'll last only a few months, but that's plenty of time to offer them in evidence. Tell the tribunal, 'Behold Exhibit A. Perhaps Yahweh saw fit to call off Isaac's private holocaust, but since then His record has been atrocious.'"

Martin grasped the thongs, damp with the boy's agonized sweat, stained with his tortured blood.

Climbing off the altar, Isaac addressed his proxy. "You are

a truly marvelous beast." He jumped free of the flames, hit the ground, and rubbed Gordon's woolly head. "I shall always be in your debt."

"Go to Hell," rasped Gordon. "You're spoiling my whole fucking afternoon."

"Is there no other way?" Isaac asked his father.

"If it were my decision, I'd let the animal live." With a single, fluid movement, Abraham unsheathed his knife and thrust it into Gordon's neck. "Do you believe that, Son?"

"I do, Father."

"Aaaiiihhh," bleated Gordon as a stream of blood, red and rich as the Hiddekel, spurted from his innocent throat.

Chapter 8

MARTIN SPENT THE NEXT MORNING lounging in a wicker chair on the steamer's afterdeck, grasping Isaac's bindings with one hand and typing into his laptop with the other. His straw Panama hat, borrowed from Father Ockham, settled down around his eyebrows, blocking the blinding sun. At length he saved the file, wiped his forehead, and smiled. Unless he was mistaken, he had finally amalgamated the ram's attack on the Binding of Isaac with the equally astute critique offered by Abraham and his son. Let Lovett try shielding his Client with the eschatological defense—oh, just let him try!

Looking up from the computer screen, he glanced across the river. Along the southern bank, a razed and ravaged city rose against a crimson sky. Fallen towers, scorched spires, seared timbers, melted domes. Its ramparts were broken and cratered, like the limestone grave markers whose inscriptions Martin's father had so obsessively sought to preserve through charcoal rubbings.

"The disciplinary defense," said Bishop Augustine, joining Martin on the afterdeck.

"What about it?"

"There, there—in the suburbs of Sodom." Augustine drew the pink itinerary from his coat and pointed toward the carbonized metropolis. "The eschatological solution may have a weakness or two, but the disciplinary defense stands tall."

Rising from the wicker chair, Martin directed his gaze along the vector of the bishop's extended finger. Beyond the city's walls lay a tract of split and blackened earth, the fissures zigzagging everywhere like cracks in a shattered mirror. A silver-bearded man in a scorched jumpsuit was making his way slowly westward, his back bent by a rucksack, his arms wrapped around a white humanoid artifact only slightly smaller than he. Dressed in a T-shirt, a prominently pregnant adolescent with straw-colored hair and a sullen countenance followed in the man's footsteps, while a second young woman—a redhead, likewise T-shirted and pregnant—brought up the rear.

The artifact was evidently heavy: every twenty paces or so, the man would pause and set it upright on the ground, leaning on it until he caught his breath. The longer Martin contemplated the thing, the more distinctly female it seemed, albeit grotesquely so, like a caryatid supporting the roof of a cubist pagan temple.

Martin knew the story well, for it had engendered his father's most notorious Sunday school lesson. "Neither look behind you nor stop anywhere on the plain," God's emissary had told the band of refugees as they prepared to flee doomed Sodom in Genesis 19:17, but Lot's wife had looked back anyway and beheld the burning city, and by verse twenty-seven she'd become—of all things—a pillar of salt.

"Keep your eyes fixed on me," Walter Candle had told his class as his brother-in-law, Martin's Uncle Wilmer, sneaked into the back of the room clutching a rolled-up poster for a late-eighties horror movie called *Hollywood Chainsaw Hookers*. Unfurling the disconcerting image—a buxom prostitute wielding a chain saw—Wilmer Scotch-taped it to the closet door. "Behind you is something God doesn't like," Walter continued. "Something God *hates,* in fact. I'm giving you the same order those angels gave Lot and his family. Don't look back at this hateful thing, children. Don't you dare peek." And within a minute, of course, a dozen children were looking back; and of these twelve, half became terribly upset (partly over the image, partly over the failure of their wills). Tommy Williams, Lucy Winthrop, and Sammy McPhee burst into tears. Douglas Hill suffered an asthma attack. By the end of the week, Walter Candle's Sodom lesson had occasioned nine reproving phone calls from the bewildered youngsters' parents.

As the midday sun beat down on the ruined city, Martin, Augustine, and the scientists forded the river and drew within hailing distance of the archetypal Lot and his crystalline wife.

"Permit me to offer you my condolences," said Augustine, gesturing toward the salt pillar with his unlit pipe.

"I lost a wife too," said Martin sympathetically, flipping open his laptop.

"My Fiona died two years ago," said Saperstein.

The Idea of Lot removed his rucksack, raised a tattered sleeve to his face, and mopped the sweat from his brow. An oblique smile played about his lips. "I'm managing," he said, a peculiar lilt in his voice.

"Don't restrain your grief on our account," said Augustine.

"I won't."

"Let your lament be so loud it rattles Heaven's gates."

"You bet." Reaching inside the sack, Lot lifted out a cocktail shaker, a long-stemmed glass, a thermos jug full of ice, and three bottles containing, respectively, lime juice, triple sec, and tequila. He filled the shaker with several ounces of each liquid, added the ice, and stirred. "On the other hand—"

"Cry tears as bitter as your beloved's transformed tissues." Augustine lit his pipe. " 'On the other hand'?"

"On the other hand, there are ways in which her present condition is not entirely a drawback." Lot pressed the long-stemmed glass against the pillar's left thigh. "Don't get me wrong." He poured the contents of the cocktail shaker into the salted glass, then raised the margarita to his lips and sipped. "I'm not saying she's become the perfect wife. Nevertheless, she now boasts both a measure of reticence and a caliber of compliance that did not obtain previously."

"Maybe *he* thinks this is a change for the better . . . ," said the redheaded adolescent.

". . . but *we* don't," chimed in her straw-haired sister, touching Martin's plasma-soaked sleeve. "Judge Candle, right? *International 227?*"

"That's me," said Martin, chewing a Roxanol.

Saperstein turned toward the young women's father. "But surely you miss the pleasures of the flesh," said the neurophysiologist.

Lot shrugged and gestured toward the pillar's crotch. "All problems have solutions."

Martin lowered his gaze. Someone had modified the pillar just below its abdomen, hollowing out a conspicuous concavity.

"You've heard of sodomy?" said the straw-haired adolescent. "Our father practices the corresponding vice, gomorry."

"Sexual intercourse with condiments," explained the redhead. Her T-shirt displayed the words BABY ON BOARD atop an arrow indicating her uterus. "I'm Shuah, by the way."

"Call me Maleb," said Shuah's sister. The motto on her T-shirt read UNDER CONSTRUCTION.

"Does anyone here know why a self-sufficient Supreme Being would fashion a material cosmos?" asked Ockham.

"Or whether Fermat really proved his last theorem?" asked Beauchamp, photographing the pillar with her Nikon.

"Fermat's what?" Shuah scowled. "Theorem? Maleb and I barely passed geometry."

As Martin surveyed the pillar, he was struck by the chilling possibility that, beneath her crust, Mrs. Lot was still conscious, buried alive like a character in an Edgar Allan Poe story. It would take a powerful argument to convince him she deserved such a fate.

Augustine cupped his palm around Lot's shoulder. "Maybe

you're still able to slake your disgusting lust, but from your *wife's* perspective this is a calamity. Divine retribution is always stern and permanent." Unhanding the old man, he allowed his fingers to brush the pillar's right buttock. "Stern, permanent—and also just. This woman was told not to look back, but she did, and now she's paying the penalty."

"Your friend is peddling the disciplinary defense," said Shuah to Martin.

"Don't buy it," said Maleb. Opening her compact, she held up the mirror and painted her mouth with phosphorescent scarlet lipstick. "For every woman who deserves the sort of punishment our mother received, there are thousands who follow the rules and *still* get shafted. Childbed fever, vicious husbands . . ."

"One sometimes hears the theory that our ordeals are like surgical incisions," said Martin, evoking a memorable metaphor from *The Conundrum of Suffering.* "Just as a doctor must cut into our bodies to excise malignant tumors, so must God cut into our souls to facilitate our spiritual growth. In both cases the patient suffers considerable postoperative pain, but ultimately it's necessary."

"God is a surgeon?" said Maleb with the sort of outraged incredulity Martin had often observed among adolescent shoplifters at the moment of sentencing.

"So the argument goes."

"Adversity builds character," Augustine elaborated, puffing on his pipe. "Discipline forges a worthy soul."

"Who the fuck are you?" asked Shuah.

"Saint Augustine, bishop of Hippo Regius."

Shuah pulled a strand of bubble gum from her mouth, stretching it taut until it snapped. "Well, Your Grace, if you'll take a minute to consider the quantity of pointless pain in this universe . . ."

". . . you'll see the cosmic surgeon has acted more like a vivisectionist," said Maleb, rouging her cheeks.

"I like that," said Martin, positioning his fingers above the computer keyboard and typing, *God as cosmic vivisectionist.*

Shuah reached toward the pillar, broke off her mother's right ear, and deposited it in Martin's hand. "Here, sir. Carry this to The Hague. Eventually it will disintegrate, but not before you've offered it in evidence. Ask the judges if they really believe that those who endure the worst tribulations are also those most needful of spiritual growth."

"Thank you," said Martin, cradling the ear in his palm. "When I was the magistrate of Abaddon, I always tried to make the punishment fit the crime."

"If you and your sister knew as much about theology as you do about incest," said Augustine, pointing to Shuah's BABY ON BOARD shirt, "you'd realize how superficial your objections are."

"Superficial?" echoed Shuah indignantly.

"Once we reach the source of the Hiddekel, everything will become clear," said Augustine.

Shuah snapped her bubble gum. "You're going to the Garden of Eden?"

"The Garden—and beyond," said Ockham.

"All the way to the pineal gland," said Beauchamp.

A concupiscent smile flitted across Augustine's face. "Perhaps you lovely ladies would like to come along."

Maleb swung her swollen belly toward Lot. "May we, sir? May we? Oh, please, *please* tell Bishop Augustine we're allowed to go."

"You must, Father," wailed Shuah. "I've never been to Eden. I hear it's beautiful this time of year."

"We'll do anything you ask," said Maleb.

"We'll forgive you for inviting the men of Sodom to gang-bang us," said Shuah.

"You were probably in a bad mood," said Maleb.

"My answer is no," said Lot, finishing his margarita.

"No?" gasped Shuah.

"No," said Lot. "I absolutely forbid it."

"But . . . why?" asked Maleb.

"Yes—why?" asked Shuah.

"Maybe I'm an old fool. Maybe my wife is made of salt. Maybe my daughters use me as a sperm bank. But the fact remains that, until God takes the Idea of Patriarchy and replaces it with something better, the power relationships within *this* family will remain unchanged. Why am I forbidding you to visit the Garden, Maleb? Why, Shuah? Because I'm your *father*, that's why."

❖

Sixty miles beyond Sodom a series of alluvial fans emerged from the Hiddekel, splitting the river into a network of channels so narrow and shallow that Belphegor needed all his navigation skills to keep the *Good Intentions* from running aground. Martin spent this treacherous passage lounging on the afterdeck, computer balanced on his knees, contemplating Mrs. Lot's right ear as he chronicled her nubile daughters' spirited attack on the disciplinary defense.

Slowly, inexorably, dusk descended, darkening the levees and straining the redness from the river. A harvest moon rose, bright and quintessential. "Just the sort of moon, I'll bet," said Beauchamp to Martin, "beneath which old Abel's brother harvested the world's first crop. Why are you staring at me like that?"

"I find it odd that a mathematician would allude to the Bible," said Martin.

"Mathematics excites me—and so does the Book of Numbers," she said with a quiet smile. "Tell me, friend, what are you hoping to accomplish, anyway?"

"With *International 227*?"

"Yeah."

"You don't approve?"

"Not really, no. When it comes to evil, I'm with Einstein. 'God is subtle but not malicious.'"

"Let me try putting it in quantitative terms. Every time we look the other way while the Defendant unleashes a plague or a tornado, the net amount of dishonesty in the world increases."

Beauchamp frowned and, bending over, grasped the iron ring affixed to the afterdeck hatch. "You know, Judge, I'm afraid I'd have to call that a white man's way of looking at things. Black people have never had the luxury of rejecting the divine order. We've never had the privilege of railing against the universe. For hundreds of years, Jesus was our only friend."

"Okay, fine—but that doesn't mean the universe is benign."

Tugging smartly on the ring, Beauchamp opened her way to the berths. "Isn't it enough that the universe *exists*?"

"No. It isn't."

"*Tsk, tsk*, Judge. That's all I can say. *Tsk, tsk*. You sure are hard to please."

As the mathematician went below, Martin set about learning whether his co-prosecutors had responded to his previous communiqués. There was no mail from Esther, but Randall had posted an elaborate message.

From: selkirk2@aol.org
To: marcand@prodigy.edu
Date: Thur, May 18, 09:35 AM EDT

First, the bad news. In response to our discovery motions, Pierre Ferrand regrets to inform us that Lovett refuses to release any depositions from his witnesses. Torvald supports this decision one hundred percent. Apparently we shouldn't be surprised. In cases like ours, where the death penalty is a possible outcome, the World Court often allows the defense to stonewall it.

Now, the good news. We have officially hired Dr. Donald Carbone, cataclysmatician, as a witness for the prosecution. He intends to augment his testimony with exhibits from the Kroft Museum of Natural Disasters and Technological Catastrophes—a photo of the smallpox virus, an iron lung, a Titanic life preserver, and so forth. At first the museum's curator, a professional jerk named Brian Maltby, refused to let his treasures leave the country, but they became a lot less delicate the minute I offered him $45,000 to label, package, and ship the stuff. It wouldn't hurt if you expressed a little gratitude, Martin, instead of accusing me of "goofing around."

I'm trying to nail down a second expert witness: Dr. Tonia Braverman, a Brown University historian who's written an eleven-hour PBS series about wars, rebellions, and massacres. A History of Havoc *will probably never be aired— the final cut was too downbeat—but I think we should make the judges watch it, assuming we're still including human depravity in the indictment. Braverman is definitely in our camp. She likes to quote Stendhal: "God's only excuse is that He does not exist." But He* does *exist, Martin, and so we need this trial.*

Lovett's behavior so angered Martin that his heart began to beat madly, rattling his implanted Port-A-Cath.

From: marcand@prodigy.edu
To: selkirk2@aol.org
Date: Thur, May 18, 11:06 AM Local Time

Lovett doesn't have a phone, not to mention a fax machine, so send the old bluffer a telegram instead. Remind him the main thing he wants from this proceeding is a "good fight."

How can we give him a "good fight" if we don't know whom he plans to put on the stand?

Sorry about the "goofing around" remark. I was terrified Carbone would slip through our fingers. Braverman sounds like a real find, and I love the idea of screening A History of Havoc *during the trial. Congratulations. Of course we're still indicting Him for human depravity. There will be no plea-bargaining in* International 227!

The instant Martin sent his message to Randall, something unexpected occurred. The text vanished in a sudden starburst, replaced by a . . . by a what? Hard to say. A kind of spherical amoeba, its outer shell shimmering with an azure light radiating from an incandescent core.

The image on the screen grew sharper.

"Greetings, Earthling," said the optic neuron, its voice pouring from the laptop speaker.

"Heavens to Betsy . . . now you've taken over the World Wide Web?"

"Only for a few seconds. How's it going, Candle?"

Martin inhaled deeply. He would never get used to these divine interventions—never. "Pretty well, actually. I found a powerful countertheodicy on Moriah and another outside Sodom—"

"Terrific."

"—along with Isaac's bindings and Mrs. Lot's right ear."

"It's good they gave you something tangible. Tribunals like material evidence."

"I don't understand why your Progenitor is helping me like this. In my final statement to the Court I'll be arguing for disconnection of the Lockheed 7000."

"He's a real enigma, isn't He? If Sarkos is the Father of Lies, Yahweh is the King of Riddles. Keep following your instincts, Judge. You're doing great. Health still holding up?"

"I can't complain."

"That doesn't sound like you."

"All right, I *can* complain. I'm weak, I'm nervous, I'm tired—"

"Hey, everybody—Martin's back!"

"—but between the Feminone and the Roxanol, I'm still on my feet."

"Go for it, sir. Bring Him to book."

At which juncture the neuron vanished, leaving Martin to stare perplexedly at his hard-drive menu.

❖

Hello, gentle reader. At last I have returned. I hope you missed me as much as I missed you.

In case you're wondering, I can assure that you Randall Selkirk was absolutely right to assume the PBS documentary called *A History of Havoc* would make a piquant prosecution exhibit. The first scene alone—the death of Robert François Damiens before the steps of Notre Dame cathedral in 1757—furnishes provocative material for anyone wishing to argue that God couldn't possibly have had sufficiently good reasons for allowing the Fall of Man. I'm proud to say that, aided by my Elias Howe sewing machine, I fashioned the very hoods worn by Monsieur Damiens's executioners—the actual executioners, I mean, not the underpaid impersonators of the reenactment.

His mind unhinged by various ecclesiastical controversies, Damiens had tried to assassinate Louis XV, a deed for which he was convicted as a regicide and sentenced to make the *amende honorable* in the Place de Grève. While the crowd gaped and gasped, an executioner mounted the scaffold, seized a pair of steel pincers forged especially for the occasion, and systematically tore gobbets of flesh from Damiens's chest, arms, thighs, and calves. A second executioner poured molten lead into these wounds, followed by a demonic potion of burning resin and boiling wax.

"Pardon, my God!" Damiens screamed to the local priest, who had come to hear his confession. "Pardon, Lord!"

The executioners next tied ropes to his upper arms and thighs, harnessed the ends to four horses, and urged the animals to a gallop. Unfortunately for Damiens, the horses were strangers to the business of quartering, and they failed to pull him apart. Growing desperate, the executioners now drew out their knives and slit his shoulders and hips. The horses tugged mightily, causing the agonized man to cry, "My God, have pity on me!"

At last his legs came off, but his arms remained in place. Again the executioners went to work, sawing through his muscles until their knives scraped bone. The horses tugged once more, and finally the right arm came loose, followed by the left. Still alive, Damiens somehow managed to sit up and survey what he'd become, a torso with a brain. He was not quite dead when they raised him aloft, threw him onto a pile of logs, and set the pyre ablaze.

To tell you the truth, I'm glad the age of the *amende honorable* is over. Being the Devil, I naturally favor capital punishment, but I believe a simple hanging or electrocution will suffice in most cases. As Damiens's death demonstrates, torture is a system too easily abused. I think it's unconscionable that four well-meaning horses were humiliated in public when the executioners could easily have taken them from their stables the night before and taught them how to quarter. If there's one thing I can't stand, it's cruelty to animals.

❖

The Idea of the Moon stood at its highest by the time the Hiddekel was reborn, each channel melding with its parent stream, whereupon Belphegor throttled down, dropped anchor, and retired to the berths. Ten minutes later a snoring sound arose: a hoarse, oddly mechanical buzz, like a Hollywood chainsaw hooker pursuing her vocation. His father, Martin recalled, had also been a prodigious snorer, a refreshing touch of corporeality in a man who otherwise seemed not quite of this Earth.

As the night deepened, Martin and Augustine sat talking atop the forecastle—or, rather, Augustine talked and Martin listened. He didn't mind. The bishop's diatribes were considerably more entertaining than Saperstein's moody silences, Beauchamp's oblique jokes, Ockham's incomprehensible cosmologizing, and Belphegor's endless enumerations of the reasons *Blood Feast* was a better movie than *The Corpse Grinders*.

Besides concupiscence, the human failing that most angered Augustine was heresy. "For thirty long years I battled the Donatists in my bishopric. I fined them, evicted them from public office, revoked their civil rights, exiled their clerics—and in the end, thanks be to God, I prevailed."

"You wiped them out?" asked Martin.

"I wiped them out. Show me one practicing Donatist in the Commonwealth of Pennsylvania."

"There aren't any."

"Indeed. I had to fight Pelagius's followers just as hard, and once again the Lord granted me victory. I'll wager not one of your friends is a Pelagian, right?"

"Not as far as I know."

"Nary a Manichaean in your crowd either."

"No Manichaeans."

"I tell you, sir, non-Catholic Christianity has no future."

"What about Protestantism?"

"Protestantism? Pshaw! Next door to idolatry, with the Bible instead of a golden calf. Believe me, Mr. Candle, Protestantism won't last over the long haul. It hasn't got the teeth."

A second noise now filled the air, as regular as Belphegor's vibrating palate. Without exchanging a word, Martin and Augustine rose and, following the insistent *thunk-thunk-thunk,* crept furtively toward the stern.

Dressed in a watch cap, pea jacket, and sailor's bell-bottoms, a gnarled, bearded man leaned over the bulwark, his hands locked around the shaft of an iron-headed ax. With each successive chop, the intruder came closer to separating the *Good Intention*'s rudder from her transom.

"What do you think you're doing?" demanded Augustine.

Startled, the ancient mariner lurched backward, swinging the ax in a wide circle and missing Martin's left breast by barely an inch.

"I *knew* I'd never get away with it," the mariner moaned.

"Explain yourself!" said Augustine.

"Perhaps I should've requested your permission—'Excuse me, might I make off with your rudder?'—but I deemed your assent unlikely."

"Of *course* you can't have our rudder," Martin snapped. "We need it to reach the Garden."

"What ails you, sir?" Augustine asked the mariner. "In the whole of Genesis, there lives no nobler hero than Noah. Your present behavior baffles me."

The Idea of Noah pulled off his watch cap and pointed toward the northern levee. Glazed with moonbeams, a mooring line as thick as a fire hose ran from the *Good Intentions* to an immense houseboat lashed to a weatherbeaten wharf. Corroded by spray, lacerated by gales, the ark had clearly seen better days. She looked completely deserted—no predators crept along her decks; no birds nested on her roof; no giraffes poked their heads through her skylights.

"Do you know what an ark is?" asked Noah. "I mean, do you really *know*?"

"An ark is a ship," said Martin.

"Wrong!" said Noah. "Wrong! Wrong! A ship has a rudder. A ship has a sail. You can steer a ship where you want her to go. But an ark? Nothing but a bottle tossed into the sea, bobbing about at the mercy of winds and currents. Even as we speak, Sarkos is making me a canvas sail. I'm picking it up tomorrow."

"You're too late," said Augustine.

"No," said Noah.

"They're all dead."

"No, they're not. I'm going back."

"They're dead—every last one."

Turning, Noah presented Martin with the sort of crazed countenance he associated with the dipsomaniacs who'd routinely paraded through the Abaddon Municipal Building during his JP days. "All I need is a rudder and a sail," said the mariner. Craggy and pitted, his features suggested the blasted terrain surrounding Sodom. "Do you know how it feels to slam the door in the faces of eighty-seven million people, guaranteeing their doom? Do you know what it's like to huddle with your wife and sons in a leaky cabin, hearing the sounds of ten thousand species as the floodwaters drag them down? Their cries fill my dreams. Their eyes haunt my sleep. I'm going back."

"Waste of time," said Augustine.

Noah slid the ax handle across his neck, balancing the tool atop his shoulders like a yoke. "You really think so?"

"Yes—and you do too." Augustine lit his briar pipe and sucked on the stem, the burning tobacco glowing red in the coagulated gloom. "Behold, Mr. Candle: the hidden harmony defense," he said, indicating the ark with a dramatic sweep of his arm. "To the outside observer—a visitor from Mars—a worldwide flood looks like a bad thing. Our naive spaceman wouldn't realize that every victim of this disaster was wicked beyond redemption. If God hadn't eradicated Noah's entire generation, the Earth today would be crawling with adulterers, sybarites, and malefactors."

"Father knows best," said Martin dryly.

"Yes, that's one way to put it," said Augustine. "Read Thomas Aquinas's *Summa theologiae*—read Julian of Norwich's

Book of Showings and Meister Eckhart's *Sermons*—and you'll see that God in His day not only tolerated floods, earthquakes, tornadoes—"

"Prostate cancer."

"—and other so-called evils, He actively *cultivated* them . . . though always, of course, for the sake of a greater good."

"If we could but grasp the divine plan," added Noah with an unapologetic sneer, "we would learn to love a lesion, make friends with anthrax, and invite tuberculosis over for tea."

"Well, let's not push it," said Augustine.

"No, *let's* push it," said Noah. "If we're not going to take the problem of evil seriously, we might as least have some *fun* with it."

"In the entire history of Western civilization," protested the bishop, "no man has ever taken the problem of evil more seriously than Augustine of Hippo Regius."

"Until I came along," said Martin.

"Don't flatter yourself."

Noah fixed his gaze on Martin. "Judge Candle, yes? *International 227?*"

"At your service."

"You've set yourself a fearsome task."

"I know."

"Not as fearsome as cramming an entire biosphere into a three-hundred-cubit ark, but still fearsome." Noah put his cap back on, pulling it down over his ears. "Once we landed on Ararat, our troubles continued to multiply—Lord, such problems! The bears couldn't stand each other. I had to become an ursine marriage counselor. The elephant was impotent. We resorted to artificial insemination. The kangaroo's mate kept having miscarriages. I've got a thousand stories. No survivors? Really?"

"No survivors," said Augustine.

"I'm going back."

"Futile, Noah. F-U-T-I-L-E."

A prolonged sigh escaped the mariner's lips. He slumped onto the afterdeck. "Here," he said at last, handing Martin the ax. "You can make better use of this than I. It will vaporize eventually, but meanwhile you should take it to The Hague. Tell the judges it's the very tool with which I felled the trees for my ark. Tell them that—in Noah's opinion—the hidden harmony defense runs counter to all our best instincts as human beings."

Martin leaned the ax against the bulwark and offered the mariner a corroborating smile. "When an upright citizen hears his neighbor has met with an earthquake or a hurricane, he doesn't stop to ask, 'Is there a hidden harmony here?' He rolls up his sleeves and tries to help."

"Exactly." With an athleticism that defied his years, Noah regained his feet and climbed onto the long, taut mooring line. "If I learned one thing from the Deluge, Your Grace, it is this: a man who seals up his ark for the sake of a greater good is a man who has ceded his soul to chaos." Slowly, cautiously, he tightrope-walked toward the rudderless vessel. "The hidden harmony defense is pornography, Bishop Augustine—pornography for priests!"

"You're wrong!" Augustine called after the retreating sailor.

"You're right!" shouted Martin.

"Read your Aquinas! Aquinas, Noah, Aquinas!"

The mariner jumped from the mooring line to the weather deck of his ark. "The moose was gay! The lioness was a lesbian! You don't know what I've been through! You simply can't imagine!"

❖

For two tedious and sleepy days the *Good Intentions* continued on her westward course, the remorseless sun pounding on her decks, the ravenous mosquitoes relentlessly pricking Martin and the scientists. The passing countryside was a parched wasteland crawling with outsized scorpions, their abdomens curving upward like scythes. Skeletons dotted the terrain as well—human skeletons, posed in tableaux alluding to various Renaissance masterworks.

"The Valley of Dry Bones," Augustine explained as the packet cruised past a deathly rendition of Botticelli's *Birth of Venus* and a meatless reconstruction of Raphael's *School of Athens*. "Ezekiel, chapter thirty-seven."

"I'm sure of one thing—those boneheads can't tell us whether Fermat proved Fermat," said Beauchamp.

"Nor do they know how the spirochetes adhere," said Saperstein.

"I'm beginning to think this expedition was a mistake," said Ockham, videotaping a flayed facsimile of Michelangelo's *Fall of Man*.

On the third day there appeared a population of skeletons who—far from behaving like the dead—had undertaken to stage *Crabs*, a musical revue that, according to Augustine, "aimed to do for T. S. Eliot's serious poetry what *Cats* accomplished for his lighter verse." Dressed in top hats and tails, the skeletons threw their arms around each other's clavicles and did a kick dance as they sang "The Love Song of J. Alfred Prufrock" to a lush, Andrew Lloyd Webber–ian melody.

> *I should have been a pair of ragged claws*
> *Scuttling across the floors of silent seas.*

The skeletons began to waltz.

> *"I am Lazarus, come from the dead,*
> *Come back to tell you all . . ."*

For Martin, *Crabs* was both highly entertaining and supremely puzzling. Had God conjured up this extravaganza merely to torment him? The ex-JP hardly needed to be reminded that a carcinomic crustacean had colonized his pelvis and thighs; the constant pain informed him of its ever-expanding authority. Perhaps *Crabs* was God's idea of humor. If so, then which was worse: getting the joke, or not getting it?

From: *selkirk2@aol.org*
To: *marcand@prodigy.edu*
Date: *Fri, May 19, 10:46 AM EDT*

I sent Lovett a telegram as you suggested, and an hour ago he called from a pay phone in Harvard Square. He gave me the identities of his three "theological witnesses" but refused to divulge anything further. In Lovett's words, "I feel no more obligated to reveal the whole of my strategy than Henry did to contact the French before Agincourt and warn them about the English longbow."

Evidently we're up against the following superstars: Bernard Kaplan (a rabbi from Fitchburg, Massachusetts), Eleanor Swann (a Yale Divinity School professor), and Brother Sebastian Cranach (a Franciscan monk living in Olean, New York). I've hired a half dozen hungry Harvard grad students—Ph.D. candidates in philosophy—to assemble dossiers on all three. The rabbi and the academic don't give me much pause, but I'm scared of that monk.

Our plan to show A History of Havoc *during Tonia Braverman's testimony has hit a snag. PBS doesn't want to give the series "a world première by default" over Court TV and CNN, and when I faxed Torvald a motion asking him to subpoena the thing, he turned us down flat. I'm hoping a serious donation will change the network's mind.*

Martin glanced up from the laptop screen. The living skeletons were animating yet another "Prufrock" stanza, singing lines that—thirty-four years after he'd first heard them in Mr. Gianassio's class—still gave him a frisson.

> *I have seen the moment of my greatness flicker,*
> *And I have seen the eternal Footman hold my coat, and*
> *   snicker,*
> *And in short, I was afraid.*

An antique hearse clattered across the Valley of Dry Bones, pulled by four horses so aged and diseased they made the carousel ponies back in Celestial City USA seem like Kentucky Derby winners. The driver reined up, hobbled around to the rear of the hearse, and yanked open the door. An oblong wooden coffin tumbled out, striking the ground and shattering to reveal the corpse of a man without any arms or legs.

From: marcand@prodigy.edu
To: selkirk2@aol.org
Date: Sun, May 21, 03:19 PM Local Time

Maybe Lovett regards himself as another Henry V, but I think of him more as Falstaff: large and self-indulgent. Is Lovett's Rabbi Kaplan the same Rabbi Kaplan who wrote that best-seller called When You Walk Through a Storm? *He's going to make a pretty sympathetic defense witness. My Aunt Bridget gave me his book, but I never read it. She says Kaplan's philosophy helped her get over Uncle Wilmer's death.*

As for the PBS crisis, I think we should offer them a donation of, say, $165,000. They can express their gratitude by giving us a Wall Street Week *coffee mug, a Big Bird T-shirt, and the right to screen* A History of Havoc *in* The Hague.

Martin was pleased to discover that Esther, too, had written back.

From: esthclute@aol.org
To: marcand@prodigy.edu
Date: Fri, May 19, 11:08 AM EDT

You said you'd like a more exotic pathology, and I think I've got just the ticket, amyotrophic lateral sclerosis: Lou Gehrig's disease. From our meetings you may recall Christopher Ransom, the young man who talks using a computerized voice synthesizer. His medical bills are horrendous, and he's been hinting he'd like a serious fee. Does $85,000 sound about right to you? I'm also working on Norma Bedloe, that woman with the defective liver who has to swallow 67 pills a day. I think she'd be sensational on the stand. The problem is that Norma plans to kill herself as soon as she figures out how to do it.

Did Randall tell you the news? God's optic neuron is no longer with us. The poor fellow simply disintegrated, in the middle of an Oprah taping. There's nothing left, but they're giving it a funeral anyway.

Martin greeted the neuron's passing with unalloyed anxiety. When alive, the creature had never quite won humankind over; that luminous little genius had made most people feel inadequate. In death, however, it would inevitably garner sympathy. *Gee, it was cute. Golly, it was smart.* And now here comes the Job Society, bent on killing its five billion brethren. The popularity of *International 227*, he feared, was about to reach a new low.

"Your friend is gone," he told Saperstein.

"My friend?"

"The optic neuron—gone to its reward."

"Lost the will to live, I suspect," said Saperstein.

"Like a honeybee cut off from the hive," said Ockham.

"I know the feeling." Martin's fingers scurried across the computer keyboard. "It hit me last November, when Barbara Meredith beat me by eleven thousand votes, and I found myself without a jurisdiction."

From: marcand@prodigy.edu
To: esthclute@aol.org
Date: Sun, May 21, 03:43 PM Local Time

Pay Ransom any amount he desires up to $100,000. Amyotrophic lateral sclerosis is just what the doctor ordered. Yes, I remember Norma Bedloe vividly. You simply must convince her to postpone her suicide. I want to make her our lead-off victim.

Shortly after the scientists went below for their customary siestas, the Hiddekel began to change. Bubbles rose from the river's depths, as if its waters had mysteriously transmuted into champagne. Coils of steam sinuated across the surface like ghosts of departed eels.

"Holy shit, it's boiling!" shouted Belphegor. "The goddamn river's boiling!"

"Steady," said Augustine. Reaching through the wheelhouse window, he laid a calming hand on the demon's shoulder. "Steady . . . steady . . ."

"The river's evaporating! We'll get stuck on the bottom!"

"You're being irrational," Augustine informed Belphegor.

"Maybe we should speed up a bit," suggested Martin, palms sweating, heart pounding.

"Good idea," said Belphegor.

"Bad idea," said Augustine. "It would annoy him."

"Him?" said Martin.

Augustine pointed north. "Him."

Directly off the *Good Intentions*'s bow, a gigantic fire-breathing creature—an uncanny amalgam of crocodile, Chinese dragon, and blast furnace—swam in tandem with the packet. Flames shot from its nostrils like rocket exhaust, imparting a brilliant red glow to the waters. Rotating on their axes, its eyes emitted sharp pulsing shafts of purple light.

"Leviathan?" asked Martin.

"Leviathan," Augustine corroborated. "The second great Jobian beast. 'He makes the deep water boil like a caldron.'"

"Our hull's gonna melt!" screamed Belphegor. "*Zizz, sizzle*—and *bang*, we're in the river, gettin' cooked like a bunch of lobsters!"

"Take it easy," said Augustine. "It's ontologically impossible for heated water to melt steel. Have we an adequate coal supply?"

"Plenty of coal, yes! That dragon's gonna cook us and eat us!"

"By nightfall he'll grow weary of the chase. Believe me, Belphegor, the law of entropy holds everywhere, even in here."

"I hate this job! I wanted to be a first baseman!"

Hour after hour, the sea monster and the packet steamer pursued their parallel courses down the burbling Hiddekel. Martin couldn't say which river dweller exuded more smoke that afternoon: the dragon or the *Good Intentions*. He knew only that the law of entropy couldn't kick in soon enough to suit him.

"'He leaves a great shining trail behind him,'" quoted Augustine, "'and the great river is like white hair in his wake.'"

Eventually Belphegor decided that ridding themselves of the monster would require nothing less than a human sacrifice, a procedure for which he blithely nominated Martin as the sine qua non. "It's basic Christianity, Your Grace," the demon explained. "We must give the Devil a ransom in exchange for our salvation."

"Basic Christianity," echoed Augustine mockingly. "Right. Except Leviathan is not Jonathan Sarkos, and Martin Candle— I assure you—is not Jesus Christ."

"You never run out of things to say, do you?" grunted Belphegor.

"There will be no more talk of human sacrifice aboard the *Good Intentions*."

As twilight crept across God's western hemisphere, the bishop's prophecy at last came true: the monster, exhausted, fell back to the packet's stern, then faded farther still, then vanished. The Hiddekel grew placid. Its waters cooled. When Belphegor offered Martin a can of Budweiser, he chugged it down eagerly. He asked for another. Only after consuming his third Bud did he begin to feel calm, though his mental picture of Leviathan remained vivid, hovering in his mind's eye like a flashbulb afterimage. Inevitably he thought of the courtroom strategy God had employed in the Book of Job. Change the subject. Pretend the topic isn't justice but mystery, then rattle your accuser with Creation's most disquieting beasts.

"I see now why it worked," he told Augustine. "I see now why Job wet his pants and repented."

❖

In the morning the Hiddekel changed once again, becoming a kind of open sewer, its odor so vile that Belphegor's Stygian breath seemed perfume by comparison. The leukocytes, poisoned, began dying in droves. The blood flow grew clotted with obese, long-tailed rats, each as big as a beaver. A prolific species of algae soon claimed the river, riding its currents like an immense carpet and covering the adjacent levees with a creamy green scum.

"The agony of Abraham moves me to tears," Augustine told Martin. "The fate of Lot's wife is wrenching beyond words.

Noah's guilt is the stuff of Greek tragedy." The bishop tapped his index finger on the pink itinerary. "When it comes to world-class victimhood, however, one name looms above all others. Here in the Country of Dung, you will meet the man who practically *invented* suffering."

This time around, the scientists declined to join the expedition. As Saperstein put it, "Job probably knows as much about spirochetes as a cow knows about Sunday."

Belphegor docked the steamer skillfully, enabling Martin and Augustine to clamber directly from ship to shore. The bishop led the way, guiding Martin through a landscape of smoldering fumaroles and smoking cinder cones. Within forty minutes their destination appeared: history's most famous dung heap, a thirty-foot mountain of ordure, guano, cow flops, buffalo chips, and coprolites, its stench so benumbing that Martin momentarily forgot the pitiless campaign the crab was waging against his pelvis.

"Hello, Judge Candle—I've been expecting you!" a raspy voice called out from above. "Come on up!"

Chewing a painkiller, Martin glanced heavenward. A cadaverous, hollow-eyed man sat on a rusty beer keg atop the heap, dressed in a shredded Crash Test Dummies T-shirt and a tattered red bathing suit. Boils and open sores speckled his skin. He was scraping himself with a Tupperware lid.

"I guess you know you're my hero!" shouted Martin toward the summit.

"I've always admired you too!" yelled Augustine. "The faith of Job can move mountains!"

"If not dung heaps!" cried the Idea of Job, gripped by a cough so catastrophic his body fluttered like a spinnaker in a gale.

Computer in hand, Martin began to ascend the holy mound. Garbage and trash lay embedded in the slope, along with dozens of castoff appliances: blenders, toasters, washing machines. With each squashy step his pulse rate quickened and his joy increased.

He laughed out loud. At long last he'd attained his idol's abode—the burning heart of sacred rage! For the scientists, only the pineal gland would satisfy, but Martin needed nothing more right now than these consecrated coffee grounds, egg shells, and banana peels, these numinous Coke bottles, disposable diapers, and dolls' heads.

Panting and sweating, he reached the summit, at which instant the Idea of Job got up from his beer keg, took him by the arm, and guided him toward a blue plastic picnic cooler. Bright yellow pus leaked from the sufferer's lesions, dribbling down his chest and crisscrossing his stomach. He looked as if he'd been tattooed with a road map.

"Keeping watch here on my heap, day after day, I naturally recall your masterful handling of the Spinelli affair," said Job. "Your sense of justice is acute."

A flush of pride warmed Martin's innards. "Thank you," he said, settling onto the picnic cooler and flipping open his computer.

Martin remembered the Spinelli case well. It revolved around the three-dollar fee charged by an Abaddonian named Schuyler Phelps for the use of the bathroom in his business establishment, Glendale Lawn and Garden Supplies. When Douglas Spinelli's aging mother ended up staining her favorite dress with diarrhea as a result of Phelps's policy, her son enacted a creative revenge. One Saturday afternoon, Spinelli strode into Glendale Lawn and Garden Supplies, paid his three dollars, entered the bathroom, and six minutes later emerged holding a paper bag containing a large and malodorous fecal sample. In full view of Phelps's shocked customers, Spinelli dumped the turd on the counter and said to the young cashier, "Here you are, mademoiselle—may I have my security deposit back now?" Phelps sued Spinelli for disrupting the store's normal operations, and Spinelli countersued Phelps for practicing a kind of gastrointestinal extortion. Martin threw the first case out of court and, turning to the second, ruled that Phelps must not only replace Mrs. Spinelli's dress but henceforth allow anyone to visit his bathroom free of charge.

The view from the dung heap was breathtaking. Scanning the neural landscape, Martin felt as if he were watching a movie flashback chronicling the last four days of his life. The Valley of Dry Bones was near enough for him to discern the living skeletons, still acting out *Crabs*. Beyond lay the docked ark, the ruins of Sodom, and Mount Moriah. Along the horizon stretched the glimmering black ribbon of the dinosaurs' mudflat.

"This heap is all mine, I'll have you know," said Job proudly. "Squatter's rights." Reaching into the dung, he pulled out a TV remote control. "For many years, I considered moving elsewhere—I even had a nice little apartment picked out, right next door to Sarkos's shop—but then we got cable, and I decided to stay." He pointed the device toward a forlorn and filthy Magnavox television set. "For the past three years, God's Idea of CBS has been producing a daytime serial of my life, *One Man's Misery*. Stick around, and we'll watch it together. My youngest daughter's in a coma. My eldest just learned she's HIV positive. Okay, sure, after the story runs its course, I'll get three brand-new daughters and seven brand-new sons—all as good as the originals, better in fact—but that's hardly *realistic* now, is it? Life is not a fairy tale."

"For those of us who permit God's grace to operate within our souls, life is *better* than a fairy tale!" Augustine called out as he started up the northern face of the heap.

"I believed that once too," said Job, activating his Magnavox. "No more."

The screen blossomed with a mid-shot of Gregory Peck playing Captain Ahab in *Moby-Dick*. "Look ye into its deeps and see the everlasting slaughter that goes on," said Peck, standing on the deck of the *Pequod* and inviting Leo Genn as Starbuck to contemplate the cosmic mystery of the sea. "Who put it into its creatures to chase and fang one another? Where do murderers go, man? Who's to doom when the Judge Himself is dragged before the bar?"

"Your protégé didn't come here to watch television," said Augustine, gaining the top of the mound. A sardonic smile curled the corners of his vast mouth. "He came to hear about the ontological defense."

"The ontological defense," echoed Job, growing suddenly lugubrious.

"Why don't you dismantle it for us? Go ahead, sir, tear it to pieces . . ."

Job shut off the TV, bit his lower lip, and frowned. "Give me a minute."

"Take all the time you want." Augustine turned, offering Martin a grin that revealed a majority of his teeth. "The ontological defense asserts, quite reasonably, that God is the only Perfect Being. All other realities, including the created universe, necessarily occupy a lower plane." Pinching his nostrils shut, the bishop plucked a moldering slice of Swiss cheese from the dung. "Because the created universe is ontologically inferior to God, it must ipso facto contain defects. If the world were flawless, it would *be* God. According to this solution"—he stuck his index finger through a hole—"reality is like Swiss cheese. Inevitably it contains gaps . . . privations . . . pockets of nothingness. You may call these holes 'evil' if you like, but God had no hand in their creation—noncreation, I should say. They occur *per accidens,* accruing unavoidably to the sheer brute fact of existence." He extracted a discarded pair of Nikes. "God certainly never *wanted* His creatures to suffer, but if He was going to fashion a cosmos bursting with plenitude and variety, a world of shoes and ships and sealing wax"—he banged the Nikes together—"then imperfections had to be part of the package."

Swiss cheese defense, Martin typed onto his hard drive. *Evil as privation.* "Can you help me out here?" he asked Job.

Placing the Tupperware lid against his chest, the sufferer scraped away the exudate of a particularly juicy lesion. "You've read my biography, Mr. Candle. 'Where were you when I laid the Earth's foundations?' God asked me, rhetorically. 'Have you descended to the springs of the sea or walked in the unfathomable deep? Have you visited the storehouse of the snow or seen the arsenal where hail is kept?' Many years later, I realized He wasn't just trying to humble me. He was reminding me that the universe *exists*. For reasons known only to Himself, a finite set of law-abiding realities occupies time and space. Most of these realities are harmless, beautiful even, but a few of them—storms, gravity, plate tectonics, microorganisms, Behemoth, Leviathan—can have undesirable side effects. This doesn't mean He *intended* such results, nor does it mean He never suspended His own rules. Occasionally, as the school bus started to hurtle over the cliff, the pre-coma God would yank it back. Sometimes He would shrink the tumor or cancel the cyclone. But whenever He did so, He inevitably absorbed a piece of the cosmos back into Himself—and if He'd kept at it, intervention after intervention, the differentiated universe would have disappeared altogether, leaving Him alone again, back on square one."

"Okay, okay, but what's the *answer* to the ontological defense?" asked Martin.

"The answer?"

"The answer."

Job sighed profoundly. He coughed up a wad of mucus interlaced with blood and spat it onto the heap. "I don't know of any," he said at last. "Do you?" he asked Augustine.

"There isn't one."

A sharp pain tore through Martin's torso. He felt as if a wild horse had just kicked him in the tits. "No answer?" he rasped, glowering at Augustine and rising from the picnic cooler. "*No answer?* You mean I traveled two hundred miles up a stinking river, got bitten by ten dozen monster mosquitoes, and listened to your stupid harangues against the Pelagians and whatnot just so I could be told there's *no answer?*!"

"You're surprised, aren't you?" said Augustine. "You're

shocked. Don't be. The ontological defense has been *centuries* in the making, beginning with Plato's classic meditations on the nonbeing of evil." Wryly he raised his right eyebrow and started to descend the heap. "We'd best return to the boat. Assuming Belphegor can work up a good head of steam, we'll be in Eden by dusk tomorrow."

Coughing convulsively, Job threw out his arms, pressed his chest against Martin's, and gave him a fervent hug. Despite the interposition of his cotton jersey, Martin could still feel the warm pus oozing from the sufferer's lesions.

"I've let you down, haven't I?"

"I'm afraid so," said Martin, breaking their embrace.

"I'd like to say I'm hurt by what Augustine just did to me"—Job settled back onto his beer keg—"but a theological humiliation is nothing compared to fourteen boils on your ass. Keep that in mind when you get to Holland."

Chapter 9

No sooner had Martin returned to the *Good Intentions* than it began to rain—a thick, cold, gray downpour echoing the dismal condition of his mood. He stared at the river. Relentlessly the drops descended, speckling the Hiddekel with concentric circles and causing it to resemble a gigantic slice of Swiss cheese. A tremulous moan escaped his lips. There had to be an answer to the ontological defense, there simply *had* to be, but he was damned if he could think of one.

The latest e-mail did nothing to lift his spirits. Esther reported that Norma Bedloe still hadn't decided whether to kill herself posthaste or wait until after she'd testified. Randall recounted a frustrating conversation he'd had with a PBS lawyer named James Foley. According to Foley, his clients would let the Job Society show *A History of Havoc* in The Hague for a one hundred and sixty-five thousand dollar donation only if the news media agreed to point their cameras elsewhere. PBS feared that people would tape the series at home, thereby cutting into the network's profits from videocassette sales. Confronted with this stipulation, Court TV and CNN had both voiced the same reaction: you must be kidding.

In drafting his reply, Martin found himself more anxious to

talk about his misadventures on the dung heap than about Randall's difficulties with public television. "We've had a major setback here—a virtually impregnable theory of evil. How smart are those Harvard kids you hired? Tell them there's a $15,000 bonus waiting for whoever can counter the 'ontological defense.'" Only at the end of his memo did Martin address the *History of Havoc* crisis. "This nonsense about wanting Court TV and CNN to look the other way during the screening is clearly just a ploy. Find out how much PBS sank into the series and offer to buy it outright. We've still got about $8,700,000 to play with."

At midnight the rain finally stopped, and by morning the *Good Intentions* had steamed far beyond the Country of Dung, reaching her destination late that afternoon, just as Augustine had predicted.

"The Garden of Eden," the bishop said to Martin and the scientists, tapping the itinerary with the bowl of his briar pipe. "Any man who seeks to solve the riddle of iniquity must eventually end up here."

On both sides of the river a dense wilderness thrived, a sprawling expanse of spastic trees and writhing vines. The aggressive stench of decaying vegetation clogged the air. If this was the Garden of Eden, it was a decidedly postlapsarian one, Martin mused—an Eden gone to seed. Cypresses and mangroves grew everywhere, their roots arching out of the water like immense rib cages, their branches laden with fruit resembling the heads of medieval maces. Along the southern shore huge spiders spun webs so vast that parrots and lemurs were becoming ensnared in them. A particularly rapacious specimen of Venus flytrap ruled the opposite bank, crushing entire cockatoos in its jaws as it went about the business of survival.

"I assume this was a less violent place before the coma struck," said Martin.

"Not really, no," replied Augustine. "It was the Fall of Man, not the stasis of God, that made Paradise a jungle. Ever since Eve ravaged the Tree of Knowledge, the universe has been a place of thorns and nettles, fangs and claws, germs and vermin."

The Hiddekel narrowed and began to undulate, as if mimicking the seductive Serpent who'd once inhabited these climes. Beyond the thirteenth bend a clearing appeared, a two-acre stretch of hardscrabble land on which creatures of manifest intelligence had established a homestead, including a bamboo hut with a stone chimney and thatched roof. The front yard featured a vegetable plot where failure was the norm—marble-sized tomatoes, cabbages no larger than carnations, string beans that looked more like strings than beans—while the side yard boasted a hammock woven of sisal fibers, slung between a pair of ginkgo trees like a disembodied grin.

Dressed in leopard skins and fig leaves, two anthropoid apes of opposite genders approached the hammock on brown, unshod feet. Their gaits were slow and halting, as if they'd only recently learned to walk upright, an impression reinforced by their prognathous jaws, beetle brows, and sloping foreheads. The male was bent and hairy. The female was similarly hirsute, her sagging breasts evoking the sandbags employed by hot-air balloonists, but her most notable feature was her abdomen: she was as dramatically pregnant as Lot's daughters.

"Hello!" called Martin. "Hello, there! Might I have a moment of your time?"

Only after the female ape had eased her gravid body into the hammock did Martin realize she was in labor. As the distracted creature squirmed and jerked, panting through gritted teeth, the male hugged her shaggy arm and lovingly kissed her palm.

"Millennia ago, that creature bent his free will toward a wicked purpose, eating the fruit he'd been told to eschew," Augustine explained, taking off his horn-rimmed glasses and pointing them toward the male hominid. "After his transgression, concupiscence infected every cell of his flesh. His semen became the carrier of his depravity, passing sin and death from generation to generation."

"The free will defense?" asked Martin.

"Indubitably," said Augustine.

"Does anyone know what species they belong to?" Ockham asked his colleagues as he focused his camcorder on the homestead. "*Homo habilis*, perhaps?"

"*Australopithecus?*" ventured Martin.

"Neanderthal?" suggested Belphegor.

"Behold his salacious gaze," said Augustine. "Note his priapic posture. With revolting regularity the rampant member he conceals beneath that leaf grows hard with blood."

"Ah . . . *Homo erectus!*" said Beauchamp, laughing.

"In point of fact, you're right," said Saperstein.

"Hello," Martin shouted again. "I'm Martin Candle, *International 227!*"

"Can't you see we're busy?" cried the male *Homo erectus*.

"Go 'way!" yelled the female.

"Come back tomorrow!" screamed the male.

"*Eeeiiiooowww!*" shrieked the female, seized by a sudden contraction.

❖

Some things never change. The process by which the male *Homo erectus* fertilized his common-law wife has endured without modification until the present day.

Return with me now to that wonderful year 2,000,000,001 B.C. It was a time of beginnings. Our Creator was working around the clock. Contrary to popular myth, the first animal to emerge from His lab wasn't a paramecium, fish, tree shrew, or any other lowly form—it was a human being. God said, "Let there be a prototype for *Homo sapiens*," and there *was* a prototype for *Homo sapiens*: a featureless creature resembling a department-store mannequin. God saw that the prototype was good, but He also saw that it lacked a way to replicate itself. Before the week was out He'd invented an encoded copying mechanism predicated on double helices of DNA. Problem: how to meld one set of chromosomes with the other?

Among His strengths in those days was His ability to delegate authority, so He put the question to the archangel Zaphiel, who forthwith consulted the rest of the heavenly host. In a matter of days Raphael, Michael, Adabiel, and Gabriel had each devised an elegant solution, but it was the strategies of Hamiel and Chamuel that Zaphiel sensed would garner divine approval. Just as Zaphiel was about to submit these two designs, I brought him a plan of my own. Beaming with a combination of deviltry and pride, I unfurled my blueprint before the archangel.

"If this is mere whimsy on your part," said Zaphiel, "I'm afraid I have better things to do with my time."

"Hear me out. My great breakthrough, as you can see, was to re-imagine the prototype as a duality: Variation One and Variation Two."

"They look the same to me."

I tapped the blueprint with the claw of my taloned index finger. "Note this detail on Variation One. Tab A."

"Don't they each get one?"

"Look closer."

"Oh."

"The system relies on Variation One periodically entering a state I call 'procreative arousal.' When this happens, Tab A stiffens with blood—"

"How baroque."

"—thereby permitting its insertion into Slot B on Two. After an unpredictable interval of enthusiastic forward and backward thrusting—"

"Backward what?"

"Thrusting."

"I don't get it."

"Trust me. After an interval of thrusting, several ounces of viscous fluid spurt from a storage compartment inside One. Adrift in the fluid are several hundred million DNA-bearing germ cells that, arriving inside Slot B, begin wriggling their tails, employing them to—"

"—scrape the inner walls and sculpt homunculi from the protoplasm!"

"—reach the terminus of Slot B, where a Variation Two germ cell awaits, likewise abrim with DNA."

"Yes, good, your way's better."

"The resulting zygote matures inside Two, becoming a viable infant within six or seven months. After month nine has elapsed, give or take a week, the infant is expelled through Slot B, whereupon it grows to adulthood, a process that consumes about two decades. So . . . what do you think?"

"It's complicated."

"It works."

"What causes the 'procreative arousal' in One?"

"It's largely an instinctual response to certain features of Two. Knobs C and D, for example."

"What's so special about a couple of mangoes?"

"Nothing. That's the poetry of it."

"Why not give Two something more intrinsically exciting?"

"Like what?"

"I don't know. Baked Alaska."

"You're not really with me on this, are you?"

"May I assume that before a One can achieve 'procreative arousal' it must wish to reproduce?"

"The arousal arrives unbidden."

"Oh?"

"Sometimes a One will even find itself aroused by *another* One, and vice-versa."

"Can they obtain relief under such circumstances?"

"That's where Slot E comes in."

"What are those bumpy things growing out of One's shoulders? Lily pads?"

"Floopers."

"They look like lily pads."

"Normally a One will keep its floopers clothed. As soon as a Two sees a pair of naked floopers, Slot B becomes—"

"—covered with blue polka dots and yellow—"

"—lubricious, thereby allowing the insertion of Tab A to proceed with minimal friction."

"Lily pads can do that?"

"It's all in the programming."

"And you really need two different versions of the prototype?"

"My first draft had five."

"Know what, Mr. Sarkos? Before I visit Him tomorrow, I'm going to slip your plan in between Hamiel's and Chamuel's. I think He'll be quite amused. Let me make a suggestion, though."

"Sure."

"Take out the lily pads. They aren't nearly as funny as the rest of it."

❖

Not only did the female hominid survive the birthing process, she was up and about within an hour of expelling and eating the placenta, making jasmine tea for Martin and his associates as they lounged on the straw mats that crisscrossed the floor of her hut. Her name was Evangeline, and for a first-time mother she was remarkably confident, as if she'd been founding the human race all her life. Clarence, the new arrival, lay prone on a comforter stuffed with cockatoo feathers, babbling to himself in a manner so sweet as to constitute, Martin felt, a prima facie case against Augustine's theory of original sin.

"I hesitate to contradict anyone as learned as you," said Evangeline, filling the bishop's ceramic tea mug from a red earthenware pot. The ape sat down. "But much of what you say in *Opus imperfectum contra Julianum* doesn't go over well with us."

"Oh?" said Augustine warily.

"When you indict my husband's seed as the ultimate source of humanity's woes, I find myself moved to defend him."

"I would assume His Grace was speaking metaphorically," said Ockham. "Weren't you?" he asked the bishop.

"Don't I wish," Augustine replied, directing his Svengali gaze toward the male hominid. "A person's depravity is every bit as genetic as the color of his eyes. When you so flagrantly abused your free will, sir, disobeying a direct order from your Creator, you polluted not only your own semen but also the semen of your progeny, the semen of your progeny's progeny, the semen of your progeny's progeny's progeny, and so on. The Fall of Man touches everyone conceived from that foul fluid— a population embracing all persons except, of course, our Lord and Savior, Jesus Christ. Every time a child is born with spina bifida, every time a maniac with a machine gun opens fire in a crowded restaurant, the tragedy bespeaks the fatal events that occurred upriver from this homestead."

Saperstein snickered unapologetically, then turned toward Martin and said, "If I were you, I wouldn't lose too much sleep over this free will defense. Evidently it derives from some sort of weird-ass Lamarckian biology."

Hope coursed through Martin's heart as he flipped open his laptop and typed, *Free will defense = Lamarckian biology.*

"It doesn't derive from *any* sort of biology," snapped Augustine. "It derives from sound reasoning and the Book of Genesis. 'In Adam's Fall, we sinned all.' "

"Through Adam's *shlong,* our race went wrong," replied Saperstein, jeering. "I'm sorry, Your Grace, but it just won't wash, either scientifically or theologically."

"My name's Adrian, not Adam," said the male hominid, untying his baby's diaper. "You folks could at least get *that* right." In the middle of the absorbent fig leaf lay a blob of excrement reminiscent of French's mustard. Adrian wrapped the soiled diaper around itself as if making a burrito and pointed it toward Saperstein. "Don't be so quick to dismiss the free will argument. By focusing on my gonads, Augustine did the solution a great disservice."

"In *your* opinion," grunted Augustine.

"Properly formulated, the *liberum arbitrium* defense emerges as one of the most potent theodicies ever devised," Adrian persisted.

Evangeline turned toward Martin, her beetle brow arching sympathetically. "Sadly for you, the defense comes in two versions: a weak form derived from Augustine's bizarre Lamarckian notions of inherited depravity, and a strong form perfected over the years by Augustine's intellectual descendents, among them Gregory the Great and Thomas Aquinas. If I were you, I wouldn't count on Lovett using the weak form."

Morosely, Martin deleted *Free will defense = Lamarckian biology.*

"I want to ask you a favor," said Evangeline, resting her callused palm on his knee. "I'd like you to make an honest woman of me."

"A tall order," said Augustine.

"Shut up," said Adrian.

"Nothing fancy," said Evangeline. "Adrian and I merely want to formalize our commitment to each other."

"I lost the election," said Martin. "I'm no longer a justice of the peace. Such a ceremony wouldn't be legal."

"If it doesn't bother you, it doesn't bother us."

"I'd be happy to help you out, sure."

"Wonderful."

"Tell me more about free will."

Evangeline raised the baby to her breast. "Although Adrian and I are often cited in connection with this solution, we're actually quite tangential to it. Forget the Garden of Eden, the

Tree of Knowledge, and my husband's supposed descent into depravity."

"I'm sick of being the fall guy," said Adrian, nodding.

"Go on," said Martin grimly.

"You should understand that the *liberum arbitrium* solution cannot account for so-called natural evil: earthquakes, tornadoes, sickle-cell anemia." Evangeline cast a sardonic eye on Augustine. "All right, *some* people would say our transgression reverberated throughout nature. Before we ate the apple, pathogenic microbes didn't exist and the world was one big Elysian Field. In general, though, if you want to explain volcanoes and such, stick with your basic ontological defense. It's a powerful theodicy."

"So I hear," said Martin wearily. "Do you happen to know any rebuttals to that argument?"

"Funny you should ask," said Evangeline. "We've been working on one for . . . how long has it been now, Adrian?"

"Four million years."

"Our hobby, you might say. If we ever find ontology's underbelly, Mr. Candle, you'll be the first to hear about it."

Adrian kissed his son on the fontanel. "Beyond natural evil, of course, lies existential evil—plane crashes, hotel fires, mining accidents—as well as moral evil, notably war, murder, rape, torture, terrorism, and slavery. To clear God's name in *those* arenas, you can't do better than the free will defense. It begins with a question. What is our most precious gift from the Almighty? Answer: our freedom. Even before the coma came, a person could be reasonably sure that, once he'd selected a course of action—simple or complex, virtuous or wicked—no divine emissary would appear and compel him to do otherwise. Now that God is non compos mentis, we can be even *more* certain of our autonomy. Whatever your other problems, Mr. Candle, you aren't a puppet. Never forget that fact."

"But there's a catch," said Evangeline. "If freedom is an absolute, no strings attached, then the unprincipled dictator in

South America must enjoy the same quality of volition as the soup-kitchen saint on the Lower East Side. The autonomy of the world's most ruthless assassin must equal the autonomy of its noblest storefront lawyer. In such a universe, I have the mundane option of lifting Clarence to my breast and feeding him, and I also have the horrendous option of wrapping my fingers around his neck and strangling him."

"Pain and suffering, to wit, are the price we pay for having real choices in life," said Adrian. "Evil is, as it were, the lesser of two evils. A hard bargain, but I don't see how God could've arranged things differently."

"Oh." Martin's stomach seemed to turn itself inside out. He shivered with nausea and despair.

"But if God in His day was both omnipotent and good, wasn't He obligated to intervene on behalf of the innocent?" asked Ockham. "Wasn't He bound to soften the Dachau commandant's heart, cool the child molester's lust—"

"Consider what you're saying," interrupted Evangeline. "You're saying our free will shouldn't be *truly* free. You're saying our moral choices shouldn't be *authentic* moral choices. You're saying we should be *robots*. That way lies madness."

"I have a question concerning your baby," said Saperstein. "Can you specify the mechanism by which one cell committed to becoming little Clarence's brain stem?"

"Huh?" said Evangeline.

Martin took a swallow of tea. The nausea persisted, wave after wave wrought by the free will defense. "Excuse me," he said, closing his computer and gaining his feet. "I need some fresh air."

"It's a fundamental biological riddle," said Saperstein. "How does an unspecialized cell—"

"All I do is gestate the things," said Evangeline.

Hobbling out of the hut, Martin stumbled through the forlorn vegetable patch and headed for the river. He paused atop the levee, studying the sanguine currents. He groaned. The beasts were upon him, the Behemoth of ontology, the Leviathan of *liberum arbitrium*, Behemoth's feet crushing his skull, Leviathan's teeth shredding his flesh.

"'Perish the day when I was born'!" he cried, quoting his hero.

He clutched his belly, leaned over the levee, and regurgitated his breakfast into the rush of donated blood.

❖

Later that morning Martin kept his promise, returning to the hut and marrying Evangeline and Adrian in a simple, nondenominational ceremony of the sort he'd performed many times throughout his career. Saperstein served as best man. Beauchamp was the maid of honor. Ockham videotaped the whole affair with his camcorder.

Annoyed by the apes' critique of *Opus imperfectum contra Julianum*, Bishop Augustine boycotted their wedding. At one point Martin glanced out the window and saw him pacing anxiously back and forth along the riverbank, wrestling with some terrible but unspecified temptation. If anyone as tormented as Augustine had ever walked into my little courtroom, Martin mused, I would've maneuvered him into psychotherapy posthaste.

The noon hour found the *Good Intentions*'s passengers gathered atop the forecastle, chatting among themselves as the pilot plied them with margaritas. Belphegor's recipe differed only slightly from Lot's. There were no limes aboard the steamer, so he'd used lemon juice instead.

"I saw a great movie the other day," said Belphegor, filling Martin's salted glass from the cocktail shaker. "*Hollywood Chainsaw Hookers*. It was on the Vomit Channel."

"Moral evil," muttered Martin bitterly. "An unavoidable phenomenon. If you want authentic freedom, you have to accept chain-saw hookers in the bargain."

"Whatever. Did any of you happen to catch it?"

"My father used to own the poster." Martin plugged his modem into his laptop. "He was a Sunday school teacher."

"I fail to see the connection," said Belphegor.

"You had to be there."

"Speaking of *liberum arbitrium*, I realize there's something *else* we should ask Him when we reach the gland," said Beauchamp. "Namely, did God have any choice in making the universe the way it is? Did He exert any free will in the matter?"

"That's good, Jocelyn," said Saperstein.

"The question, I must admit, is not original with me. I'm borrowing it from Einstein."

"No choice?" Martin fired up his computer. "That doesn't sound like God."

"Think again." Ockham imbibed his margarita. "As G. W. Leibniz noted over three hundred years ago, if God is the best of all possible deities, then He logically equipped Creation with the best of all possible physical laws. A Perfect Being would never knowingly make an imperfect world."

Saperstein tapped on Martin's modem. "Which brings us to *your* agenda. Maybe the world is ideal mathematically, but it hardly seems utopian in any other sense."

"If the opportunity arises," said Martin, retrieving his e-mail, "I intend to ask Him about His own personal theodicy."

From: selkirk2@aol.org
To: marcand@prodigy.edu
Date: Thur, May 25, 02:47 PM EDT

Your hunch was right. It turns out PBS spent $6,848,500 on Havoc, *and when I offered them a nice, round $7,000,000, they started waving a purchase agreement in my face. As for their old fears that Court TV and CNN would broadcast the series en passant, the subject never even came up.*

On Tuesday afternoon, per your orders, I sicced our hungry grad students on the ontological solution, but I don't imagine they'll bring it to bay before next week. Meanwhile, the dossiers on Lovett's "theological witnesses" get fatter by the hour. Yes, the defense's Bernard Kaplan is the same one who wrote When You Walk Through a Storm.

Patricia and I had a dreadful fight last night, and the upshot is that we're going to stop seeing each other. I'm just as glad. Her lack of faith in International 227 *was getting increasingly hard to stomach.*

The end of the Randall–Patricia affair filled Martin with profound disquiet. He wondered who'd instigated the breakup. The thought of Randall unceremoniously dumping Patricia angered him (the poor woman had suffered enough loss lately), but the alternative—Patricia jilting Randall—was equally troubling if it meant she was still carrying a torch for the ex-JP of Abaddon. Patricia deserved better than a dying man in love with his dead wife.

From: marcand@prodigy.edu
To: selkirk2@aol.org
Date: Thur, May 25, 03:10 PM Local Time

We've had another setback. Not only is the ontological solution a bear, its counterpart in the moral domain—the free will defense—appears equally unassailable. Get your young philosophers on the job right away. We're paying a $15,000 bounty to whoever can slay the Leviathan of liberum arbitrium!

Beyond our theological difficulties, I think we're in good shape. Esther has scheduled some absolutely beautiful victims.

Sooner or later Randall's Harvard kids would come up with something, Martin told himself. The thought of the ontological and free will defenses being dismantled at Lovett's place of employment, practically under his nose, filled him with unabashed glee.

From: esthclute@aol.org
To: marcand@prodigy.edu
Date: Thur, May 25, 08:36 PM EDT

The news at this end is all good. Our amyotrophic-lateral-sclerosis witness, Christopher Ransom, just signed up for our initial offer of $85,000, and our cystic-fibrosis dad is also in the bag. His name is Harry Elder, and he refuses to take any money ("I'd feel like a leech"). Best of all, Norma Bedloe has agreed to defer her suicide until after we put her on the stand. Her fee—her "legacy," as she puts it— is $110,000. If she knew how to go about the deed, I don't think she'd be so cooperative. No doctor will give her the information she requires.

Writing back to Esther, Martin found himself singing the "Prufrock" song from *Crabs*, matching the notes to the rhythm of his fingers tapping on the keyboard.

From: marcand@prodigy.edu
To: esthclute@aol.org
Date: Thur, May 25, 03:32 PM Local Time

As Randall may have told you, he has secured the services of a human-depravity specialist named Tonia Braverman and an authority on natural and existential evil named Donald Carbone. Between these two expert witnesses and your fine roster of sufferers, we've got a damn good chance of winning.

At dusk the *Good Intentions* reached the river's source, a freestanding column of donated blood shooting three miles into the air and bulking a thousand feet in diameter. The cataract fed not only the Hiddekel, Augustine explained, but three other cranial arteries as well: the eastward-flowing Euphrates, the Gihon as it rushed to circle the land of Cush, and the Pishon pursuing its southern course to Havilah. Martin had never seen such a phenomenon before, this frothing, thundering mass rising heavenward like a liquid tornado. Sipping a margarita, he bent over the transom and stared into the roiling plasma.

Something strange appeared.

A fifth river rolled out of Eden—just a brook, really, its bed filled not with blood but water. Martin recognized it. The brook's hue bespoke its identity: God's Idea of Waupelani Creek, aglow with Abaddon Township's legendary golden carp.

"Which river drains the pineal gland?" he asked Augustine.

"The Euphrates. The Gihon as well, also the Pishon—even the Hiddekel, if you want to take the long way around. Here in God's brain, all roads lead to His soul."

"What about that little one over there? Waupelani Creek— will that bring us to the gland too?"

Augustine scowled and said, "About twenty miles from here it empties into the Schuylkill and from there into the Gihon."

"I want us to follow it."

"Bad idea. Our draft's too deep. We'd run aground."

"Then I'll make the trip alone."

"Alone? On foot?"

Martin nodded.

"It'll take you three days at least," said Augustine.

"I'll camp out," said Martin.

"I don't think we should split up," said Ockham.

"Aren't you too sick to go off on your own?" asked Beauchamp.

"Of *course* he's too sick to go off on his own," said Saperstein.

"Please understand—I've got a unique opportunity here." Martin shifted his gaze back and forth among the scientists: a worried Ockham, a confounded Beauchamp, a disgruntled Saperstein. "When I was fourteen, I watched two bulldozers destroy my childhood home. It used to be a firehouse, but Dad had turned it into a really magical place, full of funny little rooms and slanted floors you could use like sliding boards. I'll bet you anything that, in God's Idea of Abaddon, my firehouse still stands."

Drawing the pink itinerary from his coat, Augustine faced Martin and ripped the paper to shreds. "Whether you visit your native township or not, we won't be needing this anymore." He tossed the confetti over the bulwark. The blood tornado caught the fragments, sucking them toward its core. "I hope you've learned your lesson, sir. Theodicy is a serious business. Ontology, free will . . . it takes more than righteous indignation to defeat two thousand years of subtle and courageous Christian thought. Perhaps you'd better pull out now, before Lovett trounces you."

"Thanks for the advice, Your Grace, but *International 227* is going to happen. Maybe if you're nice to Job, he'll let you watch it on his Magnavox. It's a much bigger set than the Devil's."

❖

At eight o'clock the next morning, after entrusting his laptop, modem, cellular phone, and theological artifacts to Father Ockham, Martin shouldered his backpack and began to trace the circuitous and shimmering Waupelani.

A ten-mile hike beneath a shining neuronal canopy brought him to the outskirts of the township's affluent northern section. As the creek wound through the parks and playgrounds— through the golf courses, tennis courts, and backyards sporting swimming pools and Japanese rock gardens—the coma's devastating legacy presented itself in stark detail. Severed power lines hung uselessly from their poles. The grass suggested the beer-stained surface of a pool table in some shabby urban saloon. Whatever glorious views and pristine vistas had once graced the divine edition of Abaddon, they had long since succumbed to His sleep.

A crab spasm detonated in Martin's right hip. He pulled the Roxanol bottle from his pocket, swallowed two tablets, and waited impatiently as the opium found its way to his brain.

He pressed on.

At noon he reached the weedy environs of his old high school. A chanting sound, cadenced and aboriginal, wafted across the field. He stopped. Listened. The noise resolved into scores of adolescent voices reciting the Twenty-third Psalm.

> *. . . Surely goodness and mercy shall follow me*
> *All the days of my life:*
> *And I will dwell*
> *In the house of the Lord forever.*

Martin resumed his journey, following the creek for another fifty yards, then pausing at the threshold of a familiar wooden footbridge. As a student, he had crossed this stout span nearly three thousand times, but only now did he see how evil it was—a lethal trap, waiting to snare some innocent Abaddonian's wife. He closed his eyes and stumbled forward. Passing over the Waupelani, he approached the glass-and-aluminum front door of his school, raised his palm, and pushed. The door broke loose and crashed to the floor, launching a spiraling plume of dust.

Like its terrestrial counterpart, the foyer of God's Idea of Abaddon Senior High featured a six-foot-wide plastic globe etched with contour lines and coordinates. Martin drew nearer. The globe, he saw, depicted not the Earth but some infant planet whose Pangaeaic mass had yet to fracture into continents.

Make a joyful noise unto the Lord,
All ye lands.
Serve the Lord with gladness:
Come before His presence with singing . . .

Psalm One Hundred grew louder, echoing up and down the empty corridors as Martin limped into the auditorium. Dust carpeted the aisles; springs poked through the seat cushions like decapitated jack-in-the-boxes; the curtains hung in tatters, as if they'd fallen prey to some voracious species of moth. Up on the stage the Idea of Mr. Gianassio strutted back and forth as he taught twelfth-grade honors English, an open copy of *The Brothers Karamazov* balanced on his palm.

"Dostoyevsky himself believed that the heart of the novel is Ivan and Alyosha's debate about the nature of God," said Gianassio, lecturing at the top of his voice lest the thundering recitation drown him out. "Ivan's examples of evil—all taken by the author from contemporary newspapers—are among the most devastating ever compiled. The peasant boy torn to pieces by hounds in front of his mother for hurting a nobleman's dog. The baby whom the Turks amuse with a shiny pistol right before blowing her head off. The five-year-old whose educated parents, angered by her bed-wetting, smear her face with her own feces, make her eat the remainder, then lock her all night in a freezing outhouse, the child beating herself on the chest the whole time, crying out for God to protect her.

"To his brother, Ivan says, 'Imagine that you are creating a fabric of human destiny with the object of making men happy in the end, giving them peace and rest at last, but that it was essential and inevitable to torture to death only one tiny creature—that baby beating its breast with its fist, for instance—and to found that edifice on its unavenged tears. Would you consent to be the architect on those conditions?'

"And Alyosha replies, 'No, I wouldn't consent.' "

Mr. Gianassio snapped the novel shut, pivoted on his right heel, and exited stage left.

The instant the chanters finished Psalm One Hundred, they launched into the Lord's Prayer. Following his ears, Martin left the auditorium, limped down the hall to Room 107, and stepped furtively inside. Two dozen students sat at their desks, eyes closed, heads bowed, hands clasped. Dissection kits and triple-objective microscopes rested atop the counters. Storage cabinets lined the walls, their shelves jammed with taxidermy specimens: great horned owl, bobcat, beaver, snapping turtle, rattlesnake. At the front of the room stood a spindly, sunken-eyed man, his fingers so tightly intertwined their tips were red with blood.

> *. . . but deliver us from evil.*
> *For Thine is the kingdom,*
> *And the power, and the glory, forever.*
> *Amen.*

The spindly man raised his head and blinked, whereupon Martin recognized Oscar Simmons, his eleventh-grade biology teacher. Without saying a word, the Idea of Mr. Simmons removed a red leatherbound New Testament from his desk drawer, opened it near the middle, and flipped ahead one page. Martin smiled. Throughout his life—every time his father had picked up a Bible—he had witnessed this startling phenomenon of a man cracking the spine of Scripture and finding himself within a page of the desired verse.

"Today's reading comes from Paul's First Letter to the Corinthians . . ."

Mr. Simmons's students lifted their eyes in unison. The coma had exacted a severe toll. With their small skulls, beady eyes, and gap-toothed smiles, they seemed descended not from healthy Abaddonian stock but from some isolated backwoods family drowning in its own gene pool, a classroom of village idiots.

"Excuse me," said Martin, stepping forward.

Mr. Simmons lowered his New Testament, cradling it protectively against his chest as he fixed Martin with a stare so feral it rivaled the stuffed horned owl's. "If you don't like what you're about to hear, sir, you may leave the room—provided you can show me a note from your mother."

"When I had you for advanced biology, you were the ultimate logical positivist. What happened?"

The teacher pointed skyward. "Out there, yes, I'm a skeptic, but in here I'm a fundamentalist Christian. My most popular course is called Introduction to Scientific Creationism."

"Prayer and Bible reading have been banned in the public schools," Martin protested. "My classmate Randall Selkirk got the Supreme Court to declare this sort of exercise unconstitutional. What you're doing is against the law."

"In God's version of reality," Mr. Simmons explained, "the Court ruled that the First Amendment permits classroom Bible reading for the purpose of ethical—as opposed to religious—instruction. 'The Holy Scriptures are a proven source of moral education, manifestly meriting a place in every student's schedule,' noted Justice Thomas Clark, writing for the majority." With a florid gesture, he directed the class's gaze toward the interloper. "Ladies and gentlemen, do we know who this is?"

"Yes, Mr. Simmons," said the students in unison, as if still reciting the Lord's Prayer. "This is Martin Candle."

"And what is Mr. Candle's project?"

"*International 227: Job Society versus Corpus Dei.*"

"And how do we feel about *International 227?*"

"It makes us mad!" said the students, rising in a body.

"How mad?"

"Mad as hornets! Mad as *Vespula maculata!*"

It took Martin only a second to realize what Mr. Simmons's class intended. Charging away from their desks, six students formed a human barricade across the doorway, while the others raced toward the storage cabinets, tore open the doors, and systematically armed themselves.

"And God created *Bubo virginianus*!" cried a busty girl as she hurled the stuffed horned owl at Martin. The predatory bird soared past his face, slashing his cheek with its talon.

"And God created *Castor canadensis*!" yelled a chunky boy, his face ravaged by acne. The mummified beaver came toward Martin, socking him in the stomach like a prizefighter's illegal punch.

"*Lynx rufus!*" shouted a lanky female student with a beehive hairdo. The preserved bobcat took to the air, striking Martin's forehead and raising an instant welt.

"*Rana catesbeiana!*" screamed a cross-eyed male student wearing a T-shirt reading MY GOD IS NOT DEAD—SORRY TO HEAR ABOUT YOURS. A glass jar containing a pickled bullfrog sailed toward Martin, missing him by inches, then hit the far wall and exploded like a land mine. The crisp, macabre odor of formaldehyde filled the classroom.

"Attention, ladies and gentlemen—attention!" shouted Mr. Simmons. "You must answer one more question. Will welts and bruises keep Mr. Candle from The Hague?"

"No!" cried the pupils.

"Will nicks and scratches stop him?"

"No!"

Moving with one mind and a single purpose, the students sought out their dissection kits. A dozen silver scalpels appeared, glittering in the pungent air. Each blade looked singularly cruel, as if recently employed in a surgical operation performed without anesthesia. Martin's muscles stopped working, frozen by incredulity and fear.

Knives flashing, the students rushed toward their visitor.

He glanced across the room. One way out, only one. Gritting his teeth, he tore off his backpack, hobbled forward, and threw himself against the window. By some miracle, the entire structure gave way—glass, rails, sash bars—shattering like a porcelain vase encountering Stuart Torvald's gavel. Martin snapped into a fetal position. God's gravity drew him down, claiming him as it had earlier claimed Corinne and her pickup truck.

Loving and deep, the Waupelani awaited. Martin cannonballed into the water and sank. His buttocks touched the sandy bottom. He arched his spine, exhaled a stream of bubbles, and surfaced just as Mr. Simmons screamed, "You'll never get around the *liberum arbitrium* defense!"

"I do not consent to the universe!" cried Martin, afloat on his back.

"Free will must be absolute!"

"I do not consent!"

He stretched out his arms, thumbed his nose at his former teacher, and let the golden currents bear him away.

Chapter 10

THE CRAB WAS ON THE PROWL again, pursuing its maleficent agenda. It jabbed one fighting claw into Martin's left hip and poked another deep into the corresponding femur. He screamed, frightening a shoal of carp so badly it disbanded and swam away in nine different directions.

Buoyed by the Waupelani, he drifted west, past the Glendale Sewage Treatment Plant, through a field of blighted sunflowers, and into the town of Kingsley. It was a poor community by Abaddonian standards, one in which the average household owned neither a dishwasher nor a clothes dryer. On both sides of the creek, damp white laundry hung from fraying ropes. He rose and clambered up the bank, the Waupelani's waters sluicing down his limbs, then drew out his Roxanol and ate three tablets.

As the holy opium suffused his nervous system, filling him with ersatz bliss, he turned and continued on foot, eyes fixed on the citizens' cluttered lots. His behavior, he realized, partook of voyeurism. Studying the Kingsleyites' backyards was not unlike peering into their bedrooms or rifling through their bureau drawers; these randomly scattered belongings—these swaying undergarments, corroded barbecue grills, and fractured plastic wading pools—were not intended for strangers' eyes. Ever the magistrate, he shuddered to behold what the local ordinances called "attractive nuisances," hazards that could easily lure and harm a passing child. A manifestly unstable tree house. A swing set that had rusted to the point of collapse. An uncovered septic tank. Why couldn't people behave more responsibly?

He cleaved to the Waupelani, footfall following footfall as he moved past the town limits, the miles dissolving in a Roxanolian haze, until eventually he reached a place he didn't want to be—the northeast quadrant of Hillcrest Cemetery. Pocked and corroded, the headstones resembled immense up-ended sponges. He quickened his pace, gimping steadily across the grounds, refusing to read any names, dates, or epitaphs. The last thing he needed to see just then was the Idea of Corinne Rosewood's Grave. He carried that stone in his heart.

At the top of a knoll a wiry man with leathery skin sat before a tombstone surmounted by a Celtic cross. His wardrobe was at once casual and austere: black sweatshirt, black sweatpants, Pennsylvania Dutch straw hat. Oblivious to Martin's approach, the man reached into a canvas satchel and drew out a steel-wool pad and a glass bottle filled with a clear fluid. He unplugged the bottle and drenched the pad. A sharp, serrated odor filled the air: sulfuric acid, Martin realized—H_2SO_4, as he'd learned to call it in Mr. Barzac's chemistry class. The man pushed the pad against the inscription and rubbed it up and down, burning a cavity in the granite.

Hearing footfalls, the man lifted his gaze and glowered. Martin froze, dazed by the shock of recognition. His throat tightened. The blood drained from his face.

"Dad?"

"No," said the Idea of Walter Candle.

"Yes. You're my father, and I'm your son."

As Martin studied the mutilated inscription, a jolt of fear tore through him, palpable as any crab spasm. MARTIN CANDLE, the stone read. Next came his birth date, MARCH 15, 1947. His death date was gone, erased by his father's acid. A BLAMELESS AND UPRIGHT MAN, the epitaph asserted.

"No son of mine would be out to defame his Creator," said Walter Candle.

"At the moment I'm merely out to find our old firehouse. Is it still there?"

"I imagine so. Haven't been to Fox Run in years. Mostly I hang out at Perkinsville First Presbyterian, teaching the youngsters about Jesus."

"The missing date, my death—what did it read?"

"I'm not supposed to tell you."

"Please."

"I *will* say this much: if you don't go back on Odradex"— Walter burned MARCH 15, 1947 from the stone—"the end will come sooner than if you do."

The sun reached its zenith, evaporating the Waupelani from Martin's skin and clothes. Unzipping his windbreaker, he reached inside and scratched the itch surrounding his Port-A-Cath valve. "I remember when you used to *rescue* epitaphs, not wreck them."

Walter gave the pad a fresh dousing of acid. "I save what's worth saving"—he went to work on A BLAMELESS AND UPRIGHT MAN—"and I erase what isn't. That's an impressive pair of bazooms you've got there."

"Estrogen-induced gynecomastia. The side effects of Odradex are even worse." Thunder boomed across Hillcrest Cemetery. Martin winced. A terminated career, an incinerated house—and now *International 227* had brought another curse upon him, his father's posthumous contempt. "Sounds like we're in for some nasty weather."

"If I were you, I'd look for shelter." Walter continued tampering with the epitaph, making it read A LAME MAN. "You don't want to get caught in a brainstorm."

"It's good to see you, Dad." Martin leaned forward, fully intending to hug his father, but the old man suddenly grew as stiff as Mrs. Lot.

"Wish I could say as much—wish I was having the same

happy feelings the father did in Luke, chapter fifteen, when his prodigal son came home. And you *have* been prodigal, Martin, wasting your energies on a vain project."

"Sometimes it's necessary to call God to account. Read Job."

"Job was pious and faithful." Walter applied the pad to the M in MARTIN. "He loved his heavenly Father."

" 'The Almighty set me up as His target,' " said Martin, quoting his hero over a second thunderclap. " 'His arrows rained upon me from every side. Pitiless, He cut deep into my vitals. He spilt my gall on the ground.' That's God's *antagonist* talking, Dad—an angry man, not a Sunday school teacher."

"All right, fine." Walter erased the A and the R. "But then Job said, " 'I repent in dust and ashes.' "

"Only after he'd gotten his day in court." A drop of thick, milky liquid struck Martin's nose. "What in the world . . . ?"

"Cerebrospinal fluid," Walter explained, obliterating the last three letters in CANDLE. The inscription now read TIN CAN. "Any minute now, the storm will be upon us."

"I wish I *were* a tin can." Martin gestured toward the vandalized stone. A second drop fell, then another, spattering his brow. "A tin can feels no pain."

"You're in pain?" asked Walter with a mixture of dry curiosity and genuine concern.

"Most of the time."

Walter blotted out TIN and CAN, then replenished his pad and capped the acid bottle. "I'm sorry, Son. Truly sorry." He removed A LAME MAN, turning the stone into a tabula rasa.

A fourth drop fell, hitting Martin's cheek an inch above the wound he'd received from the stuffed horned owl. "The worst pain doesn't come from my tumor."

"Oh, yes it does. You'd pick parental rejection over prostate cancer any day of the week."

Martin said nothing, stunned into silence by the truth of his father's words.

More fluid arrived, ten drops, twenty, fifty, and then the

storm broke, blowing across the graveyard in great diaphanous sheets.

Walter secured the acid in his satchel and struggled to his feet. "Tell your mother I miss her." Standing amid the stones, swathed in fluid, satchel in hand, he looked like Death making a house call. He faced west, and suddenly he was on the move, scurrying away through the Korean section. "Tell your sister I love her!"

Lightning flashed, zigzagging across the dome of God's left hemisphere like an immense stitch sewn by Jonathan Sarkos. Martin leaned into the wind. He took off, moving amid the stones like a skier following a slalom course. A second bolt split the sky, illuminating the inscriptions.

ABNER WHITTINGTON
DEVOTED FRIEND AND LOVING SON
1959–1988

"I'm going to return You the ticket!" he cried, raising a clenched fist toward Heaven. "I do not consent!"

SASHA REYNOLDS
1963–1967
THANK YOU FOR BRIGHTENING OUR LIVES
LOVE, MOMMY AND DADDY

"Job didn't have the data!" He stumbled past the vine-covered backhoe shed. "I've got the data!"

BRANDON APPLEYARD
1992–1999
I MISS YOU SO MUCH
ALL MY LOVE, MOMMY

"I've got the whole damn Kroft Museum, God! I've got eleven solid hours of *Havoc*! This time You won't escape!"

❖

Jehovic in its anger, Wagnerian in its sweep, the storm raged on and on, augmenting the Waupelani with so much cerebrospinal fluid that it overflowed onto the Abaddonians' lots and began carrying off their possessions. The creek became a mulligan stew of picnic tables, davenports, chaise longues, wheelbarrows, birdbaths, and badminton nets. A molded plastic playhouse floated by, a terrified orange cat marooned on its roof. A garden hose followed, riding the deluge like a satanic tapeworm.

Seeking safety, Martin climbed onto the lowest branch of a sycamore tree rooted on the border between South Hills and Fox Run. He straddled the wet bark and watched the rising tide of consumer goods. "'When a sudden flood brings death, He mocks the plight of the innocent'!" he shouted into the rain. "'O Earth cover not my blood, and let my cry for justice find no rest'!"

And then, abruptly—as if cowed by his plea—the thunder grew silent, the clouds closed up, and the lightning ceased to flash.

He descended.

Carefully, gamely, he moved along the inundated bank, the muddy waters covering his feet, calves, and knees, reaching almost to his decaying thighbones. An aluminum canoe lay caught in the cleft of a willow tree, its bottom holding a jumble of splintery paddles, tattered life jackets, and broken toys, including the Sargassia Saga's Captain Renardo and a torn inflatable sea serpent. His initial impulse was to leave the canoe alone, but then he saw that the Waupelani would soon bear it away, and he decided to act first. Salvage was not theft.

Shortly after boarding his new canoe, he realized he wouldn't have to power the vessel, merely steer it: the waters were transporting him faster than his muscles ever could. Sitting in the stern, using a paddle as a rudder, he alternately focused on keeping the canoe in the center of the stream and on trying to decide whether the Idea of Walter Candle was a person he could ever grow to love.

Waves of grief washed over Martin as he approached the juncture of the Waupelani and the Algonquin, a foamy nexus giving birth to the muddy Schuylkill River. The demonic Algonquin, he mused, spanned by the equally malign Henry Avenue Bridge. His heart pounded. Nausea suffused him. Firming his grip on the paddle, he locked his gaze on the waters ahead.

As the intersection drew near, he turned and, succumbing to temptation, peeked—a lapse he instantly regretted. Fifty yards up the Algonquin, near the southern edge of Abaddon Marsh, Corinne's Ford Ranger leaned against the levee, its cab poking above the waterline, its load bed and rear wheels submerged. A dead Irish setter, stiff with rigor mortis, lay atop the hood.

Get out of here, he told himself. Leave immediately.

He pivoted the canoe two hundred degrees, aimed the prow toward his wife's truck, and began to paddle, churning against the onrushing flood. Ten minutes later he reached the Ranger. The driver's door bore a cracked and peeling painting of a deliriously happy springer spaniel encircled by the words KENNEL OF JOY. Martin propped his elbows on the frame of the shattered window, eased forward, and peered inside.

Corinne's corpse, thank God, was gone.

A glass bowl occupied the driver's seat. Several inches away, a crayfish lay belly-up on the damp upholstery, its legs rowing back and forth in the air. Beside the crayfish a golden carp enacted a death dance, flopping and gasping.

Inside the glass bowl a tiny creature—reminiscent of a tadpole in size and shape but possessing a distinctly humanoid head—swam around and around. Its eyes bulged with fear. Its cheeks quivered with pain.

"Are you Martin Candle?" the tadpole inquired, a string of bubbles exiting its mouth.

"W-what?" he said, flabbergasted.

"You're Judge Candle, correct?"

"That's r-right. Ex-judge."

"Hello, Father."

"Father? *Father?*"

"Father," the tadpole repeated, wheezing. "It's really very simple. Your wife was pregnant when she died."

His jaw went slack. "Pregnant? Corinne? You're . . . my child?"

"Alas, that's overstating the case . . . by about four thousand billion cells."

"Oh, dear," he sighed. "We would've lost you?"

"A banner headline in the *Abaddon Sentinel. Local magistrate loses embryo. Miscarriage of justice's daughter.*"

"Daughter? You would've been a girl?"

"It's the Y chromosome that does it."

Was this happening? Was he dreaming? Even if she could claim no objective reality for herself—a hallucination inside a hallucination—he still felt an instinctual urge to nurse the tadpole through whatever illness had befallen her.

"I always thought 'Jolene' was a lovely name for a girl," he mused dreamily. "Corinne liked it too."

"I don't want a name. I want a voice."

"A voice? What do you mean, Jolene?"

"I stand before you today not as your hypothetical descendant but as the ambassador of my kind. The statistics, as you may know, are appalling: two of us sloughed off for every six who make it into the world. In all of history, there was never a more prolific abortionist than God Almighty. Make sure the tribunal learns that fact."

"Okay, but the thing is, Jolene—"

"Stop calling me that."

"—the thing is, the minute I start going after God for miscarriages, Lovett will simply counter with the Swiss cheese defense. 'If you want a differentiated, variegated, plenary universe,' he'll say, 'then defective embryos become a metaphysical necessity.' "

"You got justice for that lady whose dress was ruined. You got it for those women whose boyfriend lied about his vasectomy."

"Yes, Jolene, but they were *people*. Maybe you haven't heard, but in the outside world the ontological status of embryos is a matter of considerable controversy."

"Of *course* I've heard. I wasn't born yesterday. Cut the 'Jolene' crap." The tadpole coughed, convulsed, and spoke again. "Give us a voice, Judge. Our day in court. Justice."

"I *can't* drag miscarriages into *International 227*. It's a gigantic can of worms. I *can't*."

"Let me try another tack." A seizure coursed through her ethereal body. "Imagine a planet where—"

"Yes?"

The tadpole made no reply.

"Jolene?"

She quivered once more, nose to tail. Her eyes retracted into her head.

"Jolene!" he screamed as her limp body drifted to the top of the fishbowl. No answer. "Jolene!" Silence. "Say something!"

Cupping his hand, he dipped it into the bowl and lifted the corpse free.

"Jolene? Can you hear me?"

As Martin watched in horror, her skin fell away like a thimble slipping from Jonathan Sarkos's finger, revealing an array of tiny gelatinous organs. The disintegration continued, claiming her bones and tissues, leaving him with nothing in his hand but a puddle of water.

Dazed and exhausted, he slumped back onto the canoe seat. He picked up the paddle, oblivious to the dozen splinters that broke off the shaft and lodged in his palms. Pushing the canoe free of the Ranger, he poled forward twenty yards into a shallow lagoon where anemic bullfrogs hopped amid clusters of rotting logs. He set down the paddle, lowered his head, and, as tears squirted from his eyes, began pondering the curious fact that in the entire Book of Job the sufferer never once lamented the loss of his children.

❖

While our hero sat stupefied in his stolen canoe, I was working at my sewing machine, stitching together a pair of overalls for one of my regular customers, a Boeing aviation technician who wishes to remain anonymous.

His name is Desmond Featherstone.

The crowning event of Desmond's career occurred on August 12, 1985. At 6:12 P.M. Japan Air Lines Flight 123, a Boeing 747, took off from Tokyo's Haneda Airport. Thirteen minutes later the plane's rear bulkhead ruptured—a consequence of faulty repairs by Desmond and his teammates—causing a section of rudder to break loose and fall into Tokyo Bay. As cushions and oxygen masks flew crazily about the cabin, flight attendants instructed the passengers to put on life preservers and lean forward, heads down.

In the rear of the 747 off-duty stewardess Yumi Ochiai felt her ears pop as the cabin lost pressure. Glancing out the windows, she caught a glimpse of Mount Fuji. The stricken plane went *hira hira*, and seconds later it skidded through the foothills of Mount Osutaka, uprooting trees and crashing into the slope. *Hira hira*: who else but the Japanese would have a word for the slow, twisting fall of a leaf?

With morning's first light scores of rescue workers arrived, picking through a hellish landscape of charred metal, melted plastic, dead bodies, severed limbs, and pools of blood. Nobody imagined finding any survivors. But then a worker noticed something moving amid the wreckage. It was Yumi, badly hurt but still alive. Minutes later, another worker spotted a twelve-year-old girl caught in a tree, her injuries miraculously limited to cuts and bruises. A third worker found a mother and her eight-year-old daughter, both suffering from nothing worse than broken bones.

One of the most poignant moments I have ever witnessed occurred a year after the 747 hit Mount Osutaka and sent five hundred and twenty irredeemably depraved travelers to their graves, along with eight wicked fetuses and four sinful embryos. On July 31, 1986, the Idea of Desmond Featherstone came into my shop and asked me to make him a pair of dungarees. While placing his order, he repeatedly slid from his pocket a newspaper photo of the four Flight 123 survivors, waving it in my face. "They're all alive," he muttered tonelessly, his mouth locked in a pained smile. "They're all alive . . ."

And yet, confoundingly, from time to time I still meet people who deny that God protects the innocent.

❖

For two solid hours Martin remained in the canoe, the soggy night pressing upon him as he squeezed the splinters from his palms. High above, a crescent moon glittered in the sky like a silver sickle. The air trembled with insect serenades and bullfrog love songs. Leaving the *Good Intentions* had been a mistake, he now realized. There was no reason to believe the firehouse still stood, whereas the sooner he reached the pineal gland, the sooner he could ask the Defendant about His own personal theodicy.

A new sound arose, unexpected yet familiar, an exquisite female voice singing "The Lady of Shalott." Pangs of loss intermingled with prostate cancer shot through Martin. He seized the paddle, gasping and groaning as he jabbed it into the lagoon.

> *Out upon the wharfs they came,*
> *Knight and burgher, lord and dame,*

> *And round the prow they read her name,*
> *The Lady of Shalott.*

He looked up. Luminous with moonlight, the Idea of Corinne Rosewood danced on the far shore of the Algonquin, moving synchronously with the song. A pantherskin rug covered the ground beneath her feet, secured by her portable sound system. She wore no clothes. Cerebrospinal fluid gleamed on her naked flesh. Despite the divine coma, this vision of Corinne was no less enchanting than his memory of her terrestrial equivalent. For an entire minute he sat motionless in the stern, transfixed by her supple limbs.

> *But Lancelot mused a little space;*
> *He said, "She has a lovely face;*
> *God in His mercy lend her grace,*
> *The Lady of Shalott."*

"Martin!" she called in a choked, husky voice. Abaddon Marsh lay spread out behind her, cattails and spartina grass swaying in the nocturnal breeze. "Martin, is that you?"

"It's me!" For a fleeting instant he recalled what concupiscence was like, the sweet pain of it all. "It's really me!"

"Oh, Martin, Martin!"

As she shut off the sound system, the moon caught the halo of serum encircling her auburn hair. Firming his grip on the paddle, he stroked vigorously and sent the canoe on a direct course for his dead wife.

"I've missed you!" he wailed, weeping uncontrollably. "I've missed you so much!"

"Darling!"

"We would've named her Jolene, wouldn't we?" he shouted, tear ducts throbbing.

"Named *who* Jolene?"

"Your pregnancy. I just spoke with her."

"This brain is haunted, Martin. It's full of ghosts. Ignore them."

He dragged the canoe onto the beach, panting with a mixture of exhaustion and longing. Fiery pains traveled up and down his femurs. He didn't care. Using the paddle as a crutch, he hobbled toward Corinne, whereupon a wholly unexpected command broke from her lips.

"Stay away."

She might as well have been a divine emissary forbidding Mrs. Lot to look back.

"Stay away," she said again. "Don't touch me."

He stopped.

"I'm not being irrational—really."

He studied her exquisite feet. Sprigs of catnip sprouted from the sandy beach, curling around the edges of the black pelt. "What's this all about?"

Goose bumps grew on Corinne's thighs and breasts. She crossed her arms over her chest, rubbing each triceps with the opposite hand. "Here in the divine skull, if somebody you love arrives from the outside world, and if the two of you connect . . ."

"Yes?"

"If you touch me, I'll—"

"What?"

"—dissolve."

"Dissolve?"

"I'll dissolve, Martin. Like cotton candy. Myself, I wouldn't mind, but *you'd* be traumatized forever."

"That's crazy, Corinne. I don't . . ." He was about to say *believe you* when a memory froze his tongue. Militant little Jolene, disintegrating in his palm. "But why would He *make* such a law?"

"Insecurity, why else? He wants to be loved for what He is,

not for what He gives us." She smiled wryly, pulling a sticky strand of congealed fluid from her hair. "So, who's taking care of my animals?"

"Jenny found an eccentric old dowager on the Main Line—Merribell Folcroft. She added them to her private zoo."

"Wonderful. What about the Kennel of Joy?"

"When I left for Europe, it was flourishing."

"Any good stories?"

"The one I remember is about a seeing-eye dog up in Boston: Montesquieu the Labrador retriever."

"Montesquieu . . . perfect."

"The owner, Stephanie Brandt—she lost her vision a decade ago. Retinitis pigmentosa. Last year Montesquieu himself started going blind—inoperable cataracts—so Stephanie decided to get a second dog. Not for her, for *Monty*."

"Beautiful. Did the Kennel come through?"

"You bet—a female German shepherd named Bonnie. The three of them make quite a sight. Here comes Stephanie, walking down the street in the company of her faithful guide dog, Monty, who's being led by *his* faithful guide dog, Bonnie."

"Love it."

"Thought you would." He leaned all his weight on the canoe paddle. "I'm afraid our catnip patch has gone to seed. I've been busy."

Corinne offered a cryptic nod. "Yes. *International 227*. It's all anybody can talk about in here."

"I'm doing it for you."

"No, you're not."

"You're *one* of the reasons."

"You're doing it because, back in Abaddon, once you knew somebody was guilty, you convicted the person and made him pay. You even made *me* pay."

"I wish we could touch."

"Me too."

"I need to touch you."

"Yes."

"You have a lovely face."

"So do you."

"Next year I'll plant a new crop—I promise. Okay?"

Saying nothing, Corinne bent over her sound system, ejected the cassette, and aimlessly pulled several feet of tape from the spindles. "It's horrible being a thought," she said at last. "I hate it." Tossing the cassette aside, she stepped off the pelt and backed toward the marsh. "Good-bye, darling. Thanks for telling me about Montesquieu." She faced north, breaking into a run. "I'm dead!" she called over her shoulder. "I'm nothing! I love you!"

"Corinne!"

He took off, hobbling forward on the canoe paddle, his hiking boots splatting through the mud. Within seconds she was gone, swallowed by a field of cattails. His femurs throbbed. His pubic bones burned. He stopped and studied the cylindrical flowers. Whip handles, he decided, fixed to the lashes with which a thousand angry angels would one day flay him alive.

"Corinne!"

Again the crab attacked. Martin's pelvis flared beyond endurance. His brain shut down, seeking refuge from itself. Fainting, he fell forward into the warm silt, and as his consciousness melted away, he realized that his lips and tongue were moving, beseeching Heaven. He prayed for his father's forgiveness. He prayed for his wife's soul. And he prayed that he was about to die in his sleep—peacefully, painlessly, like a spiritually fulfilled client of the Kennel of Joy.

❖

"Wake up."

A deep voice, male and malevolent.

"Wake up," the man said again. "Rise and shine, Mr. Candle. Your journey isn't over."

Martin pinched himself, noting with mixed emotions that he

wasn't dead. The flatulence of Abaddon Marsh filled his nostrils. A pair of huge, mutant fireflies hovered before him, flashing on and off, bright red. He blinked. The fireflies froze in midair, transmuting into the eyes of Jonathan Sarkos.

"How long was I asleep?"

"Dawn is upon us," Sarkos replied, his face and shoulders lit by the crimson beams streaming from his pupils. "Your fellow pilgrims are within a hundred kilometers of the gland."

"A hundred kilometers—that's about fifty miles, right?"

"More like sixty. Aren't you Americans on the metric system yet?"

"No."

"God is. You really ought to convert."

With the aid of the canoe paddle Martin regained his feet. He fixed on Sarkos, watching him solidify in the light of the incipient sun. The tailor was seated on a horse and dressed for riding: hand-tooled cowhide boots, black vinyl slicker, spurs equipped with razor-sharp rowels. Covered with Jobian sores, his mount uncannily resembled the animals who'd drawn the hearse during the *Crabs* production back in the Valley of Dry Bones.

"Not exactly the paragon of her species, but I love her all the same," said Sarkos, patting his horse on her withers. "Ah, you should have seen the very first *Equus caballus* to roll off the assembly line—what a beast! If a camel is a horse designed by a committee, Mr. Candle, then a horse is a camel designed by God. Climb on up and hang on tight."

Martin did not move.

"*Now*, pilgrim. Get on board. Don't you trust me?"

"No," replied Martin, eating a painkiller. "I don't."

"There's no telling what you might find in the gland. An answer to the ontological defense . . ."

Grasping the cantle of the saddle, Martin hoisted himself onto the steed's bony rump.

"Forward, Mal de Mare!" cried Sarkos, stabbing his rowels into innocent horseflesh.

And so the journey began—an excruciating ride out of Abaddon Marsh, across a grassy savannah, and into the fiery core of an archetypal desert. To the east rose a line of natural obelisks, sculpted by the wind into forms suggesting a gigantic edition of Lovett's jade chess set. To the west lay a range of dunes, rolling and swelling like the waves of some vast ocean on an undiscovered planet. By gripping the saddle firmly and bathing his brain in Roxanol, Martin managed to stay on Mal de Mare, hour after hour, morning till noon till evening.

Sarkos reined up before a radiant metropolis, its watchtowers encrusted with gemstones, its walls punctuated by marble towers and golden gates. As far as Martin could tell, the city's luminosity did not trace to a public lighting system but resided, rather, in the building materials themselves. A gleaming moat encircled the ramparts, spanned by a bridge of polished obsidian and filled with a liquid suggesting molten anthracite.

"It's a city," Martin observed, slipping down from Mal de Mare.

"A city," Sarkos corroborated. "Most people's pineal glands look like lima beans. God's looks like a city." His sweeping gesture encompassed the entire southern rampart. "Behold the Idea of Jerusalem. A glorious place even today, so you can imagine how brightly it shone in ages gone by."

From his saddlebag Sarkos produced a rolled sheet of yellow parchment. He unfurled it. The intricacy of the map astonished Martin: it seemed not so much the diagram of a city as the cell-by-cell plan for a creature so complex even God in His day would've experienced difficulty assembling it.

"Your task is to get from this side of Jerusalem to the other," said Sarkos.

"You aren't coming?"

"Too busy. Big order to fill. The Idea of Joseph Smith has

just invented a new variation on Christianity, weirder even than his last one, and he needs a large supply of temple garments." Sarkos wheeled his horse around. "Find Rabbi Yeshua!" he called, galloping away. "*X* marks the spot!"

❖

As it turned out, Sarkos's map was far more lucid than Martin's initial impression allowed, and despite the city's many maddening features—its cul-de-sacs, switchbacks, and street signs written in Hebrew—he found himself limping efficiently toward the northern gate. The Idea of Jerusalem was clean, in good repair, and curiously deserted, as if all the Defendant's remaining strength were going into its maintenance, with no energy left for conjuring up inhabitants. Negotiating the gold-paved alleys and ruby-studded lanes, Martin did not meet a single person, dog, cat, or pigeon.

The spot the **X** marked was a hill of mud located a half mile beyond the gate. Sarkos's map called the hill Golgotha, and its distinguishing feature was a collection of ten thousand human skulls embedded in its sides like raisins in a fruitcake. As Martin approached Golgotha's southern slope, Saperstein, Ockham, and Beauchamp came toward him from the west, their backpacks bulging with Corpus Dei specimens. Noah's ax sat balanced atop Ockham's shoulder, adding to the wan priest's persona a dissonant note of ruggedness. The scientists' bone-deep weariness failed to mask their joy. Each bore the eager expression of a well-born Episcopalian child rushing down the stairs on Christmas morning.

"We've made it!" shouted Beauchamp. "All the way to the gland!"

"Augustine told us to hunt out a great and brilliant teacher," said Saperstein, leading the four of them up the gooey slopes. "The Idea of Rabbi Yeshua."

"How was Abaddon?" asked Ockham.

"Unpleasant," Martin replied. "Rain and graves and dead people. I never found my firehouse."

Reaching the top of Golgotha, the neuronauts happened upon a curious sight. A muscular young man wearing a white terrycloth bathrobe, a ponytail, and a crown of thorns lay spread-eagled on his back, busily pursuing the uncommon ambition of attempting to crucify himself. He had the proper tools—mallet, spikes, wooden cross featuring a plaque reading INRI—but it was nevertheless a hopeless task. Every time he managed to secure his right wrist to the wood, he had to tear it free so he could nail down the left.

"Excuse me," said Saperstein.

"Yes?" the young man replied in a peculiarly cheerful voice.

"I'm sorry to interrupt. Rabbi Yeshua?"

"Correct," said the young man. With his swarthy skin, sparkling turquoise eyes, and neatly trimmed beard, he looked like Jeffrey Hunter in *King of Kings*, Walter Candle's favorite movie after *Ben-Hur*. "Irving Saperstein, right? Plus Thomas Ockham, Jocelyn Beauchamp, and Martin Candle. Your arrival is well timed. In the old days, I had centurions to assist me . . . and, oh, such crowds—scores of mourners lining the Via Dolorosa, hundreds of lepers gathered beneath my perforated feet, eager to catch a drop of holy blood on their tongues." He stretched out fully along his torture rack, ankles together, arms apart. "Help me, Mr. Candle, would you, please?"

With monumental reluctance Martin picked up the mallet. It had the general shape and heft of Torvald's gavel. "Are you *sure* . . . ?"

"Three quick hammer blows will be sufficient. I'll hardly feel a thing."

Martin dropped to his knees, positioning a bloody spike between Yeshua's exposed wristbones. He raised the mallet.

He froze.

"Look, everybody: the man who would kill God, and he

can't hammer one lousy spike into one crummy rabbi," said Yeshua. "Do it, sir. Strike while the irony is hot."

"I can't."

"Why?"

"You're innocent."

"Oh, *that*. All right, very well—pass the tools to Dr. Saperstein over there. But mark my words, Martin Candle. Before your life is done, you'll get another chance at this, and the second time around you won't lose heart."

"I would never execute an innocent man."

"I might as well give it a try." Saperstein seized the mallet. "My people are going to get blamed anyway."

"Too true," sighed Yeshua.

"Irving, you don't really want to do this," said Beauchamp.

"You'll hate yourself in the morning," said Ockham, pulling the camcorder from his backpack.

Tools in hand, Saperstein bent over the rabbi. "Isn't it in our collective interest to make him happy?"

"It certainly is," said Yeshua. "Do it!"

"I'm steeling myself."

"Do it!"

"God forgive me!" shouted Saperstein, connecting mallet to spike.

The neurophysiologist struck again—and again.

As the steel moved through his flesh, spraying blood in all directions, Yeshua loosed screams as piercing as those of Gordon the ram succumbing to Abraham's knife.

"I'm sorry." Saperstein wiped blood from his windbreaker.

"He's sorry," said Beauchamp.

"Remorse past understanding," said Ockham.

The blood kept coming, welling up around the spike like tidewater lapping at a pylon. "I f-forgive you," said Yeshua, gritting his teeth and shivering with pain. "Really. Now, p-please . . . other wrist."

"As I understand the claims of Christianity," said Saperstein, positioning spike number two, "you aren't simply a subdeity, not merely the 'Son of God.' You are the Creator Himself."

"You've hit the nail on the head."

"Can you tell me how the spirochetes adhere to *Myxotricha paradoxa*?"

"Just drive in the spike, okay?"

"How does one embryonic cell commit to becoming a brain?"

"The spike, Professor."

"As you wish," said Saperstein, wielding the mallet.

"Aaaiiihhh!"

Wiping the sweat from his forehead, Saperstein handed the mallet to Beauchamp. "I've had enough," he said.

"Sweet Yeshua, did Fermat actually prove his famous last theorem"—Beauchamp knelt beside the rabbi's feet, positioning a spike above his overlapping ankles—"or must we settle for Andrew Wiles's solution?"

"Jocelyn, don't!" shouted Ockham.

"Go ahead!" commanded Yeshua. "Drive that sucker in!"

Beauchamp struck the spike three times, securing the rabbi's feet to the post.

Yeshua screamed and writhed.

"How might I overcome the ontological defense of ostensible divine injustice?" asked Martin.

"Which would you rather have: an answer to your question or a cure for your disease?" asked Yeshua, speaking between clenched teeth.

"A cure for my disease."

"An honest man, I like that. Sadly, I can supply you with neither."

"I thought you performed miracles as a matter of Christian routine," said Ockham, pointing his camcorder at the crucified Savior.

"Not miracles, faith healings," said Yeshua. "The first requirement for a faith healing is faith."

"I *do* have faith," said Martin.

"Nonsense. Even *I* don't have faith anymore. Elevate me, please. All my weight must rest on the spikes. Before long, I won't be able to lift myself high enough to breathe."

"If you can't help me with the ontological solution, what about the free will argument?"

"I'm not a theologian. Elevate me."

"We'd better do as he wishes," said Saperstein.

The neuronauts channeled their collective energy into the task, raising Yeshua's cross upright and pushing it deep into the mud. They secured the post by hedging it with jawbones pried from Golgotha's vast array of skulls.

"I'm thirsty," said the Savior.

Uncapping his canteen, Ockham stood on tiptoes and held the spout to Yeshua's lips. "Have some wine."

"Much obliged," said Yeshua, gulping.

"Would you like a Roxanol?" asked Martin.

"Please."

As the rabbi opened his mouth, Martin obtained a Roxanol tablet and, taking aim, tossed it skyward. The painkiller landed on Yeshua's tongue.

"Thank you."

"Mr. Sarkos led us to believe that, here in the gland, we'd learn the answers to certain scientific riddles," said Ockham.

"Mr. Sarkos is a liar."

Saperstein stuffed a stray jawbone into a Ziploc bag. "He said we'd learn the answers!"

"Life is full of disappointments."

"Here's a question you *can* answer." Beauchamp pointed to the INRI plaque. "That sign above your head—it's in all the crucifixion paintings. I've always wondered, what does it mean?"

" 'I'm Not Returning Immediately.' "

"Why is the proton in a hydrogen atom eighteen hundred

and thirty-six times as heavy as the electron?" demanded Saperstein.

"Given the imminence of my death, I should tell you how to get home," said Yeshua. "Which optic nerve brought you here, the right or the left?"

"The right," said Ockham.

"Walk east for three miles. You'll come to the Joppa Gate. It will be slightly ajar. Squeeze through. You'll find yourself at the terminus of the left optic nerve. Follow the shaft, and in an hour you'll see the chiasma."

"You mean . . . we'd have gotten here immediately if we'd followed the *left* nerve instead?" asked Ockham.

"No. Whichever nerve my visitors start out following, they always end up at the dinosaurs' gazebo. Illogical? You bet. As Dostoyevsky put it, 'If everything on Earth were rational—' "

"How are the spirochetes attached?" wailed Saperstein, eyes flashing like Leviathan's. "You know the answer! Tell me! Did God exert any free will in fashioning the universe? Please! Out with it!"

"Each time I die, it's harder than the time before."

"What's the correct value of Hubble's constant? You know it, Yeshua! I *know* you know it! Hubble, Yeshua! Hubble! Hubble!"

"Toil and trouble."

"Please! I must find out! Why turbulence? Did Fermat prove Fermat? Spill it! How many spirochetes can dance on the head of a pin? Does hydrogen have free will? Was it the chicken? The egg? Work with me, Yeshua! Stay the distance! Hang in there!"

"Happy Easter," rasped Yeshua, drawing his last breath.

The rabbi's eyes rolled into his skull, his body went limp, and his head flopped sidewards as if mounted on a discarded puppet.

A melatonin drizzle descended.

"It is finished," said Ockham softly.

"Two whole weeks in the brain of God, and not a damn thing to show for it," said Saperstein.

"My department head won't be pleased," said Beauchamp.

"At least you three can go home now," said Martin. "I've still got a war to win."

BOOK THREE

God in the Dock

❖

Chapter 11

ASIA GAVE US DOWRY DEATHS and the caste system. Africa elevated famine to an art form. North America cultivated chattel slavery for far longer than I would have dared hope; South America has done things with political oppression that I am obliged to call brilliant; Australia showed the world that the only good aborigine is a dead aborigine; and Antarctica has fabulous weather. Of all the continents that constitute planet Earth's terrain, however, Europe remains dearest to my heart and closest to my soul.

I allude here not to the sweatshops, the world wars, or totalitarian socialism (though none of these innovations has escaped my notice) but to the fact that the European imagination endowed me with a degree of glamour—you might even say *charm*—that in pre-coma times enabled me to function with extraordinary effectiveness. The concept of an Evil One is intrinsic to Islam, of course; the ancient Hebrews had their "adversary," their *satan*; the Egyptians feared a dark deity called Set; Zoroastrians believed in Ahriman, essence of destruction (forever warring with Ohrmazd, source of all things bright and beautiful). But only in Christian Europe did the Prince of Hell acquire a personality as vivid and endearing as any you will meet in a Dickens novel. And so it was that when the *Carpco New Orleans*, the *Arco Fairbanks*, and the *Exxon Galveston* steamed within view

of the Dutch coastline, my eyes welled up with tears, and soothing waves of Weltschmerz rolled through me. Schonspigel, Funkeldune, Belphegor, and I were sitting before my little Zenith
at the time, eating Hostess Twinkies as we watched the arrival
of the great flotilla on CNN. When a long-shot of Scheveningen
Harbor filled the screen, I aimed the remote control, shut off the
TV, and wept.

Europe, by God—Europe. I was home.

Netherlandian light never fails to move me. I love that sub-
stance, light. Lucifer, light bearer. When it comes to light, the
Dutch are a particularly canny people: Rembrandt, Steen, Hals,
Vermeer—and, of course, it was the Dutch who throughout the
seventeenth century permitted the Light of Reason to shine upon
Western civilization with unprecedented intensity; the Dutch
who opened their arms not only to René Descartes (of pineal
gland fame) but also to John Locke and Baruch Spinoza. Where
would I be, after all, without the rise and fall of Reason? Where
would I be if the clerics, mystics, and nonsense-mongers couldn't
point to seventeenth-century Holland and say, "Look, ladies and
gentlemen, we *tried* rationality, we *tried* skepticism, and nobody
really cared for the stuff."

Captain Anthony Van Horne, by contrast, was not pleased
to behold Scheveningen Harbor. Docking God threatened to be
an out-and-out ordeal, his severest tribulation since towing the
Corpus Dei from the Gulf of Guinea to the Arctic Circle. The
problem wasn't so much the harbor per se (though its rogue tides
and quixotic currents were conspiring to create treacherous
landing conditions) as the other vessels crowding its waters—
the dozens of commercial trawlers, private yachts, and Turner
Broadcasting cutters, not to mention fourteen gunboats belonging to the Sword of Jehovah Strike Force.

At 1615 hours the captain strode into the wheelhouse of the
Carpco New Orleans, slipped on his mirrorshades, and got to
work. The task proved even more daunting than he'd expected.
One hour into the operation his tanker nearly rammed a Belgian

trawler; twenty minutes later she almost tore a thirty-meter wharf off its pylons. But then, at last—success. Glimmering in the setting sun, the General Dynamics cooling chamber and its concomitant Lockheed 7000 heart-lung machine lay jammed against six adjacent piers, moored by an intricate web of cables and lines.

At 1845 hours Van Horne removed his mirrorshades, raised his binoculars, and looked toward shore. He cringed. Ordinarily after performing such a tricky set of maneuvers he got to reward himself with a visit to a waterfront tavern, but the mobs of newspaper reporters, TV crews, trial aficionados, and ideological lunatics crawling across the quays clearly precluded this possibility.

He spent the night in his cabin, a prisoner on his own ship, swearing that he would never again transport the body of God anywhere, no matter what they paid him.

The next morning, just as he was about to raise anchor and start leading the tanker fleet back to America, a ground force appeared: four thousand UN paratroopers who'd been flown in from Belgium the night before and dropped into the Leiden bulb fields. Like Van Horne, the peacekeepers knew their business, and by dusk the wharves were free of civilians—not one journalist or Jehovan remained. And so it was that our captain finally attained his tavern, a fake English pub on Gevers Deijnootplein called the King's Arms.

Although covetousness is not my only flaw, it seems to cause me more pain than all my other sins combined. As Van Horne sat in the King's Arms nursing a ceramic-topped Grolsch beer and thinking about his wife and child back in New York City, I suffered an attack of jealousy so acute my heart turned as green as Lovett's jade chess queen. The steady *thok-thok-thok* of the Lockheed 7000 throbbed across the harbor—a disquieting sound, at once mechanical and organic, aggravating the captain's longing for hearth and home. My jealousy grew intolerable. Van Horne took a final swallow.

Dutch beer: we simply can't get the stuff anymore. Thanks to the coma, He's forgotten the formula. And so I sit here nursing my pathetic bottle of Budweiser, reeling with envy and dreaming of Grolsch.

❖

Martin's first glimpses of The Hague, like his last of Philadelphia, occurred from within the cramped confines of a United Nations armored car. Staring out the observation port—a horizontal slot that turned the world into a Cinemascope movie—he watched the passing shops, apartments, and churches, their windows arrayed in painted shutters and blooming geraniums. UN peacekeepers appeared everywhere, erecting roadblocks, constructing ramparts from sandbags, stringing barbed wire between street signs. By the time Martin reached the Huize Bellevue, he understood why *International 227* required such a substantial budget. The soldiers alone were probably costing Lovett fifty thousand dollars a day.

Although nearly two months had passed since Martin had last received a death threat, he was still traveling incognito. The daily doses of Feminone had left him unable to grow facial hair, so instead he'd attached a crepe mustache to his upper lip with spirit gum, supplementing the deception with dark glasses and a slouch hat. This time around his bodyguards were Scandinavians: Olaf, a Swede, and Gunnar, a Norwegian, each wearing a shoulder holster crammed with an automatic pistol. As the two lean, muscular men grabbed Martin's luggage and guided him into the hotel, he sensed that in the weeks to come the three of them would be inseparable—Siamese triplets.

The lobby of the Huize Bellevue was abuzz: UN soldiers bustling about, messengers scurrying everywhere, minions trundling towers of computer printouts—activities that all seemed somehow connected to *International 227*. He started across the shiny marble floor, Olaf on his left, Gunnar on his right. As he reached the front desk, a terrible truth took hold of him. The crab had enlarged its empire, expanding into his shoulder joints and backbone. Jagged pains radiated up and down his spine, as if Jonathan Sarkos were using his vertebrae as a marimba. He popped a pair of Roxanols, chewed rapidly, and waited for relief.

Three nattily attired men approached and identified themselves in English as, respectively, Albregt Van Randwijk, mayor of The Hague, Hans De Groot, captain of police, and Pierre Ferrand, registrar of the International Court of Justice. "On behalf of our city and its inhabitants, I bid you welcome," said Van Randwijk. The mayor was round and sprightly, a Dutch Fiorello La Guardia, his trollish form encased in a black silk suit.

"My pleasure," said Martin as the blessed opium caressed his brain.

"We've put you in Suite 300," said Pierre Ferrand, a small, nervous, chipper man who failed utterly to conform to the morose, gazellelike person Martin had constructed in his mind during the course of their correspondence. "Sauna, wet bar, parlor"—he handed a key to Martin, another to Olaf—"plus two bedrooms, each *mit douche*."

"Assuming your papers are in order, why not go upstairs and treat yourself to a hot shower?" asked Hans De Groot in a gravelly voice. Encircling his girth was a Moroccan leather belt from which hung a fully equipped key ring the size of a quoit. Evidently not a single door in Holland was closed to this man.

"Swell idea," said Martin, showing De Groot his passport and wincing at how crude his American locution sounded in this elegant Old World city.

De Groot's countless keys clanked together as he shifted his weight from one foot to the other. "No hard drugs in your luggage, I presume." A miniature gold cross gleamed from the lapel of his pinstriped suit. His attitude toward *International 227*,

Martin guessed, was probably not far from the Jehovans'. De Groot would rather be jailing God's enemies than inviting them to take showers. "No assault rifles or dead bodies."

"Nothing but six changes of underwear, two linen suits, and Saint Augustine's *Opus imperfectum*," said Martin. *Along with Isaac's bindings, Mrs. Lot's right ear, and Noah's ax*, he was tempted to add, but he feared such a revelation might provoke an unpleasant confrontation with the customs agent.

"If there's anything my office can do to assist you, please give us a call," said Van Randwijk.

"I'm afraid I've brought a major disruption to your city," said Martin apologetically. "All those soldiers . . ."

"Actually, we're delighted with the whole arrangement. Every hotel, bar, and *bruin kroeg* is packed. Before *International 227* has run its course, we expect it to pump six million guilders into our little economy. This trial of yours is the best thing to hit The Hague since the North Sea Jazz Festival."

❖

Only after he had boarded the elevator, ascended to Suite 300, and stumbled into the parlor did Martin fully appreciate the intensity of his exhaustion. As the bodyguards wandered off in search of their quarters, he collapsed on the couch and fell asleep with his dark glasses and crepe mustache still in place.

Awakening an hour later, he removed his disguise and, seizing the remote control, activated the TV set. A soccer game popped onto the screen, instantly dissolving into a commercial for Oranjeboom beer. He surfed the channels, soon happening upon a Technicolor long-shot of two nineteenth-century Russians deep in conversation: the universally despised Hollywood adaptation of *The Brothers Karamazov*, he realized, captioned with Dutch subtitles.

"And if I am an honest man I am bound to give it back as soon as possible," said Richard Basehart as Ivan to William

Shatner as Alyosha. "It's not God I don't accept, Alyosha, only I most respectfully return Him the ticket."

"That's rebellion," replied Shatner.

Were the optic neuron not dead, Martin would have assumed it had arranged for this eerily pertinent broadcast. Instead he was forced to ascribe the event to coincidence.

He ate a painkiller and changed channels. A live news conference appeared: Saperstein, Ockham, and Beauchamp stood at a lectern, speaking into a bouquet of microphones. Overlaid by a Dutch translation, their voices were inaudible, so Martin had no idea what sort of spin they were according their recent expedition. All three seemed strangely cheerful, as if the journey had actually nailed down Hubble's constant or unmasked the method by which spirochetes adhere to *Myxotricha paradoxa*. Perhaps Saperstein and company were just as happy *not* to have learned these things. If nothing else, their adventure had proved that God was not about to put science out of business.

He looked out the window. The steeple of a Dutch Reformed church rose into the twilight, skewering an orange sun. He lowered his gaze. A wicker basket jammed with succulent fruits occupied the sill. Rising, he limped across the parlor, reached between two pomegranates, and retrieved a piece of elegant rice paper bearing a simple message.

Dear Mr. Candle:
Let me take this opportunity to wish you good fortune in the coming fight. I am anticipating many hours of reasoned theological debate. May the better man win!

Sincerely,
Gregory Francis Lovett

P.S. Per stipulation number two, I still expect you to take the stand as a witness for the defense.

A series of short, sharp reports filled the parlor. Gunshots? wondered Martin. An assassination attempt on the scientists by an Eternity Enterprises stockholder? He glanced at the TV. The scientists were still talking. The reports persisted. Hobbling toward the door, he wrapped his fingers around the knob.

"Hold it!" cried Olaf, dashing into the parlor, Gunnar right behind.

Martin jerked away. As Olaf opened the door, Gunnar pressed his back against the adjacent wall and made ready to ambush the intruder.

Patricia stood in the jamb, a tattered canvas bag slung over her shoulder, her slim body clothed in the primary colors: yellow cotton jersey, blue denim slacks, red silk scarf. A twinge of concupiscence arose in Martin's embattled loins.

"Howdy, neighbor."

"Neighbor?" he replied, staring dumbfounded at his visitor.

"I'm right down the hall, Suite 307. Hey, Martin, I just flew four thousand miles across the Atlantic Ocean. Aren't you glad to see me?"

"You know this woman?" asked Olaf.

"Not as well as he thinks he does," said Patricia.

"What are you doing in Holland?" Martin eased his aching pelvis onto the couch.

"I came for the light. I have a new commission, and I wanted to paint it under the same sun that inspired Vermeer."

"More trading cards?"

"*The Insect Insurrection.*" Settling down beside him, she pulled a rough sketch from her shoulder bag: a gigantic grasshopper feasting on a Burger King restaurant. "A bunch of greedy technocrats concoct the ultimate roach killer, and naturally it goes haywire, polluting the atmosphere and causing all the world's bugs to grow as big as helicopters."

"It doesn't sound very plausible."

"That's what I like about it." Patricia closed her eyes. "Spina bifida is plausible."

As Olaf and Gunnar sidled out of the parlor, Martin selected a plum from the fruit basket, grabbed his larger suitcase, and limped into the master bedroom. To his utter dismay, an immense mirror hung over the dresser. He shuddered. Whatever else he accomplished this summer, he would not achieve freedom from himself—he would not escape his bony cheeks and bloodshot eyes, his invalid's stoop and cheerleader's bust.

"I hear you and Randall showed each other a pretty good time last month," he remarked as Patricia sauntered into the room.

"Pretty good," she echoed evenly.

Setting down the suitcase, Martin thought he heard Noah's ax clank against his blow dryer. "Who broke it off?"

"Me."

"Really? Why?"

"You know why."

"Is it *romantic* loving a doomed man? Is that it? Walking corpses are glamorous?"

"Look who's talking about loving the dead." Patricia approached the mirror and pressed her palm against the glass. She stepped away, leaving a ghostly handprint. "Martin, something's been bothering me." The handprint dissolved. "Randall showed me your e-mail exchanges . . ."

He bit into his plum and frowned. "And . . . ?"

"Don't you see what this stupid trial is doing to you?"

"What's it doing to me?"

"It's warping you."

"Oh? How so?"

" 'Esther has scheduled some absolutely beautiful victims'—a direct quote from you. 'Esther has scheduled some absolutely beautiful victims.' "

"I'm tired, Patricia."

" 'Beautiful victims'? That's sick."

"Really tired."

"What does it profit a man if he wins *International 227* and loses his immortal soul?"

"Believe it or not, I have accorded this matter considerable thought." He devoured the plum all the way to the stone. "I agree with you that things have reached an odd pass when victims start looking beautiful. Given the choice between winning my case and losing my soul . . . well, it's simply no contest."

"I'm glad you see it that way."

"Damnation would be a small price to pay for a 'guilty' verdict."

"Martin, you're impossible."

A hammering sound wafted into the bedroom, the steady *thok-thok-thok* of the Lockheed 7000. He hobbled to the window and slammed it shut, sending crab spasms through his right shoulder and left femur.

"And another thing, all this cash you've been throwing around." She set his suitcase on the bed and released both clasps, each assuming the attitude of a first-class erection. "It's not right that people should get paid so much money for airing their pain in public. You're supposed to be running a trial, not a talk show."

"Witnesses receive money all the time."

"The media will call them mercenaries. Your Jobians will end up hating themselves."

"They *are* mercenaries." He considered hurling the plum stone at her, then lobbed it into the wastebasket instead. "Is there any way I can convince you to drop the present topic? I find it distasteful."

"I'll drop it if you'll let me inject you with one of these," she said, removing a 2cc vial of Odradex.

"Nothing doing."

"You're in pain."

"That's why God invented Roxanol."

"It hurts you to move—I can see it in your face. Maybe I should buy you a cane."

"Please do. Lovett owns a Malacca walking stick. We can have a duel."

Patricia sighed, replaced the vial, and absently extracted a Ziploc bag. "What the hell is *this*?"

"Mrs. Lot's right ear."

"Looks like a chunk of salt."

"Well, it is."

In a gesture that seemed erotic even to Martin's ruined libido, she untied the red silk scarf from her throat and looped it around his neck. "You really believe you're at war, don't you?"

"Yes."

"Then please accept this token. A knight should never go into battle unless he's wearing a lady's colors—right?"

"That depends."

"On what?"

"On whether the lady wants her knight to win."

"I don't want you to win, and I don't want you to lose." Patricia pulled on the ends of the scarf, drawing his face toward hers. "I just want you around as long as possible."

He smiled softly. "Remember that first time I came out to your house?" Extending his index finger, he slipped it under his silk shirt and rubbed the irritated skin above his Port-A-Cath valve. "How we sat on the rug in your studio and held each other for dear life?"

"Of course I remember."

An emphatic silence suffused Suite 300. They pulled off their shoes, climbed into bed, and slid beneath the coverlet, Patricia's head resting on his chest, her nose pressed against the valve. Martin curled his arm around her neck. The gentle cadence of her breathing, so unlike the raucous pounding of the heart-lung machine, combined with the opiate rush of the Roxanol to soothe his jangled nerves.

She began to sob.

"Dear Patricia," he whispered. "Dear, dear Patricia . . ."

"So plausible."

"Plausible?"

"Spina bifida. A tortured child."

"Yes. Plausible. Yes."

"I miss him."

He smoothed her raven hair with the flat of his hand. "Return your ticket, Patricia. I'm returning mine."

"My ticket?"

"To the universe of unavenged suffering."

"An appealing thought."

"Do it."

But instead of returning their tickets, they drifted off to sleep.

❖

Seeing the Peace Palace for the first time that sunny Saturday morning, Martin decided it looked more suited to opera than theodicy. Corinthian columns rose along a rococo facade, collectively supporting an entablature carved with grapevines. Between each pair of columns a statue of a famous diplomat—Dag Hammarskjold, Raoul Wallenberg, Benjamin Franklin, Charles Maurice de Tallyrand-Périgord—stared down at the tree-lined plaza below.

"It all goes back to 1899," Pierre Ferrand explained to Martin and the bodyguards, "when Czar Nicholas II called a conference with the aim of halting the runaway European arms race. Everyone sat around in The Hague for two weeks—drinking wine, denouncing war, and dreaming up the Permanent Court of Arbitration, forerunner of today's ICJ. For many years the thing had no home, but then the rich American Andrew Carnegie stepped in with a generous donation. The Permanent Court didn't last, but the Peace Palace did."

The plaza was jammed, a hurly-burly of locals, tourists, concessionaires, UN troops, Hans De Groot's police officers, and—

most conspicuously—the world's news-gathering organizations, their cords and cables snaking across the flagstones. Technicians swarmed everywhere, setting up cameras, positioning satellite dishes, and hopping in and out of TV-control vans. Hidden behind his crepe mustache and dark glasses, Martin approached the nearest souvenir stand and proceeded to survey its wares. Half the items bore mottoes written in either Dutch, German, or French; the rest were inscribed in English. He saw pennants reading TRIAL OF THE MILLENNIUM, bumper stickers declaring MY GOD IS INNOCENT AND I HOPE YOURS IS TOO, and T-shirts emblazoned with likenesses of Stuart Torvald and G. F. Lovett.

For a mere eight guilders he obtained a hardcover souvenir program book called *The Story of International 227*. To his everlasting relief, the vendor seemed not to recognize him.

Although the trial wasn't scheduled to start for seventy-two hours, hundreds of people had collected on the Peace Palace steps. Martin, Ferrand, and the bodyguards ascended cautiously, trying to look inconspicuous as they picked their way through the crowd. Most of the bystanders hugged sleeping bags and bedrolls, apparently intending to spend the weekend and thereby increase their chances of being seated inside on Monday. The majority looked young and bohemian; they might have been rock fans waiting to buy Guns N' Roses tickets. On the evidence of their placards, the bystanders divided evenly into two antagonistic camps. For every FREE THE AUTHOR OF FREE WILL, there was a PULL THE PLUG NOW. For every GET A JOB, JOB SOCIETY, there was a KILL ONE MAN AND YOU ARE A MURDERER, KILL A BILLION AND YOU ARE GOD.

Ferrand guided his charges through a bronze double door carved with the motto FIAT LUX. The four men lingered in the vestibule, a cavernous space appointed with medieval tapestries and Renaissance oils. "Shortly after the cornerstone was laid, Europe's leaders took time out from planning their military strategies to fill this atrium with priceless cultural treasures,"

Ferrand reported with cheerful cynicism. "By the beginning of the Great War, the Peace Palace had become one of the finest art museums on the continent."

A short journey down a marble hall, a brief ascent along a spiral staircase, and they were inside the main courtroom. The place was immense, a multileveled, oak-paneled conjunction of tables, benches, stands, docks, lecterns, galleries, translation booths, and—most strikingly—flags: three hundred at least, from every nation on Earth. TV technicians scurried about, setting up floodlights, testing microphones, dollying cameras into position. Chandeliers hung from the ceiling like bunches of crystalline bananas. Along the west wall six stained-glass Gothic windows stretched floor to ceiling, each depicting a magistrate whose decisions had reverberated with global import, including Francis Biddle of the Nuremberg Trials and John Dewey of the commission that vindicated Trotsky following his indictment by a Moscow kangaroo tribunal. For all its grandiosity, Martin felt entirely at home in this space. The Peace Palace courtroom, he realized, was nothing more than an elaborate version of his little hall of justice back in Abaddon.

He faced the judges' bench and limped down the aisle, his index finger sliding along a polished mahogany balustrade. More than ever he felt like a military commander—Napoleon himself, perhaps, reconnoitering the field on which thousands of troops would fight the next day. Where lay the high ground? On which hill should he amass his artillery? Reaching the bench, he did an about-face, fixed on Ferrand, and grinned.

"This will do."

Their final stop was the prosecution wing, a suite of twenty offices surrounding a domed rotunda like spokes on a wheel. In the center stood the human skeleton, Randall Selkirk, clutching a briefcase and speaking earnestly with the Amazon of Trenton, Esther Clute. As Martin greeted his fellow Jobians, the irony of the situation curled his lips into a smile. To the Baptists,

Jehovans, and other God fearers, the prosecution team was engaged in a byzantine and far-reaching conspiracy, when in fact its three members hardly knew each other.

"Your mustache is as phony as the disciplinary defense," said Randall, shaking Martin's hand.

"It gets the job done."

Esther explained that with the exceptions of Christopher Ransom, their amyotrophic-lateral-sclerosis victim, and Harry Elder, their cystic-fibrosis dad, the key sufferers were already in town. The first of their two expert witnesses—the cataclysmatician, Donald Carbone—would be arriving on Friday. The relevant dossiers were sitting in Martin's office, along with ten copies of the indictment itself.

Martin peeled off his mustache and scratched his itching upper lip. "Any breakthroughs from your Harvard kids?" he asked Randall.

"Nothing on ontology or free will—"

"I'm not surprised."

"—but they've thoroughly scoped out the defense's 'theological witnesses.' Just as I suspected, Brother Sebastian Cranach is their heavyweight." Selkirk added that Martin would find on his desk a dozen back issues of the *Augustinian Quarterly* and the *Thomist Review* containing the monk's articles. "Not exactly beach reading. Let's hope the judges find Cranach as impenetrable as I do."

Stepping into his office, Martin experienced a benign variety of claustrophobia. The place was like the cockpit of a jumbo jet: cramped, disorienting, and jammed with machines—telephone, computer, modem, fax, printer, copier. A combination coffee urn and warm-milk dispenser dominated the Danish-modern desk, rising from amid an avalanche of indictments, dossiers, depositions, interview transcripts, theology journals, and videocassettes of *A History of Havoc*.

While Olaf and Gunnar sat in the next room watching

dubbed *Cheers* reruns, Martin engaged in a jurisprudential frenzy, gulping down *koffie verkeerd* as he pored over the documents and worked on his opening statement. By four o'clock his stomach was rumbling audibly. So far, thank God, the crab had not undertaken to destroy his appetite.

Dusk found him sitting alongside his bodyguards in a fast-fish restaurant on Nieuwe Parklaan called Noordzee, eating a *haringsalade* and browsing through his souvenir program book. Among the highlights of *The Story of International 227* were eleven watercolor portraits depicting the "principal players" in the trial: Lovett, Martin, Randall, Esther, God, Sebastian Cranach, Bernard Kaplan, Eleanor Swann, Donald Carbone, Tonia Braverman, and Stuart Torvald. Martin's own image pleased him. The artist, a Dutchman named Van Brunt, had made him appear committed but not crazed, stricken but not terminal.

The Story of International 227 concluded with a signed article by Morris Stackpole, a philosophy professor at Binghamton University. In Stackpole's view, an odd variety of reverence lay at the heart of Martin's project. "A man who argues with God is a man who takes God seriously and thereby pays Him tribute," wrote Stackpole. "To rebuke the Almighty is to honor Him." A striking and disturbing thought, Martin decided, just the sort of perverse idea philosophers got paid for having.

On their way back to the Peace Palace they stopped off to see the famous Madurodam Miniature Town, a 1:25–scale copy of a Dutch village. Martin found it unimpressive and would have regretted the visit were it not for the modest bronze plaque in the lobby. The miniature town, the plaque explained, had been funded by J. M. L. Maduro as a memorial to his son, who had distinguished himself during the German invasion of 1940 and died five years later at Dachau.

Moral evil. A phenomenon for which, according to Saint Augustine, the Defendant could not be held responsible. "We'll see about that," he whispered to himself, raising an invisible stein of Oranjeboom beer to the memory of J. M. L. Maduro's boy. "We'll just see about that."

❖

On Sunday evening, having spent a mind-boggling afternoon studying the Kroft Museum catalog and screening the first three episodes of *A History of Havoc*, Martin convened—at Lovett's expense—a combination reunion banquet and strategy session in the Rembrandt Room of the Huize Bellevue. With the exception of those victims too busy, sick, or insolvent to travel, every charter member of the Job Society attended the event, a lavish buffet featuring roast pork, *fricandel* sausages, and other exemplars of the high-calorie Dutch diet. Looking around the hall, Martin drew considerable comfort from the familiar faces and equally familiar accessories. How could Lovett's "theological witnesses" possibly defeat the mute testimony of Norma Bedloe and her oxygen tank, Peter Henshaw and his IV drip, or Julia Schroeder and her portable dialysis machine?

As dessert was being served—those sufferers whose physicians permitted them sweets had a choice of either apple tarts or *stroopwafels* with ice cream—Martin rose and rapped his soup spoon against his water glass. The general addressing his troops: a classic scene, he mused—Henry V galvanizing his men on Saint Crispin's Day, George Patton intimidating his infantry at the beginning of the Hollywood biopic. He told his Jobians that many grueling hours of fighting lay ahead. He warned them that the World Court's protocols owed far more to international war crimes tribunals than to American jury trials. Forget Perry Mason. Forget the O. J. Simpson epic. Both the prosecution and the defense would enjoy extreme latitude in cross-examining witnesses. Objections were permitted in principle, but only a few would be sustained.

"Finally, I want to emphasize that nobody here is obligated to take the stand against his better judgment."

"Wild horses couldn't keep me from testifying," said legless Stanley Pallomar, bobbing back and forth in his wheelchair.

"Before we rehearse any interviews, I want to run my opening address past you." Martin drew a legal pad from his briefcase and, tilting his head slightly, aligned his bifocals with page one. "It's a little rough in spots, but I think it gets the job done. You tell me. Ready? Here goes." He ate a Roxanol and cleared his throat. "May it please the tribunal. The case before you, *International 227: Job Society, et al., plaintiffs, versus Corpus Dei, Defendant,* is paradoxical . . ."

❖

". . . paradoxical in the extreme," said Martin to the Western world.

He took a deep breath and planted his forearms on the lectern to reduce the pressure on his crumbling hips. The TV lights pained his irises and squeezed pearls of sweat from his brow. As he studied the bench, he realized he was also perspiring inside his three-piece linen suit—an ensemble he'd purchased right before boarding the *Carpco New Orleans*, its whiteness chosen to convey a subliminal saintliness, its bagginess to conceal his breasts. America, Great Britain, France, Holland, Italy, Mexico, Argentina, Israel, India: the nine judges—red robed, white bibbed, and bewigged, each equipped with a pair of headsets and a personal TV monitor—stared at him with hard, gelid eyes.

"It is paradoxical not only because the Defendant in His day was divine, but also because the reputation that preceded Him was impeccable. God, His partisans repeatedly told us, was good. Peaceful, they said. Merciful, loving, and just."

He winced, his voice having cracked on *impeccable* and *merciful*. He took a sip of water and vowed to get a grip on himself.

"The prosecution intends to show that exactly the opposite is true. Through the testimony of expert witnesses and ordinary victims, we shall prove that, whatever debt we may owe the

Defendant for the raw fact of our existence, He has continually acted in a fashion that must be called criminal."

Seeking to underscore this last sentence, he swept his arm toward the portrait of Francis Biddle but succeeded only in slapping the lectern microphone and creating a loud electronic thud. He gritted his teeth and pressed on.

"We shall prove that, during those millennia when God was presumably in charge of the universe, He caused or countenanced a stupefying array of atrocities."

He paused, momentarily distracted by the voice of a female translator rendering his words into French, the second official language of the World Court.

"What were these atrocities? The record is all too familiar. A complete list of the Defendant's crimes would require an indictment running to thousands of volumes. Item: in the year 19 B.C. an earthquake shook the eastern shore of the Mediterranean, slaughtering a hundred thousand in present-day Syria. Item: in A.D. 125 a plague swept through North Africa, leaving a million dead in Numidia and Carthage . . ."

Martin had three hundred and fourteen more items ready, a catalogue that excluded the great Cretaceous dying: fond as he was of Vivien and Lawrence, he felt their tragedy wouldn't move the judges. He spent a full hour reciting God's sins, periodically casting furtive glances toward the prosecution table, a massive oak slab swathed in green cloth. Esther offered an encouraging wink. Randall gave him a heartening thumbs-up. Pistols bulging from their armpits, Olaf and Gunnar smiled in unison.

"Philosophers divide human suffering into three categories. First comes natural evil. Earthquakes, tornadoes, droughts, plagues, spina bifida. Then we have moral evil—horrors committed by *Homo sapiens* in the name of historical necessity or self-defense. The Albigensian Crusade, the Spanish Inquisition, World War One, Dachau, Hiroshima, Rwanda. Finally we have existential evil—the treacherous interface between human ingenuity and the brute facts of gravity, combustion, and decay.

On August 10, 1887, an excursion train tumbled off a burning trestle in Chatsworth, Illinois, and as the cars piled on top of each other, eighty-two men, women, and children were crushed. On March 10, 1906, an explosion ripped through the Courrières coal mine in northern France, mangling, incinerating, and asphyxiating over a thousand men and boys. The evening of December 24, 1924, found two hundred youngsters and their parents jammed into a schoolhouse in Babb's Switch, Oklahoma, to watch a special holiday show. As Santa Claus began passing out presents, he knocked over a Christmas tree decorated with a lighted candle. Thirty-six children and adults perished in the resulting fire."

His voice was growing stronger. I can get through this, he told himself. I am as resolute as Job.

"But in the long run the philosophers' distinctions don't matter. What matters is whether or not our Creator in His day had good reasons for His manifest failure to prevent such tragedies."

As Martin slid his hand into his pants pocket, his fingertips brushed Patricia's red silk scarf. He pulled the scarf free, held it against his sopping forehead, and glanced toward the defense table. Dressed in a brown worsted suit reminiscent of Augustine's, Lovett raised a steaming mug of tea to his lips. His brother and aide-de-camp, Darcy—a large, veiny-nosed man with John L. Lewis eyebrows—sat disconsolately beside him, gripping a silver flask between his thumb and palm.

"Let me conclude on a personal note. As a boy I faithfully attended Perkinsville First Presbyterian Church in Pennsylvania. Throughout my youth and early manhood I had no quarrel with God. I loved my heavenly Father. As you might imagine, the journey I have taken since then has inflicted me with profound spiritual distress."

A fly buzzed through the courtroom, hurtling itself against the stained-glass portrait of John Dewey. Martin lowered his gaze and fixed on the court stenographer, a blowsy young man with a Roman nose, his fingers dancing nimbly on a computer keyboard.

"And yet, if there is one principle I came to hold sacred during my years as the magistrate of Abaddon Township, it is this: once you know someone is guilty, you must prosecute that person with unrelenting diligence. To do otherwise is to mock the name of justice. Thank you, Your Honors. For the moment I am finished."

"The tribunal will recess for lunch," said Stuart Torvald, confronting the Court TV camera with a bored and sullen face.

❖

"Do we really have to watch this shit?" asked Funkeldune, pointing toward my Zenith. He reached into the popcorn bowl, grabbed a fistful of raw kernels, and shoved them into his mouth. "We're missing *The 700 Club*."

I looked up from the sewing machine. The TV screen showed a CNN reporter standing outside the courtroom, favoring his audience with an impromptu analysis of Candle's speech. I went back to my project: a new American flag for the incinerated schoolhouse in the Idea of Babb's Switch in the Idea of Oklahoma.

"I'll have you know this is the hottest trial since the O. J. Simpson case," I told my disciple.

"Oh, gimme a break," said Funkeldune as the corn kernels began erupting in his fiery maw. *Pop, pop, pop.* "That one had sex, violence, jealousy, dogs, corrupt policemen, a likable defendant—everything. This one has three-piece suits and a lot of talk."

Schonspigel devoured a Klondike bar in one bite. "Can't we watch the Superbowl instead?"

"The Superbowl won't be on for another eight months."

"*Gilligan's Island?*" asked Funkeldune. *Pop, pop, pop.*

"No."

"*The Love Boat?*" asked Belphegor.

"Forget it."

"*Wheel of Fortune?*" asked Schonspigel.

I did not deign to reply.

❖

"Did you read this article by Morris Stackpole?" asked Martin after lunch, shoving his copy of *The Story of International 227* toward Randall and Esther.

"I thought it was a crock," said Randall.

"You don't believe that to rebuke God is to honor Him?"

"If I thought that, I'd hop on the first plane back to Boston."

"Don't tell me *you* buy Stackpole's argument," said Esther.

"I need to think it over," said Martin.

"What's there to think over?"

"I need to think it over . . ."

"The defense will make its opening statement," said Torvald, demurely readjusting his wig.

Locking his Malacca walking stick under his arm, Lovett sauntered toward the front of the courtroom. He removed a scrolled manuscript from his coat pocket and unfurled it on the lectern.

"May it please the tribunal. Let me begin by saying that the defense will not be satisfied merely to establish a lack of culpability in this case. A conventional 'not guilty' verdict would be inadequate here. Rather, we intend to prove our heavenly Father's fundamental innocence and, beyond that, His complete and everlasting perfection. We shall reveal to you a Creator who is worshipworthy in the extreme.

"If our goal were simply to protect our Client from disconnection and death, we would ask you to annul this case forthwith. We would preface our petition by arguing that judicial bodies such as the World Court are empowered to prosecute people rather than deities, and that Your Honors' jurisdiction does not extend to the numinous.

"We shall make no such request. On the contrary, we could not be more pleased that *International 227* has been convened. For far too long the best solutions to the problem of evil have been the private possession of a few cloistered theologians. It's time the public at large received the answers. Looking around this courtroom, I notice lights, cameras, microphones, and journalists. To this I say, 'Good!' Our Client has nothing to hide. He justified Himself to Job, and before the summer is out He will have justified Himself to you."

Lovett now launched into an elaborate philosophical analysis of the three qualities the pre-coma God was generally believed to possess: omnipotence, omniscience, omnibenevolence. He noted that, over the years, epistemologists had attempted to place logical limits on the Defendant's power, knowledge, and generosity. These misguided sophists liked to assert, for example, that God could not square a circle or create a stone too heavy for Him to lift. They argued that God had evidently been unable to foresee the Fall of Man—hence His righteous indignation when it occurred. In Lovett's view, such arguments were merely word games, failing to diminish the Almighty in any meaningful way.

"One popular solution to the conundrum of suffering, a solution with which I shall not waste anyone's time this summer, is essentially a compromise. This answer holds that, given the fact of evil, we cannot rationally ascribe to the pre-coma God His three traditional attributes. If the Defendant was all-knowing and all-good, He can't have been all-powerful—otherwise He would have continually intervened to end our pain. If the Defendant was all-powerful and all-good, He must have been unaware of our torment. Finally, if He was all-powerful and all-knowing, He was amoral at best and malicious at worst.

"We shall not take the easy way out. We shall not presume our Client was ignorant of human misery, nor shall we suggest

He was incapable of ending it. At the moment I wouldn't blame any of you for saying, 'The riddle is unsolvable. Either God is guilty as charged, or He was never really God.' But the riddle *is* solvable, Your Honors. The answer is satisfying but subtle. You will have to listen carefully to my witnesses—one of whom, I am pleased to report, will be Martin Candle himself, so profound is his commitment to learning the truth about human suffering. By the time *International 227* is over, you will all know why no contradiction exists between the stark reality of pain and the assumption of an omnipotent, omniscient, omnibenevolent, worshipworthy Creator. Thank you."

"So . . . what do you think?" asked Martin apprehensively.

"If I ever blow up a nursery school," said Esther glumly, "Lovett's the man I want defending me."

"Blow up ten nursery schools," said Randall, "and he'll probably take the case for free."

"The tribunal will stand in recess until ten o'clock tomorrow morning," said Torvald, lethargically rapping his Christmas gavel on the bench.

Chapter 12

THE ONLY ENGLISH-LANGUAGE NEWSPAPERS on sale in the pharmacy of the Huize Bellevue were the *International Herald Tribune* and *USA Today*, and the morning after delivering his opening statement Martin bought a copy of each for five guilders apiece. Surprisingly, *USA Today* covered recent events at the Peace Palace in greater detail than did the *Tribune*, though its treatment of Martin's performance was far less sympathetic. Whereas the *Tribune* editorial claimed that "from start to finish, Candle presented himself as a passionate student of life's deepest mysteries," *USA Today* asserted that "the chief prosecutor came across not so much as an accuser as a whiner, a man with an adolescent chip on his shoulder and a sophomoric obsession on his mind."

A passionate student of life's deepest mysteries: Martin liked that—he liked it so much he clipped the phrase from the paper and placed it in his wallet, where it became a kind of caption to his driver's license photo. Hobbling into the Peace Palace at 9:45 A.M., his right hand gripping the mahogany cane Patricia had given him the night before, he felt more certain of victory than at any time since conceiving *International 227*. He sat down, propped his cane against the prosecution table, smiled at Randall, and gave Esther an affectionate pat on the arm.

"Well, folks, here we go."

"Off to kill the wizard," said Esther.

"Did you catch Court TV last night?" asked Randall.

"No." Martin studied the head of his cane; it was sculpted to resemble a crocodile, though to his Jobian's imagination it looked more like Leviathan. "I was reading witness dossiers and back issues of the *Augustinian Quarterly*."

"They reran your whole speech."

"How did I look?"

"Otherworldly. That white suit makes you glow."

With a desultory rap of his golden gavel, Torvald convened the tribunal and invited the prosecution to examine its first witness.

Martin grabbed his cane, stood up, and limped toward the lectern. "The people call Norma Bedloe."

The witness chamber door swung open, and Martin's lead-off sufferer stepped forward, a hunched, shriveled woman in a blue print dress, a symmetrical pair of plastic tubes arcing upward from her nostrils like a Salvador Dalí mustache. Her right hand gripped the flange of an oxygen bottle: a green, lozenge-shaped metal tank that she dragged behind her like a penitential weight.

As Norma settled behind the stand, the court usher—an elfin young man with waxy skin—slapped a Dutch Reformed Church Bible into her palm and said, "Please state your name."

The witness identified herself, swore to speak the truth, and, prompted by Martin, launched into her story. A lifelong resident of Walnut Ridge, Arkansas, Norma had entered the world too soon, a three-pound preemie cursed with a malformed liver. For the past thirty-five years, her body had been relentlessly engaged in poisoning itself. Her left lung was ruined, her right ventricle damaged, her cerebellum injured, her spine wrecked. She had suffered three myocardial infarctions in as many years. She was always cold. Every day, Norma kept her symptoms under control and her pain in check by swallowing sixty-seven different pills, tablets, lozenges, and capsules.

"The problem is, half the time I throw 'em up before they can get in my blood." Norma leaned toward the witness-stand microphone, a sleek cylinder affixed to a gooseneck shaft. "That's the great fear a person like me has to live with."

"The fear of regurgitating your pills?" Martin propped his elbows on the lectern, resting his jaw between his fists.

"Right. Ever since I decided to end it all, I've been scared my stomach won't cooperate."

"You intend to commit suicide?"

Norma nodded. "No American doctor has been willing to help me out. When I realized I'd be getting a free trip to the Netherlands, I decided to book an early flight. Three days ago I met with a gastroenterologist in Amsterdam who told me exactly which over-the-counter drugs would . . . you know . . ."

"Stop your heart?" asked Martin, furtively eating a Roxanol.

"Right. As soon as I understood what he was saying, my eyes filled with tears of joy." From her dress pocket she produced a picture postcard. "He wrote the formula on the back of this card. The other side shows Rembrandt's *The Blinding of Samson*. I've probably kissed Samson a hundred times by now."

"Your final exit is scheduled for . . ."

"Soon as I get home. Three of my girlfriends will be dropping by. A kind of going-away party."

Slowly—too slowly—the sacred opium pacified the crab. "Miss Bedloe, I have just one more question. Who would you say is responsible for your suffering?"

Lovett waved his hand about in a perfunctory gesture of protest. "Objection," he said without bothering to rise.

"Overruled," said Torvald dryly.

I should hope so, thought Martin.

Norma's jaw tightened. "It's not really my place to judge Him . . . but I will say this—I think He gave me the worst damn liver in Creation."

"You blame the Defendant?"

"Yes, sir, I do. I blame the Defendant."

A sensation somewhere between exhilaration and terror washed through Martin. With Norma Bedloe's unequivocal accusation—transcribed in English by the court stenographer and echoed in French by the translator—a threshold had been crossed. *International 227* was no longer one man's private grudge match. Now it belonged to the world.

Two minutes later Lovett stood before the witness, addressing her in a manner at once gentle and paternalistic.

"You're thirty-five years old, correct?"

"Correct."

"And now you intend to end it all?"

"Right."

"That makes me very sad, Miss Bedloe."

"Nobody's asking you to come to the party."

"As you probably know, until quite recently three-pound preemies typically died within hours of their births. Some people would say it's a miracle you're here at all."

"Thank God for small favors," said Norma with a carefully practiced sneer.

"Atta girl," whispered Randall to his teammates.

"You picked a winner," muttered Martin, squeezing Esther's hand.

"Do you wish you'd died at birth?" asked Lovett.

"I get that question a lot," said Norma.

"How do you answer it?"

"Depends on who I'm talking to. Sometimes I tell people what they want to hear. Sometimes I tell 'em the truth."

"And what is the truth?" asked Lovett, smiling expansively.

"I wish I'd died."

Lovett's smile remained disconcertingly intact. "As you were growing up, did you ever ask your heavenly Father to make you well?"

"You mean . . . did I pray? Sure, I prayed. Wouldn't you?"

"Why would you beseech a God you regarded as malevolent?"

"I've never regarded Him as malevolent."

"How *do* you regard Him?"

"Hard to say. Kind of like those scientists Boris Karloff used to play in the old horror movies, always trying to discover a cure for cancer or death or something. Inevitably the experiment would backfire, after which Karloff would go off his rocker."

"You see God as a mad scientist?"

"That's right."

"Boris Karloff?"

"Boris Karloff."

"No further questions."

"Do you wish to redirect?" Torvald asked Martin.

"No, Your Honor," Martin replied, cavorting internally. Norma needed no redirection. She'd never lost her bearings.

For his second sufferer of the morning, Martin called Wanda Jo Jenkins, an earthy adolescent reminiscent of Lot's pregnant daughter Shuah.

"How old are you?" he asked Wanda Jo after she'd given her oath.

"I turn seventeen tomorrow, sir," she answered in a melodious Southern accent.

"Is that a wedding ring I see on your hand?"

"It is."

"So you're married, then?"

"I'm a widow, sir."

"Please tell the tribunal about your late husband."

In an unrehearsed but brilliantly effective move, Wanda Jo looked directly toward the bench. "Maybe you judges read about it in *People* magazine. Billy was one of those three hemophiliac brothers who got AIDS from a batch of contaminated blood factor."

"Are you referring to the so-called Atlanta Blood Center scandal?" asked Martin.

"I am, sir."

"Did Billy Jenkins know he was dying when you married him?"

"He did."

"How old were you?"

"On our wedding day I was fifteen and Billy was fourteen."

A collective gasp wafted through the courtroom.

"Where were you and Billy living?"

"Bossier City, Louisiana, but we had to go across the state border into Carthage. Fourteen-year-olds can't get legally married in Louisiana. They can in Texas."

"Were your parents supportive of this union?"

"The night before I walked down the aisle, my daddy said to me, 'Wanda Jo, normally I'd boot your butt for doin' something like this, but I gotta tell you that right now I'm probably the proudest father in the whole US of A.'"

"Did Billy Jenkins have any AIDS symptoms at this time?"

"Yes, sir. He was an outpatient at Bertram Percy Children's Hospital in Shreveport. We had to wheel his bed into the church. He married me lying down."

This couldn't be going better, thought Martin, who had himself performed four such ceremonies during his career as a JP. "That must have been a pretty emotional day for you."

"It was the happiest day of my life."

"Did you marry Billy because you pitied him?"

"No, sir. I married him because I was in love with him. And also . . . well, I knew if we didn't get married, Billy would still be a boy when he died and not a man."

"Was Billy a man when he died?"

"He was, sir."

"You were taking a certain risk, weren't you?"

"We used condoms. Billy was a great lover, very enthusiastic.

Near the end it got too painful for him because of the lesions all over his body."

Martin paused, letting Billy's Jobian sores engrave themselves into the judges' imaginations.

"Do you consider yourself a religious woman, Mrs. Jenkins?"

"Most every Sunday I attend Mount Calvary Methodist Church back home in Bossier City."

"Do you ever pray while you're there?"

"All the time."

"What do pray for?"

"I pray for God to help me find a way to forgive Him."

"No further questions."

Lovett began the cross-examination by asking Wanda Jo to describe her late husband. How did Billy dress? What were his favorite television programs? Did he have any hobbies?

The witness replied that Billy dressed like a slob, that he watched a lot of professional hockey on TV, and that he enjoyed launching toy rockets. "Once he sent up a gerbil and brought it back alive. His mom hated to see him running around with his rockets. She was afraid he'd start bleeding."

"What else did your husband do for fun?"

"Whenever I picture Billy, I see him with his nose in a book. He collected all your Sargassia stories. He especially liked *The Boy, the Bear, and the Broom Closet.*"

"Mrs. Jenkins, do you ever feel Billy is still with you in some way?"

"With me?"

"Near you. Beside you. Watching over you."

"Sometimes I hear his voice in my head. He had this wonderful scratchy voice."

"Do you think maybe he's talking to you from Heaven?"

"No, sir, I don't think that."

"Do you believe there's a Heaven?"

"No more than I believe there's an Island of Sargassia."

"Another inspired selection," Martin whispered, winking brightly at Esther.

"Thank you, Mrs. Jenkins," said Lovett. "That will be all."

❖

After the lunch recess Martin continued parading his Jobians before the bench. Orin Bromwell: multiple sclerosis. Julia Schroeder: kidney failure. Peter Henshaw: AIDS. The next day the prosecution summoned a new set of victims. Writhing around in his wheelchair, Christopher Ransom spent the morning testifying to the horrors of amyotrophic lateral sclerosis, his relentless awareness that he would soon possess "the mind of a man trapped in the body of a cabbage." That afternoon, award-winning watercolorist Carolyn Meeshaw described "losing my vision for the Almighty's amusement" at the height of her career. Shifting roles from prosecutor to witness, Esther took the stand and recounted how "one of God's beloved roundworms" had ravaged her daughter's brain.

In cross-examining these assorted sufferers, Lovett adopted the same impassive demeanor he'd employed at the outset with Norma Bedloe and Wanda Jo Jenkins. He was polite, even a tad solicitous, but he still managed to insinuate their ordeals entailed harmonies of which they were only dimly aware.

Cancer consumed the rest of the week, the whole satanic spectrum, from brain to bowel, liver to lung, breast to prostate. "Lovett might have ontology on his side," muttered Randall to his colleagues, "but we've got oncology." Especially affecting was the testimony of Frank Latham, whose twenty-year-old sister had died of Hodgkin's disease after a decade of chemotherapeutic torture. "She got so many cards and letters, the mailman started joking he wanted a tip," said Latham, voice cracking. "Everybody loved Elsa." But Martin really struck pay dirt when he put Rosalind Kreuger on the stand. Fighting tears, Kreuger told how her youngest child, Mary Lou, had succumbed to acute lymphoblastic leukemia at age nine, despite a last-ditch bone-marrow transplant. More than anything else, Mary Lou loved swimming, and in her final days she kept asking for her very own pool. "The Make-A-Wish people came through, all right, but not the way she was hoping," said Kreuger. "They bought her one of those big, round, above-the-ground pools. Mary Lou wanted a *real* pool—she wanted them to dig a hole in our yard and fill it with water. She tried to hide her disappointment, but I could still tell how she felt."

Martin spent the weekend sitting beside Patricia on the couch in his hotel suite, poring over victim dossiers, the television tuned to CNN's cogent condensation of the Job Society's first week in court. In the middle of Christopher Ransom's autobiography, the network cut to a toothsome anchorman bearing the news that on Friday afternoon—shortly before midnight, Eastern Standard Time—people's witness Norma Bedloe of Walnut Ridge, Arkansas, had committed suicide in the company of three friends.

"Such a sad story," said Olaf.

"I guess she had no other choice," said Gunnar.

"A Jobian to the end," said Martin. "You're a heroic woman, Norma."

"You wouldn't call her heroic if she'd done it *before* she testified," grunted Patricia, looking up from her sketch pad. The page displayed an immense stag beetle crushing a school bus between its pincers. "These poor people, they're nothing to you. They're pawns."

"Patricia, that's not fair," said Martin.

"You were practically drooling when Mary Lou Kreuger didn't get the right kind of swimming pool."

"Whose side are you on, anyway?"

"I'm on your side, Martin. The problem is, I'm not sure *you* are."

"I didn't *drool*."

"You drooled," said Olaf.

"You drooled," said Gunnar.

When *International 227* resumed on Monday, Martin shifted the focus from pathology to other varieties of natural evil, a strategy he pursued through Tuesday morning. Eleven different Jobians told how their lives had been irrevocably altered by what Martin called "the mindless violence of Mother Earth." Calvin Hatch was a retired auto mechanic who'd become subject to dreadful seizures after a flying hubcap struck his head during the hurricane that visited Xenia, Ohio, in 1974. Eugene West was a Hollywood screenwriter whose teenage brother had been speared through the chest by a WATCH CHILDREN sign during the great Los Angeles earthquake of 1994.

Nature's victims did not impress Lovett. Invited to cross-examine them, he sent his brother to the lectern instead. The resulting exchanges were perfunctory and unfocused. In most cases, Darcy merely had the witness repeat some inconsequential fact or other: the date of a certain avalanche, the duration of a particular hailstorm, the speed of a specific tornado.

After the Tuesday lunch break Esther took over at the front of the room, and by five P.M. on Wednesday she'd interviewed fourteen different Jobians who'd been either mutilated or bereaved by car crashes, handgun accidents, carpet-glue vapors, open elevator shafts, faulty drawbridges, and decrepit roller coasters, each such existential catastrophe featuring its own unique mix of poignancy and absurdity. June Weintraub recounted the deathbed agonies of her adolescent son, Aaron, whose Bigfoot costume had caught fire during a campfire skit in the Catskills. Marilyn Stonebury described standing outside Our Lady of the Angels Parochial School in Chicago with two dozen other parents on December 1, 1958, all of them listening to their dying children's screams as flames consumed the building. Hands protruding directly from his shoulders like a seal's flippers, forty-year-old Malcolm Beale told what it was like to go through life as one of Europe's eight thousand "Thalidomide babies."

In cross-examining the existential victims Lovett managed to exude compassion while still holding his theological ground. The theme he developed was as straightforward as a geometry proof. Existential evil variously traces to human arrogance, negligence, and stupidity. The Defendant was not to blame.

On Thursday and Friday, Esther guided the tribunal across the vast, cratered continent of moral evil. Sheila Rabinowitz's twelve-year-old daughter had been raped and eviscerated by a serial killer in San Diego. Bruce Kadrey's preschool son had been pulverized during the 1995 terrorist bombing of the Alfred P. Murrah Federal Building in Oklahoma City. On the final day of his Vietnam combat tour, Stanley Pallomar had stumbled into a booby-trapped howitzer round, losing both his legs, the fingers of his left hand, and large chunks of his chest. The war hero testified from his wheelchair, listing from side to side like Brandon Appleyard's Godzilla punching doll. Esther saved her most affecting moral witness for last: Xavier Mrugamba, a maimed Rwandan expatriate who'd miraculously survived the genocide of 1994 and now lived outside London. When the Hutu youth militia invaded his homestead near Kigali, Xavier had begged them not to dismember his family alive with machetes, and so the soldiers invited him to take his wife and two children into the backyard, bind their hands, and hurl them screaming down the latrine wells . . . which he did, whereupon the Hutus hacked off his arms and left him for dead.

Lovett declined to interview the victims of moral evil, and this time he didn't even send Darcy onto the field. Moral evil is an unavoidable consequence of human free will, ran Lovett's tacit argument. Leave our Client out of it.

Martin cast an anxious gaze toward the bench. None of the judges seemed particularly engaged in the matter at hand; they all looked as if they'd rather be reviewing the testimony in an international boundary dispute. Had this flood of melodrama offended them? Had they been put off by Norma Bedloe's baleful liver, June Weintraub's roasted son, Malcolm Beale's phocomelia, and Xavier Mrugamba's mutilation? Time to switch strategies, he decided. Time to stash the sufferers and hand the case over to the professionals.

❖

From the photograph in the catalog of the Kroft Museum of Natural Disasters and Technological Catastrophes, Martin had concluded that Dr. Donald Carbone was tall, but the man now crossing the courtroom looked decidedly squat. Martin inspected the catalog photo, soon realizing his mistake: the shot had been taken at the museum itself, and the racing car alongside Carbone was a three-fifths-scale replica of the Mercedes-Benz that had spun lethally out of control during the 1955 Grand Prix.

What he lacked in stature, the sociologist affected in swagger. Settling behind the stand, he exuded a measure of vanity that Martin would have found insufferable in a witness for the defense. Upon being sworn in, Carbone magisterially informed the tribunal that he ran the Disaster Studies Department at Bowling Green State University in Ohio, where he held the Poincaré Chair in Applied Cataclysmics.

"Disaster studies," said Martin as the crab locked a fighting claw around his left shoulder. "That's a relatively new field, correct?"

"At the risk of sounding immodest, I would have to say I invented it."

Turning away from the lectern, Martin surreptitiously consumed two Roxanols. "Please tell the tribunal something about disaster studies."

"Our argument is simple." Carbone seized the witness-stand mike, pulling it level with his mouth. "By analyzing history's worst events through the emerging science of cataclysmics, researchers can learn how the human psyche functions under stress and also gain unique insights into nature's primary patterns."

"Events such as . . . ?"

"Plagues, famines, earthquakes, plane crashes, circus fires," Carbone recited breezily, his voice rising and falling with incongruous musicality. "Stroll through our museum—I'm referring to the Kroft Museum of Natural Disasters and Technological Catastrophes—and you'll catch on right away."

As the opium reached his cerebrum, forcing the crab to relax its grip, Martin gestured toward five heaps of bric-a-brac stacked against the west wall. It had taken Randall and Esther the entire weekend to haul the evidence into the Peace Palace and arrange it atop the exhibit table. "Dr. Carbone, do you recognize those artifacts over there?"

"They are all display items from the Kroft Museum."

Limping toward the exhibits with the aid of his crocodile cane, Martin selected a three-foot-square blowup of a transmission electron-microscope photograph labeled PEOPLE's EXHIBIT A-1: PASTEURELLA PESTIS. The image suggested a population of dispossessed worms lying on a sidewalk following a rainstorm.

"What's this?" he asked, bearing the blowup to Carbone.

"The bacterium that causes bubonic plague, enlarged one thousand times. Normally that picture hangs in our Hall of Epidemics."

Martin faced the Court TV camera and thrust the bacterium photo forward, making it register dramatically on the judges' personal monitors. Always lead with your ace, he thought, setting the photo beside the stand. "Your Honors, the prosecution is offering in evidence People's Exhibit A-1: *Pasteurella pestis*."

"Does the defense have any objections to the admission of *Pasteurella pestis*?" Torvald asked Lovett.

"We do in principle, Your Honor, but we want Mr. Candle to enjoy the widest possible latitude in developing his case."

"You may proceed, Mr. Candle," said Torvald.

"Please tell the tribunal about the Plague."

"Several notable outbreaks occurred before the fourteenth century, but when people talk about 'the Plague,' they generally mean the great epidemic that began in 1347," said Carbone animatedly. "Words fail, really. The stench of decaying bodies pervaded every major European city. Half the population of Florence died in six months. Fifty thousand corpses were thrown into one mass grave outside London. In southern France they ran out of burial space, so the Avignonese pope, Clement VI, had to consecrate the Rhône River."

"One of the murals in your Hall of Epidemics depicts peasants hanging fifty dogs en masse," said Martin, assuming the lectern.

"People got the mistaken idea that dogs harbored the infection, so the animals were systematically slaughtered. The strategy backfired—killing the dogs eliminated the main predator of the rats whose fleas really *did* carry the bacterium."

"Another mural shows a band of penitents whipping themselves."

"In 1350 Pope Clement organized a mass pilgrimage to Rome. He thought God might smile favorably on such a conspicuous display of faith, but the flagellants merely helped to spread the disease farther."

"The Plague lasted almost four years, correct?"

"It finally petered out in 1351, after killing twenty-five million men, women, and children."

"Did you say twenty-five million?"

"Twenty-five million."

Martin cocked a sardonic eye toward the photo. "That wasn't the last humanity would hear from *Pasteurella pestis*, was it?"

"In 1664 London was a teeming metropolis of about five hundred thousand. By September of 1665 you could walk down the deserted streets at midday and see house after house boarded up and marked with a red cross."

"Boarded up? Why?"

"The city officials were imprisoning stricken Londoners inside their own homes. Our plague diorama features one such doorway. You can still read the message over the painted cross. 'Lord have mercy on us.'"

Martin returned to the exhibit table and retrieved an electron-microscope photo labeled PEOPLE'S EXHIBIT A-2: *TREPONEMA PALLIDUM*. Dozens of corkscrew-shaped pathogens filled the circular frame. "What have we here?" he asked, holding the image before the Court TV camera.

"The spirochete that causes syphilis."

"A particularly virulent strain of syphilis rampaged through Europe in the late fifteenth century, correct?"

"The doctors had never seen anything like it. They had their patients drink snake blood, sometimes vulture broth mixed with sarsaparilla. One army surgeon was forced to amputate the genitalia of five thousand infected soldiers."

Martin spent the rest of the day and all of the following morning filling the record with microbes from the Kroft Museum's maleficent zoo. The diphtheria bacterium. The cholera bacterium. The smallpox virus. The measles virus, still racking up an annual body count of 880,000. HIV, presently responsible for 550,000 deaths each year. *Plasmodium*, the malaria protozoan, currently occasioning 1,000,000 corpses per annum.

On Tuesday afternoon Randall took over the task of recording what he called "the biological weapons deployed by the Defendant in His relentless war on humanity." People's Exhibit A-27 was a two-foot-long plastic model of the mosquito *Aëdes aegypti*, vector of the dreaded yellow fever virus. Holding the model in his lap like a pet, Carbone explained that from 1793 to 1798 yellow fever killed about 12,700 British soldiers in the French colony of Saint Domingue. Exhibit A-31 was a loaf of bread made from rye contaminated with ergot, a disease caused by the fungus *Claviceps purpurea*. In 1722 nearly 20,000 Russians died in excruciating pain after eating ergot-contaminated bread. Exhibit A-34 was a cloth face mask worn by a San Francisco dock worker during the great influenza epidemic of 1918–1919. The masks did no appreciable good, but the city fathers still made them mandatory. Worldwide death toll: 22,000,000.

On Wednesday morning Martin returned to the lectern, a

piercingly familiar object now; he knew its every nick and whorl. He put aside the tiny universe of pathogens and began addressing the larger-than-life fact of planetary upheaval, leading the judges through the Chamber of Earthquakes and Volcanic Eruptions.

People's Exhibit B-1 was the fractured skull of a child who'd been crushed along with 20,000 other victims by the great Spartan earthquake of 464 B.C. Exhibit B-9 was a smashed bell from a Byzantine church destroyed by the quake that leveled Antioch in A.D. 526, killing 150,000 Christians. As the day wore on, Martin stepped up both the pace of his presentation and the audacity of his rhetoric, using Kroft artifacts to document how the Defendant had "inflicted His seismic wrath" on forty-eight separate population centers between 1456 and 1999. The great Lisbon earthquake of 1755, which did so much to nurture Enlightenment skepticism concerning divine justice, slaughtered 75,000, including hundreds of worshipers gathered in the cathedrals for All Saints' Day services. The worst disaster in the history of Peru occurred on May 31, 1970, when a powerful quake shook the region around Chimbote. The debris, ash, and subsequent famine claimed 60,000 lives and orphaned 5,000 children. A survivor radioing for assistance moaned, "We have no medicine. No food. All night long, the women have cried and prayed. Some men were cursing, raising their fists to Heaven."

"Raising their fists to Heaven?" said Martin.

"That's what the survivor reported," said Carbone.

Martin passed the evening in the company of Patricia and his bodyguards, studying the Kroft Museum catalog while the others watched the day's highlights on CNN.

"You've got to ease up a bit," said Patricia as she drew the wings on a giant dragonfly that appeared to be attempting sexual intercourse with a jetliner. "You're indulging in overkill."

"*God* indulges in overkill. *I* indulge in facts."

"All those plagues and earthquakes—it's making people numb."

"Your friend has a point," said Olaf.

"If we didn't know you personally, we'd be tempted to change channels," said Gunnar.

"Numb?" wailed Martin. "*Numb?* What about the diseases I *didn't* introduce? What about tuberculosis and typhus? What about Chagas's disease? Do you know how many people Chagas's disease kills each year? Seven hundred thousand! Whooping cough—three hundred and sixty thousand! Hepatitis B—two million!"

"The judges are bored," said Patricia. "You can read it in their faces. Enough already with the earthquakes."

"We're finished with the earthquakes."

"Good."

"Tomorrow we do the volcanoes."

On Thursday morning Randall once again assumed the task of examining Carbone. He pointed toward People's Exhibit B-63, which appeared to be a plaster sculpture of a young boy. "What have we here?"

"A five-year-old victim of the Mount Vesuvius eruption that wiped out Pompeii and Herculaneum in A.D. 79," Carbone replied merrily. "There are ninety-eight such figures in existence. Our museum owns sixteen. Many of Pompeii's citizens, you see, were buried alive in molten ash. After it hardened, their bodies decomposed, leaving natural molds behind. To get an object like that one, an archaeologist merely had to pour liquid plaster-of-Paris into the cavity, let it solidify, and chip away the ash."

"So Exhibit B-63 isn't really a sculpture, is it?"

"No, Mr. Selkirk, it's a casting—a kind of three-dimensional photograph of a child dying in agony as hot gases sear his lungs."

Thus began the cavalcade of volcanoes, twenty-five in all, for a total of over 3,000,000 victims—from the explosion that rocked the island of Thera in 1628 B.C. to the vaporous geyser that shot out of Cameroon's Lake Nios in 1986 and subjected 2,000 villagers to a painful, choking death. As the interview progressed, Martin found himself scoring each eruption according to the

number of corpses it created. A respectable 15,000 for Sicily's
Mount Etna in 1169; a boffo 53,000 for Japan's Unsen in 1793;
a pathetic 1,200 for the Philippines' Mayon in 1814; a solid 36,000
for Indonesia's Krakatoa in 1883; a disappointing 6,000 for
Guatemala's Santa Maria in 1902. Particularly spectacular was
the June 8, 1783, eruption of Iceland's Mount Laki, which killed
9,000 outright and obliterated the sun with ash, triggering a famine so intense that starving horses cannibalized one another and
humans were reduced to eating rope. No less impressive was the
explosion that tore apart Martinique's Mount Pelée on May 8,
1902, and sent a gigantic flaming gasball barreling through the
capital city of Saint Pierre. Amazingly, many of Pelée's 35,000
victims were discovered with their clothes unburned. The su-
perheated cloud had moved too quickly to ignite the material,
though it did have time to vaporize the Martinicans' blood and
make their brains explode.

After lunch, Esther took over the examination, inventorying
the Transportation Tragedies Room. Exhibit C-11 was the
smashed altimeter from a Venezuelan DC-9 that unexpectedly
lost height on March 16, 1969, and hurtled into a Maracaibo
suburb. All eighty-four passengers died, and a family of five
sitting around the dinner table was annihilated when the plane
plowed through their home. Exhibit C-13 was the rear door
from the U.S. Air Force transport that left Saigon on April 4,
1975, filled with Vietnamese children, beneficiaries of a plan to
rescue the war-torn country's orphans. After the door in question
blew out, the plane crash-landed in a rice paddy. Fifty orphans
strapped into the cargo hold were squashed on contact, while a
hundred and twenty-two others eventually died of their injuries.

The next day, having placed twenty-four air disasters on the
record, Esther spotlighted what she called "the Defendant's ac-
quiescence to scores of maritime catastrophes." Exhibit C-31 was
a manacle recovered from the wreck of the *Sisters*, a British slave
ship capsized by a gust of wind on May 17, 1787, during a voyage

from Africa to Cuba. Four hundred and ninety-seven captive blacks were drowned, chained in their berths. Exhibit C-45 was a compass from the freighter *Mont Blanc*, which was cruising out of Halifax Harbor on December 6, 1917, its hold laden with TNT and benzine, when it rammed into the merchant ship *Imo*. The blast hurled the *Imo* onto dry land, leveled two square miles of the town, and left hundreds of children dead beneath the collapsed walls of their schools and orphanages.

Martin spent the lunch recess in his office, perusing the Kroft Museum catalog while talking on the phone with Patricia.

"How do you think it's going?"

"You really want to know?"

"Well, yes."

"You're overplaying your orphans. First the Chimbote quake, then that plane crash in Vietnam, then the Halifax Harbor explosion."

"Too many orphans? You can't have too many orphans."

"Too many orphans, Martin. You'd better cool it."

That afternoon, Esther finally exhausted the Transportation Tragedies Room, filling the record with evidence from twenty-six famous railroad, automobile, and subway wrecks. Exhibit C-68 was the transmission from a Mercedes-Benz that skidded crazily during the Grand Prix at Le Mans on June 11, 1955, shooting over the dirt wall and landing on the crowd. Flying debris sliced through scores of victims and decapitated two children before their parents' eyes. Exhibit C-72 was a sign indicating Moorgate Station, a terminal of the London subway system. On February 28, 1975, a six-car train inexplicably accelerated as it neared the end of the Moorgate tunnel, smashing headlong into the wall. The impact killed forty-one passengers and telescoped the first fifteen seats into a two-foot mass of metal, flesh, and bone.

"At one time we exhibited the metal mass itself," Carbone elaborated, "but that turned out to be a bad idea."

"Too grisly?" asked Esther.

"Too tempting. Visitors were always breaking off little bits and taking them home as souvenirs."

❖

At 5:15 P.M., shortly after adjourning the tribunal for the weekend, Torvald guided Martin and Lovett into his private chambers in the lowest basement of the Peace Palace.

"What the hell do you think you're doing, Candle?" Torvald demanded in a tone of tenuously suppressed rage.

Martin glanced around the judge's quarters. Books lined the walls, giving the subterranean room the atmosphere of a bomb shelter for intellectuals. "What do I think I'm doing? I think I'm making the people's case, Your Honor."

"You're making the whole world sick to its stomach, *that's* what you're doing. This Carbone person you dug up, I believe he's some sort of sadist. Have you noticed his smile? Damn it, Candle, this is a *family* show. Get me? Every evening, right in the middle of prime time, Court TV beams the day's events into fifteen million homes. Three thousand political-science teachers across America are having their students watch us as an assignment. Do you grasp what I'm saying? No more soldiers getting their peckers cut off! No more squashed orphans! No more beheaded children!"

"I wish you were less worried about offending bourgeois taste, Your Honor, and more concerned about justice."

"That ghoul leaves the stand by Tuesday afternoon at the latest. Am I being clear?"

"Just because your friend's scientific expedition came to nothing, Dr. Torvald, you don't have to take it out on *me*."

"Tuesday afternoon. Is that understood? Tuesday afternoon!"

"We've still got our fires to do. We've still got our famines."

Eyes ablaze with opium and frustration, Martin turned toward Lovett. "You told me you wanted a 'good fight.'"

Lovett frowned thoughtfully, methodically tapping his Malacca walking stick against the floor as if transmitting Morse code. "Come, come, now, Your Honor," he said at last. "Let's give the Devil his due."

"You really think we should?" asked Torvald.

"Yes."

"Your logic eludes me."

"Assuming the Court finds my Client 'not guilty,'" said Lovett, "the last thing we want is Mr. Candle telling the press that you and I squelched crucial evidence. This trial must solve the problem of evil once and for all—no loose ends!"

"How much more time were you planning to spend with Carbone?" Torvald asked Martin.

"Seven and a half days."

"I'll let you have three and a half."

"I need six at least."

"All right, *four* and a half. Four and a half days, tops—and the minute anybody else loses his dick, I'm shutting you down on the spot!"

❖

As the second week of Carbone's testimony unfolded, Martin gave the tribunal a whirlwind tour of the Fires and Explosions Wing. "During the past three centuries the Defendant has practiced His skills as an arsonist on a myriad of public buildings and private enterprises," he said, an assertion he proceeded to document through twenty-two separate exhibits, including a melted school bell, a scorched circus pennant, a blackened baptismal font, a charred hotel register, a carbonized pair of opera glasses, and a blistered miner's hardhat. On the afternoon of January 9, 1927, hundreds of children were crowded into the

Laurier Palace movie theater in Montreal to watch a festival of comedy shorts. Shortly after a Hal Roach two-reeler called *Get 'Em Young* flashed onto the screen, a fire broke out in the projection booth, and seventy-eight children were crushed in the resulting panic. "Would you please repeat the title of that film?" asked Martin, rolling his eyes heavenward. "*Get 'Em Young,*" replied Carbone. On July 6, 1944, a matinee performance of the Ringling Brothers Circus ended abruptly in Hartford when the main tent caught fire. Desperate parents trapped in the highest bleachers resorted to tossing their children onto the escaping mob below. One hundred and sixty-eight people perished that day, including many of the hurled youngsters. On August 9, 1965, a firestorm ripped through an underground Titan II missile silo near Searcy, Arkansas. Of the fifty-three civilian workers making repairs inside the silo, fifty-one were broiled alive. "If it hadn't been for God, I don't guess I'd ever gotten out," said one of the two men who escaped.

Wednesday found Martin returning to the horrors of nature, frantically documenting "the Defendant's wanton deployment of hurricanes, tornadoes, deluges, blizzards, and killer fogs," an investigation that continued through Thursday morning and ultimately embraced one hundred and six artifacts from the Storms and Floods Pavilion. On May 31, 1889, torrential rains inundated the valley around Johnstown, Pennsylvania, and at 3:10 P.M. the Lake Conemaugh dam burst under the pressure, loosing 20,000,000 tons of water upon the city. An outlying stone bridge blocked much of the floating wreckage, creating a thirty-acre sanctuary to which scores of survivors flocked. At 6:00 P.M. the heaven-sent island caught fire, incinerating two hundred people. On September 8, 1900, a record-breaking rainstorm descended upon Galveston, Texas. When the Catholic Orphanage Asylum began to crumble from the force of the flood, each nun tied eight babies to her waist and set out for dry land. The sisters' corpses were recovered with the drowned orphans still lashed in place. On September 16, 1928, a lethal hurricane struck West Palm

Beach, Florida. In the swampy terrain around Lake Okeechobee, families fled the deluge by climbing trees, parents holding their children on their backs. Reaching the upper branches, the refugees were horrified to find that displaced water moccasins had sought shelter there as well. Hundreds of people who'd managed to survive the storm subsequently died of snake venom.

"I thought you were cooling your orphans," said Patricia that night, pointing toward the Court TV replay.

"Cooling your orphans would be a really excellent idea," said Olaf.

Martin set Dr. Tonia Braverman's dossier aside and looked Patricia in the eye. "Those orphans were tied to *nuns*."

"What the hell difference does that make?" asked Patricia.

"If I have to explain it . . ."

"Torvald said no more orphans."

"No more *squashed* orphans."

"Oh, for heaven's sake."

"Cool the damn orphans," said Olaf.

"For your own good," said Gunnar.

"If you folks don't like it here in Holland," said Martin, "you can always go home."

Martin concluded the Carbone interview by madly covering forty-two relics from the Gallery of Droughts and Famines. People's Exhibit F-3 was a caldron of the type in which abducted children were cooked for food during the great famine that depopulated Egypt from 1199 to 1202, a result of low rainfall at the source of the Nile. Exhibit F-7 was a blighted potato of the sort that constituted the inedible Irish crop of 1845. In 1846 the plants blackened and withered once again. The sound of weeping echoed throughout the countryside as women stood sobbing in the stinking fields, knowing another year of hunger, cold, and cholera lay before them. By the time the crop recovered—in 1851—1,030,000 people were dead of starvation, disease, or exposure following eviction. The last Kroft Museum artifact Martin offered in evidence, Exhibit F-42, was one of the cloth scraps used to swaddle the hollow-eyed, swollen-bellied children who poured into the Ethiopian relief camps by the thousands from 1983 to 1988. The famine followed the worst drought in African history: whole rivers and lakes simply vanished. By the time the rains came, over 1,000,000 innocent victims lay dead.

"Dr. Carbone, I'm about to ask you the most important question of this entire interview."

"I'm listening."

"Can you name any occasions on which the Defendant acted to mitigate one of the tragedies commemorated in the Kroft Museum?"

"No, Mr. Candle, I cannot," the witness replied firmly.

"Not a single instance of divine assistance?"

"Not one."

Martin swabbed his sweaty brow with Patricia's red silk scarf. "On behalf of the entire prosecution team, Dr. Carbone, let me thank you for your meticulous and exhaustive testimony. We have no further questions."

Torvald laid his palm against his wig, closing his fingers around the longest curl as if squeezing a bovine teat. "Professor Lovett, you may begin your cross-examination."

Walking stick in hand, the defense counsel strutted up to the lectern wearing a gigantic Augustinian smile. In one continuous gesture he removed a gold watch from his suit coat, ascertained the hour, shut the lid, and deftly repocketed the timepiece.

"On the first day of your testimony, Dr. Carbone, you mentioned a pilgrimage organized by Pope Clement VI during the great fourteenth-century plague. Are you prepared to argue that, for Clement and his fellow bishops, my Client's role in the epidemic was that of a criminal?"

Carbone redistributed his weight from his left buttock to his right. " 'Criminal'? They wouldn't have used that word, no."

"Even at the height of the Plague, people didn't blame God. They never put Him on trial, correct?"

"True enough."

"Is there any evidence that Pope Clement questioned God's right to discipline sinners through penalties and tribulations?"

"Popes rarely question God's right to do anything."

"Two weeks ago you also discussed the so-called great plague of London. Would you please explain the connection between this event and a disaster to which you did *not* testify—namely, the great fire of London that began on September 1, 1666?"

"You're asking about the relationship between . . ."

"The plague of 1665 and the fire of 1666."

"Many historians believe the fire can be credited with ending the plague. The flames cleansed London of rats, their fleas, and the bacterium itself."

"Do *you* believe the great fire of London ended the great plague of London?"

"Yes, I do."

"How long did the London fire last?"

"Five days."

"Five days? That's quite an inferno. Why do you suppose the prosecution never put it on the record?"

"I don't know."

"How many Londoners perished in the 1666 fire?"

"There were eight documented deaths."

"Did you say eight?"

"Correct."

"Only eight people died in a five-day urban conflagration? That sounds like a miracle to me."

"It probably didn't seem miraculous to the eight victims or the hundred thousand left homeless."

"Let's double Carbone's salary," whispered Randall to Martin.

"At one point you testified that between 1793 and 1798 yellow fever killed thousands of British soldiers in Saint Domingue," said Lovett. "What were those soldiers doing in the colony to begin with?"

"Keeping the peace."

"Keeping the peace . . . is that all? Weren't they in fact attempting to quell a slave rebellion?"

"The slaves were in revolt, yes."

"Whose side do you believe the Defendant was on—the slaves' side or the British troops'?"

"Objection!" shouted Martin, rising. "The question calls for speculation by the witness."

"Overruled," said Torvald.

"I have no idea whose side the Defendant was on," said Carbone. "I'm a sociologist, not a theologian."

"Isn't it reasonable to suppose He was on the slaves' side?" asked Lovett.

"If I were God, and I wanted to communicate My low opinion of the slave trade, I would certainly select a more efficient medium than yellow fever."

"But you aren't God."

"True enough. Then again, neither are you."

For the rest of the day and continuing until the Tuesday lunch recess, Lovett exploited the Carbone interview to develop three interconnected themes: the victims of history's worst natural disasters rarely held the Defendant responsible; the sufferers commonly believed they were being justly punished for their sins; and the tragedy in question could sometimes be interpreted as serving a greater good.

Ice water condensed in the pit of Martin's stomach. Were the judges buying this bald, audacious, and—he had to admit—ingenious attempt to discredit the Kroft Museum evidence? Hard to say. Their expressions were utterly opaque, as indecipherable as the mind of Corinne's armadillo.

The prosecutors spent an entire afternoon redirecting their star witness. Prompted by Randall, Carbone theorized that the relative lack of Jobian indictments throughout history was really no mystery. (As long as God was presumably in power, His victims had nothing to gain by criticizing Him, and everything to lose.) Carbone went on to explain why sufferers have traditionally regarded their ordeals as fitting retribution. (The alternative interpretation—a malevolent Creator—is intolerable.) And while a few select disasters might indeed have contained hidden blessings, this was manifestly not true for the majority of horrors documented in the Kroft Museum.

On August 3, 2000, at 4:45 P.M., having given ninety-six solid hours of testimony, Dr. Donald Carbone, sociologist and cataclysmatician, was dismissed.

"That creepy little troll has singlehandedly won the war for us," said Esther as the witness waddled out of the courtroom. "Everything we do from now on is icing on the cake."

"I'm not so sure about that," said Martin.

"Who can argue with the great influenza epidemic, for chrissakes?" said Randall. "Who can argue with the Johnstown flood? Who can argue with the Irish potato famine?"

"Counsel for the defense just did," said Martin morosely, "and he hasn't even opened his case."

❖

The prosecution's second expert witness, Dr. Tonia Braverman, was as tall and willowy as her predecessor had been short and squat. While Braverman was Carbone's physical opposite, in the realm of ego she was—for better or worse—his twin. Curling her arm around the mike like a chanteuse performing a torch song, the historian explained that, besides "conceiving, founding, and directing" Brown University's Institute for Understanding Human Depravity, she was also the "associate producer, principal writer, and voice-over narrator" of an ill-fated public television series called *A History of Havoc: Three Thousand Years of War, Cruelty, and Injustice*. Completed two years earlier by the celebrated documentary filmmaker Bruce Kelvin, whose nine-hour chronicle of the Great Depression had won four Emmys,

A History of Havoc had yet to run on PBS, although a VHS edition was currently available in stores throughout North America.

From the exhibit table Martin procured a boxed set of videocassettes, the lid swathed in blood red felt and stamped with gold letters. Slipping out the first tape, he held it before the witness. Braverman's poorly lit dossier photo had failed to do her justice. For all her pouches and wrinkles, she had obviously been attractive in her day, and Martin imagined her coming across to the *International 227* audience as a kind of gracefully aging talk-show hostess.

"Why was *A History of Havoc* never broadcast?"

"The whole matter is in litigation, and I'm not free to discuss the details. All I can say is, when the PBS executives previewed the series, they were horrified."

Martin snapped his fingers, prompting Randall to stride down the aisle pushing a utility cart containing a television monitor and a VCR.

"In researching the historical dimension of the people's case, we were tempted to disregard moral evil and concentrate solely on what the insurance companies in their wisdom call 'acts of God,'" Martin told the judges as Randall positioned the monitor before the Court TV camera. "Then we considered our predecessors. Job, you will recall, experienced moral evil in the form of the Sabaeans who murdered his herdsmen and stole his oxen. And, of course, the rabbis who tried the Defendant at Auschwitz were indicting Him for the depravity He allowed to flourish in Nazi Germany. May it please the tribunal: the prosecution is offering in evidence People's Exhibit G-1, *A History of Havoc*— an eleven-hour television series written by Tonia Braverman and directed by Bruce Kelvin."

"Excuse me, Mr. Candle," said Torvald. "Are you saying you expect us to sit here and watch a TV documentary about atrocities for the next two days?"

"Yes, Your Honor, I am," said Martin, inserting the tape.

"This is a court of law, not Le Grand Guignol."

"I'm aware of that, Your Honor."

"How does the defense feel about the prosecution introducing this sort of sensationalistic material?" Torvald asked Lovett.

"The defense has nothing to hide."

Martin pushed PLAY.

Episode one, "The Altars of Antiquity," began with an eight-minute teaser, and before it was over everybody knew exactly why PBS had declined to air the series. Through a montage of antique engravings intercut with staged shots, the prologue depicted the ghastly death by quartering of Robert François Damiens that occurred on March 2, 1757, in the Place de Grève. As the executioners split open Damiens's hips, Braverman asked, voice-over, "Why is *Homo sapiens* the only animal that tortures its own kind?"—the first in a string of sententious questions the historian would pose during the episode. "Why are we the only species that makes war on itself?" she continued from the monitor as the horses tore off Damiens's legs. The sociopolitical naiveté of the series did not trouble Martin. With its factual accuracy and encyclopedic sweep, *Havoc* was exactly what the prosecution's case required. "Why do we call atrocities 'inhuman' when in truth they constitute one of our most salient traits?"

The remaining one hundred and ten minutes of "The Altars of Antiquity" chronicled the period from the destruction of Nineveh in 612 B.C. through the sack of Rome by the Visigoths in A.D. 410. In an especially powerful sequence, Braverman and Kelvin dramatized the persecutions orchestrated by Nero in A.D. 64. Blaming the Christians for the great fire of Rome, a conflagration he himself probably started, Nero subjected them to horrendous public executions. "While thousands cheered, believers of all ages were torn to pieces by hungry tigers and wild dogs in the city's open-air theaters," narrated Braverman. "The emperor also loved to hold nocturnal chariot races in his private gardens, illuminating the spectacles by smearing Christians with pitch and setting them ablaze." No less graphic was the filmmakers' restaging of the first-century Jewish revolt against Rome, which climaxed in A.D. 73 when Titus, heir to the imperial throne, besieged Jerusalem with 80,000 men. After weeks of fighting around the outer walls, the Romans dislodged the city's defenders, who then took up new positions within the temple complex. As the Roman army stormed into the central court, the defenders stood shoulder to shoulder, certain that a miracle would spare them. Six thousand Jews died in the slaughter that followed.

After lunch the prosecution played episode two, "The Great Darkness," covering the period from 476 to 1453. The late twelfth century found Richard the Lionhearted leading the Third Crusade in Palestine. When the vanquished defenders of Acre refused to pay any tribute money until 3,000 prisoners were released as promised, the Christians responded uncharitably. "On the afternoon of August 20, 1191, the captive soldiers were marched onto a plain in full view of the defeated Islamic army," narrated Braverman. "Richard gave the order, and the Crusaders systematically murdered the Muslims with swords and lances." Seventeen years later the Pope was again preaching a crusade, this time against fellow Christians: the Albigensians of southern France. The most famous line to come out of the Albigensian Crusade was spoken when a mercenary army led by northern French barons entered Béziers, a city populated by both Catholics and heretics. In the middle of the bloodbath, a Catholic soldier asked how he might tell the Albigensians from the faithful. "Kill them all," his superior commanded him. "God will know His own."

Later that afternoon Martin had the tribunal watch "Impalers, Inquisitors, and Insurrectionists," Braverman and Kelvin's version of the Renaissance, beginning with the reign of Vlad II Dracula, prince of Wallachia. A typical day in Vlad's life occurred on April 2, 1459, when he entered Brasov with his troops and for no particular reason ordered all the townspeople impaled on wooden stakes. As his career progressed, Vlad had the objects of his paranoia variously skinned alive, hacked to pieces, and disemboweled, but impalement remained his signature depravity. "To make the process totally excruciating, the prince demanded that each stake traverse its victim vertically and that its point be rounded and oiled." Compared with their account of Vlad the Impaler, the filmmakers' treatment of the Spanish Inquisition seemed tasteful and restrained. The enterprise began in 1478, when King Ferdinand obtained a papal bull permitting him to hire professional torturers to counteract the supposed nefarious activities of Jews, *conversos*, Muslims, and heretics throughout his country. Friar Tomás de Torquemada became the first Grand Inquisitor. "His techniques for eliciting confessions were generally unimaginative—shredding his victims' flesh on the rack, desocketing their arms via the *garrucha*—but he got the job done." Throughout episode three Kelvin cut to snippets from the witch craze that infected western Europe during the fifteenth and sixteenth centuries. The phenomenon started officially in 1484, when Pope Innocent VIII issued a bull empowering Heinrich Kramer and James Sprenger, two respected theologians and experienced torturers, to travel across the continent diagnosing "the disease of heresy" and punishing its practitioners. "The number of accused witches burned at the stake following the bull of 1484 is unknown, but many historians favor a figure approaching seven hundred and fifty thousand."

"It's too much," said Patricia that evening, gesturing toward the Court TV replay. "We get it, okay? History is written in blood. You don't have to show us any more."

"Listen to your friend," said Olaf.

"I'm going to place every last second of *A History of Havoc* on the record," Martin insisted, glancing up from Harry Elder's dossier. "Every last second!"

"Let me guess," said Patricia. "You're about to shovel the Third Reich down our throats and—what else?—Bosnia, right?"

"I didn't invent the twentieth century."

"Neither did God."

"The point is debatable. That's why I came to Holland."

The following morning Martin played episode four, "The Teeth of Reason," which charted the evolution of iniquity from the Protestant secession through the horrors of the French Revolution and the subsequent carnage of the Napoleonic Wars. In 1524 Germany erupted in chaos when the downtrodden peasants, fired by the spirit of the Reformation, turned on their ruling princes. The imperial army responded with great efficiency, surrounding the rebels completely on May 15, 1525. "Just as the peasants were about to give up, a rainbow appeared, convincing them they enjoyed divine protection," narrated Braverman. "When they refused to surrender, the government troops butchered them to the last man." Forty-seven years later an equally terrible bloodbath occurred when France's Catholic king, Charles IX, permitted his zealous supporters to attack the Protestant Huguenots, who were allegedly plotting against him. On the night of Saint Bartholomew's Eve, August 23, the royalists locked the gates of Paris and painted crosses on the Huguenots' doors. The following morning Charles's troops began dragging the branded families from their homes and slicing them apart with swords. Protestant children were thrown screaming into the Seine. The massacre ended only after tens of thousands had been killed.

Episode five, "Progress toward Perdition," catalogued the various moral evils that infected the optimistic and industrious nineteenth century, including the slaughter of countless Native Americans, the War Between the States, and the grisly demise of the Paris Commune during Bloody Week. The year 1865 brought the notorious Fort Pillow Massacre, in which three hundred captured Union soldiers, mostly black, were shot to death by a Confederate general who was later elected a grand wizard of the Ku Klux Klan. Eleven years later came the so-called Bulgarian Horrors, perpetrated by Turkish irregulars, the Bashi-Bazouks, as they sacked the ostensibly rebellious town of Batak, continuing their assault even after realizing the defenders were mostly women and children. The Turks split apart the Bulgarians' skulls and decapitated the lucky ones outright. Pregnant women enjoyed no protection. The Bashi-Bazouks ripped open their wombs with bayonets, leaving both mother and fetus to die in the mud.

That afternoon the judges watched the climactic episode, "The Loom of Ruin," which packed into its hundred-and-eighty-minute running time the whole dreadful saga of the twentieth century. Among the events covered in the first hour was the 1916 German offensive against the Allied fortress of Verdun. For ten successive months, both armies endured relentless barrages of bullets, artillery shells, and poison-gas canisters. "When the shooting finally stopped," said Braverman over a tracking shot displaying heaps of slaughtered infantrymen, "the lines remained essentially unchanged, and more than a million soldiers were dead or wounded." Equally gruesome was the filmmakers' presentation of the horrors surrounding the Bolshevik Revolution, including the 20,000,000 Russians killed by influenza and starvation between 1914 and 1924 and the 100,000 butchered by the Reds during the civil war of 1918 to 1922. The second hour of "The Loom of Ruin" focused on the evils accruing to World War Two, including the Holocaust that consumed nearly half of European Jewry between 1933 and 1945. At Auschwitz, the Nazis were eventually herding up to 6,000 victims a day into chambers marked BATHS AND DISINFECTING and releasing poison gas into the air. "As the panicked prisoners stampeded over one another, their corpses became piled to the ceiling," narrated Braverman. On August 6, 1945, the American B-29 *Enola Gay* dropped the atomic bomb called Little Boy on Hiroshima, Japan, instantly killing 75,000 civilians. Survivors ran screaming through the streets, their scorched skin hanging from their bodies in black strips. "In the days that followed, radiation sickness tortured thousands with nausea, fever, and uncontrolled bleeding. Pregnant women gave birth to malformed babies, and the leukemia rate soared." The final hour catalogued the barbarities of the postwar years, from the Soviet Army's brutal repression of the 1956 Hungarian uprising through the epic feud still smoldering among Orthodox Serbs, Catholic Croats, and Bosnian Muslims in the former Yugoslavia. Particularly memorable was the on-camera testimony of a Cambodian refugee, Kim Nu, who told how she and her family had just sat down to dinner on a hot summer evening in 1976 when machine-gun bullets blew apart the door and tore off her grandmother's face. As Kim and her baby brother looked on, Communist soldiers entered the hut, kicked their father to death, and shot their mother between the eyes. "Such attacks characterized the process through which Pol Pot consolidated his power after defeating the Lon Nol government," narrated Braverman. "By the time the Vietnamese toppled Pol Pot's regime, an estimated three million Cambodians had been murdered outright by the Khmer Rouge or died in disease-ridden concentration camps."

Martin shut off the TV, secretly ate a painkiller, and steadied himself on the lectern.

"Three million Cambodians?"

"Three million."

"Dr. Braverman, I must now ask you a crucial question. Thinking back on all the atrocities you've documented here—the crusades and the massacres, the impalings and the gassings—can you identify a single instance in which the Defendant intervened on the victims' behalf?"

"There were many cases in which people *expected* divine assistance. The sack of Jerusalem, the German peasants' war . . ."

"But is there any evidence He *did* intervene?"

"None that I know of."

"Zero evidence?"

"Zero."

"Thank you, Dr. Braverman."

Invited to cross-examine the witness, Lovett predictably kept it short. The subject, after all, was moral evil, a regrettable but unavoidable by-product of human free will.

"Dr. Braverman, do you really believe the Defendant never entered history with the aim of relieving His creatures' pain?"

"That is my conclusion, yes."

"Have you ever read the Gospel According to Saint Matthew?"

"I've scanned parts of it."

"When was the last time you 'scanned' Saint Matthew?"

"Three years ago. We were hoping to include Christ's crucifixion in episode one, but we couldn't get an angle on it."

"Is there by any chance a New Testament in your hotel room?"

"I don't know."

"May I make a suggestion? When you return to the Huize Bellevue tonight, go to the front desk. A Revised English Bible will be waiting for you, placed there by my brother. It's yours to keep. Take it to bed with you. Read the Gospel According to Saint Matthew. It can't do you any harm, and you might even learn something. I have no further questions."

❖

The following morning Martin stood before the bench, raised himself to the fullest height his friable hips permitted, discreetly swallowed two Roxanols, and solemnly addressed the judges. "The great Prussian military theorist Karl von Clausewitz once remarked, 'A single death is a tragedy, a million are statistics.' " He cleared his throat and fixed on Torvald. "Von Clausewitz was wrong, Your Honors. A million deaths are a million tragedies. The people call Harry Elder."

Martin's cleanup sufferer was cherubic and sprightly, the sort of smiling, open-faced man from whom you'd be happy to buy a used car. He approached the stand wearing a blue polyester suit at least two sizes too small and clutching a stuffed ape dressed in a tuxedo.

"What do you do for a living?" Martin asked Harry after the witness had given his oath.

"I manage a Kay-Bee toy store in the town where I live—New Castle, Delaware."

"What's that in your hand?"

"My son's favorite stuffed animal."

"A gorilla?"

"Orangutan, actually. His name's Ozzie."

"Please tell the tribunal about your son."

Harry adjusted the orangutan's cummerbund. "Right from the beginning, Duncan was a sickly sort of kid—colds, earaches, diarrhea. First Dr. Wendell said it was normal, then he said it was asthma, then he gave Duncan a test for cystic fibrosis. It came back positive."

"Cystic fibrosis is caused by a mutated gene, correct?"

"That's right."

"What does this gene do?"

"It manufactures huge amounts of mucus that turn your child's lungs into breeding grounds for bacteria. It also wrecks his pancreas, so he has to take enzyme pills before he can digest his food. My wife and I are both carriers, but we didn't know that until Duncan got diagnosed."

"When a husband and wife are both carriers, will their offspring inevitably get CF?"

"No. Our first child, Emily, she's just fine."

"Go on."

"A few hours after we got the news, Janet and I crept into Duncan's room while he slept. 'We're sorry,' we kept telling him, over and over. He was only two years old. 'We're so sorry . . .'"

Undoubtedly the worst aspect of cystic fibrosis, Harry explained, was the way it required you to torture your own child. To dislodge the mucus, Harry had to place Duncan on a sloped board twice a day and beat him with a cupped hand on his back, chest, and sides, all the while ordering him to cough. "It's over!" Duncan would start screaming halfway through. "It's over, Daddy, it's over!"

"Eventually Duncan figured out that not every child in the world gets pounded on," said Harry. "He kept asking me, 'Will I have to do this after I'm all grown up?' "

"What did you say?"

Harry blanched. "I told him there'd be no more poundings after he was . . . all grown up."

Every six months, Duncan needed to spend ten days in New Castle Children's Clinic, where he received antibiotics intravenously to combat the pseudomonas and other bacteria attacking his lungs. In Harry's view the only advantage of these hospitalizations was that somebody else had to beat his son.

Duncan's condition remained stable for four years. Then, on the day after his sixth birthday, his left lung collapsed, and the doctors had to insert a tube in his chest and pump up the deflated organ.

"He was terribly ill from then on—arthritis, pneumonia, weak heart, liver problems—but he kept on being himself, eager to play with his sister, happy in his own way. The twelfth time he entered the hospital, I promised him we'd all go to New York City after he got out. He'd always wanted to see *Cats*."

"Did he get his wish?" asked Martin, wondering how Duncan would have reacted to the production of *Crabs* currently running in the divine cranium.

"Two days after Thanksgiving. The city was absolutely dazzling—Christmas lights, sparkling snow. I had to carry him into the Winter Garden Theater. He stayed awake for the whole show. As we were leaving, he said, 'You know what I'd like for Christmas? A kitty of my very own.' The minute Duncan was back in New Castle, he wrote a letter to Santa Claus. The letter ended, 'I promise I'll take real good care of my kitty, Santa, even though I'm very sick.' "

On the first of December, Duncan's left lung collapsed again, and he returned to the hospital. A week later, just as he was about to be discharged, his right lung collapsed.

"It was more than Janet and I could stand. We both started crying right there in the hospital. And you know what Duncan did? He brushed away my tears and said, 'Don't be sad, Daddy. Christmas is coming.'"

After Duncan finally got home, Harry and his wife began to suspect their son wouldn't make it through the holidays, so they visited their local Humane Society and picked out a black kitten with a white star-shaped patch on her head. The accompanying note from Santa explained that Starshine had been getting mighty lonely at the North Pole, so it seemed best to place her with her new family right away.

"I'd never seen Duncan looking happier. He was hurting pretty bad, but happy. He and Emily and Starshine rolled around on the floor for hours, which made Duncan cough a lot, but he didn't seem to mind. Later, he said to Emily, 'You know what Starshine does for me? She makes me forget about my disease.'"

Three days before Christmas, Duncan was seized by terrible pains. Dr. Wendell came over and gave the screaming boy a shot of morphine, and soon he dozed off. Emily wanted to know if Duncan would be returning to the hospital that day, and Janet told her no, Duncan was going to die. Emily's jaw went slack. Was this really the end? Yes, Janet explained, it was the end. Then the three of them—Harry, Janet, Emily—sat down on the rug beside Duncan's bed and began talking quietly while he slept, reviewing his life. Shortly after they finished, he awoke.

"Have you ever seen a child die, Your Honors?" asked Harry, turning toward the judges. "Duncan kept sitting up in bed, but then he'd fall back on the sheets, right next to Starshine and Ozzie, and then he'd sit up again, and then he'd fall back." The witness was sobbing now. His words lodged in his windpipe. "And all this while his eyes were open, darting back and forth from me to Janet to Emily, and his whole face was glowing with such unbelievable love. He sat up one last time, threw his arms around me, and stared straight at his sister. 'Merry Christmas, Emily,' he said. Those were his final words. 'Merry Christmas, Emily.' His eyes were still open, only now they were blank. And that is how death came for my little boy, Your Honors— on a bitter cold morning in December, in New Castle, Delaware, when he was eight. We buried him in the local cemetery, and every Sunday I visit the grave, and I cry the way I'm crying now. He was the bravest person I ever knew, and if I've made you understand that, well, then it was worth my coming all the way over here across the Atlantic Ocean."

The witness pulled a handkerchief from his pocket and unashamedly blew his nose. The French translator wept. Tears ran down the stenographer's cheeks.

"Thank you, Mr. Elder," said Martin. "I have no further questions."

❖

Lovett began the cross-examination by asking Harry whether Duncan had ever wanted to know the reason for his suffering.

"Once I remember him asking, 'Daddy, does God hate me? I think God must hate me very much.'"

"How did you reply?"

"I don't remember."

"You don't? Your son was asking an awfully important question. What did you tell him?"

"I'm sure I said God didn't hate him."

"Might you have gone so far as to say God loved him?"

"I might have."

"Mr. Elder, do you wish your son had never been born?"

"Objection!" shouted Martin.

"Overruled," said Torvald.

Harry balled up the handkerchief and stuffed it back into his pocket. "Never been born? I don't think I've ever been asked that before." He stared at the orangutan. "No," he said at last. "No, I'll always be grateful I had Duncan, even if it was for just eight years."

" 'Always be grateful,' " echoed Lovett. "To whom are you grateful?"

"I'm not grateful to anybody. I'm just . . . grateful."

"How can you be grateful if—"

"You want me to say I'm grateful to God. But I'm not."

"Mr. Elder, let me draw your attention to the March 13, 1998, issue of *Parade*, which profiles a research scientist named Arthur Jablonsky." Lovett flourished the magazine in question before the Court TV camera. "His team has pinpointed the gene on the seventh chromosome that causes cystic fibrosis, and they've even found a way to manufacture a healthy substitute. Do you know what Dr. Jablonsky says is motivating him?"

"I have no idea."

"He is driven by, quote, 'my desire to do God's work.' What do you make of that?"

"I don't believe I make anything of it."

"Mr. Elder, did you ever tell your son he'd be rewarded with eternal life in Heaven?"

Harry scowled. "I might've said something like that."

"I don't think the tribunal heard you."

"I said, 'I might've.' "

"Did Duncan ever ask you any questions about Heaven?"

"Most kids have questions about Heaven."

"Did Duncan have any?"

"As I recall, he wanted to know whether he'd be getting his wings right away."

"What did you tell him?"

A bright crimson flush crept across Harry's face. "What did I tell him, Dr. Lovett? I'll tell you what I told him. 'Duncan, you'll get your wings on the very first day, and after that you'll be our guardian angel, looking down at our house through Heaven's big glass floor, watching over me and Mommy and

Emily until we can come and join you.' *That's* how I answered my sweet, beautiful, tortured child."

"And did you believe yourself?"

"No."

"Why did you lie to your son?"

"Objection!" cried Martin.

A strange distension overcame Harry, so that his suit seemed to grow yet another size too small. "What kind of question is that?" he moaned, not so much speaking the words as spitting them. He swatted at the witness-stand mike, knocking it askew. "What the hell kind of question is that?"

"Withdrawn," said Lovett crisply, doing an abrupt about-face and starting back to the defense table. "Thank you, Mr. Elder. You have supplied me with all the information I need."

"The prosecution may redirect," said Torvald.

"I have just one more question," said Martin, limping up to the lectern. "If these nine judges find the Defendant guilty, would you urge them to disconnect the Lockheed 7000?"

"Pull the plug?" asked Harry.

"That's right. Pull the plug."

"I don't even have to think about it."

"Yes?"

"I would *beg* them to pull the plug."

"Thank you, Mr. Elder. You may step down."

"Please call your next witness," said Torvald.

"We have no more witnesses, Your Honor," said Martin.

"You mean—the people rest their case?"

"Yes, Judge Torvald. On the corpse of Norma Bedloe, the suffering of Billy Jenkins, the toll of *Pasteurella pestis*, the ravages of Vesuvius, the evil of Vlad the Impaler, the depravity of Pol Pot—and the grave of Duncan Elder—the people rest their case."

Chapter 13

HAVING SAT THROUGH over a thousand Methodist church services without ever experiencing a numb posterior or the urge to yawn, I can honestly say I am not easily bored. If Candle's team had been only slightly less systematic in getting our Creator's peccadilloes on the record, I would have received these statistics with the same enthusiasm a baseball fan brings to the lore of batting averages. Earthquakes, after all, are music to my ears. Plane crashes make me come. But enough is as good as a feast, to quote Mary Poppins. Halfway through Donald Carbone's testimony, my ennui grew so acute I grabbed the tools of my trade—needle, thimble, thread—and began to indulge in the seamster's equivalent of doodling, continuing my improvisations through the interviews with Tonia Braverman and Harry Elder.

The results, I must say, were impressive: a series of samplers illustrating fourteen great moments from the Passion of Martin Candle, a kind of nouveau Stations of the Cross. Sampler number two, *Bad News*, depicted our hero in Dr. Hummel's office, receiving his diagnosis. Sampler number nine, *Good Grief*, showed him kneeling atop Corinne Rosewood's grave, leaning a bunch of lilacs against the stone. For sampler number twelve I stole a title from my favorite Dutch master, Rembrandt. I called it *The Night Watch*.

Our hero could not sleep. Lying on his bed in the Huize Bellevue, he tossed and turned like a beached flounder. As the clock crept toward three A.M., he rose and—not against his will, but not wholly with it either—got dressed, donned his disguise, seized his cane, and limped into the hallway. He descended to the lobby. He went outside. A silvery sliver of moon hung over The Hague, riding the midnight sky like a cutting from God's big toe. A stray mongrel dog padded past. The air reeked of geraniums and hyacinths. Candle stumbled along Raamweg, quickening his pace as the crooked street melded into Haringkade.

Despite the hour, Scheveningen Harbor was crowded: a polyglot conglomeration of vigil keepers, relic seekers, UN infantrymen, Hans De Groot's police officers, and soldiers from the Sword of Jehovah Strike Force. It took our hero forty-five minutes to elbow his way down Pier 15 and draw within view of the Defendant's waterborne cooling chamber. Three docks away, the heart-lung machine pursued its perpetual obligations, groaning and chugging as it irrigated the Corpus Dei with His creatures' loving blood.

"So, Sir, it is done," muttered Candle, assuming the stance I so skillfully captured in *The Night Watch*: cheek pressed flat against the cold Lucite, hand arched over a chamber rivet. "I have held up Your record for all the world to see, every last massacre and volcano."

Our hero glanced to his left. An apple-cheeked nun in a white wimple and black habit knelt on the raft, ticking off beads on her rosary, eyes locked shut in prayer.

"And now I must tell You something. The Stackpole editorial in *The Story of International 227* is wrong. There is no piety in my enterprise, Sir, not one jot of reverence. 'To rebuke the Almighty is to honor Him.' Sorry. I don't think so. 'A man who argues with God is a man who takes God seriously and thereby pays Him tribute.' No, Sir. Get somebody *else* to play that part."

He looked to his right. A grieving bohemian with a ponytail, gold earring, and macramé headband cupped his palm over the waxy turret of a red taper, sheltering the fragile flame.

"Am I being clear, Sir?" Candle rubbed a patch of itching skin above the Port-A-Cath valve. "This is war. My army takes no prisoners."

Our hero stood silently before the Defendant. 3:55 A.M. The nun's veil fluttered. Her tears glittered in the moonlight. 4:10 A.M. The bohemian's taper blew out. He made no attempt to relight it.

Turning, Candle lifted his hand from the rivet. He smiled at the nun, winked at the bohemian, and began the long, slow, painful walk back to his hotel.

Later that night, his brain cradled in Roxanol, Candle dreamed he was still inside the divine cranium. He was sitting on the floor of Adrian and Evangeline's hut, prodding the two hominids for an answer to the ontological defense.

"It's very simple," said Evangeline, suckling her baby. She reached into her nursing bra and removed a fistful of Scrabble tiles—borrowed, she explained, from her dinosaur friends, Vivien and Lawrence. "As the coma reaches its climax, we shall suffer total desiccation. The milk will evaporate from my breasts. My husband's vesicles will lose their semen." She laid the tiles in front of Candle. The letters spelled out ARID APES. "We shall become . . ."

"Arid apes?" said Candle. "What does that have to do with the problem of evil?"

"Isn't it obvious?"

"No."

Whereupon the dream dissolved.

He awoke in stages, sifting illusion from truth like our Creator separating light from darkness at the beginning of time. Illusion: the answer to the ontological defense lay in the odd expression ARID APES. Truth: ARID APES was a random outpouring from his subconscious, devoid of theological significance.

Then again, maybe not. Maybe the dream had issued from the same confounding quadrant of God's psyche that had already supplied him with such sterling rebuttals to the eschatological, disciplinary, and hidden harmony solutions. ARID APES . . . did the term actually mean something, apart from the fact that Adrian and Evangeline were evidently destined to meet a dry and undesirable fate?

❖

At 10:17 A.M.—as the pearly Dutch sunlight filtered into the courtroom, illuminating Francis Biddle's stained-glass portrait—Martin ate a painkiller and Lovett opened the case for the defense.

The professor's first witness was Bernard Kaplan, the rabbi from Fitchburg, Massachusetts, who'd been inspired to write a personal theodicy following the loss of his eleven-year-old son, Jeffrey, to a brain-stem tumor. Much to Kaplan's surprise, *When You Walk Through a Storm* became not only a *New York Times* best-seller but a source of solace to millions of readers both Gentile and Jew.

"Please tell the tribunal something of your philosophy," said Lovett, striding toward the lectern.

"You have to understand, I'm a rabbi, not a Talmudic scholar." Kaplan nervously twisted a cuff button on his blue seersucker suit. He was a smiling, disheveled gnome, his light brown hair frothing outward in a manner that evoked the second visiting potentate in Jonathan Sarkos's Nativity movie. "Until *Newsweek* called my book a 'theodicy,' I'd never even heard that word."

To Martin, the rabbi's modesty seemed wholly genuine, his humility totally without guile. He would not enjoy dismantling this nice man's worldview.

"Nevertheless, you ended up tackling some pretty tough questions in *When You Walk Through a Storm*," said Lovett.

"I wanted my readers to grasp a strange but soothing truth. Many things that initially seem wrong turn out to be necessary when we shift perspectives. 'Why does carrion smell so bad?' the student asks the Zen master. And the master replies, 'If you were a vulture, it would smell like chocolate.' "

"Did you know that Christian theologians call this the hidden harmony defense?"

" 'Hidden harmony'? All right. Fine. I was very moved by Mr. Elder's testimony last week—how he had to keep pounding on his son's chest. A visitor from Venus might think Mr. Elder was abusing the boy, when in fact he was keeping him alive."

Martin opened his briefcase and drew out the loose-leaf binder he'd obtained that morning in the hotel pharmacy, its cover decorated with Franz Hals's *The Jolly Toper*. Turning to the first page, he wrote, *Call his bluff. Ask about Auschwitz.*

"In your book you give the example of lightning striking a dead tree and starting a forest fire," said Lovett.

"Our first instinct when we see a burning forest is to douse the flames," said Kaplan, "but ecologists now tell us such fires are part of nature's rhythms. They clear away dead trees, allowing sunlight to filter down and stimulate new growth."

"Your book also includes a discussion of termites."

"Homeowners hate them, but this would be a pretty sterile planet if we didn't have lots of termites out there in our forests, converting dead trees to loam."

"The man's obsessed with trees," whispered Esther.

"The arboreal defense," grunted Randall.

"Termites murdered my wife," muttered Martin, scribbling frantically in his loose-leaf binder.

As the August sun arced across the sky, the rabbi reeled off a dozen additional examples of ostensible evils in which an ultimate good lay concealed. Throughout this long speech Martin kept his eyes fixed on the judges. They were a grim and twitchy bunch, continually removing their headsets to scratch their ears or brush the sweat from their temples: a phenomenon he chose to interpret optimistically. All nine men, he decided, were bored out of their skulls.

Among Kaplan's more vivid illustrations was a catastrophe that had arisen not far from The Hague. On October 1, 1574, the North Sea had come crashing through the dikes and rolled across the western plain. From the Dutch perspective this disaster was actually a godsend, for the people were then in rebellion against their overlords in Madrid, and a vast Spanish army had surrounded Leiden. The deluge broke the siege, saving many innocent lives.

"Let's return to Jeffrey for a moment," said Lovett. "That is, unless . . ."

"It's all right."

"At one point in *When You Walk Through a Storm*, you suggest that even a child's death can involve unexpected blessings."

"As horrible as it was to see that tumor destroying Jeffrey, completely horrible . . . all that pain . . . he was so brave." The witness's voice failed. He lifted his hands, hid his grimace behind his open palms, and sobbed.

"Perhaps we should stop."

"No. *No.*" Kaplan slid his palms away. A tear trail streaked each side of his face. "The truth is that, for the other parents in my congregation, Jeffrey's suffering was . . . well . . . a kind of gift." He looked past Lovett and focused his moist eyes on the bench. "Why do we love our children, Your Honors? Because they're *vulnerable*, that's why. Remove that vulnerability, that awful chance of losing your boy to some monstrous twist of fate, and you've sacrificed the very thing that gives a father's love its edge. Think about it. It's a trade-off—a terrible, white-hot trade-off—but I'm willing to make it."

"Are you saying you've become reconciled to Jeffrey's death?" asked Lovett.

"I shall never become reconciled to Jeffrey's death."

"Thank you, Rabbi Kaplan. I have no further questions."

After the lunch recess, Torvald invited the prosecution to

interview the witness. So here it comes—my first cross-examination, thought Martin, approaching the exhibit table with the
best approximation of a strut that exhaustion and the crab allowed. He tucked both his crocodile cane and his Jolly Toper
binder under his arm, took hold of Noah's ax, and limped up
to Kaplan.

"Do you know what this might be?"

"It's an ax," said the witness.

"The very ax Noah used to built his ark. His prototype presented it to me when I toured the Defendant's brain. In a month
it will be dust—otherwise I could probably get fifty million
pounds for it from the British Museum. Are you aware, Rabbi
Kaplan, that the hidden harmony argument is sometimes evoked
to explain the great Deluge recounted in Genesis, chapters six
through eight?"

"No, but I can imagine . . . the Flood was a necessary
purgative—right?—cleansing the Earth of sinners and clearing
the way for a more virtuous generation."

"Very good." Martin smacked the flat of the blade against
his open palm. "Chop, chop, chop, and down go the gopher trees
Noah will need to set the saving remnant afloat. Let me ask you
something: does the Flood story fit your notion of how a benevolent Creator ought to behave?"

"Objection," said Lovett. "Rabbi Kaplan has already stated
he's not a Biblical scholar."

"Overruled," said Torvald.

"Thank you, Judge, but I'll withdraw the question anyway,"
said Martin smoothly. "I'd rather talk about the *witness's* book."
He set the ax on the stand, hobbled up to the lectern, and opened
his binder. "This morning, Mr. Kaplan, you told the tribunal
that forest fires sometimes prove benevolent in the long run."
Lubricated by sweat, his bifocals slid down his nose. He pushed
them back into place and glanced at his notes. "Now, putting
aside the question of ultimate ecological necessity, let's consider
a common occurrence with forest fires: an innocent fawn trapped

in the flames. Before long the animal is horribly burned, and over the next three days it dies a slow, agonizing death. Are you saying that behind the fawn's seemingly gratuitous suffering there lies a greater good?"

"I'm saying there *might* be a greater good."

"What sort of greater good?"

"If I knew, then the fawn's suffering wouldn't be 'seemingly gratuitous,' would it?"

Martin was taken aback by this riposte but managed to remain unflustered. "Quite so . . . but let's have a crack at it, okay? Let's imagine, for example, that the fawn is hosting a new species of pathogenic bacteria. Released into the human population, these germs would cause a plague ten times worse than the Black Death."

"That wouldn't explain why the fawn needs to be roasted alive," said Kaplan thoughtfully.

"Maybe only intense heat can kill the bacteria."

"I don't think that's very plausible."

"Neither do I. How do you feel about the Nazi concentration camps of World War Two?"

"What?"

"I said, 'How do you feel about the Nazi concentration—' "

"How do I feel about them? They were probably the greatest evil of this century."

"Why did the Defendant allow these camps?"

"Objection," said Lovett.

"Overruled," said Torvald.

"I'm willing to talk about my son, Mr. Candle, but not *this*."

"Here's a theory for you. All the people who died in the camps—Jews, Gypsies, homosexuals . . . children—every one of them was plotting to manufacture and disperse a lethal chemical capable of wiping out life on Earth. By permitting the Holocaust, God prevented the extinction of a hundred thousand species, including our own. What do you think?"

"I think your theory is obscene."

"So do I—the hidden harmony defense is invariably obscene . . . 'pornography for priests,' as God's Idea of Noah puts it. Question: suppose one of the dikes protecting this city suddenly ruptured. Can you picture it? The North Sea starts pouring into the streets, sweeping away thousands of victims. How would the people in this room react? Would they sit around saying, 'Maybe this is 1574 all over again. Maybe there's a greater good here'?"

"I doubt it."

"What would they do?"

"They would probably grab the nearest sandbags and try to repair the breach."

"Right. And yet you're inviting us to imagine some arcane justice in the world's pain. To which I can only reply, 'If this is a hidden harmony universe, Rabbi Kaplan, then why do we try so hard to *change* it?' By your reasoning, a person who puts out a fire, cures a disease . . . or lifts a sandbag against a flood—this person may actually be opposing the divine will, correct?"

A shudder passed through Kaplan, head to toe. Martin prayed that the witness's distress was registering clearly on the judges' personal monitors. "All I can say is, in my line of work, the idea of a greater good is astonishingly helpful. As a rabbi, I'm obligated to comfort people."

"Indeed you are, sir. Indeed you are. No further questions."

Stifling a smile, Martin limped back to the prosecution table.

"Great job," said Esther. "You blew him out of the water."

"We'll be hearing no more about hidden harmonies," said Randall.

"One down and four to go," said Martin.

❖

When the trial resumed the next morning, Lovett called Eleanor Swann, a Yale Divinity School professor whose published works included a scholarly history of Gnosticism and a three-volume annotated translation of the Dead Sea Scrolls. She was slender and sharp featured, the sort of formerly pretty woman whom advancing age has made beautiful. Her diction was like her physiognomy, compact and efficient. Sentence by sentence, metaphor by metaphor, Swann constructed a lucid and compelling argument to the effect that adversity fosters spiritual growth.

"Disciplinary defense," muttered Randall.

"Piece of cake," whispered Martin. Opening his binder, he turned to a blank page, picked up a pencil, and carefully printed, ARID APES. Was it an anagram, perhaps? A SAD PIER, he wrote. DRIP EASE. SAID RAPE. None of these variations seemed remotely relevant to the ontological defense.

In confronting life's hardships, Swann explained, people often discovered within themselves "unexpected reserves of patience and compassion." Alluding to Lovett's own *Conundrum of Suffering*, she called the pre-coma God "a cosmic surgeon" who reluctantly but dutifully inflicted pain "while He repaired our souls with His divine scalpel." As the examination continued, the professor made dozens of learned references—Saint Augustine's *Enchiridion*, Gregory Nazianzenus's *Discours*, Martin Luther's *Werke*—though these embellishments didn't seem to impress the judges, who so far appeared as benumbed by Swann's presentation as they'd been by Kaplan's.

Raise the stakes: bring in AIDS, Martin wrote.

At 12:47 P.M. Torvald, yawning, declared a lunch recess.

"I'm sure we can all understand how suffering strengthens a person's character," said Lovett after the tribunal reconvened. "Nevertheless, a skeptic might ask why misfortune is distributed the way it is. Last month we heard from a man who lost his legs in Vietnam. Why was he so badly hurt while thousands of his fellow soldiers returned home whole? Was Lieutenant Pallomar in particular need of spiritual growth?"

"The problem of seeming randomness presents a formidable

challenge to the disciplinary defense," said Swann with a frigid smile. "So formidable that in many instances one must supplement this explanation with an eschatological argument."

"According to which our spiritual growth continues . . ."

"After death. Christian eschatology holds that anyone who exits the present world unscathed will undergo various disciplinary trials upon entering the next. Conversely, a person who dies with a highly developed soul—Lieutenant Pallomar, say—will receive a perfect body right away."

"The eschatological argument has a venerable history, does it not?"

"Oh, yes. I'm particularly moved by Bishop Origen's concept of *apocatasis*, according to which even the Devil can be saved."

"Origen cut off his own balls," Martin informed Randall.

"Prostate cancer?"

"Faith."

"Thank you, Professor Swann," said Lovett. "I have nothing further."

With her fiery gaze and eloquent gestures, the witness reminded Martin of the cleverest person ever to appear in his courtroom, Rhonda Fischer, a Glendale aerobics instructor whose spouse had been cheating on her for fifteen years. Shortly after 9:30 P.M. on July 4, 1992, the town's residents watched enthralled as a thirty-foot-long aluminum trellis rose into the nocturnal sky, the climax of the annual fireworks display. Earlier that day, Fischer had managed to tamper with the materials, so that when the trellis was ignited, instead of reading HAPPY ONE HUNDREDTH BIRTHDAY, GLENDALE, the brilliant orange sparks spelled out, for all of Abaddon Township to see, HELEN AMBROSE IS FUCKING RHONDA FISCHER'S HUSBAND. So impressed was Martin by Fischer's resourcefulness—and so moved by her pain—that he punished her vandalism with the lowest allowable fine, sixty-five dollars.

Martin left the prosecution table gripping his binder and swathed in self-confidence, his ears ringing with the husky voices of Lot's daughters trashing the disciplinary defense and the enraged bleatings of Gordon the ram savaging its eschatological counterpart.

"I'd like us to climb down from Heaven for a moment and talk about the present vale of tears," he informed Swann as he limped toward the exhibits.

"As you wish."

He retrieved the Ziploc bag containing Mrs. Lot's right ear, approached the stand, and, disclosing the relic's identity, asked Swann whether she regarded the salinization of Lot's wife as a good example of the disciplinary defense in action.

"It's a puissant little parable." Swann examined the ear with an expression that alternated between curiosity and revulsion. "As I interpret it, the woman lacked moral fiber—otherwise she wouldn't have looked back on Sodom."

"She needed to be taught a lesson?"

"Right."

"So along comes Professor Lovett's cosmic surgeon, inflicting an instructive variety of suffering on the disobedient woman?"

"Yes."

Taking the ear from the witness's grasp, Martin hobbled up to the lectern. "Dr. Swann, are you familiar with the dictum, 'Let the punishment fit the crime'?"

"I suppose so."

"Do you believe Mrs. Lot's punishment fit her crime?"

"Objection," said Lovett.

"Overruled," said Torvald.

Swann swallowed hard. Martin hoped the judges were studying their monitors closely. "Well, no," she said cautiously, "but I imagine it fit in *God's* eyes."

"The hidden harmony defense was yesterday. This morning we're doing the disciplinary defense." Martin opened his binder atop the lectern. "Would you like to know what Lot's daughters think of it? They told me, quote, 'If you'll take a minute to consider the quantity of pointless pain in this universe, you'll see that the cosmic surgeon has acted more like a vivisectionist.'"

Swann winced. "I am sure Lot's daughters possess many virtues, but they are not trained theologians."

"Have *you* ever taken a minute to consider the quantity of pointless pain in this universe?"

"That's a loaded question."

"Then give me a loaded answer."

"Objection," said Lovett.

"Sustained," said Torvald.

"Withdrawn," said Martin, slamming the binder shut. Got her on the run, he thought. "Would it be accurate to say the disciplinary defense traces to the old ideal of retributive justice?"

"I suppose it does . . . yes," said Swann guardedly.

"All those serious thinkers you cited—Augustine, Nazianzenus, Luther—wouldn't they argue that suffering represents well-deserved retribution for sin?"

"Fair enough."

"If these theologians came back today, they'd probably interpret the AIDS epidemic as God's punishment for the sin of homosexuality, true?"

"I don't believe homosexuality is a sin."

"I didn't ask you that. I asked you whether Augustine and company would interpret AIDS as divine punishment."

"Objection," said Lovett. "The question calls for speculation."

"Overruled," said Torvald.

"They might interpret AIDS as divine punishment, yes," said Swann.

"Now . . . suppose Augustine noticed that people sometimes get AIDS for reasons other than controversial sexual activities," said Martin. "Last month the tribunal heard from the widow of an adolescent named Billy Jenkins. What would Augustine say to a hemophiliac like Billy whose AIDS bears no relationship to his conduct?"

"I don't know."

"Use your imagination. What would he say?"

"I'm not here to defend Saint Augustine."

"All right—what would *God* say to a hemophiliac who got AIDS?"

"I don't know that either."

" 'Ooops'?"

"I cannot presume to speak for God."

" 'Sorry, Billy, guess you got hit by some friendly fire.' "

A peal of quavering laughter issued from the gallery.

"In instances where the victim appears to be innocent, one does best turning to eschatology," said Swann, inhaling through clenched teeth. "God permits suffering in this world so we might be perfect in the next."

As Martin approached the exhibit table, he experienced two concurrent crab spasms, one in his left pubic bone, the other in his right shoulder. He slipped a Roxanol between his lips and, reaching out, obtained Isaac's leather bindings. Limping to the stand, he dangled the bindings in front of Swann like a mischievous boy attempting to frighten his little sister with earthworms.

"Can you tell me what these are?"

"Thongs?"

"The very thongs with which Abraham bound Isaac's wrists together." Returning to the lectern, Martin set down the thongs and rubbed his palm across them, as if molding a pair of clay snakes. "No doubt you're familiar with the case. It's an eschatological classic. Yahweh demands a blood sacrifice, and Abraham goes ahead and builds an altar, lays Isaac on top, and picks up the knife. At the last minute, Yahweh calls it off. Question, Dr. Swann: what do you think of a God who would put His creatures through an experience like that? Is He benevolent?"

"Objection," said Lovett.

"Overruled," said Torvald.

"Among other interpretations, the story of Abraham and Isaac can be taken to mean that suffering is a temporary condition," said Swann. "In the fullness of time, the substitutional ram will appear and justice will prevail."

"All's well that ends well?" said Martin.

"Right."

"Jam tomorrow?"

"In a manner of speaking."

"Life is Hell, but then you go to Heaven?"

"That's one way to put it."

Martin pointedly encircled his wrist with a thong, then pulled the binding taut. "Despite different philosophical outlooks, the various players on Mount Moriah all agree that the problem of evil cannot be solved through appeals to a Christian afterlife. In the ram's words, 'A father doesn't have the right to sexually molest his children throughout the winter simply because he intends to take them to Disneyland in the spring.'"

"Christianity teaches that people suffer because they're born into a fallen world." Swann's elegant fingers writhed around each other in a Laocoönian tangle. If the Court TV director knew his stuff, Martin decided, he was ordering the videographer to zoom in. "God is not the culprit. God is our salvation."

"Have you ever heard the maxim, 'Justice delayed is justice denied'?"

"Everybody's heard that maxim."

"Have you?"

"Yes."

"Do you believe that justice delayed is justice denied?"

"I imagine I do . . . yes."

"Would you mind repeating that for the record? You believe that justice delayed . . ."

"Objection," said Lovett. "Leading the witness."

"Withdrawn," said Martin tartly. "No further questions. Thank you, Dr. Swann."

He sauntered back to the prosecution table, grinning so prodigiously his face was starting to ache.

"You ate her for breakfast," said Randall.

"Three down and two to go," said Martin.

❖

Eighteen hours later Lovett stood before the bench, speaking glibly and smiling seraphically, as if the case for the defense were still as sturdy as the dikes holding back the North Sea.

"It is one thing—I'm sure Your Honors will agree—to understand how the great theodicies operate on an abstract plane, and quite another to see them touching people's lives. No solution to the problem of evil can ease a victim's pain in the telling alone, but only when coupled to the grace of God. The defense calls Amos Brady."

"Who the fuck is Amos Brady?" whispered Randall.

"I don't know, but I think Lovett's about to unleash his secret weapon," said Martin, defiantly opening his binder to a blank page.

The witness, a stooped and wizened man in a frayed cardigan sweater, entered the courtroom with the sort of sauntering gait the elderly commonly affect by way of denying their inveterate exhaustion. His saintliness, though palpable, was of a decidedly earthly sort: a Francis of Assisi who preached the Gospel not just to the birds in the trees but also to the grubs in the ground. As the interview got under way, the tribunal learned that Brady was an eighty-year-old retired aluminum-siding salesman who lived with his wife and sister-in-law in Minatare, Nebraska.

"Do you consider yourself a religious man, Mr. Brady?"

"When I was a boy, my parents kept dragging me to Lutheran Sunday school. I liked the music. It wasn't until my son was born, though, that God appeared in my life as well. I actually saw Louis enter the world—this was 1963, when they were just starting to let fathers in the delivery room."

"Did Louis seem all right to you?"

"He was purple as a grape and all tangled up in the umbilicus. But the part that's etched in my mind forever happened when the nurse turned to the obstetrician and said, 'He looks Downsy around the eyes.'"

"'Downsy'? What did the nurse mean?"

"She meant Louis had Down's syndrome. She meant he was a 'mongoloid idiot,' as they called those kids back then."

"Did you and your wife speak with a pediatrician that day?"

"We did. He said Louis would be severely retarded and susceptible to all sorts of infectious diseases. Our boy would never be able to dress himself, use the toilet, or know who me and Charlotte were. It'd be best all around if we put Louis in a state mental hospital and pretended he'd died at birth."

"What did you say to the pediatrician?"

"We told him, 'Excuse us, Doc, but we have to give Louis his first bath.'"

For the next ninety minutes Amos Brady catalogued the enervating realities of raising a Down's syndrome child. The uncomprehending relatives and the unsympathetic bill collectors. The beshitted underwear and the chronic earaches. By the time he was nine, Louis could tie his shoes, speak in complete sentences, and read *Pat the Bunny* all by himself. In his adolescence he became an expert at finding the nests of baby rabbits whose mothers had been preyed upon, then raising the bunnies to adulthood and selling them to pet stores. Throughout his twenties Louis held down a job mopping the floor at Emilio's Pizzeria in Gering.

"What you're describing sounds like a miracle," said Lovett.

"Charlotte and I had help."

"Whose help?"

"Objection!" cried Martin.

"Overruled," said Torvald.

"We had the good Lord's help," said Amos.

"Aren't you mad at the Defendant for burdening you with a Down's child?" asked Lovett.

"Louis was a blessing, not a burden." Amos absently tore a pill from the cuff of his sweater. "Sure, there were times when we wanted to give up, but it made us better human beings . . . slower to pass judgment—know what I mean?—more understanding of the other person's faults."

Lovett stared directly into the witness's luminous eyes. "Is your son still alive, Mr. Brady?"

"These days, the typical Down's kid can expect to live anywhere between thirty-five and fifty years. Louis wasn't as lucky as some. He died last October, at age thirty-seven."

"That hardly seems fair."

A solitary tear slid down Amos's cheek. "We miss him a lot."

"I imagine your faith sustains you."

"The last time Charlotte and me visited Louis's grave . . . he's buried at Clearview Cemetery in Scottsbluff, and the last time we visited—I swear this is true—a rabbit came hopping onto the grass in front of the tombstone, a little brown bunny like the ones Louis used to raise. It started nibbling the clover."

"You took this as a sign?"

"Louis was using the bunny to tell us he's doing just fine up in Heaven."

"Thank you, Mr. Brady. The witness is yours, Mr. Candle."

Martin rose stiffly from the prosecution table and muttered, "I feel like I'm about to kick a puppy."

"Or a little brown bunny," said Esther.

Forcing a self-assured smile, Martin limped to the lectern, set down his cane, glanced at his notes, and said, "Hello, sir."

"Good morning."

"Down's syndrome is a genetic anomaly, correct? Your son was conceived with three twenty-first chromosomes, whereas most children have only two."

"That's right."

"Why do you suppose the Defendant failed to engineer the human germ cell so it would always divide normally?"

"I thought you'd ask me something like that. You want to hear my answer? I'll tell you. There's never been a time in history when Down's kids weren't with us. It happens once every seven hundred births, which means you could go out right now and find about ten million cases worldwide. The way I figure it, anything so common must be around for a reason."

"And what is the reason?"

"I believe God sends Down's kids to Earth to teach us about love and gentleness and joy."

"Okay, but let's focus on the children themselves for a moment. Isn't it wrong that they should go through life feeling inadequate and defective?"

"Louis was a happy boy. He looked a little funny, sure, with his thick tongue and crinkled ears—his Downsy eyes—but I'll tell you a true fact: he was the kindest person I ever knew."

"Suppose scientists one day figure out how to correct Down's syndrome in the womb . . . would that be a good thing, Mr. Brady?"

"I guess so. A good thing? Sure."

"So given the choice between the status quo and a universe without Down's syndrome, you'd opt for the latter, correct?"

"Uh-huh."

"But didn't you just say we need Down's kids to teach us about love and gentleness and joy?"

"You're trying to make me contradict myself."

"No, Mr. Brady, I'm trying to understand whether fixing Down's syndrome *in utero* would fulfill God's plan or thwart it. Can you enlighten us on this matter?"

"Objection."

"Sustained."

"No further questions."

The prosecution team spent the lunch recess in Martin's office, where Pierre Ferrand provided them with *koffie verkeerd* and fish sandwiches. The coffee was flat. The mackerel had no savor.

"You did your best," said Esther, laying a soothing hand on Martin's shoulder.

"We can bounce back from this," said Randall. "I *know* we can."

"*We're* supposed to have the sympathetic victims," Martin moaned. "Not Lovett—*we* are."

When the tribunal reconvened, the defense called Mona Drake, a dimpled young woman with a pageboy haircut and a chronic smile, though the first thing Martin noticed about her was her wheelchair. The strategy, he had to concede, was brilliant. Harry Elder, witness for the prosecution, had seen his own son die—and so had Amos Brady, witness for the defense. Stanley Pallomar, witness for the prosecution, was imprisoned in a wheelchair—and so was Mona Drake, witness for the defense.

"Tit for tat," said Esther.

"Lovett has no shame," said Randall.

As Mona's testimony unfolded, the tribunal learned that, two weeks after her sixteenth birthday, she'd dived into a shallow lagoon off Chesapeake Bay and broken her neck. In a strong, mellifluous voice—a voice abrim with bravery and devoid of self-pity—she described how God had taught her to accept her quadriplegia, a process that climaxed with her decision to become a commercial artist.

"Before my accident, I was really good at drawing. My friends called me Mona *Lisa* Drake. So I had the talent—I simply needed to connect it to the parts of me that still worked."

"Your lips . . ."

"My lips, tongue, and teeth."

"Could you give us a demonstration?"

"Certainly."

"Are we to be spared nothing?" groaned Randall as the defense counsel inserted a drawing pencil between the witness's jaws.

Pulling a sketch pad from his briefcase, Lovett flipped back the cover, approached the stand, and positioned the blank sheet in front of Mona. The pencil dangled like a cheroot. She lowered her gaze, pressed the pencil point against the page, and began to draw. Within one minute a comic portrait of Lovett himself emerged, a caricature capturing not only his Alfred Hitchcock features but also his blustery persona.

After Mona had finished creating her cartoon, Lovett informed the tribunal that her work was now selling regularly to publishers of calendars and greeting cards. He took out a scrapbook containing photostats of her most recent illustrations, holding it before the Court TV camera and slowly turning the pages. This artist, Martin saw, had no fear of schmaltz. Her sense of kitsch was keen. A mischievous puppy dug up a flower bed; a kitten stalked a grasshopper; a rabbit painted rainbows on an Easter egg. If Patricia was watching in her hotel room, she was probably throwing up.

"One more question, Miss Drake," said Lovett, returning to the lectern. "Do you think you've gotten a raw deal in life?"

"I'll give you my personal philosophy, sir. I believe our lives don't truly begin till after we reach the Great Beyond. God wanted me to see that the present world can't make a person truly happy, so He sent a broken neck my way. Okay, sure, the dark despair that followed wasn't much fun, but it got me appreciating what the Gospels teach about immortality. When I finally reach Heaven, and suddenly I can walk—I mean, imagine how *thrilled* I'll be, compared to some woman who was always on her feet."

"Thank you, Miss Drake. Your witness, Mr. Candle."

Martin's cross-examination of Mona was perhaps the single most exasperating experience of his life. The further the interview progressed, the more he felt like Brer Rabbit slugging the Tar Baby.

"Do you ever feel angry about being a quadriplegic?"

"If it wasn't for my accident, I never would've dared to try breaking into commercial art. It's a very competitive field."

"Are there times when the frustration of quadriplegia makes you think the Defendant might be cruel?"

"Know what I believe, sir? I believe Jesus has a great big bottle, bigger than you and I can imagine, and He collects all our tears inside it. Not a single tear we shed in this life goes unnoticed by our Lord and Savior, Jesus Christ."

❖

For eight days running Lovett cleaved to the same devastating strategy, systematically canceling out each of Martin's Jobians with an equally unfortunate sufferer who knew for a fact his Creator was benevolent.

"God's character witnesses," snarled Randall.

"Where does he *find* them?" growled Esther.

Continuing its exploration of existential evil, the defense paraded an impressive array of human wreckage—dozens of ingratiating God fearers who'd been irretrievably twisted by car crashes, train derailments, falls, fires, fumes, explosions, and grisly misadventures with power tools. In every case the witness explained how his tribulations had furnished him with a stouter heart, a stronger will, or a sturdier soul.

When it came to natural evil, Lovett flourished ten cancer patients, each insisting that his pains were as nothing compared to what Christ had endured on the cross. Staying with the theme of pathology, the defense next carted out a scrappy thirteen-year-old hemophiliac lad . . . the pious father of a preschool girl suffering from spinal meningitis . . . an eleven-year-old Mormon boy whose congenitally deficient T-cells required him to live inside a glass bubble as if he were a goldfish . . . and a winsome pair of adolescent female Siamese twins who said, in unison, "Together we are forging our separate lives."

Turning at last to moral evil, Lovett drew heavily on the Vietnam War—four mangled vets, three bereaved siblings, and six melancholic widows, each more maddeningly seraphic than the one before—then wound up with a rape victim who averred, "Because I have God's love in my heart, I am able to forgive my attacker."

The cross-examinations, predictably, went nowhere. Interviewing a woman whose husband had died during the Tet Offensive, Martin got her to admit to envying those Vietnam wives whose men had returned home safely, at which juncture she recounted how her grief had inspired her to found an orphanage in Dong Ha, so that "thanks to Jack's sacrifice, hundreds of Asian children are getting the love they need." Reviewing the testimony of a teenage girl whose little brother had fallen head first from a twenty-fifth-story window in midtown Manhattan, Martin maneuvered her into calling the accident "difficult to understand," but then she began recounting "all the evidence I've been noticing that Barry is living happily in Jesus' arms." Speaking with a testicular cancer patient who had less than three months to live, he managed to elicit the man's apprehension over his ten-year-old daughter's future, but then the witness added that soon he'd be "standing alongside the angels, supervising Sally's life from above."

We're losing ground, Martin reluctantly confessed to himself, staring at his latest batch of ARID APES anagrams. A SEA DRIP. PEA RAIDS. DIS A PEAR. We're losing the battle, he begrudgingly admitted. We're losing the whole damn war.

❖

So disoriented was Martin by Lovett's use of countervictims, so troubled in his heart and confused in his soul, it took him several minutes to realize the defense had once again changed strategies. The present witness wasn't a sufferer but a monk: Brother Sebastian Cranach, a portly, bald Franciscan who lived in a monastery, wore leather sandals and a brown wool robe, and taught evening courses in Church history at Saint Bonaventure University.

"Holy shit, it's Friar Tuck," whispered Esther.

"Nine articles in the *Augustinian Quarterly* and a dozen in the *Thomist Review*," said Martin, staring at the east wall. Rain spattered the windows—an ominous sound, like a drum cadence heralding the approach of Vlad the Impaler's army. "I think we're in for a rough time."

"You'll send him packing," said Esther.

"I appreciate your faith," said Martin.

Cutting through the haze of his despair, he focused on the interview. Cranach was explaining how a complex, differentiated universe must ipso facto contain defects.

"Ontological defense," grunted Randall.

"We knew it was coming," moaned Martin. Behemoth was upon them. The slavering beast had arrived. REAP AIDS, he wrote. PAID ARSE. RIDE A SAP.

"Like a cut diamond, this solution boasts many beautiful facets," said Cranach, his pronunciation so florid and precise it seemed the audile equivalent of Old English typography. "It includes, first of all, an epistemological facet: a theory of human knowledge. As Lactantius put it in the fourth century, 'Good cannot be understood without evil, nor evil without good.' "

"If everything were red," said Lovett, "then *red* would be a meaningless concept."

"Exactly. Epistemologically speaking, our ability to know happiness, pleasure, and contentment depends entirely upon our firsthand experiences with sorrow, pain, and misery."

Observing Cranach's bulky frame and imperious demeanor, Martin recalled the equally overbearing defendant in the case of *Abaddon Planning Commission versus Wilcox*. In the spring of

1992, Herbert Wilcox, a Perkinsville orthodontist, had dug a swimming pool on his front lawn without obtaining proper building permits; Martin ruled that Wilcox could keep his pool, but he had to admit the whole neighborhood every Saturday and Sunday afternoon, supervised by a lifeguard hired at the defendant's expense.

"But none of this accounts for the *amount* of evil we see all around us," said Lovett with fake dismay.

"Yes. Quite so." Cranach slipped a hand under his robe and scratched the apex of his abdomen. "Which brings us to the aesthetic facet of the ontological defense: the theory that for all its ugliness this is still—in G. W. Leibniz's memorable phrase—'the best of all possible worlds.' "

"One doesn't hear that argument much these days."

"Let's assume for a moment that Leibniz—who invented the infinitesimal calculus, after all—was no fool. Does a best-of-all-possible-worlds theory get us anywhere? I think it does. Permit me to offer a simple visual aid." With consummate nonchalance, Cranach drew a raisin bagel from his sleeve. "When we buy a bagel at the delicatessen, we know we're being charged for the dough, not the hole, so we're perfectly happy to hand over our money. When we look at the rest of reality, however, we tend to focus on the negative: the necessary fact of privation, the hole in the cosmic bagel."

" 'Cosmic bagel'—is he serious?" whispered Randall.

"Saint Augustine makes the same point using Swiss cheese," muttered Martin.

"The world, we must remember, is beautiful in the main and benevolent overall," said Cranach. " 'And God saw that it was good.' Our planet abounds in glorious sunsets, golden beaches, soaring mountains, children's laughter, ecstatic lovers, faithful dogs, loyal friends . . ."

"Tasty raisins," said Randall.

"The best of all possible bagels," said Esther.

"Manifestly the work of a loving Creator?" asked Lovett.

"Manifestly." Reaching into his robe, Cranach pulled out a matchbook. "If the Defendant were guilty as charged, the world would be, ontologically, a far more sinister place. It would not be Leibnizian but Lovecraftian: a great big hole with little or no bagel." He tore off a match and ignited it. "Consider the phenomenon of fire. For thousands of years this miraculous chemical interaction warmed our homes, cooked our food, frightened away our enemies, and brightened our nights. Destructive fires occurred, but they were the exception, not the rule."

"That fact wouldn't prove very comforting to a woman whose daughter died in, say, the 1911 Triangle Shirtwaist Company fire," Lovett noted, feigning bewilderment.

Cranach blew out the match. A curlicue of smoke drifted toward the chandelier. "Quite so. Which is why the ontological defense includes a third, mechanistic facet. The instant God resolved to make a physical cosmos, He realized it must be governed by laws: combustion, gravity, motion, and so on. Far better for those laws to cause hardships on occasion than for the universe to be anarchic. Take the case of bone." In a gesture more appropriate to Harpo Marx than a Franciscan monk, the witness slid an entire human femur from his robe. A jolt of envy shot through Martin: unlike his own thighbones, this one appeared entirely free of cancer. "Our skeletons are amazing inventions," Cranach continued, "strong enough to support our bodies, yet light enough to let us move around." Assuming the posture of a circus strongman intent on bending a crowbar, he snapped the femur in two. "The brittleness of bone doesn't mean the pre-coma God was incompetent or malign. It merely means that when fashioning our frameworks He was bound by the limitations inherent in matter. One could offer a similar analysis of our planet's crust . . ." The witness flourished a cream puff, tearing away the cellophane wrapper as smoothly as a magician performing a card trick. "If God had made the ground so hard that earthquakes and volcanic eruptions never occurred"—he poked his thumb through the cream puff's shell—"then farming, mining, and road building would be impossible. The same point could be advanced concerning wind, rain, and bacteria. Each phenomenon is fundamentally benign, even though it sometimes entails such undesirable side effects as hurricanes, tornadoes, floods, droughts, and plagues. In every case the so-called evil is occurring *per accidens*. The Defendant is not responsible."

"But surely the pre-coma God could have suspended a natural law when He saw it was causing pain," said Lovett.

Cranach responded to this challenge pretty much as Job had done back in the divine brain: yes, the Defendant could have broken His own rules, but the more He did so, the more disorderly the universe would have become, until its utter randomness drove its inhabitants mad. "Which is not to say He *never* intervened. For all we know, there were hundreds of times when He looked down, noticed that a famine or a flood was in the offing, and willed it out of existence."

"There might have been a thousand such times," said Lovett.

"Or a million," said Cranach.

"Or none at all," muttered Martin.

"The catastrophes you've mentioned so far all exemplify natural evil," said Lovett, glancing at Cranach as if the witness had just dealt him a straight flush. "What about moral evil? Shouldn't the Defendant have stepped in whenever a child was about to be molested or a massacre about to occur?"

"No."

"No?"

Here it comes, thought Martin, the second great Jobian beast, the Leviathan of *liberum arbitrium*.

Lovett and Cranach spent the rest of the day on a meticulous presentation of the free will defense. From his conversation with Adrian and Evangeline, Martin already knew the basics: if free will is to be a fully functional virtue, then it must belong to everyone, including those who would exploit it to swindle, plunder, rape, and kill. Cranach's elaboration proved both erudite and nuanced, peppered with references to Augustine's *De libero arbitrio*, Gregory the Great's *Moralia*, Saint Anselm's *De casu diaboli*, and Thomas Aquinas's *Summa theologiae*. When at last the lecture was done, Martin understood as never before the argument's iron logic. Given the alternatives of creating either robots wired to eschew iniquity or autonomous beings blessed with real choices, God had rightly opted for the latter.

"It seems to me the free will defense handles not only moral evil but also existential evil," said Lovett.

"Absolutely. The gift of *liberum arbitrium* permits us to produce many impressive if prideful inventions: railroad trains, ocean-going ships, opera houses. All these inventions involve a potential for disaster—trains collide, ships sink, opera houses catch fire—but we're prepared to assume such risks in the name of progress and creativity."

"Better to build an airplane, even though it may succumb to gravity, than to remain forever on the ground, confined by our Creator's loving desire to protect us?"

"I couldn't have put it more cogently."

"Thank you for your enlightening testimony, Brother Sebastian. I have nothing further."

❖

When Martin awoke the following morning, the crab awoke with him, fastening its claws around his femurs and biting voraciously into his shoulders. Cancer patients have two kinds of days, he remembered Blumenberg telling him—bad days and terrible days. This was going to be a terrible day. He consumed four Roxanols and began to dress, all the while staring at the fifty 2cc vials of Odradex on his bureau. Did this forbidding ocher fluid really have the power to cure him? Could it truly end this agony forever?

Take a vial, said his pain. *Just one vial won't cloud your mind.*

"Not till I've had my shot at Cranach," said Martin out loud.
Go ahead.
"No."
Take a vial, Martin. Curse God, and live.
"I can't. No. My Jobians are counting on me."

At 9:35 A.M., as Martin started across the Peace Palace plaza, his goal of spending the whole day cross-examining Cranach began to seem nothing but a preposterous fantasy. Fiery spasms tore through his pelvis and spine like lightning bolts hurled by the pre-coma Jehovah. Each upward step was an ordeal. Sensing his distress, Olaf and Gunnar slid their hands under his armpits, lifted him two inches off the ground, and carried him bodily into the courtroom.

Before Torvald could call the tribunal to order, Martin convened a colloquy comprising Lovett, Randall, the judges, and himself: the sort of hiatus the Court TV reporters loved, he mused—an opportunity for them to wallow in Louis Brady's bunnies, Mona Drake's calendar art, and related insipidities. Lovett agreed that Randall could cross-examine Cranach, provided Martin took over the instant he felt equal to the task.

Eyes aflame with nihilistic zeal, Randall strolled up to the prosecution table and appropriated a portion of Esther's breakfast: a doughnut dusted with confectioner's sugar.

"Let me guess," she said. "The cosmic doughnut?"

"By the time I finish with Cranach"—he faced the lectern and started away—"he'll be wearing it through his nose."

Randall began by feeling out the ontological defense. "The universe, okay?" he said, holding up Esther's doughnut for Cranach and the rest of the world to see. "Now, my question to you, sir"—he placed the doughnut to his eye, like a monocle—"is this: why does there have to be a hole at all? Why couldn't God have created a cosmic waffle instead?"

Cranach loosened the belt of his wool robe. "Even an omnipotent being must obey the demands of logic. The pre-coma

God could not have purged Creation of matter, energy, and physical laws without simultaneously annihilating it. Leibniz, please remember, argued that ours is the best of all *possible* worlds. You're asking—illogically—for God to have made the best of all *impossible* worlds. A flawless universe wouldn't be a universe at all. It would be God Himself."

"You haven't answered my question." Randall screwed his index finger through the doughnut hole. "Why aren't we living in a cosmic waffle?"

The witness responded by evoking Leibniz again, whereupon Randall tried his waffle metaphor once more, and then the two of them went around and around this same metaphysical mulberry bush a dozen more times, and before they knew it an hour had elapsed.

ARID APES, Martin wrote. IS A DRAPE. A DESPAIR. PARADISE. PARADISE?

PARADISE!

A sudden excitement overcame him, a spasm of delight radiating through flesh more accustomed to pain. Paradise . . . Elysium . . . Heaven . . . yes! "I've *got* it," he whispered.

"Got what?" asked Esther.

"The answer to the ontological defense. The free will theory too, now that I think about it."

Having failed to make a dent in ontology, Randall began hammering away at *liberum arbitrium*. "If freedom is a gift from God, and if that gift inevitably causes cruelty and injustice, then why isn't He responsible for those evils?"

"Thomas Aquinas addressed that problem seven hundred years ago," said Cranach. "In a brilliant melding of the free will argument with the ontological defense, Thomas reasoned that the average individual sooner or later loses touch with the divine harmony of the cosmos. This lapse is not itself an evil. It is not even a phenomenon. It is simply a *privation*: an ontological gap that occasionally inclines a person to behave wickedly. But if human sinfulness proceeds from a non-event—from a hole without a cause—then the question of agency becomes meaningless, and God cannot be held accountable."

"I see," said Randall morosely.

When the lunch hour arrived, Martin realized he was much too tired to leave the table, so he asked Esther to bring him a snack from the nearest Nordzee. She returned with a *haringsalade* accompanied by French fries suspended in mayonnaise. Martin ate eagerly, and a few minutes later his energy level rose. Whether this improvement traced to the food, the opium, or the fact that he'd finally deciphered *arid apes*, he really couldn't say. He knew only that he was ready to tackle Cranach.

"I imagine you believe in Heaven," said Martin, staring fixedly at the witness while steadying himself on the lectern.

"Quite so."

"An amazing neck of the woods, I hear. An ideal world."

"True enough."

"Then I'm confused. Doesn't your ontological solution argue that an ideal world cannot exist?"

Cranach remained imperially unperturbed. "Heaven isn't like other places."

"But it can still be distinguished from God. Correct?"

"More or less."

"Which forces me to conclude either that Paradise is flawed or that the ontological solution is bogus. Is Paradise flawed, Brother Sebastian? Is there a rusty hinge on the pearly gates? Does Gabriel's harp have a broken string?"

"If Heaven contains flaws—"

"Or perhaps there's a child somewhere: one lonely, wretched, abused child—Ivan Karamazov's tortured five-year-old, locked away in a freezing outhouse, screaming for help."

"If Heaven contains flaws, they aren't what we normally regard as flaws."

"Then why can't *Earth* contain flaws we don't normally

regard as flaws? Why can't it have slithy toves and borogoves instead of meningitis and Buchenwald?"

"You're assuming an analogy between two different ontological planes."

The crab clawed its way into both of Martin's pubic bones. He grimaced, groaned, and said, "Maybe so, but—"

"There's no 'maybe' about it. The Kingdom of God is completely discontinuous with the material cosmos."

Martin mopped his eyes with Patricia's scarf, fighting both his pain and the fear his pain instilled. Oh, hell, he thought, there's an answer to my answer. "Nevertheless, we have to—"

"Ergo, no contradiction exists between the ontological solution and the promise of Christian redemption."

"In your opinion."

"In my opinion—*and* in the opinion of the Holy Catholic Church."

"Let's move on," said Martin, forcing the words between his clenched teeth. "The so-called free will defense states that most *liberum arbitrium* creatures must eventually wander into error. And yet your Holy Catholic Church exists primarily to celebrate an exception to this rule. Jesus Christ had free will. True?"

"Among his other assets."

"Then it follows—does it not?—that the defense fails. Or did Jesus sometimes wander into error?"

"Jesus was—"

"Perfect. Exactly. Did the dishes, kept quiet in libraries, never burned a witch at the stake."

"Of *course* he was perfect," said Cranach. "He was divine."

"Yes, but he was also a *man*. A man, sir. Deny that, and you're committing the Docetist heresy." I've nailed him, thought Martin. Checkmate. "You're not a Docetist, are you?"

"Nobody's a Docetist anymore. What are you saying, Mr. Candle? Are you saying God should have populated the cosmos with nothing but emanations of Himself?"

"A planet of Jesuses might be pretty boring, but I'd prefer it to one featuring, say, Vlad the Impaler and Pol Pot."

"You must understand that Christ cannot be grasped apart from the Godhead. He was not a *'liberum arbitrium* creature,' as you put it. He was not a 'creature' at all."

The crab bit clean through Martin's coccyx. He moaned, gritted his teeth, and hugged the lectern as if it were a handrail on the Heaven to Hell roller coaster. "Then what was he?"

"You know perfectly well what Jesus was. He was God incarnate, Mr. Candle—God incarnate."

Martin gasped, partly from the crab's predations, partly from Cranach's recalcitrance: a long, low, whistling noise he feared the judges would interpret not as a cry of pain but as an admission of defeat.

"No further questions."

❖

As Martin eased back into his chair—slowly, carefully, so as not to antagonize the crab—Lovett told Torvald he felt no need to redirect the witness. I blew it, thought Martin. I failed to defeat ontology and freedom, and now they're on the loose. In his mind he saw the beasts attacking his courageous Jobians: Behemoth stomping Christopher Ransom into the dust and crushing Wanda Jo Jenkins's head between his jaws, Leviathan chewing off Stanley Pallomar's remaining arm and incinerating Harry Elder with a single fiery sneeze.

"The defense—at long last—calls Martin Candle."

With the aid of his crocodile cane, he rose. Aiming himself toward the stand, he realized a fever now possessed him, twisting reality into odd, elongated shapes, as if God had constructed the world from Silly Putty instead of wood and clay. His progress down the aisle was halting, each step attained at the price of a spasm. In its entire career as his private torturer, the crab had never behaved with such Torquemadan zeal. Shivering, he sank into the witness chair, rested his cane on his knees, and blatantly lobbed four Roxanols into his mouth.

The usher came forward. Martin grasped the World Court's Dutch Reformed Bible, each shift of ligament and bone triggering an explosion of pain. He swore to tell the truth.

"You appear to be unwell," said Lovett, his voice reverberating off the paneled walls.

Martin nodded. "I'll get through this."

"Perhaps we should postpone the interview."

"I said I'll get through it."

Lovett marched up to the usher, secured the World Court's Bible, and returned to the lectern. "May I assume you're familiar with the Book of Job?"

Martin ground his molars together, seeking to dislodge any stray grains of Roxanol and deliver them to his brain. "I've read it fifteen times."

"Then I'm sure you remember that dramatic moment in chapter thirty-one when Job requests an audience with his Creator. 'Let the Almighty state his case against me . . . I would plead the whole record of my life and present that in court as my defense.' Shortly afterward, God appears, and the first thing He says is, 'Where were you when I laid the foundations of the Earth?'"

Martin leaned forward and said, "As a matter of fact, His first line is, 'Who is this whose ignorant words cloud my design in darkness?'"

Cracking open the Bible, Lovett licked his index finger and flipped ahead one page. "Indeed . . . but what I want to know is, how would you answer the question?"

"Which question, the first or the second?"

"Where were you when God—"

"Laid the foundations of the Earth?"

"Yes."

"Are you kidding?"

"No."

"I didn't exist when God—"

"How unfortunate for the rest of us. If you *had* been there, you could've told Him how to do it properly—or am I over-estimating your opinion of yourself?"

"Objection!" shouted Randall, leaping up.

"Overruled," said Torvald.

"I might have kibitzed a bit, yes," said Martin, rubbing his eyes. Lovett's face looked narrow and warped, as if reflected in a hubcap.

"Please explain to the tribunal why the universe contains three spatial dimensions and not two or four," said Lovett.

"What?"

"Tell the tribunal why the universe contains exactly three spatial dimensions."

"I've never really thought about it."

"If *I'd* made the universe, I think perhaps I would've given it *four* spatial dimensions. More is better, right?"

"If you say so."

"Why settle for three when we could have four?"

"I don't see what you're getting at."

"Scientists now tell us that the ultimate particles of reality, quarks and so on, are knots in space-time. You can't make a knot in two dimensions because there's no 'over' or 'under,' and—here's the rub—you can't make a knot in *four* dimensions either—a 'raveling,' yes, but it won't hold. So it turns out this four-dimensional cosmos of ours would be a disaster, and God in His day knew best."

"I've never questioned His math, Professor. My quarrel is with His morality."

"Do you know what would happen if the 'strong nuclear force,' the interaction that binds atomic nuclei together, were slightly more intense?"

"I have no idea."

"God did. He knew that if He were to make the strong force only two percent greater, protons would become *di*protons, resulting in a variety of hydrogen so unstable our universe would consist entirely of helium. If He'd made the strong force five percent *weaker*, the deuteron couldn't form, and so there'd be no deuterium, a situation—"

"I'd rather discuss Deuteronomy than the deuteron. Let's talk about God urging the Israelites to go out and mercilessly slaughter the Hittites, Amorites, and Canaanites."

"—a situation that would preclude the main nuclear reaction chain used by the sun, thus canceling all life on Earth. But we *do* have life on Earth, don't we? Tell me: if I were to hand you a jar full of prokaryotic cells, the sort found in pre-Cambrian blue-green algae, could you change them into eukaryotic cells— animal tissue, that is, complete with nuclei, nucleoli, mito- chondria, and Golgi apparatus?"

"Of course not."

"Of course not, and neither could the brightest biologist at the University of Amsterdam. But *God* in His day could do it, and over the eons He put that power to use, so that our pre- Cambrian algae ended up sharing the planet with arthropods, brachiopods, sponges, worms, fish, reptiles, cats, dogs, and gi- raffes. Do you know anything about giraffes, Mr. Candle?"

"Not much."

"As you might imagine, a giraffe's blood pressure must be very high—otherwise, the blood could never make it up that eight-foot neck. But there's a problem. When he bends down to drink, he's going to black out from all that squeezed fluid in his brain. So how do we prevent this?"

"Don't ask me."

"*God* knew how to prevent it. Through evolution, inter- vention—whatever—He equipped the giraffe's circulatory system with a pressure-reducing mechanism, the *rete mirabile*." Reaching into his suit coat, Lovett took out a squat cardboard cylinder capped with a hot-pink lid. He marched up to Martin. "Do you know what's in here?" he asked, setting the cylinder on the stand.

"It says, 'Play-Doh,' " Martin replied, wistfully remembering the night he and Patricia had fooled around with Brandon's Play-Doh in her studio.

"Exactly. Children's Play-Doh. Now—I'd like you to take this Play-Doh and use it to fashion a living creature. Nothing fancy. Not a frog or a snake or any other vertebrate—but perhaps you could give us a slug. Is that asking too much? Could you please favor the Court with a real, live, wriggling slug?"

"Oh, for heaven's sake."

"You can see where I'm heading, yes? If the Defendant knew how many dimensions the universe must contain—if He knew how strong to make the subatomic forces and how to turn pro-karyotic cells into eukaryotic cells and how to keep giraffes from blacking out—if He knew all these things, then maybe He knew some *other* things as well. Is that possible?"

"I'm not questioning His *power*, Dr. Lovett. I'm positively in *awe* of His power."

"Answer the question. If God knew all these things, is it possible He knew some other things too?"

"*Some* other things, yes."

"Perhaps He even knew why the fact of evil does not imply malice on His part. True?"

"Objection!" cried Randall.

"Overruled," said Torvald.

Martin steeled himself. "I'm willing to concede He's innocent until proven guilty. I'm *not* willing to concede He's innocent until I can make a slug out of Play-Doh."

"Thinking back on Brother Sebastian's testimony, do you recall him saying bacteria are 'fundamentally benign'?"

"I remember that, yes."

"Are you as well disposed toward bacteria as Brother Sebastian?"

"I suppose so."

"In *The Conundrum of Suffering* I suggest that we are to the divine as bacteria are to us. We matter in our own way, but we're insignificant alongside God. Tell me, have the *Lactobacillus acidophilus* in your intestines ever accused you of mismanaging their universe?"

"Not to my knowledge."

"What would you think of an intestinal bacterium that put you on trial? Might you not regard it as misguided?"

"If I knew my microbes were in trouble, and if I were capable of helping them, I would certainly intervene."

"Most admirable. Might you not even incarnate yourself as one of those germs—assuming you had the ability—the better to understand their predicament?"

"Assuming I had the ability . . ."

"Good for you." Lovett held out his palm like a bellboy soliciting a tip. "Give me your hand."

"What?"

"Your hand. Please."

Cautiously, reluctantly, Martin extended his palm and inverted it, pressing Lovett's skin with the gentle but steady force his father had taught him to employ when making gravestone rubbings.

"You're in pain," said Lovett.

"Yes."

"Metastatic prostate cancer—one of the worst catastrophes imaginable."

Martin nodded. "It's pretty bad."

"Do you feel anything besides your pain?"

"I can feel your hand."

"Listen, Mr. Candle. Forget that confounding object moored in Scheveningen Harbor and concentrate instead on the Eternal Entity who rules the universe even as we speak. Can you perceive God's grace rushing from the heart of Creation, passing through my gnarled fingers, and pouring into your afflicted flesh?"

"No." Martin had to admit that a quivering sensation was now suffusing his palm, as if he were gripping a power sander or a motorized drill. "Not really." For whatever reasons, the throbbing in his pelvis diminished slightly, and his fever seemed to drop at least one degree. "I wish I could, but I can't."

"You feel nothing?"

"Nothing." This was merely some insidious variety of hypnosis, Martin decided, akin to what he'd experienced thirteen months earlier standing atop the Defendant's cooling chamber. "Leave me alone."

"God loves you, Martin Candle, and I love you as well." Lovett withdrew his palm and backed away from the stand. "That will be all. Thank you for your testimony."

Seizing his crocodile cane, Martin stood up. The entire courtroom was spinning, around and around like the Four Horsemen of the Apocalypse carousel. He was vaguely aware of Torvald asking Lovett to call his next witness, and of Lovett saying he had no more witnesses.

"Does the defense rest its case, then?"

Martin took a tentative step forward, a second step, a third. It seemed as if he were crossing an especially ephemeral stretch of Abaddon Marsh, a tract so soft that if he advanced any farther he would sink all the way to the other, the infernal, Abaddon.

"The defense rests its case, Your Honor."

A loud, serrated scream spewed from Martin's throat, wrought by some irreducible mixture of cancer and bewilderment. He dropped his cane. He pressed his sternum. His legs failed, his vision dimmed, and as he toppled to the floor a Voice filled his skull, its bassy vibrations spiraling toward the center of his soul as God Himself said, distinctly, "Let there be night."

Chapter 14

AT THE RISK OF SPOILING my reputation, I shall admit I felt sorry for Martin Candle as his bodyguards carried his unconscious form out of the courtroom and bore it down the street to Saint James Hospital. Consider our hero's plight. Lovett had just treated him with imperial condescension before the entire world, he had bobbled his great opportunity to slay Behemoth and Leviathan, and the cancer had reached its cruelest crescendo yet. I actually shed a tear, something I hadn't done since 1965, when Pope Paul VI ruled that even the crime of deicide should enjoy a statute of limitations, and so the world's Jews must no longer be persecuted for having—in the Church's opinion—murdered Jesus Christ two thousand years earlier.

Thanks to Holland's robust system of socialized medicine, our hero entered Saint James with minimal bureaucratic fuss. As Funkeldune likes to say, "It's easier to get admitted to the average Dutch hospital than to the men's room of the average American gas station." Later that afternoon, acting on orders from an oncologist named Van der Meulen, the bodyguards brought Candle up to Suite 1190, where the nurses gave our hero a shot of morphine, rubbed him with alcohol, and put him on an IV drip that suffused his system with saline solution and broad-spectrum antibiotics. Within the hour he rallied, becoming alert enough to tell Van der Meulen the bald-faced lie that he was injecting himself each day with two cc's of Odradex-11 via his implanted Port-A-Cath.

By sundown he was permitted to receive visitors. In a manic burst of energy, Candle spent his first evening at Saint James dictating his closing argument to Selkirk, who dutifully entered each word in our hero's computer and converted the speech to hard copy via the hospital's laser printer.

"*Now* will you take your medicine?" asked Patricia Zabor, drawing a syringe and a vial of Odradex from her shoulder bag.

"It's all over, isn't it?" said Candle resignedly. "All over but the shouting."

Zabor filled the syringe with two cc's, leaned toward the adjustable bed, and, parting the halves of Candle's robe, slid the needle into the valve protruding from his chest. "I won't pretend I'm not furious with you." She pushed the plunger. "We should've done this *weeks* ago."

Before the drug kicked in, fuzzing his mind and abridging his diction, Candle managed to read over his speech four times. He liked it. "The final *j'accuse* of a dying Job," he told Zabor.

There was no question of Candle giving the speech himself, and with Lovett's blessing the task fell to Selkirk. At 10:15 the next morning this angry middle-aged man stood before the bench and read Candle's words with predictable aplomb: Selkirk was, after all, a person who at age seventeen had convinced a Pennsylvania district court to outlaw classroom prayer. The speech's basic theme was that, while Lovett and his witnesses had indeed supplied the Defendant with "alibis of a certain sort," the circumstantial evidence against Him remained overwhelming.

" 'Our position is simple: no being is above the law,' " Selkirk read. " 'In rendering a "guilty" verdict, you will be helping to heal millions of broken, bleeding, blameless hearts around the world. In disconnecting the Lockheed 7000, you will be striking a blow for temporal justice, human dignity, and the other noble ideals to which this Court is consecrated.' "

"Good Lord, he's actually doing it," I said. "He's asking them to pull the plug."

Funkeldune devoured a slice of pepperoni pizza and said, "Where are the Ring Dings?"

"You ate them," said Schonspigel.

" 'Thank you, learned judges. The world awaits your decision.' "

Lovett's closing argument contained nothing I hadn't heard before, either during the trial or in the course of my checkered career. He began by reviewing the disciplinary, eschatological, and hidden harmony solutions, according them barely ten minutes apiece. The soul of his case, clearly, lay in the one-two punch of ontology and free will, and he spent the rest of the afternoon recapitulating "these venerable and invulnerable defenses."

"Are we out of pork rinds?" asked Funkeldune.

"We've been out of them for a week," said Belphegor.

"It's really very simple," said Lovett. "Moral and existential evil together constitute the cost of human freedom, while natural evil is the price we pay for having a material world in which to exercise that freedom."

"I *know* we've got more Skittles," said Funkeldune.

"We don't," said Schonspigel.

"Let me conclude by emphasizing that the events of this past summer are unique. Never before in the annals of arrogance, never in the history of hubris, has there been such a trial. Although we have all referred to God as 'the Defendant,' Mr. Candle has conceded on the stand that our Creator is unlike any Entity ever indicted in a court of law. 'Who is this whose ignorant words cloud my design in darkness?' asks the Voice from the Whirlwind in Job 38:2. Be careful, Your Honors. Move slowly. Every star in the firmament is watching you. To render a 'guilty' verdict in this case would be to claim for yourselves a quality of knowledge far beyond what mortal minds possess. Do not cloud God's design with ignorant words!"

"Doritos?" asked Funkeldune.

"Gone," said Belphegor.

"And so we come to the end. The day after tomorrow I shall fly home to Cambridge, Massachusetts, where I am scheduled to teach an undergraduate course on the medieval epic and a seminar on the *Mabinogion*. Several days into the semester a student will doubtless come running up to me, agog with word of your decision. I shall listen to this young person with bated breath . . . but no matter what the news—guilty or not, disconnection or status quo—two irrefutable facts will sustain me: I spoke truthfully in The Hague, and God's love reigns supreme, forever and ever, amen."

"Don't tell me there's no more popcorn," said Funkeldune.

"There's no more popcorn," I said, aiming the remote control and obliterating the last live closeup of Gregory Francis Lovett that would ever appear on a television screen.

❖

Although Martin had never been a father, he assumed that waiting for the World Court's decision in *International 227* was rather like anticipating the birth of a child. When will the creature come? Will it be healthy or sick, calm or colicky? The closest equivalent in his experience was the ordeal of sitting in Vaughn Poffley's TV room on Election Night, watching the local returns while nervously consuming beer and pretzels.

Three hours before his plane was scheduled to take off from the Amsterdam airport, Lovett appeared at the hospital smelling of aftershave lotion and bearing a fruit basket even lusher than the one he'd left in the Huize Bellevue two months earlier. To Martin's drugged sensorium, the fruit seemed at once surreal and erotic, like a snack Hieronymus Bosch might have packed for

Little Red Riding Hood to take on her first *déjeuner sur l'herbe*. Patricia plucked a glistery apple from the basket and bit off a chunk. Martin selected a luscious green pear.

"Eat of your own free will," said Lovett, smiling gently.

"Free will," echoed Martin, struggling to overcome his Odradexian stupor. "Right."

Lovett bent over the adjustable bed and squeezed Martin's hand. There was no electric buzz today, no jolt of psychic energy. "How're you feeling?"

"I highly recommend cancer. It's worth it just for the drugs."

"Are you in pain?"

"Yes."

"I'll pray for you."

"I'd appreciate that." This was not entirely untrue. "Take a banana. Take two. You and Darcy might get hungry on the train to Amsterdam."

"I'm sorry I treated you harshly during your testimony."

"All's fair in love and theodicy."

Lovett snatched up a banana, pocketing it as he might a large ballpoint pen. He grabbed a second banana, started for the door, then turned toward Martin and flashed a lopsided grin. "They've started taking bets."

"Bets?"

"In London they'll give you ten-to-one odds if you dare wager on a unanimous conviction."

"Sounds like you've already won."

"You know what you'd better do now, Professor?" said Patricia.

"What?"

"You'd better get out of here before I bounce this apple off your fucking head."

Lovett fled.

The arrival of the deliberation phase dramatically rekindled flagging public interest in the Trial of the Millennium. All around the industrialized world, people talked of little else.

During the first week following the judges' withdrawal, Western civilization's news-gathering apparatus did an admirable job of sating its audience's appetite for eschatological gossip—a feat the journalists accomplished despite the unavailability of the two principal players. Thanks to a cadre of personal servants supplemented by the Harvard campus police, Lovett managed to preserve his privacy, teaching poetry by day and sipping claret on Mount Auburn Street by night. Martin, meanwhile, remained holed up in Saint James Hospital, periodically issuing press releases to the effect that he was a mortally ill man incapable of giving a coherent interview.

Randall and Esther, by contrast, made themselves available to every television camera and radio mike that came their way. Whenever Martin surfed the channels, he saw his teammates' talking heads. Their promiscuity annoyed him. Didn't they understand the cosmic meaning of the war in which they'd just fought? If a Jobian crusade wasn't sacred, what was?

"Win or lose, we did what needed doing," Randall informed a Court TV reporter.

"If only one judge ends up agreeing with us, we'll feel victorious," Esther told CNN.

Equally eager for media exposure was the Sword of Jehovah Strike Force. Exploiting the human species's endless fascination with fanaticism, the TV reporters cast the organization in a sinister light, portraying them as hayseed zealots who at any moment could transmute into urban guerrillas. The more Martin saw of the Jehovans, the more he agreed with this assessment— particularly after a CNN interview with a West Virginia snake handler named Jasper Hooke.

"If them judges say He's guilty and then try to disconnect Him, I suspect we'll have to take action," Hooke told the reporter.

"Are you implying there might be violence?"

"Let me put it like this." Hooke patted his twelve-gauge shotgun. "If my people had been around on Good Friday two thousand years ago, them Romans never woulda got away with it."

Both Captain Hans De Groot of The Hague Metropolitan Police and General Jacques Mazauric of the United Nations peacekeeping brigades assured everyone that order would prevail no matter what the tribunal decided. The media reacted skeptically: even if Scheveningen Harbor and its environs stayed quiet, disturbances might erupt elsewhere around the globe.

"Good heavens, aren't they *ever* going to make up their minds?" moaned Martin, flicking off the TV.

"Relax," said Patricia. "Give them time. They'd never even *heard* of ontology till you came into their lives."

While everyone on Earth except Torvald, his eight colleagues, and the ICJ usher was banned from the deliberation chambers, the courtroom itself remained open to the media. The two dozen journalists who staked out the place soon found their initiative rewarded. Twice a day, the usher would ascend from the bowels of the Peace Palace, remove an object from the exhibit table, and bear it away to the judges. "They're grappling with existential evil," a CNN stringer told his audience after the tribunal asked to see a charred tent fragment from the 1961 Gran Circo Norte-Americano fire. "They're debating the hidden harmony solution," concluded an *NBC Nightly News* reporter after the usher delivered Noah's ax to the chambers. "They're pondering the disciplinary defense," a Court TV commentator announced after the judges requested Mrs. Lot's right ear.

When no other *International 227* story presented itself on a given day, the media resorted to covering the various sweepstakes that had emerged in the trial's wake. The biggest such game originated in London—the Royal Millennial Fortune Hunt, which quickly attracted sixteen million pounds to its trove by offering favorable odds on the entire matrix of possible outcomes: unanimous acquittal, split-decision acquittal, split-decision conviction, unanimous conviction with disconnection, unanimous conviction without disconnection. The hundred-million-franc Prix de Paris, by contrast, operated on a lottery principle. Winners would be randomly selected from among a subset of ticket holders who'd accurately predicted each judge's vote.

As the tribunal entered its third week of deliberations, Dr. Van der Meulen brought Martin a startling piece of news. They were planning to sign him out. According to the latest C-125 results, their patient had undergone a "quasi-remission."

"Quasi-remission? What's that?"

"It's like a remission," said Van der Meulen, "only we don't call it that, because it isn't. It's a quasi-remission. Keep taking the Odradex. With any sort of luck you'll be enjoying a *real* remission when they announce the verdict."

The next day Martin left Saint James Hospital and moved back into the Huize Bellevue—a smaller suite this time, a single room in fact, as Lovett had understandably stopped paying the prosecution's bills. He dismissed Olaf and Gunnar, thanking them for their professional services and also for the unsolicited but often useful critiques they had accorded each of his daily performances in the Peace Palace.

"I must be honest with you—I'm playing the Royal Millennial Fortune Hunt," Olaf admitted. "I've got two hundred guilders riding on a split-decision acquittal."

"I've wagered three hundred on a unanimous acquittal," Gunnar confessed. "If you'd made a stronger showing against Brother Sebastian, we might've hedged our bets."

So intense were the side effects of the Odradex, Martin could no longer write postcards, read the newspaper, or carry on an intelligible conversation. Hour after hour he lay in bed, watching television and drinking *koffie verkeerd*. The trial received scant attention that week. Most of CNN's energies were going into an intertribal war in the Transvaal, while Court TV had elected to cover the case of a young mother accused of baking her preschool daughter's head into a mince pie and serving it to her ex-husband.

"Moral evil," noted Martin.

"Give it a rest," said Patricia.

Then, on September 17, 2000—at ten A.M.—Pierre Ferrand called a press conference on the Peace Palace steps and told the reporters exactly what they wanted to hear. In twenty-four hours the International Court of Justice would reconvene, at which time the judges would reveal their decision.

"Are you feeling well enough to make the trip?" asked Patricia.

"I'm feeling well enough to prosecute God all over again," Martin replied, though in truth the crab was back, devouring what remained of his pelvis.

❖

Only after entering the Peace Palace courtroom for the last time did Martin realize how profoundly he was going to miss it. He had spent some of the most meaningful hours of his life among these mahogany balustrades and stained-glass judges. Apart from the Lovett brothers' conspicuous absence, the place looked the same as always. The exhibit table was still jammed with artifacts from the Kroft Museum and relics from the divine cranium. Martin fixed on the plaster casting of the young Vesuvius victim—the Roman boy and Patricia's son, he figured, had died at about the same age—then shifted his gaze to the notorious door from the Vietnam-orphan plane crash. At last his eyes alighted on Noah's ax, its chopping edge gleaming like the razor-sharp guillotine blade featured in Braverman and Kelvin's treatment of the French Revolution.

"All rise," said the usher in a voice so solemn he might have been a Judgment Day angel commanding the saved to ascend.

Everyone stood up.

One by one, the red-robed, white-wigged judges filed in, each as stiff, sour, and expressionless as an Easter Island statue.

Tucked under Torvald's arm was a stack of fan-folded computer paper.

"Resume your places," said the usher.

Everyone sat down.

Torvald took out a pair of tortoiseshell reading glasses, put them on, and set the computer printout on the bench before him. He cleared his throat. He scowled. "I shall begin by revealing that you will hear no minority opinion this morning." The judge stared straight into the Court TV camera. "We are of one mind concerning the Defendant's guilt or lack thereof."

" 'Guilt or lack thereof,' not 'guilt or innocence,' " muttered Randall. "That's a good sign."

"Maybe," said Martin, eating a Roxanol.

"This summer the tribunal heard arguments for and against five different theories of evil," Torvald read. "Despite the thoughtful testimonies of Rabbi Bernard Kaplan and Dr. Eleanor Swann, we found ourselves quickly discounting the so-called hidden harmony, disciplinary, and eschatological defenses."

"Good for you," mumbled Randall.

"The ontological and the free will defenses, by contrast, detained us for six days running . . ."

"Uh-oh," said Esther.

"Shit," said Randall.

". . . after which we decided that they, too, fail to solve the problem of pain. Anyone wishing to know how we reached these conclusions can consult the forthcoming edited transcript of our deliberations, scheduled to appear in English as a mass-market paperback from Bantam Books and in French from J'ai Lu."

"Did you hear that?" gasped Randall. "Did you *hear* that?"

"He's throwing them out!" shouted Esther. "Every last one!"

Joy flooded through Martin's ruined bones. He resolved that, assuming things continued going against God and Lovett, he and Patricia would take the express train to Amsterdam that night and patronize the priciest restaurant they could find.

"So where does this leave us?" said Torvald. "After many hours of wearying discussion and withering debate, we decided that *International 227* boils down to a single question. Once the Defendant set the universe in motion, should He have impressed His will directly on its workings for the sake of reducing His creatures' pain?"

"Fair enough," said Martin.

"Folks, we're sittin' pretty," said Esther.

"The more we thought about divine intervention, the more we realized what a complex transaction it is. An omnipotent deity, we saw, has three choices open to Him. One: continual intervention to eliminate all unhappiness. Two: secret and selective intervention to prevent egregious evils. Three: no reliable intervention whatsoever, even in the face of extreme and unmerited suffering.

"We did not linger over the first alternative. Imagine a universe where, thanks to God's incessant manipulations, nothing unpleasant ever occurs. Under this regime, if a thief steals a million guilders from a bank, another million instantly appears in their place. If a maniac fires an assault rifle into a crowded restaurant, the bullets melt into thin air. If a fire levels an orphanage, an identical building materializes on the spot, with all the children miraculously restored to life. Any fool can grasp the sterility of such a world. Any schoolboy can see its pointlessness, not to mention its absurdity. The God who echews option one—in short—is not a God we can rightly condemn."

"Oh, yes He is," said Randall.

"Take it easy," said Martin.

"Which brings us to option two: secret and selective intervention to prevent egregious evils. At first blush this seemed like an attractive alternative. 'If we were the pre-coma God,' we told ourselves, 'that's how we would have behaved.' But eventually we noticed the catch: option two, we saw, sets in motion a chain reaction of impossible expectations."

"This had better be good," said Esther.

"Egregious evils are not egregious in themselves but only in relation to other evils. If the Defendant had caused Hitler and Stalin to perish in the womb, there still would've been Goering—wouldn't there?—as well as Mussolini and Franco. And if He'd aborted *these* tyrants, then we'd be pointing to Pol Pot—right?—along with Idi Amin and Slobodan Milosevic. The same pitfall awaits those who say America's plans to obliterate Hiroshima cried out for cancellation from on high. If God had delivered Japan from the A-bomb, instead we'd be focusing our Jobian indignation on the razing of Dresden—wouldn't we?—not to mention the Bataan death march, the My Lai massacre, the Lisbon earthquake, and the eruption of Vesuvius . . . until eventually we're indicting Him for bush wars and brushfires—then crooked politicians and poison ivy—then schoolyard bullies and bee stings. Divine intervention, the tribunal concluded, is the slipperiest of all possible slopes."

"I can't believe I'm hearing this," groaned Esther.

"It's rigged," seethed Randall. "This whole damn trial is rigged."

"And so we come to option three: no manifest or reliable intervention whatsoever, even in the face of extreme and unmerited suffering. Was the tribunal able to reconcile itself to such a regime?" Tovald took a swallow of water. "In a word, yes."

A courtroom, Martin had always believed, should be a temple of reason and decorum. It was this conviction—and this conviction alone—that now prevented him from pounding his fist on the table and smashing his waterglass on the floor.

"Consider the alternative: a universe devoid of gratuitous catastrophe. In such a universe, plane crash victims never elicit our sympathy, for we know they deserve their fates. Famines never occasion herculean relief efforts, for we realize mass starvation is cosmologically necessary. Cancer and Down's syndrome never inspire us to probe nature's secrets, for we understand pathology is essential to the divine plan. To wit, only by building random annihilation into the scheme of things could the Defendant have secured a world containing charity, compassion, courage, patience, self-sacrifice, and ingenuity."

"Not to mention the March of Dimes," snorted Randall.

"Easter Seals," grunted Esther.

"Jerry Lewis telethons."

"The Ronald McDonald House."

"The United Way."

"UNICEF."

Aphasic with rage, Martin said nothing.

"Thus ends *International 227*," said Torvald. "The Defendant is not guilty. Justice has been served."

"Justice has been screwed," said Randall.

A low, coarse, surflike sound washed through the courtroom, rising and falling and then rising again. Joyful shouting, Martin realized—the cheers of the mob outside the Peace Palace.

"This afternoon the tribunal will formally cede the Corpus Dei to its previous owners, Eternity Enterprises," said Torvald. "Our fond hope is that they will once again make God's material form the Main Attraction at Celestial City USA, offering solace and inspiration to millions of disheartened pilgrims around the world."

Martin felt as if someone had stuck a needle in his Port-A-Cath valve and injected his soul with strychnine.

Torvald rapped his Christmas gavel on the bench with uncharacteristic enthusiasm. "The Court stands adjourned until November thirteenth, when it will hear opening statements in *International 228: Kingdom of Liberia versus United States Merchant Marine*."

❖

"What do you suppose he's thinking?" asked Belphegor. His scaly finger pointed toward my television, which just then displayed a closeup of Candle's pale and trembling face.

"He's thinking it wasn't supposed to end this way," I replied.

"Once Job finished trying God, he was rewarded handsomely: new house, new herds, new kids, stock options. Candle gets a shit sandwich on stale bread."

The camera zoomed out. Leaning on his crocodile cane, our hero rose from his chair, hobbled toward the exhibit table, and caressed the blade of Noah's ax. For a moment I thought he intended to commit a particularly garish variety of suicide, but then I saw he had something more ambitious in mind.

"I'm sick of looking at that clod," said Schonspigel as Candle tossed his cane aside and, grasping the ax, lifted it off the table. "I wish they'd bring back the snake handler."

The camera zoomed in. Candle stared into the lens and gave the Western world a cryptic smile.

"I've always wondered: are snake handlers in it for the religious ecstasy or merely for the ritualized masturbation?" asked Funkeldune.

"They're in it for the thrill—the pure Nietzschean thrill," I answered, pressing my palm against the TV screen.

The image dissolved from Candle to the exterior of the Peace Palace. A CNN reporter stood on the steps, asking a beautiful young American exchange student her reaction to the verdict.

"I thought it was awesome," she said.

"Every time the rattler strikes and doesn't kill you," I told Funkeldune, "you grow a little stronger."

❖

Ax in hand, Martin emerged from the Peace Palace into the muted morning light. Within seconds he was surrounded by sufferers: two dozen official Jobians augmented by about four hundred equally unfortunate victims. As always, the rich, textured diversity of the damned impressed him—these stalwarts with their walkers and wheelchairs, their oxygen tanks and IV drips—but at the moment their most striking quality was their restlessness. A dark, menacing expectancy hung in the air, as if a thunderstorm were due to arrive or a North Sea dike about to break.

Riser by riser, spasm by spasm, he began his descent, the mob parting around him like a turbulent sea yielding to the prow of the *Carpco New Orleans*. Even the reporters moved back. Occasionally a victim reached out and touched his sleeve, as if some arcane therapeutic power suffused the garments of the world's most famous dissident.

He set his foot on the middle step and paused, surveying the spectacle through a fog compounded of Odradex and Roxanol. Just beyond the sufferers a second crowd had collected on the plaza, a mob of deliriously happy foot soldiers in the Sword of Jehovah Strike Force. They laughed, sang, clapped, and moved their limbs in a manner seemingly inspired by the snakes they loved to touch. "Hosanna!" they whooped, blowing into plastic replicas of Joshua's city-busting trumpets. "Hosanna! Hosanna!"

"You did your best!" shouted Stanley Pallomar over the din.

"You put up a hell of a fight!" yelled Julia Schroeder.

Bedecked in full riot gear, a deployment comprising United Nations peacekeepers and Hans De Groot's police officers stood at attention, rifles snugged against their shoulders, separating Jobians from Jehovans like the Waupelani winding its way through Abaddon Valley. The ubiquitous news media lent to the scene an atmosphere of artifice: a passerby might have fancied himself on the set of a Hollywood epic—cameras, lights, swarming extras. Martin half expected to hear Cecil B. DeMille yell, "Action!"

"It's all my fault!" He resumed his downward journey. "I'm the one to blame!"

The press corps, he could tell, wanted to rush him, reeling off a thousand questions. It was the ax that kept them away. Band by band, violet to green to yellow to red, an iridescent spectrum fanned outward from the blade, arcing across the plaza like the rainbow with which Yahweh had sealed His very first covenant with *Homo sapiens*. Whether the glow originated in the ax itself or in the fevered soul of the man who held it, Martin couldn't say. He knew only that this antique tool was about to perform its most momentous task yet.

"You're being too hard on yourself!" called Harry Elder.

"Job would've been proud of you!" shouted Rosalind Kreuger.

At last Martin reached the plaza. Defying his disease, countermanding the crab, he raised the weapon high above his head. "Was justice done this day?" he cried.

"No!" responded the Jobians in unison.

"And is this day over?"

"No!"

"And will justice be done this day?"

"Yes!"

"Sufferers, form your ranks!"

With a consensus bordering on the uncanny and an efficiency partaking of the miraculous, the mob began to move. Swiftly, surely, the Jobians became what Martin had always known they were: an army. As the divine ax pulsed and shimmered, he took command of a force Alexander of Macedon would have been honored to lead. Instead of a chariot host, he had a hundred and fifty-five paralytics in wheelchairs. Instead of an infantry, he had two hundred and twenty invalids armed with crutches and walkers.

"Forward—march!"

He shouldered the ax. A spontaneous cadence arose, *ratta-ta-tat, ratta-ta-tat, ratta-ta-ratta-ta-ratta-ta-tat*: the emphysema victims, drumming on their oxygen tanks with crocheting needles and ballpoint pens. His army rolled, limped, and staggered down Patijinlaan toward Raamweg, cutting through the normal lunchtime congestion of cars, bicycles, motor scooters, taxis, and trams, the Jehovans following close behind, monitoring the sufferers' march like wolves reconnoitering a sheep ranch. Reluctantly the UN troops joined the parade. The peacekeepers, Martin saw, were in a bind. If they attacked immediately, they would come across on television like Charles IX's royalists perpetrating the Saint Bartholomew's Day Massacre. If they waited too long, they would miss their chance to prevent whatever strange variety of mayhem was about to erupt.

" 'Though I am right, God condemns me out of my own mouth'!" chanted the Jobians as Martin led them around the corner and down Raamweg. " 'Though I am blameless, He twists my words'!" A spiraling violet beam corkscrewed outward from the ax blade and disintegrated in an explosion of sparks. " 'The land is given over to the power of the wicked,' " they screamed, tromping past the Huize Bellevue, " 'and the eyes of the judges are blindfolded'!"

By one o'clock their destination was in view: Strandweg and the harbor beyond. A bewildered battalion of UN peacekeepers stood guard along the beach, protecting both the cooling chamber and the Lockheed 7000. Seagulls soared across the breakers, nattering and screeching. The incoming tide issued a low, coarse whisper, like some obscene secret falling from the lips of Jonathan Sarkos.

Martin slid the ax from his shoulder and, grasping the handle with all ten fingers, pointed the blade toward the peacekeepers.

"Charge!"

And so it began: the United Nations versus God's victims, a melee to satisfy the most sadistic CNN viewer. Fists collided with jaws. Shields smashed into walkers. Bayonets dueled crutches. Tear-gas canisters detonated, spraying their noisome fumes across the harbor. The cacophony grew ever louder, assailing the TV audience with groans of pain, cries of dismay, and the sickening thud of nightsticks breaking ontologically vulnerable bone. The United Nations had the law on its side, but the Jobians had their bitterness. Forming the sort of wedge with which the Spartans had opposed Persian moral evil at Thermopylae, they advanced down Pier 18 toward the Lockheed 7000, squeezing the UN troops against the guardrails.

Debilitated by decades of sea spray and a succession of termite infestations, the boards disintegrated, dumping the peacekeepers into the surf. Within minutes the North Sea suggested the site of a maritime disaster straight from the gravamen of Martin's case—the wreck of the *Sisters*, perhaps, or the sinking of the *Larchmont*.

Jagged bursts of blinding light shot from the ax as, hips aching, femurs throbbing, shoulders burning, Martin broke from his army, hobbled to the end of the wharf, and scrambled down onto the raft. For a full minute he stood breathless in the shadow of the Defendant's cardiovascular system. The steel-plated pump was running at full tilt, roaring and hissing as it siphoned the donated blood into the four aeration domes, through the Corpus Dei, and back to the domes again. Spewing steam, the bellows contracted and expanded like some vast primordial bladder. Seagulls perched on the maze of transparent pipes, pecking away in hopes of tapping the briny nourishment that flowed beneath their feet. The last time Martin had been this close to the Lockheed 7000, it had lain deep within the central Florida earth, but now it was completely exposed, like the organs of a gutted whale strewn across the *Pequod*'s flensing deck. So naked, he thought. So vulnerable.

Mark my words, Martin Candle. Before your life is done, you'll get another chance at this . . .

Panting and wheezing, a CNN videographer appeared: a barrel-chested man in a white matador's shirt and black beret. A portable TV camera lay athwart his shoulder. Rooting himself to the raft, he zoomed in on the Man Who Would Kill God.

With an ear-splitting shriek Martin stumbled toward the seam that joined the main pipe to aeration dome number one. A cyan river roiled within the viaduct, leukocytes hurtling themselves against the Plexiglas like fruit bats crashing into a picture window. Here was the place to strike, he thought—this spot, yes. He lifted his weapon aloft.

" 'O Earth cover not my blood . . .'!"

He brought the ax down hard. The blade glanced off the Plexiglas; golden sparks peppered his cheeks. He attacked his target a second time, more passionately than before. The pipe held firm.

"Try again!" yelled the videographer, twisting the focus ring.

Once more Martin raised the ax. He summoned all his strength.

"'. . . and let my cry for justice find no rest'!"

He struck. The vein split. A geyser of O-positive blood shot skyward, turning instantly from dark blue to bright red as it hit the radiant Dutch air.

He continued the assault: an easy job now—*chop, chop, chop*, and a hundred shards of polymer pinwheeled away, leaving the seam in ruins, the Defendant's essence gushing through the breach. Hot steam rose from the liberated plasma. The vapors smelled like burnt molasses. With tsunami strength the blood splashed against Martin; it drenched him head to toe, knocking him sideways and forcing him to replant his feet. The fluid was relentless, unstaunchable, gallon upon gallon spilling across the raft, tumbling over the sides, and soaking the befuddled troops as they climbed out of the surf. And still he chopped, striking a blow for Corinne, a blow for Brandon, for Norma Bedloe, Billy Jenkins, Duncan Elder, Louis Brady, Mona Drake, and the plaster-cast boy from Pompeii, *chop, chop, chop*, fashioning a flood with the very ax that had enabled Noah to flee the Deluge. The waters of Scheveningen Harbor turned red.

"Terrific stuff!" cried the videographer, shaking the blood from his arms.

As the hemorrhage eddied around Martin, engulfing his thighs and warming his hips, he noticed something odd. The blood was alive . . . sentient, conscious, a creature unto itself, like some amoeboid monster from a fifties sci-fi movie. Crawling willfully out of the surf, it metamorphosed into a wave as awesome as the one that had ravaged Japan's northeast coast in 1896, People's Exhibit B-72. The videographer pivoted, focusing on the wave. He grinned with glee. He trembled with delight. The blood hit the dikes and broke, rushing over the levees and flowing down Strandweg and the thoroughfares beyond—Gevers Deijnootweg, Schokkerweg, Jacob Pronkstraat—sweeping away bicyclists, motor-scooterists, and pedestrians in a scene that recalled the 1642 rebel attack on the Yangtze river dams in episode four of *Havoc*, a seminal act of terrorism that had inundated Kaifeng.

"Spectacular!" shouted the videographer, zooming in.

The longer Martin stared at the cataract, the more obvious the explanation became. For nearly three years this blood had inhabited holy neurons. For over a thousand days it had fed the thoughts of a failing Providence. Of *course* it had acquired a mind of its own.

Within minutes the whole of Scheveningen stood transformed. Red streets, red lanes, red parks, red plazas.

A frightening truth seized Martin's soul. The blood wanted him. Its resolve was absolute. Already a strand of clotted plasma had sinuated from the breach and encircled his waist like a tentacle. He laughed maniacally, running his tongue around his sticky lips.

"No!" he cried as the slimy plasma lifted him off the ground and the ax fell from his hands.

"Jesus!" whooped the videographer. "Jesus, that's beautiful!"

The blood drew Martin into the pipe, a pungent place, empty but for a shallow creek roiling along the bottom. His ears rang with the booming of the pump. His nostrils twitched with the burnt-molasses odor. For an instant he thought of the eighteenth-century Parisians vacating the Place de la Révolution to escape the guillotine's stench. As the blood swept him into aeration dome number one, he pressed his palms against its walls, tacky with drying plasma. He tried cursing God aloud, but the syllables lodged in his throat, and suddenly he was moving, blood borne, his free will evaporating and his consciousness dissolving as the glutinous serpent carried him toward the dark core of his Creator's unbeating heart.

Chapter 15

SECONDS AFTER CANDLE STORMED OUT of the courtroom, Schonspigel picked up my Elias Howe sewing machine and, by way of editorializing on Torvald's ridiculous and wrongheaded verdict, hurled the device at my television set. The picture tube imploded in a shower of glass. There was something profoundly satisfying about Schonspigel's action, though it made a mess and left us incommunicado. An entire day passed before word of the divine hemorrhage reached my shop.

We experienced the symptoms before knowing the cause. They were subtle at first. When I went to make a new nylon tent for the Idea of the Gran Circo Norte-Americano (the previous one had caught fire during the matinee of December 17, 1961, and incinerated three hundred Brazilian children, People's Exhibit D-20), my fingers grew so palsied I couldn't thread the needle. When Funkeldune attempted to roast the Jehovic archetype of witchfinder Heinrich Kramer for lunch—let the punishment fit the crime, I always say—the oven refused to stay lit. Eventually it became clear a major disaster was upon us, the worst since the great coma. On Sunday morning Belphegor took his fishing pole down to the Hiddekel, returning posthaste with the information that the river had disappeared. A few hours later Schonspigel set off for Jerusalem, where he planned to spend the day eating Cheese Doodles and watching crucifixions, and the instant he caught sight of Golgotha the entire mound of skulls dissolved before his eyes. Finally, come dusk, my dinosaur neighbors from across the mudflat turned up dead in the backyard.

It was Augustine who told us what had happened. "Did you hear the news?" he screamed, rushing into the shop like a man taking refuge from a blizzard. "He pulled the plug!" Elaborating, the bishop explained that Candle, maddened by the verdict, had gone on a rampage, attacking the Lockheed 7000 with Noah's ax. The liberated plasma had flooded the town, staining it a hideous maroon and causing damages estimated at sixty-five million guilders. "An ocean of blood!" cried Augustine, at which instant I noticed all his teeth had fallen out. "I looked at my television set and I said, 'Even John the Divine never beheld such an apocalypse!'"

❖

Gradually, spasmodically, the light seeped back into Martin's brain. He opened his eyes. He was supine, he realized—and scared. Already he could sense the crab at work, flexing its claws and working its jaw. Bit by bit, his trip through the heart came back to him. The thundering systoles, the emphatic diastoles, the warm blood carrying him forward like a log in a sluice. Moaning, he slid his hand into his pants pocket. His grateful fingers touched plastic. He pulled the bottle free.

Rotating his head side to side, he studied the great vault of the Defendant's brain, His neurons twinkling feebly in the ashen sky. The solar archetype had lost its grandeur; it looked less like the sun than like a red light in a bordello. To Martin's right rested the ruins of Noah's ark, piled against the riverbank in a mass of frazzled hemp and fractured timber. To his left: the ancient mariner himself—his remains, rather, the Idea of Noah's Corpse. Martin tried to stand. Pain detonated in his shoulders and sacrum. He sank back, opened the bottle, and ate five Roxanols.

The mud was soft and cool. How long the river had been absent he couldn't say; he knew only that it was gone, forever fused with the sanguineous flood he'd loosed upon the harbor. Again he attempted to rise, inch by painful inch, until at last he stood erect. He coughed. Hans De Groot was coming for him—of this he was certain. He could almost hear the clangs and jangles of the police captain's key collection. Martin's second sojourn in The Hague, he knew, would be quite unlike his first: he pictured himself standing before the judges' bench, this time as the defendant, on trial for the Crime of the Millennium.

A squadron of vultures soared past the sun, darkening the divine cranium. He turned and hobbled east. The farther he advanced along the riverbed, the drier it grew, eventually becoming an arroyo so desolate it might have been a gully on the moon. Imagined footfalls dogged his steps. Ghostly voices assailed his psyche.

The tribunal finds you, Martin Candle, guilty as charged . . .

Rounding a bend, he came upon an unexpected scene, outré even by the norms of intracranial travel. A naked Saint Augustine sat atop the corpse of Behemoth, which in turn lay sprawled across the carcass of Leviathan. Death had bloated both monsters, turning them into zeppelins of putrescence. Augustine had no eyes. His dormant briar pipe dangled between bare gums.

" 'Who can open the doors of his face?' " Martin muttered, eulogizing Leviathan in the words of Job's biographer. " 'Out of his mouth go burning lamps, and sparks of fire leap out.' "

"Candle?" inquired the bishop, his articulation compromised by his toothlessness. "Martin Candle?"

"Hello, Your Grace." He stole a glance at Augustine's unclothed crotch. The organ that had inspired the saint's groundbreaking meditations on concupiscence was among the largest a man could hope to receive. "I was afraid I'd never see you again."

"It's certain I'll never see *you* again." Augustine gestured toward the hollow sockets in his skull. "You and your infernal ax."

"There's no telling where a man's free will might lead him," Martin replied dryly. He shifted his gaze back to the monsters. Leviathan wanted for a throat. Behemoth had been eviscerated, his intestines lying before him in a great ropy pile. "I'm sorry about your eyes."

Augustine pulled his horn-rimmed glasses out from behind Behemoth's ear, angrily broke them in two, and tossed the pieces aside. "They're certain to give you the chair for this, and I don't mean the Thomas Aquinas Chair in Medieval Philosophy at Princeton." He raised his right eyebrow independently of the left. "I have a message for you . . . a communiqué from beyond oblivion. No doubt you remember those two opinionated hominids, Adrian and Evangeline. Before they died—"

"Desiccated. Arid apes."

"—they said to tell you, quote, 'We really thought we'd cracked the ontological defense, so we sent you our answer. We're sorry it had to arrive encoded. We're even sorrier it failed. You're an upright man, Martin Candle.' Unquote."

Drawing Patricia's scarf from his pocket, Martin interposed it between his nose and the odor of the rotting flesh. "What happened to your pets?"

"They quarreled over the question of God's psychic integrity. Behemoth argued that our Creator must be bipolar, otherwise He would've had no motivation for bringing the universe into being. Leviathan held that a bipolar Supreme Being is metaphysically unstable, hence not 'supreme' at all. They came to blows." Augustine poked Behemoth's hide with the bowl of his pipe. "Have you ever been tempted to suck on the ears of an immense hippopotamus?"

"Not really, no."

"I have known such urges. Did you ever want to mash a sea

dragon's scale with a pestle, stick it in your pipe, and smoke it?"

"Perhaps you should see a psychiatrist."

"I tried that once."

"And ... ?"

"It didn't help."

Martin faced upriver, toward a horizon that among its other virtues probably lay beyond the radius of the monsters' stench. "You'll forgive me if I don't stick around." Stepping away, he limped west. "Your pets have started to turn."

"Good-bye, Martin Candle. Fare thee well. I must confess something, though. I never really liked you."

❖

At dusk the landscape grew familiar, the territory Augustine had termed the Country of Dung. Empty soup cans, broken beer bottles, and discarded automobile tires cluttered the riverbed. Gasping, sweating, Martin fought his way to the crest of the levee. A lone, molting vulture wheeled across the sky, its feathers drifting down like black snow.

He headed north. Within an hour he reached the place where four months earlier he'd come face-to-face with his alter ego. At the base of the dung heap, sandwiched between the Magnavox TV and a discarded Whirlpool clothes dryer, rose a pietà of surpassing strangeness. Dressed in a white lace wedding gown, the Idea of Corinne sat on Job's lap, his right arm curled around her neck. Three bluebottle flies circled above her face. A smile lay frozen on her lips. She was as motionless as Behemoth.

"Hello," said Martin, surveying Job's abode. The dung heap had degenerated. Rust had reduced the smaller appliances— toasters, blenders, coffeemakers—to fragments of cancroid metal. The pile of disposable diapers was now a shapeless plastic mass.

"We saw the whole show," said Job, glancing toward the TV. He still wore his shredded Crash Test Dummies T-shirt and ratty red bathing trunks. "Trial, verdict, hemorrhage, everything." The lesions on his chest had dried up—not because they were healing, Martin realized, but because the divine cranium itself was drying up. "You were an able prosecutor. I couldn't have done better myself. You look terrible."

"I know," said Martin, uncertain whether Job was referring to his crooked physique or his bloody suit.

"Pulling the plug . . . tell me how it felt. Like justice, perhaps?"

"Not exactly, no."

"Then . . . how?"

"More like revenge."

"I was hoping it felt like justice."

"Sorry. No. Revenge." A blast of fecal odor hit Martin, an obscene inverse of the lavishly perfumed bulb fields he'd experienced during his sojourn in Holland. Crouching beside Job, he stretched out his hand and shooed the flies from his wife's brow. "Is she . . . ?"

"Yes. Try not to grieve too much. She's only an idea."

"I know," said Martin, eyes welling up with salt water. A tear broke free, tickling his cheek as it fell. "But she's so convincing."

Job nodded. "God was always good with the details." He shifted the corpse's weight from his left knee to his right. "She had a final request."

"Let me guess. I'm to make sure the Kennel stays in business."

"Bingo."

"Heaven knows what I'll do if the donations stop rolling in. I'm unemployed, and Lovett no longer finances my projects."

"You'll think of something." A gentle breeze wafted across the dung heap, tousling the corpse's auburn hair. "Do you know what her last words were? 'Tell Martin I'm proud of him.' "

"I hope you're not just saying that."

"I've never told a lie in my life. No, wait, there's one exception: my most famous line, as it happens—usually translated as 'I despise myself and repent in dust and ashes.' I never repented, sir. Not in dust, ashes, cow flops, dog doody, or anything else."

"Corinne really said she was proud of me?"

"Her last words. And do you know what *my* last words will be?"

"What?"

" 'To close the gap between jurisprudence and justice would require a canon of a hundred million laws,' " said Job.

"Yes, exactly—a hundred million laws, like a map so accurate it was as big as the territory that it . . ."

Martin didn't bother finishing the sentence. The man was dead, stone dead, his prophesy fulfilled.

"Job? Job?"

Silence.

As Martin gained his feet, a relentless entropy overtook the landscape. Flop by flop, chip by chip, maggot by maggot, the great stinking mound dissolved, until nothing remained but a modest pile of peach stones, orange rinds, egg shells, and coffee grounds. Robbed of all ontological status, the bodies of Job and Corinne succumbed as a unit, devolving irrecoverably from divine ideals to sacred notions to mere supernatural fancies. Their abandoned clothing littered the ground like mayfly husks.

The sun expired. The wind died. A spasm of homesickness shook Martin's soul. He wanted to be back in Abaddon again, savoring a Monday-night NFL game with Vaughn, arguing about capital punishment with his sister, or simply sitting beneath a weeping willow on the banks of the Waupelani, watching a school of golden carp flash beneath the pellucid waters like a sunken cache of pirates' doubloons.

He swallowed a painkiller and lay down atop his dead wife's

wedding gown, soon falling asleep despite his burning bones and the lingering odor of the vanished dung.

❖

The next morning, shortly after Martin awoke, a solitary ram wandered onto the scene, alternately pawing the ground and sniffing the refuse. He was as large as a pony, with moist nostrils, a black face, and two horns spiraling eternally inward like cross sections of a conch. Sauntering over to the peach stones, he began to gobble them down.

"Gordon?"

"Morning, Mr. Candle," said the ram lugubriously, without looking up from his breakfast. "These peach stones are lousy. The pits."

"I thought you were . . ."

"Dead? Every day at three o'clock I return to Mount Moriah and Abraham slits my throat. Rain or shine. Winter, spring, summer, or fall, holidays included. It's not a life—you should've pulled the plug years ago." He fixed Martin with his rheumy eyes. "You've been summoned, friend. Climb on my back."

"Summoned? Where?"

"Climb on up. You've probably never ridden a ram before. The worst part, I'm told, is the fleas. They're only ideas, but they're very *definite* ideas."

Although Martin was braced for an ordeal, riding Gordon proved far less stressful than his last such experience: his journey on Jonathan Sarkos's horse from Abaddon Marsh to the pineal gland. Gordon's gait was rapid but steady, and the abundant wool made a wonderfully cushy saddle. The promised fleas never materialized. Extinct, Martin guessed. Killed by the hemorrhage.

Within two hours they reached the outskirts of Jerusalem, its sparkling spires and phosphorescent ramparts spreading toward the horizon like an elaborate Christmas diorama. The ram slowed to a canter, then to a trot. Before them lay a range of rocky hills that a team of talented and tireless sculptors had converted into a necropolis.

Dismounting, Martin approached the nearest tomb—a cottagelike edifice that, with its blank marble walls and opaque windows framed by functionless bas-relief shutters, partook equally of the quaint and the macabre. It was like a playhouse for dead children. Although he'd never encountered this particular tomb in person before, it still felt familiar, figuring as it did in the various Jesus epics his father had collected on videocassette. The door was a granite disk, riddled with air vents and big as a millstone, but like everything else in the posthemorrhage brain, it was extremely tractable. Gordon merely had to nudge the stone with his snout and it rolled away, making a soothing rumble as it turned.

"This crypt belongs to Joseph of Arimathea," said Martin.

"Correct."

"Is Rabbi Yeshua here?"

Gordon lethargically shook his head. "It's deserted."

"Deserted? You mean he's been resurrected?"

"Don't let it get around. The last thing we need in this skull is another religion. It's hard enough coping with Judaism. Right now he's on the hills outside Bethany, trying to ascend. Expect him back by midnight. Meanwhile, make yourself at home. There's a cot, a commode, a well-stocked larder—everything you could possibly want. I'd join you inside, but I'm scheduled to be sacrificed in an hour. *Au revoir*."

For Martin, the interior of the Arimathean's tomb owed less to the New Testament than to the culture of recreational vehicles. A red velvet divan occupied the far corner, adjacent to a four-poster bed roofed by a gold silk canopy. A refrigerator stood against the opposite wall. He peeked inside. Cold chicken wings, a German chocolate cake, a pitcher of iced tea, six-packs of Rolling Rock and Guinness stout. Assembled from oak planks and trimmed in brass, the commode was as luxurious as a throne.

He had just poured himself a glass of iced tea when a balding, portly man turned back the stone and entered. Dressed in spotless tweeds and wielding a Malacca walking stick, the visitor looked astonishingly like G. F. Lovett, though his complexion was pastier and his paunch less pronounced.

"Professor Lovett?"

"Surely you jest. It's a major accomplishment for G. F. Lovett to cross Harvard Square at ten o'clock each morning so he can lecture his undergraduates on *The Romance of the Rose*. He's not about to show up *here*."

"The *Idea* of Professor Lovett?"

"Ahhh . . ." Sauntering over to the refrigerator, the visitor obtained a Guinness stout and a chicken wing. "Normally I'd be snugly ensconced on the Idea of Mount Auburn Street this time of day, taking a nap."

"What brings you here?"

"An engraved invitation," replied the Idea of Lovett, flourishing a piece of heavy stock embossed with black letters.

Like two Civil War buffs refighting the Battle of Gettysburg, Yeshua's guests proceeded to hash over the recent trial, a project they pursued throughout the afternoon and well into the evening. Martin offered Lovett a begrudging congratulations on his victory. Lovett complimented Martin on his tenacity but chastised him for "cheap jokes at the expense of Eleanor Swann's dignity." As the antagonists polished off the chicken wings, they found themselves agreeing that Torvald's final speech was no Gettysburg Address. His argument amounted to nothing but a clumsy recapitulation of the hidden harmony defense seasoned with a dollop of ontology, so superficial it seemed plausible to suppose he'd tuned out nearly everything that had followed Bernard Kaplan's testimony. The judge's gimcrack theodicy was a proper monument to neither side of the controversy.

❖

At midnight their host appeared, his entrance heralded by the groan of the granite disk. A luminous white shroud flowed downward from his shoulders. He boasted the same handsome features as always, but the hemorrhage had left him looking drawn and anemic.

Lovett, flustered, loosened his tie and hid his Guinness behind the four-poster. Limping confidently up to Yeshua, Martin gave him the most vigorous handshake he could manage. The perforation in their host's right wrist was large and ragged, like the fleshy wake of a dumdum bullet.

The three of them sat on the divan.

"Fate has appointed me the bearer of sad tidings," said Yeshua, tugging absently on his ponytail.

"My disease?" said Martin.

Yeshua nodded. "It's beyond the reach of everything. Feminone, Odradex, radiation, prostatectomy, divine intervention."

"Everything," Martin echoed. He blanched, seized by the now-familiar sensation of sinking through Abaddon Marsh. He'd never really doubted his illness would be the death of him, but hearing the verdict from Yeshua's own lips brought the truth irredeemably home. "I was hoping I'd been summoned to . . . you know."

"Receive a cure? Sorry. Not possible." Yeshua closed his piercing blue-green Jeffrey Hunter eyes. "You're here to learn the solution, Mr. Candle. You deserve to know it." He opened his eyes and spun toward Lovett. "*You* deserve to know it too, though now I'm using 'deserve' in rather another sense."

"That would be the ontological solution, right?" said Lovett breezily, retrieving his hidden Guinness. "Maybe Torvald didn't buy it, but it stands to reason *you* do."

"The ontological?" said Yeshua, incredulous. "The *ontological*? Do you really think your terrestrial counterpart is living in the best of all possible worlds? Where I come from, an eighth grader would be ashamed to enter planet Earth in a junior high school science fair."

"There's more to the ontological defense than its Leibnizian facet. If the universe is to be predictable, it must be governed by laws."

"Okay, but then why did our Creator keep those laws *hidden*? Why didn't He *tell* humanity that rats bring plague, mosquitoes carry malaria, and obstetricians should wash their hands? The ontological defense is a loser before it's out of the gate."

"No, you're wrong. Imperfections are inherent in matter. The Creator had no choice but to—"

"Shut up, Lovett," said Yeshua. "You give me a pain in the ass."

"Are you perhaps alluding to the free will argument?" asked Martin.

Yeshua screwed his face into a sneer. "If free will is such a good thing—if it's the blessing that can reconcile us to Hiroshima and Auschwitz—I'd like to know why there's so *little* of it."

"Have you noticed that whenever a debater gets desperate, he drags out Hiroshima and Auschwitz?" grumbled Lovett.

"Hiroshima and Auschwitz," echoed Yeshua tauntingly, extending his tongue and aiming it at the professor. "Hiroshima and Auschwitz, the big H and the big A, H and A, HA, HA, HA!"

"What do you mean 'why there's so little of it'?" asked Martin.

"Most animals don't have free will," said Yeshua. "Neither do the destitute, the addicted, the senile, the stupid, or the psychotic. If *I* were God—which, by the way, I am, as Brother Sebastian pointed out during his testimony—I wouldn't go around touting the merits of freedom until I'd made the stuff generally available." Rising, he procured a Rolling Rock from the refrigerator, the bright green bottle slick with condensation. "Beyond the question of distribution, of course, there's a purely mathematical flaw in the free will defense. Can we honestly say human free will leads to an ever-expanding community of autonomous beings? When Pol Pot exercised his *liberum arbitrium* by putting half his nation in jail, the aggregate quantity of freedom in the universe actually *decreased*."

Martin said, "Surely you're not about to resurrect the hidden harmony, the disciplinary, or the—"

"Don't worry."

"So what *is* the solution?"

Yeshua sneezed.

"God bless you," said Martin.

"I intend to," said Yeshua, opening his Rolling Rock. He curled his hand around the dislodged cap and fixed Lovett with an iridescent stare. "*You* know, Professor."

"I haven't the foggiest—"

"Oh, yes you do."

"No."

"Oh, yes."

Lovett was trembling now. His face assumed the color of Swiss cheese. He set his Guinness on the floor.

"The Church fathers were fully conversant with the best of all possible theodicies," said Yeshua. "Saint Ignatius apprehended the answer, and so did Bishop Polycarp, Philo of Alexandria, Justin Martyr, and Saint Anselm, though none of them had much stomach for it. Neither do I, as a matter of fact."

"The last time we met, you insisted you weren't a theologian," said Martin.

"*International 227* has sparked my interest." Yeshua flipped the bottle cap into the air like a coin. He caught it, palmed it, and took a swig of beer. "I've been reading up."

"Surely not . . . ," rasped Lovett.

"Yes."

"Dualism?"

"Dualism," Yeshua confirmed, grinning ear to ear. "The Manichaean heresy, the Gnostic dichotomy, the Albighensian blasphemy, the Mephistopheles hypothesis—call it what you will."

Lovett's pallid face reddened, a flush flowing all the way to the hairless dome of his head. "I cannot accept a dualistic God."

"Oh? We accept *you*, fat boy—HA, HA, HA!"

Barely had this last speech escaped their host's larynx when something astonishing occurred: more astonishing, even, than the sentient tide that had recently descended upon Scheveningen. A lycanthropic change overcame Yeshua. Lock by lock, his hair dissolved, leaving him balder than Lovett. His neck thickened, his lips swelled, his eyebrows proliferated, his forehead ballooned, his eyes turned bright red.

He grew seven inches in as many seconds.

Martin and Lovett gasped in unison.

"No," wailed Lovett.

"Jesus," moaned Martin.

"Indeed," said Jonathan Sarkos, his hairy shoulders and broad back bursting the seams of Yeshua's shroud. "I am what I am. I am Christ and Antichrist, God and Satan, Heaven and Hiroshima, Arcadia and Auschwitz." Smiling devilishly, Sarkos lumbered up to Lovett. "Get it, fat boy? God is a duality. Dr. Jehovah and Mr. Hyde." He lobbed the bottle cap into his mouth and chewed. "Allow me to tell you a bedtime story. It's called 'The Day the Gas Chambers Malfunctioned at Auschwitz.' On second thought, why bother? You know the plot: the title gives it away—I'm surprised Braverman and Kelvin left it out of their overblown epic. Can you imagine how it feels to be a seven-year-old Jewish child, standing in line with hundreds of other Jewish children, waiting your turn to be thrown alive onto an open fire?" Swallowing the bottle cap, Sarkos swerved toward Martin. "Don't you see? It's the only solution that can possibly work. No other theory comes close. Of *course* God has a dark side. Not just dark—evil. Radically, radically evil."

"Why didn't you tell me this the last time I was in His brain?" demanded Martin. "If I'd walked away with a deposition from you arguing for a dualistic—"

"A deposition from *me?* From the *Devil?* Torvald would've shredded it on the spot."

"I'll have you know I passed up a meeting of the Beer and Beowulf Society to come here tonight," said Lovett scoldingly. "I must admit, I expected something more enlightening."

"Tough cookies," said Sarkos. "You aspired to be God's advocate, you got the job, you performed admirably. But God's advocate was ipso facto *my* advocate. Theodicy's a sucker's game, Professor. When Yahweh was operational, humanity's obligation wasn't to *worship* Him, for chrissakes. It was to celebrate His creativity and stand forevermore opposed to His malice. And anybody such as yourself, anybody who sought to shoehorn an omnibenevolent God into the same universe with Auschwitz . . . that person, Dr. Gregory Francis Lovett—that person did the Devil's work for him."

"The real Lovett should be hearing this—not the Idea of Lovett, the *real* Lovett," wailed Martin. "It's not *fair.*"

"It's not fair," Sarkos agreed, transmogrifying back into Yeshua. He rested his turquoise eyes on Martin. "Not fair at all."

"Maybe the Almighty has His weaknesses, but ultimately He's our only hope," said Lovett. "Without our heavenly Father, we wouldn't know what love is."

"Wrong again," said Yeshua. "Have you never owned a dog? Dogs are experts at love, and yet they know nothing of God."

"Not fair," said Martin, "not fair, not fair . . ."

"What about all those witnesses I called?" protested Lovett. "What about my cancer victims—and courageous young Mona Drake, drawing pictures with her teeth? *They* don't think God has a dark side."

"Fascinating," said Yeshua. "A psychologist would call it 'identification with the aggressor.' Battered children do it. So do beaten wives. The most memorable outbreak occurred in the concentration camps, when certain prisoners began acting like their guards: the salute, goose-step, Nazi uniform, everything.

No matter how cruel the abuser gets, the victim keeps responding with a twisted sort of hero worship. In this fashion he maintains a modicum of control over his situation."

"So I was right to pull the plug?" asked Martin.

" 'Mark my words, Martin Candle,' " replied Yeshua, quoting himself. " 'Before your life is done, you'll get another chance at this . . .' Which doesn't mean I'm about to let *you* off the hook either. In your own way you're as sorry a phenomenon as Lovett here. Bitterness is not a philosophy, friend. Outrage is not an ethic. Stop counting corpses and reach a truce with the universe, or you'll be stuck on the dung heap forever."

"But the universe is full of pointless suffering."

"Pointless," Yeshua agreed.

"The Court has already found in my favor," said Lovett caustically. He walked straight up to Yeshua, clasping the Savior's shoulders with both hands. "It doesn't matter *what* you and the Devil think."

"Take your hooks off me."

The professor backed away.

"Maybe we could reopen the case," said Martin.

"The case is closed . . . forever," said Yeshua.

"No, it isn't. I could mail a new petition to Ferrand."

"It's closed, Mr. Candle. End of story. Curtain."

"How do you know? How? How?"

Instead of answering, Yeshua finished his Rolling Rock, shape-shifted into Sarkos, and then became Yeshua again.

"I wish you'd stop doing that," said Lovett.

"What makes you think I have a choice?"

"Aren't you the architect of free will?"

"No, Professor, I'm the architect of the known universe. Cheer up. We four are doomed, but life goes on. The eternal Footman is breathing down our necks, but babies keep arriving outside this brain. The sky is falling, but the chocolate cake in the refrigerator tastes like God Himself baked it—which, as a matter of fact, I did."

❖

Martin slept on the bed that night, Lovett on the divan, their host on the floor. With the approach of dawn the cancer patient's dream visited him once again. Martin's subconscious carried him to his little courtroom in Abaddon. Standing before the bench, Dr. Blumenberg confessed to exceeding the posted speed limit on Welsh Road but said he shouldn't have to pay because he'd recently made the magistrate well. Martin refused to waive the fine, but he reduced it from a hundred dollars to eighty-five.

As the sun's first rays slanted through the air vents, casting on the rug a pattern resembling Corinne's favorite constellation, Canis Major, Martin awoke. He stumbled to the refrigerator, took out the pitcher of iced tea, and filled his glass. Head to toe, a remorseless fever coursed through him. The crab feasted greedily on his shoulders, thighs, and pelvis.

Setting six Roxanols on his tongue, he ground them to pieces and washed down the grains. He looked around. His roommates were gone. The hemorrhage had evidently destroyed the Idea of Lovett: the professor's worsted suit lay in a rumpled pile under the divan. The white shroud was nowhere to be seen, a circumstance suggesting that Sarkos a.k.a. Yeshua might still be alive—a thought Martin found both disturbing and comforting.

"Dualism," he muttered. "Yes. Of course."

Turning back the stone, he experienced a strong premonition that someone was waiting for him on the other side. Gordon, perhaps, or Lot, or one of those loopy Scrabble-playing dinosaurs.

He was not prepared to meet himself.

But there he stood, all right—the Idea of Martin Candle, leaning on the driver's door of his Dodge Aries and dressed in a white linen suit covered with crusted blood.

"Martin?" said Martin, stepping into the feeble morning

..le raised his left hand, seeking to determine whether he
..:holding a mirror image.
..oth of the Idea's hands stayed in place. "Hello, buddy."

"What're *you* doing here?"

"I've been elected to drive you home. You'll finally get to see
your childhood fire station again."

"We were right all along, weren't we?" A crab spasm seized
Martin's frame, rattling every bone. His fever climbed another
degree. "God was guilty. The best defense is the Manichaean
heresy, which isn't a defense at all, it's—"

"Never mind about that."

"—an indictment."

"We'd better hit the road. De Groot is storming through
Jerusalem even as we speak." The Idea opened the rear door,
extending his trembling index finger to indicate that Martin
should enter. "I would help you, but if you touch me I'll disintegrate."

"I've heard about that rule. It applies only in cases where
the individuals love each other."

"Indeed."

"You mean . . . ?"

"Yes, Martin, I love you. Not everybody can say that about
himself."

Slowly he eased his enfeebled body into the car, gritting his
teeth so hard he half expected to crack his molars, until at last
he felt the soft velour upholstery cradling his spine and hips.

As the Idea climbed behind the steering wheel, Martin realized a second passenger occupied the backseat—a frail septuagenarian dressed in a black sweatshirt and a straw hat.

"Dad?"

The old man said nothing.

"Dad?" inquired Martin again. "Dad?"

Slowly, with the sound of a wrought-iron gate pivoting on
rusty hinges, the Idea of Walter Candle turned. Martin shuddered. Since their last meeting his father's face had undergone

a degeneration so profound it was nearly synonymous with his skull.

"I saw your performance in the Peace Palace," said Walter. "What did you think?"

"The white suit was an excellent choice. Too bad you got blood all over it."

"I mean, what did you think of my arguments?"

"Clever. Not as clever as Dr. Lovett's, but still clever."

"You . . . you agreed with the verdict?"

"Well, yes."

"God has a shadow side, Dad—just like everybody else. His guilty half was . . . guilty."

"Do you remember the lesson I used to teach about Jonah and the whale?"

"Jonah? I guess so. Sure." The image returned in a sudden rush: Martin and his Sunday school classmates huddled inside a sweaty canvas tent while his father pumped in the sounds of surf and the stench of three-day-old pollacks. "You borrowed an army tent from Billy Tuckerman's father."

"And do you remember the *point* of the Jonah lesson?"

"I'm not sure."

"I was hoping you'd remember the point."

"Give me a minute."

" 'A whale can swallow a man, but only God can swallow a whale.' You tried to swallow a whale, Son. It got stuck in your throat."

"Stuck in my throat," Martin echoed in a corroborating tone. "And if I had it to do over again, I'd still hunt Him down."

"It hurts me to hear you say that."

"I'm sorry."

"You shouldn't have killed Him."

"I can understand your feelings."

"It's *embarrassing*."

"He wanted it, Dad." Inexorably Martin's fever took hold of

him. His heart hurled itself against his rib cage. "All those tornadoes, and no real defense . . . He *wanted* it."

Blackness seeped through Martin's brain like ink jetting from a quintessential squid.

❖

When at last his consciousness returned, he found himself sitting in a pile of freshly cut grass, each blade damp with cerebrospinal dew. He blinked—once, twice, a third time—inhaling the vivacious fragrance of mentation mixed with chlorophyl. He recognized his environs: the front lawn of his parents' old homestead, the building miraculously restored to its prebulldozer state—Abaddon Fire Station Number One, a weathered mass of brick and clapboard comprising a two-engine barn, a dozen improvised living spaces, and a broken siren. Four stout sugar maples commanded the side yard, shedding their coat hanger–shaped seedpods. His Dodge sat abandoned in the driveway, doors wide open, giving it the appearance of an immense four-barbed fishhook. Walter's wardrobe lay on the backseat in an amorphous mass. A blood-spattered suit coat hung over the steering wheel.

"Martin! Martin Candle!"

He swiveled his torso, triggering crab spasms in both shoulders. As Patricia ran across the lawn, he inevitably recalled his first glimpse of her: a lithe, attractive woman charging through Hillcrest Cemetery in a mourning dress, looking for the right funeral. Today she wore a more customary ensemble: yellow turtleneck, blue jeans, tennis shoes. A few yards behind her, Randall stood with his hands in his pockets, dazed by the primordial banality of God's Idea of Fox Run.

"Patricia, is that *you?*" asked Martin.

"You bet."

"Not merely the *idea* of you? Not your twin sister?"

"Darling, it's me. We had a hell of a time getting in. Some day I'll tell you the whole story."

"This brain of His is the craziest place," said Randall, approaching. "I just visited our old school, and—you'll never believe this—everybody was reciting the Lord's Prayer. It's like *Abaddon School District versus Selkirk* never even *happened*."

"I'm in a bit of a fix right now," said Martin. "I can't seem to get up."

His friends knelt beside him, setting their hands firmly against his shoulders and beneath his thighs. Their palms were sticky with cerebrospinal fluid. Lifting him off the grass, they bore him into the backyard, two acres of suburban verdancy permeated by the divine perfume of his mother's rose garden. To the preadolescent Martin, this labyrinth of bushes and pathways had always seemed the most tactile place on Earth—Mom's garden with its smooth petals and sharp thorns, its crumbly dirt and prickly-footed Japanese beetles. He wished he could walk through the maze once more, touching everything, but it was not to be. The crab owned him completely now, flesh, blood, and bone.

They laid him on the Waupelani's eastern bank, in the shade of a weeping willow. The creekbed was empty, sucked dry by the hemorrhage. And suddenly he was ten years old, wading through the water in galoshes, turning over one flat rock after another. Often as not, the anticipated payoff followed: a confused crayfish, sitting beneath a cloud of water-borne dirt and wondering what God-like entity had deprived it so unjustly of its home.

"It's good to be back," said Martin, becoming fifty-three again.

"I'm fond of Abaddon, I truly am," said Randall. "My classmates tried to kill me, but that would've happened no matter *where* I was living—Cheltenham, Lower Merion, Philadelphia."

"In Philadelphia they would've succeeded," said Martin.

"Your bedroom's all ready," said Patricia. "Fresh sheets, clean pillow cases, a morphine drip. Just say the word."

Willow leaves fell everywhere, narrow green blades dropping *hira hira* through the August air. "I pulled the plug," said Martin. "I made Him bleed all over Holland."

"Yes, Martin—your popularity has never been lower," said Patricia.

"Listen, friends, I was right all along. I got this straight from Yeshua. The only solution that works is the Manichaean heresy." The crab was on the move, Martin realized, making ready to attack his sacrum. "God wasn't completely evil, of course, not even *mostly* evil. I mean, look at my mother's roses, and the oceans, and all those stars—*none* of us could have brought that off. Nevertheless, His worshipworthiness remains problematic and—*aaaiiihhh!*"

The spasm abated as quickly as it had arrived. He closed his eyes, sucked in his breath, and told his friends what they were doubtless expecting to hear.

"I'm ready for the drip."

❖

The room was radiant with memories—and far more crowded than Martin had expected, the most densely populated deathbed scene he'd witnessed since the time he married two AIDS patients, Trevor Hood and Richard Erwin, in a Chestnut Grove hospice. The Idea of Siobhan Candle stood by the nightstand, arranging red roses in a green cut-glass vase. The Idea of Jenny Candle leaned over the edge of the mattress, offering her brother a steaming cup of Constant Comment, but it was a hopeless proposition: the man who'd failed to swallow God could no longer even swallow tea. The Idea of Vaughn Poffley sat astride a palomino rockinghorse, meticulously lettering MARTIN CANDLE FOR MAGISTRATE on a piece of Bristol board with a green felt marker.

"It's time we started planning your comeback," he said.

Martin shifted his gaze. His ex-fiancées fidgeted near the bureau, randomly removing and then replacing his Superman pajamas, Bugs Bunny T-shirt, Phillies baseball cap, and Mickey Mouse Club beanie.

"Every night we got together and watched the replays on Court TV," said the Idea of Robin McLaughlin. "You were *terrific*."

"Sensational," said the Idea of Brittany Rabson.

Lifting his head, he saw that his tissues were being hydrated, his cells nourished, and his spasms managed by three different IV drips. He felt like a UFO abductee whose captives had dissected him alive, hanging his organs all around their spaceship on aluminum poles. Gradually the morphine worked its miracle, flowing through his veins like warm butter, transforming his pain-racked bones into an enchanted and uncharted archipelago. He flopped his head to one side, surveying the precious geegaws of his youth. A cyclopean teddy bear named Warren stood in the corner. Martin's Revell plastic models—a Messerschmitt, the HMS *Bounty*, the aircraft carrier *Forrestal*—sat atop the bookcase. Below lay *The Hobbit, The Adventures of Tom Sawyer, Through the Looking Glass,* and a dozen Hardy Boys reprints; his passion for jurisprudence, he realized, had emerged at an early age. The floor was strewn with dominoes, checkers, Monopoly deeds, and murder implements from Clue.

At some point Hans De Groot must have entered, for an ominous metallic sound now filled the room, keys jangling against keys. Seconds later Martin heard the police captain's gravelly voice, informing him he was under arrest. With unrestrained glee De Groot specified the charges. Evidently half the population of Scheveningen was suing Martin for damages, and that was the least of his troubles: in a rare collaboration between Catholicism and Calvinism, the Holy See and the Kingdom of the Netherlands had petitioned the World Court to put the ex-JP on trial for deicide. Preliminary hearings would begin in two weeks.

Martin cranked his head in De Groot's direction. The police captain sported the same pinstriped suit he'd worn on the day they met. "Are you . . . truly De Groot . . . or merely . . . ?"

"Don't worry, Candle—I'm real as a stubbed toe." The captain rattled his keys. "In my opinion we ought to extradite you right now, but some important people sent telegrams, including Dr. Lovett, so for the moment we're leaving you alone. Enjoy that soft bed while you've got it—your next stop is the gallows. I hope they let me tie the noose."

"You can't talk to my son that way," said Siobhan Candle, swabbing the *Forrestal*'s flight deck with a feather duster.

"I'm . . . not guilty." Sweat covered Martin head to toe. He felt like a marathon swimmer greased in preparation for a shot at the English Channel. "Ask . . . Yeshua. God is . . . duality."

"Hear that, Captain?" said Siobhan. "A duality—so there."

A vicious and voracious truth bored its way, wormlike, into Martin's mind. His illness had attained a new level of iniquity, breaking its morphinian bonds. "Ontological . . . doesn't . . . hold up," he gasped.

"You're absolutely right," said his sister.

"Lousy defense," said Randall.

"No damn good at all," said Vaughn.

"Free will . . . doesn't . . . either."

"Swindle," said Robin.

"Flimflam," said Brittany.

"Stop . . . humoring me!" cried Martin. The crab had procreated, releasing thousands of progeny into the farthest reaches of his flesh. "Stop it! Stop it! Stop! Stop!"

Randall's mouth opened. His lips moved, but his words were overpowered by an unexpected noise: a rhythmic *clop-clop-clop* resounding throughout the fire station.

"Horses," moaned Martin.

Patricia bent beside him. "Horses?"

"Horses . . . from . . ." From where? The Four Horsemen of the Apocalypse carousel? No. "Stables."

"Stables?"

"Executioners' stables. I'm . . . regicide, Patricia. I killed . . . King . . . it's . . . not . . . working."

"What isn't? The free will defense?"

"The morphine."

The mattress dissolved, the room dissolved, the fire station dissolved. March 2, 1757. The Place de Grève. He lay face-up on a scaffold, dressed only in a loincloth, each of his limbs roped to a different horse. De Groot crouched near him, a saw-toothed knife locked in his palm.

Grinning, the police captain slipped a black linen hood over his head. "The Devil made this for me," he explained.

A second executioner leaned into Martin's field of vision, his crimson irises blazing through the eye holes in his hood. "A perfect day for an *amende honorable*, Monsieur Damiens!" said Sarkos a.k.a Yeshua. "The nightingales are singing in the belfries of Notre Dame!" The torturer held up his knife, its serrated blade glistening in the morning sun. "Hardly a cloud in the sky!"

"I'm not Damiens," moaned Martin.

"Forward!" shouted De Groot. "Forward!"

The four horses moved, straining against the ropes. Cancer pains tore through Martin's joints.

"Forward! Forward!"

"You've got the wrong man!"

"Oh, dear," said Sarkos a.k.a. Yeshua mockingly. "Oh, dear, oh, dear, he's not coming apart. Whatever shall we do?"

Acting in tandem, the executioners went to work with their knives. They operated methodically, precisely, cutting the cancer from Martin's hips along with considerable quantities of muscle, sinew, and bone. The pain was explosive, relentless, beyond excruciation. He screamed until he thought his throat would rip.

"Dualism!" cried Martin. His left leg vanished. "He's guilty!" His right leg deserted him. "Dualism!"

"Tell it to the judges," said De Groot, savagely hacking into his prisoner's left shoulder.

Martin was about to reply when a great knot of half-digested chicken rolled upward from the depths of his stomach. Free will, he thought, clamping his jaws shut. Blocked by his *liberum arbitrium*, the rising tide of vomitus lodged in his gullet. He sat upright, lungs pleading for air, teeth locked in suicidal defiance.

As his left arm flew off, he fell back on the mattress—just like Duncan Elder, he thought, poor little Duncan, murdered by cystic fibrosis. In a great thundering rush everything poured out of him: his dinner, his bile, his blameless blood. The vomitus smelled like Job's dung heap. The bile bubbled like the waters of Leviathan. Steam rose from the blood.

And so it was that on August 28, 2000, Martin Candle of Abaddon Township, Pennsylvania—legless, one armed, naked, supine—flung his remaining hand toward Heaven, splayed his fingers, and respectfully returned his ticket.

❖

Unlike yours truly, Candle never stood trial for his crimes. After leaving eighteenth-century Paris he entered oblivion forever. It was the Idea of Robin McLaughlin who first noticed. To the assembled vigil keepers she said, simply, "He's gone now. I know it. Our dear, sweet Martin is gone." The official certificate from The Hague coroner's office read "disseminated metastatic prostate cancer," but in fact he'd succumbed to an acute case of hopeless causes.

As for the future faced by myself, Yeshua, Isaac, Lot, and the rest of us, I must say it looks desolate. Between the coma and the hemorrhage, we've probably got about a week. Much as I hate to admit it, humanity will get along perfectly well without me. Any species that could invent the twentieth century entirely on its own doesn't need a Prince of Darkness.

Right now we're throwing a party, the blowout to end all

blowouts, a combination Mardi Gras, New Year's Eve celebration, and Roman orgy. Eat, drink, and screw Mary, for tomorrow we die. Schonspigel's kick-ass heavy-metal band, the Bulgarian Horrors, is providing the entertainment. You should see Saint Augustine break-dancing. Blind. The noise is so loud, I can hardly hear myself think. Writing these last few paragraphs will drain me, sapping away energies I might otherwise have employed in making sampler number fifteen, *Amende Honorable*.

At least I know how it will end.

Patricia Zabor has our hero's corpse cremated in The Hague. The ashes are delivered to her sealed in a white porcelain urn no larger than one of Siobhan Candle's flower vases. Zabor spends the entire flight home—Amsterdam to London, London to Philadelphia—holding the urn in her lap.

Once back in Abaddon Township, she arranges for Candle's remains to be buried in Hillcrest Cemetery, right next to Corinne Rosewood. His funeral is as well attended as was his swan song in Jehovah's brain, and it attracts the same audience—with the exception of Brittany Rabson, laid up with the flu. It rains throughout the service. Placing him beside his one true love is the hardest thing Patricia Zabor has ever done. The marker reads A BLAMELESS AND UPRIGHT MAN, though I believe he would have preferred A PASSIONATE STUDENT OF LIFE'S DEEPEST MYSTERIES.

On her way out of the cemetery, Zabor visits her son. For a full hour she kneels beside the grave, weeping in the rain. The stone says, as always, I MISS YOU SO MUCH . . . ALL MY LOVE, MOMMY.

Later that day she goes to the Federal Express office in Perkinsville and ships the completed, camera-ready paintings for *The Insect Insurrection*. Her editor at Apex Novelty Company is ecstatic. He gives her a thousand-dollar bonus.

The following Sunday, Zabor and Randall Selkirk end up at the same matinee performance of a Broadway play—a revival of Archibald MacLeish's *J.B.*—and soon afterward they begin dating again. Before the year is out they are married in a simple ceremony conducted by the Abaddon Township justice of the peace, Barbara Meredith. If Candle had gotten to know the woman, Zabor decides, he wouldn't have liked her very much. For Meredith it's just a job.

In a few minutes my better half will take over and perform a minor intervention. With a wave of his hand Yeshua will cause five hundred thousand dollars to vanish from the coffers of Sargassia, Incorporated, and reappear on the books of an equally worthy but far less profitable enterprise, the Kennel of Joy.

Somewhere out there, a happy dog is barking. Can you hear her? I can. She's a feisty Border collie, born and raised in the concrete heart of Pittsburgh. Her name is Crumpet, and she is dying of ovarian cancer. For the first time ever, Crumpet has been permitted to assuage her genes. Ears flapping, eyes flashing, she is herding two dozen sheep across the south meadow of the Hostetler farm in central Pennsylvania. Not ordinary sheep, mind you: large, serious sheep—sheep as big as Gordon the ram. And all of them, Crumpet notices as, darting and swerving, she brings the flock safely home . . . all of them are doing exactly what she wants.